C000263344

# provoke

AVA HARRISON

*Provoke*
Copyright © 2022 by Ava Harrison
Published by AH Publishing

All rights reserved. No part of this book may be reproduced or transmitted in any form by any means, including photocopying, recording or by information storage and retrieval system without the written permission of the author, except for the use of brief quotations in a book review.

This book is a work of fiction. Names, characters, places, and incidents are products of the author's imagination or are used fictitiously. Any resemblance to actual persons, living or dead, events or locations is entirely coincidental.

The author acknowledges the trademark status and trademark owners of various products, brands, and/or restaurants referenced in the work of fiction, which have been used without permission. The publication/use of these trademarks is not authorized, associated with, or sponsored by the trademark owners.

*Provoke*
Cover Design: Hang Le
Photographer: Chris Davis
Model: Olly Hines
Editor: Editing4Indies
Brit Check Editor: Readers Together
Content Editor: Royal Reads
Proofreader: Comma Sutra, Jaime Ryter

For those who need a little grumpy/sunshine in your life . . .
This ones for you.

Keep your face always toward the sunshine and
the shadows will fall behind you
—Walt Whitman

# chapter one

## Charles

"**B**LOODY HELL, AMANDA. NOT HERE," I bark to the annoying woman who has attached herself to my hip for the evening.

Can this night get any worse?

This woman is handsy. And not in a good way.

Typically, that would be more than welcome, but tonight, I'm not feeling her.

*Pity.*

It's not that she isn't insanely beautiful. She is.

Wavy brown hair hangs to the top of her small breasts, and her toned legs go on forever. Not an inch of her is soft. She's all hard lines and muscle.

Definitely my type.

Although, I don't have a definitive preference when it comes to the opposite sex.

"It's Mandy," she croons.

I cringe at the awful sound.

*Mandy* is too much, and I can tell she wouldn't be up for any of my rules.

One night. No numbers exchanged. No repeats.

I made that mistake one too many times in London, and I have no plans to repeat it here in the States. This is my clean break. My do-over.

I'm too busy for relationships and wouldn't be good at one, even if I wasn't constantly working.

*Which I am.*

Mandy has practically growled at any woman who's looked my way, which only furthers my suspicion that she'd be clingy if I gave in to her roaming hands and took her into the offered VIP room.

I'd spend the next month dodging her advances, and I have absolutely no time for that.

"Charles," she whines in what could quite possibly be the most ear-piercing sound I've experienced in some time.

I glare over her head at my supposed friend. The man responsible for this setup. He promised me top-shelf drinks, a night of relaxation, and a beautiful woman who would be more than happy with one night of sex. Complete rubbish.

He failed to say that he only knew petulant models who drink the most expensive champagne on an empty stomach and practically piss all over their target of the night. Me being said target.

He chuckles into his fist at my glare, and I manage to refrain from pummeling him.

Paxton Ramsey is an arrogant son of a bitch, but a good man. His friend, Mathis, owns the club, which he takes full advantage of regularly. He has a reserved VIP room every Wednesday night to schmooze clients. This week, there was a cancellation, and I was the lucky recipient of a night out on Pax's dime.

"Charles, you're ignoring me."

My eyes close as I attempt to rein in my growing irritation with the exasperating woman. When they open, I'm met with Mandy's green eyes piercing into me with barely restrained anger.

Perhaps this one is more than a little clingy. I'm not into the whole fatal attraction foreplay vibe that Mandy is throwing my way.

"I need to use the little girl's room," she says, pursing her lips.

An audible breath rushes through my chest, and Pax hears it loud and clear, if his barely restrained laughter is any indication.

Mandy doesn't seem to notice as she swishes her hips in the most exaggerated fashion when she saunters out of the room.

"Christ, Paxton. What have you done?" His head falls back, and he bellows in laughter.

I'm sure this entire situation is quite hilarious if you're on the outside looking in. His hand pops up as he works to get himself under control.

"I'm sorry. It's just—" He falls forward, wheezing in glee. I'm ready to shake the amusement out of him.

"Right, then. Go on and get it all out, mate." I smack my lips together, not amused in the slightest at his absurd reaction to my distress. "Are you quite finished?"

His head shakes back and forth. "She's never acted like this. What can I say? You bring out the crazy in women, Cavendish."

"This night has gone all to hell," I say, shaking my head.

"The night's still young, my friend. I'm happy to help you ditch Mandy. I'm tired of her moaning myself."

"Oh, she's whining on, all right."

He grunts. "Alex and the guys are on their way. She has a history with him. Give me an hour, and I can have her well and truly distracted, if you know what I mean."

"I'll gladly vacate this room for Alex if it means being rid of her. Just tell me when."

Sitting back in my chair, I stretch my legs and get comfortable. Our server enters, handing me another scotch on the rocks.

I tip my head in thanks, receiving a coy grin in return. This woman would no doubt be a perfect replacement for Mandy.

"Don't even think about it," Pax says, watching the girl leave with her empty tray tucked under her arm.

"Sod off. You have no say at this point, mate. I choose her."

"You want to tango with Mathis? Have at it." He takes a swig from his beer bottle. "I'm not losing my VIP status because you decided to fuck the help."

"She's the owner's girl?"

His eyebrow rises. "They're *all* his girls. Off-limits."

We sit in companionable silence for several minutes, each sipping on our drinks. The bass from the music pumps through the room as the night begins to pick up. Outside this room, the party rages like it does every night at Club Silver.

"The party is here, boys." Alex steps through the curtain with Mandy curled into his side.

The son of a bitch was right.

Pax leans toward me. "Told you. And it didn't even take an hour."

I grin, nodding my head in admiration. "I believe I owe you now."

He slaps my leg, smiling. "Let's go. There are plenty more ladies to charm, and I need you as my broody wingman." He turns back to the room. "Boys, enjoy yourself. Drinks are on me."

He stands, and I follow him through the chiffon curtain that hides each VIP table. The scene is just as I suspected. Scantily clad women move their bodies in time to the music while men watch on in ravenous delight, eager to score.

My eyes sweep through the throngs of people gyrating on the dance floor. No part of me wants to be in the middle of that chaos. I've never been one for the clubs. I've always found it to be the worst sort of place to decompress, but every now and then, I step outside my comfort zone for the sake of Pax.

He's been a good friend since I've made this city my home for the last three years. And where he goes, I go, if and when I decide to venture outside my office.

Pax enjoys Silver more than the average person, so it's become my stomping grounds by proxy. It's more than the discount his friend provides. He lives for the loud music and over-eager women. I prefer the chase.

I'm about to tell my friend I'm calling it a night when my eyes land on a woman directly across from me, sitting at the bar with two others.

She shines like a beacon in the crowd, drawing my attention without effort. Golden hair falls down her back in waves, stopping midway to her arse. Her bright smile literally lights up the room as she laughs with her companions. I wonder what the man beside her said to draw such an authentic delight from the woman. They seem well acquainted but not a couple. He leans into her as though that's exactly what he's angling for, but her body language doesn't scream lust when she looks at him.

The glow about her is alluring and utterly hypnotic, but it's not for him.

She's so unlike every other girl in Silver tonight. Understated, but still the most beautiful girl in the room. Her red sundress flares at her thighs, accentuating her hips and showcasing her lean legs. She's breathtaking.

As if I've willed her eyes toward me, she looks up, and our gazes connect. My blood flows uncomfortably to my cock, and I have to force myself not to adjust my growing hard-on. Damn. She's ethereal in a way very few others are.

*A ray of fucking sunshine.*

I'm so enchanted by the woman that I don't sense Mandy at my back until her hand lands on my shoulder, and her lips are pressed against my ear.

"It could've been you tonight, but I can tell when a man is not interested."

*Thank fuck.*

I turn to look at her, not wanting to come off as intentionally rude, given she's acquainted with Pax. "It's not you. It's me."

"The age-old excuse." She offers me a tight-lipped smile, nodding briskly. She doesn't buy my words, but I can't be bothered to care. I've done my part in offering a reason that's not as harsh as reality.

"It was nice to meet you, Charles."

"Likewise, Mandy." I grab her hand and raise it to my lips. "Enjoy your night."

She steps back into the enclosed VIP room, and I sigh in relief at her retreat.

"Let's go before she changes her mind," Paxton quips, motioning toward the crowd. "There are fish aplenty, and they won't murder you with a pickax in your sleep."

"You don't say," I grunt, picturing the whole scene that Pax has laid out.

Mandy would play the perfect psycho.

"Don't you worry. I'll find you a good one." He smirks.

I turn my head in the direction of the blonde, but her eyes are no longer pointed toward me. She's back to talking with her friends as though our moment never happened.

It's for the best, based on the ridiculous reaction I had by simply looking at her.

Women like her are bad news for men like me.

Strings. Attachments. Promises.

The things I cannot offer.

Tonight, I'm looking for Mandy 2.0, minus the madness.

# chapter two

Raven

"CHEERS TO MY FRIEND, CONQUERING THE WORLD!" LILY hands me a glass of champagne.

With a shake of my head, I look at the effervescing liquid and let out a chuckle. "What happened to our usual martinis?" My brow rises in question. "Since when do we drink champagne?"

"Today, we're celebrating that you're one step closer to conquering the world."

I roll my eyes. "I got a new job. I didn't cure *cancer*." My heart tightens in my chest. "Plus . . ." I take the drink in my hand but don't lift it to my mouth. "Is it really right to celebrate *today*?"

"You managed to snag the job of a lifetime."

"Yeah, but the timing." Despite how exciting it is, it feels bittersweet. Today is the five-year anniversary of my father's death.

"He would have wanted you to celebrate." Lily offers me a small smile. She's trying to get me out of my head.

If anyone knows how much my father meant to me, it's her and our other friend, Asher. They both have been my friends since before Dad died.

We all met the first day of freshman year.

Lily was my roommate, and our friend Asher . . .

We met him that first meal in the cafeteria, and after a heated debate over whether sweet potato fries or tater tots were better, he's never left our side.

Which is why they showed up at my apartment today, forced me to get dressed, and dragged me out. Which I appreciate. Still, I can't help the heavy feeling in my heart.

He should be alive to celebrate with me. "I know, but—"

"No buts. This is why Asher and I forced you to come out. You deserve this job, and there is no way we were going to let you stay home feeling sad while eating a whole pint of ice cream."

"I wouldn't eat the *whole* thing."

"You forget Asher and I have been with you every year. Sometimes you eat two pints."

My free hand reaches out, and I take hers in mine. "Thank you."

"For what?"

"For always being there. You and Asher . . . I don't know how I would have made it this far without you." My throat feels dry, and I can feel my vision become fuzzy from the unshed tears. I blink, and one slips down my cheek.

Lily gives my hand a squeeze. "There will be none of that. No thank you and no tears."

"Fine. Speaking of Asher, where did he go? He was just here, and now, he's gone."

She blinks several times, taking a sip of her drink. "Why would I know?"

Inclining my head, I give her a look that says I'm not buying it. Her head swivels around the room, evading my heavy stare.

*Like she doesn't know where he is.*

We might all be best friends, but Lily . . . well, she's been in love with him the whole time.

I narrow my eyes at her. "Are we really still playing this game?" Lily's eyes widen as she nervously chews on her bottom lip while toying with the ends of her long, red hair. "Oh, there he is now," I say and wave Asher over.

From the corner of my eye, I notice that Lily sits up a little straighter. Her shoulders go back, and her breasts jut out as she straightens the collar of her black button-down dress.

Unfortunately for Lily, Asher's a player. At this stage of his life, she has no shot with him.

"Hey, hey, there's my girl," he says, gliding up beside me. "Getting wasted without me?"

I shrug.

"Harsh." He laughs.

"Lily's trying to keep my spirits up."

Asher's smile drops, and he wraps his hand around my shoulder. "He would have been so proud."

"Thanks," I mouth back and then hold up my glass. "You drinking?"

"You know it." He drops his arm from around me and starts to wave down the bartender.

Asher orders himself a beer and pulls up a barstool. "Congratulations, Miss Raven Bennett. You're officially employed."

"I've been employed before," I reply.

"Sure, but that didn't count."

I lift my brow at his words. "Oh, yeah? Why not?"

"You worked part time while getting your MBA. This is the real deal now."

I groan. He's right. I have a great résumé, but I've never worked full time at a company like this.

Despite my credentials, my previous work experience, and the internships I have had, I'm still starting at the bottom.

Don't get me wrong, I'm ecstatic at landing a job, but it's basic compared to the level of knowledge I have.

"You're an advertising analyst now."

"I'm a glorified assistant." I sigh, laying my head on Asher's shoulder. "The thought of running errands and grabbing coffee for the higher-ups makes me want to gag."

"It won't be that bad," Lily assures lamely, scooting her barstool closer to Asher. "You've always been able to charm your way into better seats at the corporate table."

"Yeah," Asher agrees, taking a long pull from his Heineken. His eyes drop to my legs and linger a tad longer than acceptable. "You're special, Raven." He eyes me a little too appreciatively for a friend, and my stomach drops.

Shit.

I don't like that look. It reminds me of the way Lily looks at him.

"Been there, done that gig. It's not too bad. The climb will be quick for you. If someone like me can get promoted, then you most definitely can." He shrugs, taking another sip. "Let's be honest. You're far more intelligent than me."

"And better looking," Lily quips, raising her glass and leaning over Asher to clink it against mine.

"Definitely," Asher agrees. "Pity we're going to be working for competing companies. You would've been a killer addition to our firm. But between you and me, Cavendish Group is a really good alternative."

"You don't say." My words are dry. Cavendish Group is the best, and Asher knows it. He'd cut off his right arm for a chance to work there. Said so himself before he was offered a position with Bauer Marketing.

"Plus, rumor is they have the most amazing café inside their building. Good coffee every day. What more can you ask for, really?"

I laugh. "You know me too well."

"Can I get a job there?" Lily chimes in.

Asher and Lily talk about who knows what, and I zone out.

Thoughts of my father creep into my mind. Closing my lids, I see him in my head. The way he used to smile down at me. Always so proud.

His absence never gets easier.

When my hands shake, I know I need a distraction so I don't fall apart. Dad wouldn't have wanted that. He would want me to have fun.

Opening my eyes, I lift my glass to my mouth and down the remainder of my drink. As soon as the bubbles hit my lip, my shoulders uncoil.

My gaze moves across the room, taking in the sterile place. It's void of color, modernistic, and made to attract the wealthy. Little alcoves line the far wall, hiding the elite patrons of Club Silver behind white chiffon curtains.

Men like the ones I'll be running errands for at Cavendish.

Wealthy. Entitled. Arrogant.

A curtain slides open, and two well-dressed men appear like models being unveiled. The air is practically sucked from the room at their presence. There's something about the magnetism they possess even from across the space, and I'm not the only one to notice. Several heads are turned in their direction.

Women whisper and gape, making their ogling far too obvious, if the darker-haired man's smirk is any indication, as he peruses the room. His head nods toward a table of women decked out in glitzy dresses that barely cover their asses. Jewels drip from their necks and arms, making me wonder what the hell they've done in their lives to be so successful at such a young age.

They can't be much older than me.

At twenty-six, I feel like I've gotten a late start, but it couldn't be helped. When your father gets sick, it changes the time frame.

My eyes stray from the darker-haired man to the one who nearly knocks the air from my lungs. He's tall and broad-shouldered, but trim at the waist. His suit looks tailored to his body like a well-fitted glove.

He's imposing and beautiful. Even from here, the cut of his jaw gives the impression he's been carved from stone by a master carver.

Pure perfection.

As if manifested, his head turns toward me, and our eyes lock. My breath hitches, and my stomach flips. He holds my gaze, and I don't so much as take a breath through the encounter.

It's unlikely he's actually looking at me from clear across the room, but I refuse to turn away. An exotic beauty, dressed to the nines, walks up from behind him, placing a hand on his shoulder and whispering something into his ear.

My stomach twists with jealousy. I don't understand.

I don't know this guy, and he's so far out of my league, it's depressing.

A small smirk spreads over his handsome face, and my body reacts in ways it never has before. It's as though he can sense my envy, and he's lapping it up.

Holy. Shit.

"Raven?" Lily asks, drawing my attention away from the stranger and back to my friends.

My head shakes as I try to knock myself from the trance I've been in. To wipe away the lust that one look from a handsome stranger caused.

"Huh?"

"Are you ready to start your job?" she asks, eyes narrowed in on me.

I blink several times, considering her question. "Yes, but—"

"But what?" she presses.

"If I'm being honest . . ." I bite my lip.

"Always."

"I'm pretty nervous about the whole thing. I'm happy I got the job, don't get me wrong. And I know I'm qualified, but I still can't help but worry. What if I mess something up? Am I good enough? What if I screw up this chance? You know what I mean?" *These are the moments I miss Dad the most.* He would sit me down at our kitchen table, offer me a cookie, and tell me exactly why I deserve this. His lips would part into a large grin, and I would believe him.

"Whoa. You didn't take a breath there." Asher chuckles, and I welcome the joke. It pulls me away from wallowing.

*He wouldn't want me to.*

Lily eyes me curiously before offering a comforting smile. "Don't worry. You'll be fine. You were always the smartest out of us three."

I take a deep breath, willing my racing heart to slow.

"I have no doubt that you'll kick ass." Asher's smile is wide and reassuring.

I return the smile, grateful for my friends, especially Ash. He always believes in me, even when I don't. It's what I love most about him.

"He's right, you know. You're really good with people, and you're amazing at all this advertising and marketing stuff. You see things that a lot of people don't."

My hands rise. "Okay. Enough flattery, guys. I'm fine. I swear."

Asher raises one eyebrow as though to say, *yeah, right.*

"I mean it," Lily continues.

Wanting to change the topic, I gesture to the bar. "Anyone for shots?"

"I'm in," Asher says.

We both turn toward Lily and wait for her to refuse. But she just laughs. "I'm definitely in."

"Good, I like drunk Lily." Asher grins.

"I've missed this," I confess. "We don't go out together nearly enough."

"I've missed this, too," Asher agrees. Then he beckons the bartender and orders a round of shots, plus fresh drinks to chase them down.

We all knock them back with a grimace, and Lily and I quickly wash them down with our fresh glasses of champagne.

*We'll be hurting tomorrow.*

"Ah, I remember why I don't like shots now." Lily's grimace causes Asher and me to burst out laughing again.

"To the new job!" we shout.

"And drinking to the new paycheck," Lily yells over the music.

My eyes roam back to the VIP room, hoping for one more peek of the handsome stranger, but he's long gone.

# chapter three

Raven

NOW ON THE DANCE FLOOR, THE EFFECTS OF THE SHOTS ARE going to my head.

The place is packed for a Wednesday, and sweat-glistened bodies move all around us.

Still, we've created a perimeter with Asher in the middle, shielding us from the gyrating couples practically dry humping.

Silver has transitioned a lot over the past couple of years. There has always been a higher echelon clientele in the VIP areas, but nowadays, everyone in the place is swathed in high-end wear and dripping with diamonds and watches that cost more than my first car.

The club is now the hottest spot in the city.

It's practically a speed-dating location for the rich and famous.

Luckily for us, Asher has connections.

Well, at least his family does.

He's from a wealthy family, oozing in old money. His connections are limitless in the city of who you know. While I'd never say that to his face because he's determined to make his own way, it's the truth. Asher will never have to beg and plead for top positions with his last name.

Nepotism is alive and well in these parts.

"Oh, my God, Ash. Whatever you are trying to do there is not a dance move worthy of Silver," Lily barks in laughter as he continues with his less than stellar imitation of a lawn sprinkler.

Lily leans forward in hysterics at his antics as Asher is many things, but a dancer, he is not.

"I'm going to pee. Stop it!" I yell at the moment when one song stops and another starts.

Everyone looks at me, and the three of us burst into more laughter. We're acting like high schoolers, but it's what I need.

Starting a new chapter in my life has me confused. One part of me is excited about the future, and the other is already disenchanted by a career I haven't even begun. Despite Lily's and Asher's reassurances, I'm nervous about what's to come Monday.

I'll be miserable if they have me running pointless errands and shut me out of the idea process.

"Okay, I really am going to pee," I say, needing to get out of the fray for a few moments.

"Yeah, me too. Sorry, Asher," Lily calls, chuckling as she follows me through the crowd of people still dancing.

"Girls," Asher mumbles as he turns towards the bar.

Like always, there's a line for the ladies' room. Lily and I take our spots behind two women complaining that VIPs should have a separate bathroom at the back of the club. My head turns to Lily, and I roll my eyes. Her hands fly to her mouth to smother a giggle, but it's too late.

The women turn around, glaring down at us. They aren't that much taller, but their five-inch stilettos make them appear as though they are.

I quirk one eyebrow at the pair as if to say, *do you have a problem?* They sneer, turning back to the front. Staring at the one woman's profile, I realized she was the girl with the gorgeous man outside the VIP room.

I can't help but sweep my eyes over her in complete jealousy.

She's wearing a waxed metallic dress that is easily more expensive than anything I own. It hugs her curves like a glove, showcasing a body that likely hasn't seen a carb in years. She's sexy and glamorous.

Looking down at my own dress, straight from Amazon, I can't help but feel inferior in every way. And I hate that. I'm not a jealous girl. I'm not someone who begrudges others for their success. I'm the girl who fixes crowns and cheers on my fellow women.

Apparently, not tonight. Here I am, hating her—a stranger—for simply being good enough for a man I've seen once in my life from across a crowded room. She'll get swept up in him tonight while I head back to my meager apartment alone.

It's pathetic.

"Hey, can I talk to you?" Lily asks, pulling me from my inner pouting.

She shifts on her feet unsteadily, alerting me to the fact she's clearly drunk and all her inhibitions are loose. I have no doubt in my mind that she wants to talk about Asher.

"Of course. What's up?" I say, ushering her forward as the line moves.

"Well . . ." she starts and seems unable to finish.

"It's about Asher, isn't it?" I ask, hoping to help her along in the right direction.

She nods. "Yeah. But not just that. It's about you and Asher." My head cocks back in incredulity.

"There's no me and Asher, Lil."

She sighs, and I want to shake her. "Would you ever want there to be?" she asks timidly.

An unladylike snort rips through me, and the two women in front of us turn, wearing matching looks of revulsion. I smirk, only managing to infuriate the pair more, before turning toward Lily.

"Are you crazy? No way. He's like my brother." My nose scrunches up in mild disgust at the thought. "I know you think he likes me, but it's only because we've known each other for so long. Trust me, nothing is going on between us, and there never will be." She blows out a breath in relief, and I smile.

"I know." She leans in and hugs me tight. "Thanks, Raven. You're my friend, and I wouldn't have done anything to get in the way if I wasn't sure you weren't into him like that."

I smile. "Talk to me about this anytime, okay? I promise you—Asher is permanently friend-zoned."

The line moves again, and the raven-haired girl of the evil pair in front of us drops her clutch. I lean down without thinking and retrieve it for the woman who can't even be bothered to offer thanks.

Money does not equate to class.

Lily leans in and whispers. "Uh . . . Raven, do you know that guy?"

I follow Lily's gaze toward the men's restroom.

The handsome man from the VIP room is directly ahead and looking straight at me.

He's even more devastating up close. A healthy dose of scruff, trimmed to look tidy but sexy as hell, gives him an air of brutish authority. A shiver runs down my spine, and my cheeks warm as I peruse every inch of the man unapologetically. A grin spreads across his face, which only manages to make him more roguish.

I quickly avert my gaze.

"No. I've never seen him before in my life." I'm not sure why I lie. I haven't actually seen him for more than a minute here in the club, but there had been a moment. At least on my end.

*Only your end, Raven.*

"Well, he obviously has his eye on you."

My head shakes back and forth. "No, he doesn't," I say and feel the color rush to my face again. "He's with her." I motion toward the bathroom where the two girls have disappeared. The man was long gone.

"Who?" she asks, looking around, face scrunched in confusion. "Are you blushing? You never blush."

"I'm not blushing. It's just warm in here," I say, fanning my face with my hand.

She chuckles. "Whatever you say, girl. Not that I'd blame you. That man was oozing sex."

My eyes close of their own volition. The image of the guy seared into my mind like a dream I'm not ready to let go of. I internally groan at how ridiculous I'm acting.

He's a handsome man, but I'm in New York City. A place that's crawling with attractive, successful guys at every corner. My reaction to him is nothing more than my body's way of rebelling against my self-imposed drought.

I've kept myself free of distractions, determined to focus on finishing up my degree and landing the job of my dreams in a competitive landscape full of impressive applicants. I've worked my ass off to graduate from Columbia Business School with my MBA, and I did it.

Men complicate things. Sex complicates it even more. So, for the past few years, I've avoided both.

"This is taking so damn long," someone barks from behind.

My eyes snap open to see that the line is still over ten people deep.

This is ridiculous. I let out of huff. "I can wait. You?"

"Yeah. Maybe the line will be shorter in a bit."

"Probably not. But we'll probably be drunker and not care as much." I laugh.

"I don't know how Ash likes this place. The people are so damn rude." A groan escapes Lily's lips.

"It's not so bad. We're having fun," I say, and she shrugs in response. "This is Asher's world, Lil. If you want a future with him, this will be your world, too."

Her cheeks stain a pretty pink, and her eyelashes flutter. "I guess."

I smile at my friend, hoping like hell I'm not leading her down a dead-end path with Ash.

We step away from the line, turning to walk in the opposite direction, narrowly knocking into the girl behind us. "Sorry," I offer, and she doesn't so much as grunt.

We're walking back through the crowd when I see the man standing at a tall table surrounded by more insanely gorgeous women. The first girl is nowhere to be seen.

Ugh. Typical. He probably took her for a ride in the VIP room and has moved on to the next pretty girl who looks his way.

He grins at my obvious scrutiny, and in complete embarrassment, I spin around so my back faces him.

"God. Take me home now." I cringe.

"What?" Lily's voice is concerned but confused.

"The guy from earlier caught me staring at him," I groan.

Lily's eyebrows waggle. "You should go talk to him."

"What? No." I shake my head wildly. "I don't even know him. That sounds like a terrible idea."

Lily grins, crossing her arms over her chest as though she's about to lecture a child. "You're scared," she teases, and my eyes narrow on her.

"Well, with my luck, he will probably end up being a mass murderer. He's probably stalking victims right now as we speak. In fact, he's probably a vampire." I bare my teeth in emphasis.

She throws her head back and laughs at my horrible acting.

"Come on, drama queen. Let's have a good time."

Lily spins me around and pushes me toward the bar, marching us right to Asher. He passes us each another round of shots. As much as I don't need it, I take it, relishing the burn as it slips down my throat.

"What took you so long?" Asher yells over the music.

"The line was long." Lily's shoulders shrug, earning her a broad grin from Asher. "And we didn't even go."

I gesture toward the dance floor. "Let's move," I say, grabbing Lily and dragging her out into the middle of the room just as the song changes to an old-school rap that's making a comeback in popularity. She doesn't fight it as both our inhibitions are lowered.

Lost in the haze of my buzz, I dance with abandon, not caring who's watching.

I feel carefree.

Beads of sweat drip down my neck, but I don't stop. I can't.

With the adrenaline running through my veins, all my worries from earlier are gone. My hands are thrown into the air as I swing my hips more daringly.

I spin around to find Lily, and my eyes lock on the same man again.

His eyes penetrate me from across the room. I watch as his tongue darts out, running across his bottom lip in a way that's sexy without trying to be.

From beside me, Lily nudges my arm, and I look over at her. "He really is gorgeous," Lily yells a little too loud. "You need to go talk to him."

Two hands grab my hips, pulling me back into a firm chest. I know immediately, based on Lily's expression, that it's Asher.

"Don't be silly. She's celebrating with us," Asher shouts. "A club is the worst place to meet a guy. Especially a good one."

"You're at a club, and you're a nice guy," Lily snaps.

I smile at my friend, twisting out of Ash's grip. "You're right, Lil. I should. And he does look . . . *nice.*"

Asher's arm snaps out, grabbing mine. "How the hell can you tell from here? He could be a serial killer."

"You're ridiculous," I accuse. "He's a vampire," I deadpan. "Get it right. Plus, look at him."

"Yeah. What about him? You can't tell anything about someone by their looks. Women liked Ted Bundy. Look how that ended."

Lily chokes on air. "Raven's right. You are ridiculous.

Nothing is wrong with her talking to a guy at a club. It doesn't mean she's leaving with him."

I nod at Lily in thanks for coming to my defense.

Asher scoffs but drops my arm.

I offer one last smile to Lily and turn to head toward the guy, but he's gone. *Again.*

Clearly, it's not meant to be.

# chapter four

Charles

**M**Y MOBILE NEVER FAILS TO BUZZ AT THE WRONG TIME, BUT this call can't be ignored.

I'm working my way to the front of the club, desperate to find an area free of the noise, which seems impossible at the moment. Silver is packed to the brim tonight.

"Kennedy, give me one moment. I'm trying to locate a quiet place," I yell down the line, hoping that this hiccup won't ruin Cavendish Group's chances to represent the hottest brand in the country.

Paxton recently alerted me to a sort of hidden hallway, where a few very private restrooms for important clients are kept, and it's not long before I'm sliding behind the wall and finally able to hear myself breathe.

I yank on the doors, but they're all locked.

"Shit," I bark under my breath, growing agitated.

I've waited for this call for two weeks, and they choose now? Just my luck.

Walking swiftly down a back hallway, I continue to search until I find an unlocked door. It's pitch black, save for the light streaming in.

The cloakroom is currently out of use due to it being summer. A few white sheets are hung along the racks, and a stack of extra chairs sits in the back corner. Otherwise, it's bare.

Entering, I quickly shut the door and breathe out a sigh of relief when the noise from outside is snuffed out, leaving me able to hold a conversation.

"Kennedy, I apologize. I'm currently entertaining clients at Club Silver, and the noise was deafening."

"No worries, Charles. I appreciate you taking my call at this hour. We just got word today about a new product launch, and it's moved up our timeline. A strategic advertising campaign is a priority."

This account would mean huge things for the company and our investors. I've been attempting to pitch to Diosa for six months.

Cavendish Corporation is a staple in the United Kingdom, but this branch, Cavendish Group, is different. This is a new company set up here in the States. We are the new kids on the block, scrapping for our piece of the pie.

I'm fortunate enough to have friends in high places that jumped on board immediately with me, helping with the competitive edge. But I'm still an outsider in this city.

Landing the high-end line, Diosa, will change all that. The owner of Diosa is the fashion designer of the decade. Working with them would ensure we're the crème de la crème of boutique advertising.

Every model, superstar, and athlete worth their salt is coveting one of Diosa's signature limited edition pieces, but the Diosa label doesn't just include couture fashion. Middle-class America is running to Macy's for their sister company's everyday wear under the Icon line and to every mall for their AlteredX fitness apparel. They're dominating the various markets.

When we represent them as their sole advertising team across all labels, it will be game, set, match for us with our competition.

Getting this pitch ensures it because I know we have the talent to land the account if I can only get in front of them.

"You name the day and time, and my team will be there to pitch."

"No need. This is a formality, Charles. We've seen what you can do. Drew has been raving about you for months."

I'm going to owe Drew a year's worth of scotch for his endorsement. It undoubtedly made the difference. He's well-connected and on a first-name basis with Diosa's owner, Sergio De Rosa.

"We just need to finalize the contract."

At her words, a smile I didn't realize I was capable of rendering breaks across my face.

"Brilliant," I croon. "Tomorrow? First thing in the morning?"

I hear shuffling on the other end as Kennedy likely shifts through her planner. Diosa is old school, relying on word of mouth, runways, and fashion magazines. They are still working on their digital marketing plan as the previous two have failed. As their head of marketing, it's one thing I'm going to stress to prioritize as part of our reinvigorations to their company.

"That's perfect. Come by the office then."

I nod, although she can't see me. "I'll be there."

"Thanks, Charles."

The line goes quiet, and I know Kennedy has already disconnected the call. It's ten o'clock, well past business hours, but the successful never sleep in this city.

Kennedy Ryker hasn't climbed to the most sought-after and highest-paid assistant in fashion by working nine to five. She's a powerhouse and Sergio's right-hand woman.

I pace the floor of the small room, not sure what to do with this renewed energy. That one phone call has changed the game. Cavendish Corporation is already a lucrative company in my home country, but this account makes this division the premier advertising agency in the US.

I'm practically bouncing off the walls, and I need to compose myself. One does not get to my level without the ability to remain grounded. We'll have our work cut out for us. Landing the account is one thing. Executing a flawless campaign is another entirely.

I'll need to hire additional help immediately.

Pulling up my contacts, I hit favorites and find my assistant, Shelby. Her husband, Brad, will likely want to wring my neck for calling at this hour, but it can't be helped. She's worked just as hard as I have trying to land this deal. I know her worth, and I won't let one minute more go without telling her the news.

"You rang?" she drawls, voice full of sleep and something similar to annoyance.

"Shelby. Darling," I murmur, attempting to ease her ire with charm.

"Since when do you attempt flattery? Better yet . . . why are you even attempting? What do you want at," there's a beat, and then she continues, "after ten?" Her voice pitches in question.

"I'm so very sorry, love, but it couldn't be helped. I know you'd have my balls if I didn't call you, no matter what time it was. We landed Diosa."

"What?" she yelps, and I hear Brad in the background asking if everything is all right. "Fine, babe. Go back to bed," she says to him. "Why did you wait so long to call me?"

"Kennedy just called me," I explain. "I finalize the contract tomorrow morning."

"Charlie, this is amazing," she shrieks.

I cringe at the nickname. She is the only person other than my mother who I've ever allowed to get away with calling me Charlie. After the incident that shall not be discussed, the name is tainted.

"You know I despise that name."

"Consider it payment for calling me in the middle of the night." I can practically see her rolling her eyes at me while she says it.

"It's not the middle of the night, you old crone."

She chuckles, knowing full well I'm teasing. I adore her. "And now, you'll be bringing me coffee tomorrow at my apartment."

"That's not how this arrangement works, love. You're my employee." I pick at my fingers, waiting for her to insist that coffee is deserved for this intrusion on her off time.

We've done this dance many a time before.

"It's how it works now. Unless, of course, you want to start the Diosa account without an assistant."

It's my turn to roll my eyes. Shelby Donaldson isn't going anywhere. I pay her exceptionally well for her experience and intuition on how to run my office.

"Fine. I'll bring your favorite black tar in the morning. Now, for the reason I called," I say, getting us back on track. "We need to hire four more analysts. One for Diosa and three to manage Icon and AlteredX."

She groans down the line. "We couldn't have discussed this in the morning?"

"No," I drawl. "I need you ready to make this happen first thing as you walk in while I'm gathering your coffee."

"Fine. We need an account manager more than we need another analyst." She sighs, and I know she's right. We're already stretched with the addition of two more restaurants owned by my friends and now clients, Drew and Bailey Lawson.

"All right, then. Make it happen."

"The analyst starting Monday has an impressive résumé." She blows out a breath. "She just graduated from Columbia with her MBA, but her internships and part-time work would be perfect for this account."

"Internships? Part-time experience? That won't cut it. This is Diosa we're talking about. I need someone impressive. We need someone with experience."

The line is silent, and I know that's Shelby's passive-aggressive way of showcasing that she doesn't agree with my assessment but will allow me my opinion as the owner.

"Perhaps we can switch her department. Seems she would be better suited for the Diosa analyst position?" I offer to appease her.

"I'll see what we're working with on Monday."

"No, tomorrow is already going to be wasted by not having the extra hands. I need her to start sooner. We'll hold an all-staff meeting to discuss this account while you and I iron out the details. We've had too many struggles as of late not to do this right from the start."

"Fine," she snaps. "Again . . . all things we could've discussed in the morning." She moans. "I'm tired. You owe me a scone now, too."

I swear, some days . . . if she wasn't so good at being my right-hand . . .

"Good night, Shelby."

Clicking the phone off, I hope she's able to get back to sleep. She isn't wrong. All of this could've waited until morning. I'm just too excited—not that I'd admit that to anyone—and needed to share the news with someone I know would care.

It's pathetic that the only person I have in the office to tell is my assistant.

*You pushed them all away because of her.*

I turn for the door, eager to push thoughts of my past from my mind. There's no room for that when something so positive has happened.

A celebration is in order, but not tonight. There's too much to do, and I need rest. My turn of the door handle is met with resistance.

"What the fuck?"

I jiggle the handle again, but the door won't open.

My hands drift blindly over the only thing standing between me and sleep. There's a keyhole on this side of the door. Meaning it's a double-cylinder lock, and I'm officially stuck.

*Son of a bitch.*

Fist banging against the metal, I call out to anyone close enough to hear, but I know it's no use. The hallway was empty and secluded from the main club. Nobody is going to hear me. Not until the music ceases its deafening level or the club closes for the evening.

Either way, my much-needed night of rest won't be happening unless Pax decides to actually check his phone for a change. When he's "entertaining," his phone is practically a paperweight.

"Fuuuck."

I make my way to the back, lighting the area with my mobile's torch feature, remove a chair from the stack, and take a seat before sending off a quick text to Pax.

**Me: Locked in cloakroom. Back hallway. Need help.**

It isn't until after I hit send that I realize how ridiculous this situation is.

Things better go off without a hitch tomorrow. My entire career rides on it.

The door handle jiggles, and I smirk.

"Thank God."

Paxton found me. I may actually kiss the bloke.

When the door pushes open, it's not Paxton's large frame shrouded in light but the backside of a woman backing into the cloakroom as though she's hiding from someone or something.

A mass of blonde waves stops mid-back, and the light streaming in overhead creates a halo effect that has me transfixed. Blinded by the beauty before me, I miss my opportunity to catch the door.

The door clicks shut, and an audible sigh escapes the woman and me simultaneously.

"Well, isn't this an unexpected turn of events?"

# chapter five

Raven

*Five minutes earlier . . .*

I'M NOT SURE WHY I THOUGHT THE LINE TO THE LADIES' ROOM would be any less ridiculous this time around. But here I am again, still *waiting*. And those extra shots didn't help.

Such a high-class establishment really needs to work on its flow.

With a huff, I admit defeat. *I might as well just go home.* It will probably take less time to get there then for one of these damn bathroom stalls to be free.

I step out of line and turn, running straight into a firm chest. The man grunts at the impact, and for a few quick moments, I see stars. Shaking it off, my eyes move up, meeting a pair of hazel eyes rimmed in blue.

"Hello there," he says, smiling down at me.

I recognize him instantly as one of the men outside the VIP room. He's very attractive but a bit too playboy for my liking.

Don't get me wrong, I love a good flirt, but this guy looks like he's brokering hookups in his sleep. The charisma oozing off him screams player with a big ole capital P.

"I'm sorry. Per usual, I wasn't paying attention."

I offer him my most dazzling smile, and it seems to work. He's grinning ear to ear.

"Where are you off to in such a hurry?" His eyes remain locked on me, and I have to refrain from rolling my eyes at his lame attempt at conversation.

I lean in conspiratorially, ready to ruin his game. Guys like this are typically easy to chase away. All you have to do is make them uncomfortable.

"Well, you see . . . this setup isn't working for me," I say, gesturing to the restroom and line. "So, I figured I'd find a dark alley. It'll be faster that way."

His head lolls back, and he barks out a laugh.

Not what I was expecting.

Typically, when you talk to guys about anything bodily, they run for the hills.

He wipes under his eyes. "You're funny."

I shrug. "I was only half teasing. That bathroom line is ridiculous. Guess it's time to call it a night."

"No alley in your future after all?" His eyes sparkle with mirth.

"No. I'm not the dark alley sort of girl."

I can't help but wonder where his friend went. Which girl is he currently entertaining? Why am I even thinking about a guy I've never seen up close?

I need help.

"That, I'm glad to hear. It's not safe for any woman." The man's tone is serious, as though he needs to warn me further.

It makes me curious about this guy's story. What has he seen or been a part of to have such a reaction to a strange woman joking about heading to the alley?

"Noted. I'll refrain from loitering in dark alleys. In the meantime, I need to find my friends so they can escort me to less unsavory places. Like my apartment."

His stoic features soften, and a smile spreads across his face.

"Good luck finding your friends. I'll be sure to tell Mathis you're not a fan of the restroom situation."

I shake my head. "Silver is incredible. It's just the clientele doesn't understand the concept of in and out."

"Fair point." He grins. "Be careful not to bump into anyone else."

I chuckle. "I shall endeavor to pay attention." I offer one last smile and turn to leave.

"Miss," the man calls out, and I turn with one brow raised.

He takes a step toward me and leans in. "There is another private restroom just back off that hall. It's for VIPs."

My eyes narrow. "Is that a thing?"

He nods. "At Silver, there is." His hand lands on my shoulder, twisting me in the opposite direction. "Just past those stairs is a hallway you'll miss if you blink. Go behind the wall and look for the metal doors. Those are the bathrooms."

My head bobs in confirmation that I'm following his directions.

"Don't let anyone see you."

It occurs to me that I don't know this guy and having him send me off to some deserted hallway sounds suspect.

I raise a brow. "Why exactly aren't *you* using this uber-secret VIP restroom?"

"Guys understand in and out."

"Touché. But if I end up being dragged into a back alley and stuffed into a van due to this tip you've offered, I will curse you for eternity."

"You are something. No kidnapping will ensue. You have my word."

I narrow my eyes playfully at the man. "We'll see."

He chuckles. "But truly, don't let anyone else see you go that way. Mathis wants that hallway to remain a secret."

"I won't," I say, unsure how I can possibly keep that promise in a place as packed as Silver. "I owe you."

"A fruit basket will suffice," he says, grinning widely, but it drops quickly, and his eyes dart around the area as if he's ensuring nobody can overhear us. "If you run into anyone and they ask what you're doing, tell them you're a guest of Paxton Ramsey."

"A fruit basket it is." I grin. "Thank you, Paxton. I appreciate your hospitality. Perhaps you should run the place."

He grunts. "I'll keep that in mind, Miss . . .?"

"Just call me Raven."

One side of his mouth lifts as he appears to mull over my name, finally deciding it's suitable.

"Nice to meet you, Raven. Enjoy your night."

Just like that, Paxton is off and linking arms with a beautiful blonde swathed in diamonds and barely covered by a red micro mini dress.

I don't waste time heading toward this elusive VIP restroom. I need to empty my bladder, grab a glass of water from the bar, and call it a night.

Paxton wasn't kidding when he said the hallway was hard to find. It's set up like something out of *Labyrinth*, a movie I once watched with a kid I babysat in high school. It's like an illusion. Looks like a wall, but really, it hides a secret hallway.

Very cool.

"Metal door," I say out loud, recalling Paxton's directions.

I open the first metal door in the hall I see, and there is a bathroom here, thank goodness! In and out in no time. Once I leave the bathroom, I start to head back to my friends when I hear voices from the opposite end of the hallway and begin to panic.

Paxton told me not to get caught.

My eyes scan the area, landing on another metal door. *Another bathroom, perfect.*

I rush to it and exhale in relief when the doorknob wiggles. I twist the knob and back myself into the room just as two people round the corner.

I click the door shut quietly and wait in the dark for a few seconds, hoping I wasn't seen.

"Well, isn't this an unexpected turn of events?"

My breath hitches, goose bumps rise over my arms, and tingles work their way down my spine.

Intoxicating is the only way to describe the sophisticated, sexy-as-hell British voice washing over me and turning my stomach to jelly.

Holy. Hell.

I have no clue who the man is or why he's sitting in the dark room, but the way my body reacts to the stranger I've yet to see is concerning on all levels.

"What are you doing in here?"

The man chuckles. "I could ask you the same thing, love. Except, I know why you're here."

I turn around to face him despite the fact I can't see even an inch in front of me. "Is that so? Why, pray tell, am I in this pitch-black shoebox with a strange man?"

He huffs. "Strange man? Don't play coy. You followed me here."

A choked laugh bursts from my chest. He's insane.

"I did no such thing." My voice pitches. "Follow you? I don't even know who *you* are."

"Well then, my mistake." The humor in his voice puts me at ease.

He doesn't sound like a psycho. Then again, what does a psycho actually sound like?

I watch too much true crime and way too many Netflix documentaries on serial killers. My overactive imagination is getting the better of me.

This is just a man. In a dark room. Alone.

There has to be a reasonable explanation, just like I have. I'll tell him I was still looking for the bathrooms. "I was told this is a private VIP restroom. What's your excuse for hiding in the dark?"

The man does something akin to a snort. "This is hardly the toilet," he says. "You've found yourself locked in a cloakroom, love. We're stuck."

"A cloakroom?" The words are barely a whisper. "Locked?"

I can't see anything, and that fact causes anxiety to surface.

"Locked," he repeats.

I spin around, hands fumbling to locate the doorknob, but when I finally find it, the air whooshes from my chest.

He's right. It won't open.

The heady feeling from moments ago is gone, and fear is taking root.

"Where are you going? I told you . . . we're stuck."

I turn slowly, back pressing against the door.

*Calm down, Raven.*

No such luck. Fear has me in its clutches and has effectively cut off my air supply. I'm not sure if it's the man's proximity or my slight claustrophobia kicking in, but I'm losing my cool.

My hands ball into fists, and my eyes slam shut as I work on my breathing.

The chair screeches across the tile floor as it sounds like the man stands.

Here I am, alone in this tight space, with a guy I haven't even seen. What if he hurts me? What if I'm left for dead? Body convulsing and breathing ragged, I try my best to calm myself, but it's no use.

The man comes closer until his body is practically hovering over me.

"Damn," he says into my neck.

"W-What are you doing?"

"Looking for a switch. There has to be—" His words are cut off when a light overhead beams down on us. "There we go."

My knees give out, and I slump toward the ground, but the stranger manages to catch me under the arms, hauling me up and pressing me against the door.

"Calm down." One hand continues to hold me up while the other lifts my chin. "Breathe. You'll be all right."

His voice is like honey, slipping around me in a cocoon of warmth. My breathing slows, and the panic ebbs.

"Good girl. Keep breathing. In through your nose, out through your mouth. I've got you."

With every passing second, my body relaxes, and he presses into me further.

When I'm completely calm and under control, the nearness of the man becomes more evident. My eyes open, and my breath hitches.

It's him.

"You," I say breathily, looking up into the bluest eyes I've ever seen.

He smirks down at me, showcasing two dimples. "Ah, so you *were* eyeing me up."

My cheeks heat, and embarrassment builds. "You can let me go now," I say, meeting his gaze.

"Right, then," he says, backing up and putting several inches between us.

I straighten my dress and run a hand through my hair, wondering if I look as horrible as I feel.

"You look fine."

My eyes sweep over his gorgeous face. Chiseled cheeks, strong jaw, straight nose . . . the stuff of gods. My head dips to the ground, feeling entirely off-balance.

"I thought I was going to have to attempt resuscitation in the dark, love. You were quite out of sorts."

"Raven."

His eyes narrow in on me.

"My name is Raven. Not love."

"Raven." He tests out the name, lips pursing. "Well . . . now that you've found me, perhaps we should make the best of this current situation."

"I wasn't looking for you. Paxton told me—"

His brows shoot up. "Paxton," he drawls. "I see my mate's made good on his promise. I must say, he's managed to—what is the American saying—*hit the ball out of the park* this time."

"What?" I ask, head shaking in confusion.

"Never mind. That doesn't matter," he says, taking two steps and invading my space expertly. "I'm just glad you followed his instructions and decided to meet me here after my phone call."

"Your call?" I ask, completely dumbfounded by what he's saying.

"You look confused, but if it's okay, I'd like to kiss you now."

"I . . . I . . . okay," I fumble my way through saying. Did this hot as hell guy just ask to kiss me?

His large, solid chest is pressed against mine before I can react further, palm caressing the side of my face. I don't even know how it happens, but his lips are pressed against mine, and I'm molding to him like it's the most natural thing I've ever done.

My mouth opens to his, allowing his tongue entrance. A whimper escapes me, and he reacts by grabbing my leg with his free hand and lifting it around his hip, pressing his erection into my core.

Even through his pants, I can feel he's larger than any man I've ever been with.

"Oh, God," I yelp out at the feel of him as his lips begin roving over my neck.

It's been so long since I've kissed a man, let alone whatever this is we're doing. It feels so good. Too good.

He's a complete stranger, and I'm in a locked closet, practically thrusting myself against him.

This is wrong.

I have to stop it.

His hand grabs the hem of my dress, gliding it upward, bunching it above my hip, baring my thong-clad ass in the process. When his hand runs over my ass, I about lose my mind.

His touch is lighting a fire in my core that's never been lit before. The need is excruciating at the moment.

"Tell me you want this." His British lilt is husky and hot as hell.

"I—"

He runs his finger up the outside of my panties, and I shiver in response. My answering moan fills the small space.

"Words, Rae."

Rae.

The name is like ice water being poured over my head. Only one man has ever called me that, and he's gone.

"What's wrong? Why are you pulling away?" he asks.

These men are all the same. Wealthy. Insanely attractive. Arrogant. Players.

I'm about to push him off me when the door flies open, and I fall backward. Two large arms catch me before I hit the ground.

"Whoa there, Raven. Nice to see you again." Paxton grins down at me. "I must say, you're a bit of a wrecking ball."

"Paxton," the man nearly growls. "Your timing is impeccable, like always."

Paxton's grin somehow widens at that as he lifts me to stand.

"Thank you," I say, running my hands down my dress. "You came at the perfect time. I think I'll add balloons to that fruit basket."

"That so?" he asks, looking at his friend, smirking like a loon. "How about chocolate bars instead, Raven? Better for the environment and all that."

I nod in response. "Obviously. Environment. Yeah. I'll sneak in just one then. I'm sure my friends are looking for me," I say, not meeting either man's eyes. "I better go find them."

"Raven."

I don't look at the stranger or Paxton as I turn my back and rush down the private hallway.

"Good night," I call out, never turning back.

My name is called several times before I slip out from behind the wall into the chaos of Silver.

Am I a chickenshit for running?

Probably.

Was it for the best?

Absolutely.

# chapter six

Raven

MUSIC BLARES THROUGH THE SPEAKER NEXT TO MY BED, AND I internally curse myself for setting an alarm on one of my last days off.

Not that I'm too upset. I still managed to sleep in. It's eight, and my internal clock is typically set at six o'clock on the dot.

It's been a nuisance on the weekend for years, but today, my body cooperated.

My pounding head brings awareness to why I was able to make it to eight. From the copious amounts of champagne and far too many shots consumed last night, I'm lucky I didn't get sick. It's been a very long time since I've had that much to drink.

After being locked in the closet and almost losing my mind by way of a kiss with a stranger, I found Asher and Lily, ordered two shots of shitty tequila, and chugged them both back, one after the other.

My friends looked at me like I'd sprouted a second head, but I didn't utter a word of what occurred in that closet, and neither one of them asked me why I was guzzling tequila like it was water.

Thankfully for me, they were both three sheets to the wind themselves and oblivious to my shame. Not that I had any real reason to be ashamed. I hadn't had sex with the guy. We simply kissed. It was mind-blowing and earth-shattering, but it ended right before everything got out of hand.

*Saved by Paxton.*

I should probably look the guy up and send him that fruit basket.

The phone on my nightstand begins to ring, and I don't even need to look to know it's my mother. The fact that she hasn't heard from me already this morning likely has her in a panic.

She knew I was going out with Asher and Lily, and there's no doubt she's afraid I didn't make it home last night. She's a worrywart. Always has been, but even more so now that it's just her and me.

"Hey, Mom," I say, cringing a bit at the volume of my voice.

There's a reason I typically don't drink that much. The hangovers are not worth it.

"Hi, darling. I was starting to worry. You typically call me before seven."

My mother is the master of managing to make me feel guilty without even trying. She's a wonderful, loving mom, but knowing she's alone, I have this self-imposed guilt every time I feel I've let her down.

Her worried tone causes the guilt to kick in.

"I'm sorry. I'm just waking up." I rub at my temples, trying desperately to rid myself of the jackhammer taking up residence in my skull. "It was a long night. Didn't get home until late." I've reverted to talking in clipped phrases because my aching head can't take full sentences right now.

"Hmm," she drones. "I'm not surprised. You *were* out with Asher after all."

"Mom," I scold. "We've discussed this. He's my best friend."

It's not that she doesn't like Asher. She's just always thought his motives for hanging around me weren't in line with mine. He's my best friend. The one I count on. The person I tell every secret to.

He's never been quite like that with me in return.

He always holds a piece of himself back, and Mom believes it's because his feelings go far beyond friendship, and he's not being honest with me.

Yet another person in my life who's hell-bent on ruining my relationship with Asher. Because him having feelings for me like that would ruin everything. They'd never be reciprocated. Ever.

"I know. You trust him," she drawls. "I just worry he'll break your heart."

"He's not going to break my heart because it's not his to break."

She sighs. "My darling, friends can break us just as easily. Sometimes, it even hurts more."

I know she remembers how her own friends managed to break her, and it makes me sad. She and my dad had a very active social life and a group of friends who were more like family. When my dad was diagnosed with cancer, they all rallied around her.

They gave her strength when she needed it the most. Their husbands were my dad's best friends, and his death came fast. Rocking all of us to the core. It was a blow that none of us would've ever been prepared for.

After the funeral was over and life had to go on, they all went on with their lives, leaving her behind.

The calls stopped.

The invitation to events ceased.

She was forgotten and left to suffer alone.

"Do you want me to bring you an iced coffee? Or maybe one of those little sandwiches from Starbucks?" she asks, drawing me back to the conversation.

The thought of food makes me queasy. "No, thank you. I have a busy day today. My last hurrah before work starts."

"My baby girl, starting her first job at a major advertising firm." She breathes in deep. "Your dad would have been so proud." Her voice is soft, and I can hear the sorrow in her words.

"Are you okay, mom?"

"It never gets easier. But I'm happy you were able to celebrate last night. It's what he would have wanted." The line goes quiet for a beat. "What are you up to today?" Her voice resumes its usual cheerful pitch as she changes the subject.

"I want to get some stuff done around here before life as I know it ends."

"Don't be so dramatic, darling. You'll have your weekends."

I snort. These types of jobs almost never have normal hours. Am I supposed to have my nights and weekends? Yes. But having worked several internships and part-time roles with large companies, I saw firsthand how overworked and underpaid people in my position are.

"Need help?" she asks, steering the conversation elsewhere.

When I moved to the city, my mom followed. After losing my dad and then her friends, she had no reason to stay in Michigan. She packed up the things that mattered most and followed me to the East Coast.

She lives in a tiny loft in Elizabeth, right across the river. It's a little more affordable and still close enough to drop in whenever she feels like it.

In fact, I'm shocked she didn't just swing on by today.

"As much as I appreciate it, I have a lot of errands to do. But if I get done early, I'll head your way," I offer, hoping not to have hurt her feelings. "Maybe we can have dinner?"

"I'd like that."

My phone beeps in my ear, alerting me to an incoming call. I pull the phone from my ear and see a number I don't recognize.

"Mom, I'm getting a call on the other line. I'll call you back?"

"Sure. Call me later."

I push accept before the call goes to voicemail.

"Hello, this is Raven."

"Hi, Raven. This is Shelby from Cavendish Group. How are you?"

"Oh, hi," I say, sitting up too quickly, causing the room to spin. "I'm doing well. Thank you. Is everything okay with my paperwork?"

I'd sent the last of my paperwork over yesterday and was told they'd call if there were any issues.

"Fine. Fine. We've had some huge developments for the company, and we need you to start tomorrow."

Tomorrow? I had so many plans for these next two days, and they're shot to hell with one call.

And so it begins.

"Sure," I say, pulling open the drawer to my nightstand and pulling out a notepad and pen. "Same start time?"

"Actually, could you be in at seven?"

*It's a test.*

These types of things are always a test in corporate America, and if I want to climb that ladder quickly, there's no way I could say anything but, "Absolutely. I'll see you at seven."

"Perfect. We need to discuss some changes in your employment and get all the necessary paperwork sorted before an all-company meeting at nine."

I shake my muddled head, questioning if I heard her wrong.

"I'm sorry, did you say changes in my employment?"

"Oh, sorry, I should've led with that." She chuckles. "This new opportunity for the company has opened some vacancies. Based on your résumé and stellar references, we believe you'd be a perfect fit. We can discuss the specifics tomorrow, but it would be a promotion to a bigger account, not a lateral move."

"That's . . . incredible."

"I'm glad you're open to it," she says, cutting me off. "We'll see you tomorrow at seven."

I can tell from her fast and clipped tone that she's in a hurry.

*Move along, idiot. Let the poor women go.* "Thank you," I offer, sounding dumbfounded.

"Thank you, Raven. Enjoy your day."

I place my phone on the white table, along with the pen and

paper, and sit against the headboard, sliding down until my head hits the pillow.

There are so many questions I should've asked before hanging up that call, but they'd all eluded me at the time.

Being caught off guard is the worst.

But I can't complain. It's taken years for some of my friends to be offered better positions, and here I am getting a better gig before I even start?

It sounds too good to be true. Which means it probably is.

I groan, hating that I'm being robbed of my last few days but ready to start earning real money. My mom has been paying for my apartment, and I know it's been a stretch for her, even with my father's life insurance money.

I'd tried to convince her we could live together to save, but she insisted I have the experience they'd always promised me. City living in a place of my own because I've never been fond of the idea of sharing a space with a roommate. My mom would be the only one I'd make an exception for.

I close my eyes, giving myself permission to rest today. All the projects I wanted to get done can wait. Sleep is more important. As I drift off, all I see are cornflower eyes and a devilish smirk.

⸺⸺◆◆⸺⸺

"I can't believe you already managed to snag a better position. You've got to be the luckiest girl I know, Raven," Lily says, stuffing a forkful of lo mein into her mouth.

After lying down for another hour, I got up and tackled my list. With the help of my mom, who insisted on coming into the city, and Lily, I managed to get two days' worth of stuff done in one.

"Her father and I have said that since she was born," my mom says, smiling widely. "She was born under a full moon, after all."

"I'm not sure it's lucky to be born during a full moon, Mom."

I take a bite of the chicken and rice my mom brought us and moan in appreciation.

Mom scoffs. "Nonsense. Full moons are magical."

"I agree," Lily says, nodding her head.

"Kiss ass," I whisper under my breath, sharing a smile with Lily.

My mom makes work of cleaning up the empty food cartons and carrying them the two steps to the kitchen. My place is one big open space, and my bedroom is separated by a row of foldable white panel wall dividers. It's small but cozy.

I'm lucky to afford this in the city.

"I need to go, lovies," my mom says, heading toward me with her arms outstretched. "Tomorrow will be here far too quickly for my liking." Pulling me into a tight hug, she places a kiss on my temple. "Good luck tomorrow. You make me proud."

I inhale, taking in the scent that is all Teresa Bennett. Jasmine with a hint of citrus and cedar wood. I squeeze her back, wishing she'd stay but knowing I'll need to get to bed soon myself.

My mom is home.

She's my comfort, and it's always hard to let go, even when I know I'll see her soon.

After experiencing the loss of my dad, the reality that life isn't promised is a dark cloud that hovers above, spoiling even the best of days.

"Love you, Mom."

"Love you, baby girl." She wipes a tear from under my eye. "Why the sad face?"

"I just wish Daddy were here."

Her sharp intake of breath always comes at the mention of him. The hurt from his absence never quite abated. I doubt it ever will. He was her soul mate, and love like that doesn't come around twice in a lifetime.

Or so she says.

"He's so proud of you. You know that, right?"

I nod, unable to form words, emotion threatening to tug me under.

This is a happy time, and I refuse to have it spoiled because I'm unable to celebrate what I do have. A mom who loves me fiercely and a friend that's willing to give up her one day off to help me organize my messy apartment.

I stand tall, take a deep breath, and offer a genuine smile. "Thanks for dinner."

Her hands rise to my shoulders, squeezing. "I'm glad I got to spend the afternoon with you two."

I walk her to the door and offer one last hug and smile before shutting the door and turning on a sigh.

When my eyes meet Lily's, she's staring at me with a look I can't quite place.

"What?"

She shrugs. "You've been a bit off today. And I know it's not just about your father. Care to tell me why?"

I walk past her, heading to the chair, and swipe the carton of lo mein from her hands.

"Hey! I wasn't done with that," she whines.

"Calm down, killer. I just want a small forkful."

I scoop one small pile onto my paper plate and pass the carton back to her.

"Okay, you have your lo mein . . . now spill," she snaps.

I take a bite, ignoring her words and averting my gaze.

"I'm not letting this drop," she presses. "Where were you for almost twenty minutes last night? You came back looking like you were in shock and slammed two shots of tequila."

Okay, so she did notice.

I blow out a breath and decide there's no reason to hide what occurred from Lily.

"Remember that guy you saw looking at me?"

Her eyes widen, and she nods like a lunatic.

"Well . . . I sort of got locked in a closet with him."

"What?" she yells, jumping to her knees and scooting toward me. "How the hell did that happen?"

"I was using a private restroom that someone told me about, but when I stepped out, I heard someone coming. I was told to not be seen, so I ducked into what I thought was another bathroom, but instead stumbled into the closet that locks from the outside."

Her hands fly to her mouth, covering her glee-filled squeak.

"Tell me all the gory details."

I take another bite, clearing my plate.

"Not much to tell," I say around a mouthful. "We made out, and then someone found us."

Lily's nose scrunches. "You made out? That's all?"

I roll my eyes. "What did you expect, Lil? I'm not the kind of girl who has sex in a closet in a club."

She grunts. "That may be so, but with that guy? You should've made an exception. He was easily the hottest guy I've ever seen, Raven."

She isn't wrong. I agree wholeheartedly that he is a caliber far beyond what I'm accustomed to attracting.

"Then it's a good thing I didn't embarrass myself by throwing my body at him."

She snorts. "You're an idiot for not throwing your body at him."

I press my lips together and narrow my eyes at her.

"What? It's not like you'll ever see him again."

"That's exactly why I didn't. I have standards."

She blows out a breath. "Are you waiting for a ring?"

"Not a ring . . . but a commitment? Yeah, I think I'll hold off for one of those."

"Last I checked, you said you didn't have time for commitments."

Damn Lily, always calling me out on my bullshit.

"I'd make time for the right guy," I say, picking at my fingernails.

"How will you ever meet the right guy when you're constantly pushing away any that comes along?"

"I resent your words of wisdom right now."

She chuckles. "I'm just saying, it's okay to let loose every now and then. Having consensual sex with a gorgeous man isn't a crime, Raven."

"He called me some other girl's name," I say, voice pitching. It's a bit of a lie, but she doesn't need to know that Rae was what he used.

Her eyes widen. "Why didn't you lead with that? That's a whole other matter entirely."

"Now you see," I say, swiping my hand out. "I stopped before it went too far because the guy likely slept with another woman earlier in the night. He's a player."

She blows out a breath. "Well, that's a disappointment. In that case, I'm glad you left him with blue balls."

I choke on the water I just swallowed. "Who said anything about that?"

"You left him in a closet where you'd just been making out hot and heavy." She shrugs. "It's unlikely he didn't have them."

My head shakes as I laugh at my friend. "Oh, my God. Let's talk about something else. *Anything* else."

And we do.

We talk for another hour about life, but my mind is back in that closet with the sexy stranger the entire time.

The fact is, if he hadn't called me Rae, I probably would've given myself to him. And I'd likely be regretting it today.

I'll likely be dreaming of him for months to come because you don't forget guys like that.

Player or not.

He is something otherworldly, and that sort of sex appeal is tough to shake.

Those beautiful blue eyes and dimples to die for could make any strong woman cave.

# chapter seven

Raven

S ITTING AT MY NEW DESK AT MY BRAND-NEW JOB IS EXCITING. But truth be told, I feel like an imposter.

It's like I'm watching a movie of myself or am involved in a very real dream.

I keep running my hands over the wooden desk, wishing someone could take a photo of me to send to Asher.

How dorky would that be?

Very.

Plus, I have a feeling that wouldn't go over well in this place.

A few people have been less than kind today, making me wonder if it has anything to do with my change in position. Were they originally hoping to snag the promotion?

So, yeah, nope.

There will be no pictures.

I don't want to come across as the childish new girl taking selfies in her unearned office.

My phone pings, and I look to see a text from Asher.

**Asher: How's the day going?**

**Me: You must have ESP because I was thinking about you . . .**

**Asher: Oh, yeah? This I've got to hear . . .**

I reread that last text I sent, cringing at the way it might come across. Lily and my mom have burrowed so deep in my head that I'm now freaking out that I'm sending mixed signals. It sucks. I've never worried about this sort of thing with Asher. I've always been myself and said whatever I wanted without thought. Now, I'm analyzing everything.

**Me: Well . . . less about you and more about sending you a selfie of my new desk.**

**Me: I HAVE A DESK!!!!!!**

**Asher: That's a lot of exclamation points. This desk must be special . . .**

**Me: It is! I already got a promotion!**

I arrived ten minutes before seven, and Shelby met me at the door. She ushered me into an office and said it was mine if I wanted it. Not a cubicle like I was originally given, but an actual office.

**Asher: What the hell? How did you manage that?**

**Me: Let's get together and chat.**

**Asher: For sure!**

**Me: I'll text you later.**

I put my phone down, eager to use these last few minutes before the all-staff meeting to go over my new position. Instead of being one of five analysts, working little jobs for many accounts, I'm the lead advertising analyst for a new client that Cavendish picked up.

She couldn't disclose who the account was until after the president, Charles Cavendish, announced it to the execs, but she assured me it was a huge opportunity. One that could lead to a much bigger role, a lot sooner than expected.

The only caveat is that I'm unable to meet the account manager—my new boss—as interviews are still underway. The thought of taking a job before meeting the person I'll spend most days with is a little disconcerting. What if I don't like him or her?

I shake off that thought, eager to make this work. It's a

once-in-a-lifetime opportunity. The pay is double what I was originally offered, and the experience is crucial for further opportunities.

It's an exciting working environment.

My door is open, and I can hear people talking, phones ringing, and ideas floating. It's exactly what I hoped for.

There's a knock on my doorframe, and I look up in time to see Shelby.

"How's it going so far?" she asks, taking a step inside the door.

I offer a smile and motion for her to take a seat across from me. She doesn't need to ask permission, of course, but it seemed like the right thing to do.

She smiles wide and takes the offered seat.

"So far, so good," I say. "For the most part."

She raises a perfectly sculpted eyebrow. "For the most part?"

I fold my hands on my desk and lean in. "I've researched my new position as much as I can, and now, I'm not entirely sure what I'm supposed to be doing."

I've just clicked on random folders and opened my desk drawers a million times, trying to at least look busy for the past thirty minutes.

She nods. "Once the meeting is over, you'll be watching HR modules for the rest of the day," she offers. "We've also promised Mr. Keller that he could use you until we're able to fill your role." She grimaces but quickly schools her face back into neutral.

It's obvious that Mr. Keller isn't well-liked around here. I dodged a bullet by not having him as my superior, which, come to think of it, could be the reason some have been prickly toward me. I can't blame them. He's not the friendliest of men.

He was tasked with getting me situated in my office. He spent about five minutes pointing out various things and then stormed from the room, barking orders at everyone in earshot. They all seem a little afraid of him, and it's no wonder.

"They're ready for the meeting," Mr. Keller barks from the other side of the door. He completely ignores Shelby, directing his next words to me. "I'd like you to take notes. As head of our division, it's important for me to remember everything that goes on, and as head of the division, I simply cannot listen adequately *and* take notes. I'll have to rely on you, despite the fact you've been here for two seconds."

His disdain is evident, but I don't let it get me down.

Plastering on the biggest, brightest smile I can muster to the cranky, old man, I nod my head. "I'll do my absolute best, Mr. Keller."

The corner of his lip tips up in what looks like more of a sneer than anything else, but I don't let my smile drop. He practically growls and walks away.

I notice that he likes to use the words "head of the division" as often as he possibly can. Completely unnecessary since I'm not his direct report, so he has no need to enforce his authority over me. But men like him use fancy titles to compensate for other lacking areas.

"That man is insufferable," Shelby says under her breath, but I don't miss it.

An unladylike snort rips from me, and I quickly cover it with my fist.

"Sorry," I say with a lopsided smile.

She grins. "Well, we best be on our way before he comes back in here, whining some more."

"Yes, of course," I say, pulling out a notebook and two pens from my desk. Always good to be prepared.

I follow her out of my office and down a narrow hall until we reach the floor lobby.

"We'll take the elevator," she says, pressing the button and waiting in silence for the door to open.

We don't say another word the entire ride up to the floor with the largest conference room.

The air is thick with tension, and I wonder what's to come that has Shelby so nervous. She'd made whatever account Cavendish has picked up a very good thing, but the way she's acting now has me wondering.

"Are you okay?" I ask, knowing it's none of my business.

She looks straight, never once looking my way. "Fine. I'm not a fan of tight spaces."

I relax, feeling relief that her current mood has nothing to do with the upcoming meeting.

The relief gives way to the memory of the last time I found myself in a tight space, in the dark.

A sexy stranger.

His hands.

His tongue.

The way he made me feel.

That's until it all came crashing down.

I sigh. "I'm not a huge fan either," I admit. "If the lights went out in here right now, I'd freak. But it's all good. It's almost over."

She looks at me out of the corner of her eye and offers a tight-lipped smile.

"Thank you."

I shrug. "I did nothing."

The doors ding open, and a flurry of activity greets us. People mill about the hallway, making small talk. Their voices are full of excitement as they discuss who they think the new account is.

"That's enough," Shelby chastises, not harshly, but enough to get their attention. "Mr. Cavendish won't be happy if you're not all in your seats and ready for the announcement."

They scurry off, heading toward two glass doors that open into a large conference room. There are easily fifty people taking seats, and I can't help but be amazed at how quickly Cavendish Group has grown. They only opened a few years ago in the United States.

Charles Cavendish Sr. is a legend in the United Kingdom, but here in the States, his son is a bit of a mystery.

Rumor is he should've been taking over the UK office reins from his ailing father but, instead, opened this division in the US.

There's little to be found on the internet about him. He's very elusive, but word travels fast in business.

It's why I wanted to work with Cavendish. Creating a growing company while staying out of the spotlight himself.

It speaks highly to his work ethic if he's able to pull the clients he has without being like every other flashy marketing executive in the business. There's so much potential under that kind of leadership, and I could learn a lot in this job.

I quickly find a seat in the first row at the end and wait for the meeting to proceed. A woman next to me offers a small smile.

"New girl?"

"Yes. Hi. I'm Raven," I say, offering my outstretched hand to her.

She takes it in her hand, squeezing gently. "I'm Liz. Welcome on board. I've been working for Cavendish for three months. Short time, but let me know if I can help."

"How do you like it?" I ask, curious to know if the company as a whole is better than what I've seen in regard to Keller.

"It's wonderful," she says. "Of course, there are a few assholes in the bunch, but overall, the environment is fantastic. Execs listen to everyone's ideas, and credit is given where it's due."

"Good to know," I reply.

"Rollout meetings are a big thing. How exciting to experience one on your first day," Liz says, smiling over at me.

Asher had told me as much. He said every time a new client is announced, the office's excitement builds. Ideas are shared, and in some cases, celebrations occur.

"I'll be working closely with the new client, so I'm excited about this."

"Ah . . . that's why they're staring," she says, looking around.

That's when I notice a few people staring, whispering behind their hands.

"Don't pay them any attention. They're all jealous because they're not good enough to get the promotion."

I blow out a harsh breath. "Not exactly how I wanted to start."

"Never mind them. They weren't going to get it regardless of you. Most of these runners will only ever be just that. At least here at Cavendish."

"He's coming," someone announces to the room as footsteps sound down the hallway.

The air shifts, and everyone quiets, sitting up a little taller. I find myself doing the same while I open my notebook and prepare to take notes.

"We have lots to discuss, so I'll need your undivided attention. Hold all questions until the end. Is that clear?"

"Isn't he absolutely spectacular?" Liz whispers to me.

My head lifts, eyes landing on the owner of the company. The elusive Charles Cavendish.

The room spins, and I feel a bit faint.

"Are you all right?" Liz murmurs, her hand landing on my leg.

I close my mouth as I realize it's hanging open.

It's him.

The man from the club—the handsome stranger from the coat closet.

A part of me expects him to react when he sees me, but his eyes merely trail over me without recognition. I narrow my eyes to make sure it's him. But there's no denying that the man in front of me is the same man from Silver. I'd seen him up close and personal. Had his tongue down my throat, hands all over my body.

All sorts of emotions begin to rage through me.

Excitement.

Nervousness.

Irritation.

*He didn't even recognize me.*

I sit for the next fifteen minutes, listening to him speak. He's been going on about shifts in management due to the upcoming news, and I frantically write down as much as I can.

I'm so distracted by his presence that I know I've missed half of what's important.

Mr. Keller is going to be more than displeased with my first assignment, but I couldn't care less at the moment. This turn of events is just too much.

The man at the front of the room is too much.

*The* Charles Cavendish is *my* sexy stranger.

My new boss.

What the hell are the odds?

The room erupts, pulling me from my internal wonderings.

My eyes glance around the room, taking in the excitement and trying to catch wind of what I missed.

Liz puts me out of my misery, leaning in. "He scored Diosa Clothier."

My breath hitches.

This can't be real. Sergio De Rosa is a legendary designer. The recent growth of his brand has been sparking rumors all over the web. Their digital campaigns have been failing for their athletic wear. This could be a huge turning point for them. Landing this account is next-level, and I'm going to be working on it.

This is a game changer.

A goofy smile spreads across my face as I digest how massive this news is. But it quickly falls when my eyes land on Charles. He's staring right at me, eyes narrowed.

He does know exactly who I am, and he's not happy to see me.

# chapter eight

Raven

M R. KELLER LOOKS OVER MY NOTES, GRUNTING IN DISAPPROVAL. We're back at my desk, and I'm trying to get Mr. Keller to go away so I can focus on the HR web training, but he's bound and determined to make me as uncomfortable as he can manage.

"I can't read this chicken scratch," he bemoans, throwing the paper onto the desk in a huff.

I chew on my bottom lip, trying my hardest to remain positive. "I'll type them out for you," I offer, hoping to appease him.

I've already decided that I don't like Mr. Keller, but I'm going to force him to like me if it's the last thing I do. Even if it's useless. I'm not working for him much longer.

I inhale, basking in the knowledge that soon I'll be working directly with De Rosa. The ideas are already percolating, and I'm so excited to brainstorm with the team. Whoever that consists of.

The heady feeling is washed away, thinking back on that unpleasant stare down by Charles Cavendish.

My nerves are shot.

It was awful. I'd lowered my eyes quickly when I realized he wasn't going to look away first and kept on writing with a smile plastered across my face.

What could he possibly have been thinking? I tortured myself with that question for the remainder of the meeting.

He clearly put together who I am and was likely as caught off guard by my presence as I was his.

Luckily for him, I'm a professional, and a little kiss in a dark closet, fueled by booze and tiredness, will not impact my work ethic. I'll kick ass in this job, and that one little slipup at Silver will be long forgotten.

It has to.

It's day one, and I can't mess up this opportunity.

"Helloooo. Earth to Miss Bennett," Keller hisses.

"I'm sorry. What did you say?" I pop my head up to look at his round, ruddy face.

"I said, make sure that you do." He stalks from the room.

My body deflates, and I sink back into the chair, wondering how long I'll have to put up with this man.

Sighing, I fire up the next web training module and hit play. This particular video focuses on proper work etiquette.

It's common-sense material—or should be—so my mind wanders to things it has no business wandering to.

Strong jaw, straight nose, cheekbones chiseled from stone, muscles flexing under my touch, tongue caressing mine . . . memories permanently etched into my mind.

Charles Cavendish.

Lucky for me, my stomach chooses that moment to growl, and for once, I appreciate the distraction.

It's just after eleven, and I haven't yet been told when I can take a lunch break. People have been coming and going since the meeting, but I figure I can't just walk off on my first day.

Thankfully, I'm smart enough to have thought ahead and brought food. I pull out the sandwich and stuff it into my mouth. I'm eating it so quickly that I hope nobody sees me. I'm unsure of the protocol here. Can we eat at our desk? Is there a cafeteria?

Worse than not knowing what's allowed, I definitely don't want to scare anyone off on the first day with my less than proper food shoveling.

As I'm just about to swallow my last bite, and I'm wiping crumbs off my shirt, Shelby and Charles—no, Mr. Cavendish—walk by. Neither spares me a look, and for that, I'm grateful.

They stop just past my door, and I wonder if they're aware that I can hear every single whispered word.

"Not acceptable, Shelby. She just graduated. Past internships are not enough to have prepared her for this account. I won't have it."

"With all due respect, Mr. Cavendish, you don't have any other options." Shelby's tone is sharper than one would expect, being as though she's addressing the CEO of the company.

"What about Liz Montoya? Or Persephone Adams?"

I bristle when it becomes obvious they're discussing my qualifications, and he clearly finds me lacking. Is this because of my lack of experience or what occurred at Silver?

"Liz was just put on Mr. Lawson's new accounts, and Persephone . . . well, let's just say she's a complete idiot. Incapable of following directions if her life depended on it." She sighs. "Charlie, listen to me. Experience doesn't always equate to talent. Raven Bennett is talented. Her references are glowing."

Charlie? It doesn't suit him at all, but then again, I don't know him. Having one's tongue down your throat does not equal familiarity.

He grunts. "Who are these glowing references?"

She begins rattling off the list of references I supplied, which is an impressive list if I do say so myself.

"All right," he says.

"Megan Hall," she continues. "Frank LaBlanc."

"I said, all right," he snaps. "You've made your bloody point. Let's get this introduction over with, shall we?"

My hand darts out, swiping away every last crumb from the desk as I pull the notepad toward me. Once that's in order, I grab the bottle of water to the side and quickly take a sip, hoping to wash down any remaining food I have in my teeth. I'm just swallowing when Shelby walks through my door with a brooding Charles Cavendish on her heels.

I straighten in my seat, trying my best to look thoroughly enraptured by the notebook containing my chicken scratch.

"Raven, I'd like to introduce you to our CEO, Charles Cavendish."

I stand, doing my best to act as though this is the first time I'm meeting him. I extend my hand, willing it not to shake. "Pleasure to meet you, Mr. Cavendish. Raven Bennett."

His eyes narrow in on my proffered hand, and I thank God that Shelby isn't paying him any attention and, therefore, has not noticed his icy demeanor toward me.

Eventually, the ass takes my hand in his and offers a too-firm shake. "The pleasure is all mine, Miss Bennett," he says through his teeth.

Shelby looks at him, pulling a face, but he ignores her, continuing to glare directly at me. With a shake of her head, she turns back to me. "We came to see how you're settling in."

I plaster on the cheeriest, fakest smile I can muster. "Everything's going incredibly," I say. "I've been doing some homework. Between HR modules and researching Diosa, the ideas are already flowing."

Charles grunts, and Shelby's mouth pinches together. I can tell she's embarrassed by his behavior, but I refuse to show either of them that I'm bothered by it.

I somehow manage to beam brighter, and eventually, her pinched expression relaxes into a smile.

"That's wonderful, Raven. I can't wait to hear what you've come up with."

"She's an analyst, not the account manager," Charles directs to Shelby, completely ignoring me.

I'm done allowing him to treat me like I'm invisible. I get it, I caught him off guard, but he did the same to me. We're professionals, and it's time he starts acting the part.

"An advertising analyst worth her weight brings fresh ideas

to her superiors, right?" I look directly at him when I say it, and I don't miss the way his jaw clenches and eye twitches.

He's not used to being challenged. Well, buckle up, Mr. Cavendish, because this girl isn't going to be cowed by your obtuse attitude and hoity-toity hotness.

"Well said, Raven," Shelby offers in encouragement.

I really like this woman. Not only is she kind, but she doesn't take his shit, no matter who he is.

"Perhaps an *assistant* to the *assistant* of Diosa Clothier should worry more about her appearance and less about ideas."

Shelby gasps, probably realizing that her boss is a walking, talking HR nightmare.

A whooshing sound echoes through my ears as I try to breathe through my annoyance and calmly have him clarify what he's implying about my appearance. "I'm sorry?"

He motions toward my chest, and my eyes widen. "You have crumbs all over you, Miss Bennett."

My face heats, but I push down the embarrassment and swipe my shirt, ridding it of the breadcrumbs.

"I'll endeavor to be more presentable in the future." I look toward Shelby. "I was unsure when and where I'm to eat lunch, so I ate here so I could continue to work. It won't happen again."

"We'll see," he says, turning toward the door. "There's a meeting for the Diosa team in ten. Be there on time."

He strides from the door, leaving Shelby and me alone. She crosses her arms, watching him disappear around the corner.

"Raven, I'm so sorry. He's a bit stressed since landing this new client and the growth of Cavendish Group in such a short time."

I smile, hoping to ease her worry. She's likely fretting that I'm about to quit, leaving them even more short-staffed. Oh, the trouble this woman probably endures at the hands of her boss.

"No worries, Shelby. I've worked with a few men like Charles Cavendish. It's nothing I can't handle."

Her shoulders appear to relax, and a loud breath escapes her lips. "Well, I'll work to get him under control."

With that, she spins on her heels and stalks off after him.

Something tells me he isn't going to make my job easy, but I refuse to allow him to mess this up for me. He was equally involved in the situation at Silver. I won't allow him to pin this all on me.

———————•✦•———————

"Diosa needs someone like Summer Smith to represent their brand. A rising pop star who's currently the darling of the media. It's perfect."

A man with greasy hair and too-thick eyebrows addresses the room filled with suits.

Since the team that will lead Diosa is not quite assembled, Charles invited the C-Suite to attend a meeting about the campaign so the ball can get rolling. Shelby instructed me when I arrived to take notes for her.

I listen as this new face to me drones on for several minutes about the potential this pairing could have. I write down everything that's being said and manage to refrain from rolling my eyes when he outlines Summer Smith's highlights.

It all sounds like something he's gotten directly from a tabloid.

*How is any of this relevant to Diosa?*

Outside the fact that she's the most popular singer of the year, what does she bring to the label as a whole? More importantly, what does the label bring to her? I've yet to hear how this fits Summer.

Diosa is elegant, and Summer Smith is the epitome of a cool girl. She's a better fit for the AlteredX athletic brand.

Even I know more about her than this stuffy suit does, and I didn't even know we were going to be discussing her today.

Mr. Keller interrupts a few times to have his say, and it's obvious he doesn't know jack about her either. In fact, I question why he's even here.

I stifle a groan but eventually realize they will lose a big client if they continue down this route. I try to keep my mouth shut, opening and then closing it and biting my lip. But eventually, I can't take it anymore, and I raise my hand.

Mr. Keller glares at me, motioning for me to put my hand down, but I act as though I don't see him, keeping my hand up and smiling at all the suits staring in my direction.

"Miss Bennett, do you have a question?" the greasy-haired man leading the discussion asks while sounding annoyed.

A few of the suits chuckle under their breaths, but I stuff down the embarrassment and forge on. I didn't get this far in life by allowing some assholes to run me off.

Mr. Keller clears his throat. "I'm not sure Miss Bennett is ready to offer ideas in front of this management team, sir."

I shoot him an annoyed look before masking it behind a wall of fake cheer. "I assure you and Mr. Cavendish, I wouldn't waste anyone's time by offering ideas I feel bring nothing to the table."

Charles's eyes narrow, and his hands ball into fists.

My presence is definitely not wanted by him, and that fact not only annoys me, but it also bothers me for reasons beyond the boss factor. And I don't like those feelings.

"Well, then, Miss Bennett, get on with it. I'm the CEO of the company and have things to do with my time."

The CEO of the company.

What a damn egomaniac. I bet everyone in the room would be interested in knowing what the CEO does to strangers at clubs in coat closets.

"I think it's best she gets more training under her belt, sir," Mr. Keller says. "She didn't mean to put her hand up."

My head snaps to him, nose scrunching up. I can't stop my annoyance from showing.

Charles raises his eyebrows at Mr. Keller and then turns to me.

"Did you mean to put your hand up?"

This is getting ridiculous. For a man who has better things to be doing, he surely is wasting his own time asking worthless questions.

"I didn't raise it by accident, sir."

Laughter breaks out around the room, and I feel a deep blush form on my face. This is not the sort of first-day impression I was hoping to make. Not only is Keller making a fool out of us both, but I've clearly made an enemy of the boss. The whole room has to see his disdain.

He leans back, elbows resting against the desk, looking bored and incredibly sexy in the process. It manages to throw me off my game and muddle my brain, so I look away. My eyes scan the room, looking for someone willing to offer a smile of encouragement.

"Then please, get on with it." I look up at him. He's grinning, surely prepared to watch me make an even greater fool of myself.

I take a deep breath and repeat the mantra, *you've got this*, at least three times in my head. When I'm finally calm, I take one more deep breath, straighten my shoulders, and dive in.

"Summer Smith is huge with the younger crowd. She's a style icon, but her personal brand is relaxed, casual, and a bit hipster. Her Instagram and Snapchat following is insane, but beyond her music, it's due to her mystic and yoga posts."

"Your point?" Mr. Keller snaps, and for a change, that glare of Charles's is directed at him.

"Go on, Miss Bennett," Charles directs, looking back at me with a slightly less annoyed glance.

"She likes to be in the limelight, and she wants everyone to know who she is, so she'll take this deal, but Diosa isn't going to be a fit for her to be the ambassador of the whole brand. AlteredX? Perhaps, if we tie it into her yoga posts."

"Interesting," a gray-haired man sitting next to me says without out any hint of sarcasm.

"I know the demographic interested in Summer Smith, and they're not Diosa clientele on a daily or even yearly basis. She's AlteredX."

"What would you suggest?" Charles asks, his eyebrow lifting. He's looking at me with a renewed sense of interest, and it's hard not to be distracted by his intense blue eyes and the dimples showcased by the barest of smiles.

I'm still annoyed with him for his attitude toward me, but I can't help but melt a fraction when he gives me a chance to showcase my creativity. I only met him once, and he's already quite possibly the most infuriating person I've ever met, and still, I find him incredibly handsome. That truth I hate above all.

"She's been on the scene for several years, and her brand is still very immature. She's ready to evolve and grow her fan base. Her recent album is more mature and soulful. Diosa can help her brand mature as well."

"How?" Charles crosses his arms, giving me the stage.

"Start her with AlteredX to capitalize on her current fan base, then work with her new album to cross into the other brands. In the meantime, find other talents that already fit the mold for Diosa. Someone who needs to show their everyday side. Maybe a model or movie star?"

He pushes himself away from the desk, standing up straight and running his hands down his suit.

"Put together some ideas for me. Because, clearly, you know more about this pop singer than I do. And I don't mind admitting that."

"Yes, sir."

My eyes meet his, and I offer a nod before collecting my things to head out and get started.

"And Rae," he calls to me, making my shoulders stiffen at the mention of the name that ended our time in the closet. "Don't disappoint me . . ."

He leaves that sentence hanging as though he wants to add words to it. If we weren't in a room full of his employees, he would've said don't disappoint me *again*.

I hope his balls were blue for days.

# chapter nine

Raven

I WALK BACK TO MY DESK ON A CLOUD OF HAPPINESS.

He listened to me. Charles Cavendish, the CEO of Cavendish Group, gave me the opportunity to put together a plan.

This is my shot to prove that I deserve to be taken seriously. Because *the seven minutes in heaven* with him didn't help my case.

Seeing him in that room was a shock. Of all the people in all of New York City to make out with in a closet, it had to be him.

Just my freaking luck.

His frosty demeanor toward me was a bit much, but I couldn't let it get to me. He is the owner of this company and was surely just as taken aback as I was. I can understand that. He likely feared I'd tell the others in the office about our rendezvous, but I wouldn't. Ever.

I care about what my colleagues think of me, and I'd never want them to accuse me of getting this job because I threw myself at the boss. Because I most certainly didn't.

He was the one who practically ravaged me. At least that's what I'm going to tell myself. It's less humiliating that way.

Maybe he'll take me aside and speak to me about it when we're alone. Clear the air and start anew.

I shudder at the thought. I seriously hope he drops it and never brings it up again.

Mr. Keller storms in, looking like he's about to rip my head off. I gulp, preparing for his wrath.

"Uh, hi, Mr. Keller. I was just about to type up these notes for you."

"Raven," he grits through his teeth, spittle flying out of the corner.

He looks deranged, and it makes me wonder how he got this job in the first place. I might not know Charles, but he doesn't seem the type to suffer fools, and this guy is making a complete ass of himself.

"I am *not* at all happy with the way you conducted yourself in that meeting. You do realize that you made me look like a complete idiot in there."

A few heads peek over the cubicle walls, watching the showdown.

I wish he'd lower his voice.

I don't need to be the talk of the office on my first day.

"I'm so sorry, sir. That was not my intention. I saw an issue, and I didn't want things to implode on Cavendish if the company went down that road. I hoped you'd be happy that I bring some knowledge to the company's biggest client to date."

Okay, so that last part probably could've been left off if Keller's lobster red cheeks and clenched teeth are any indicators. He looks feral.

He took my words exactly how they'd been intended—as an insult. The fact is, none of the higher-ups did their research. They'd simply wanted to mesh two superstars together without a semblance of brand cohesiveness.

"You thought I would be happy about you basically making me look like a fool? Did you honestly think that I would come out of that meeting and thank you?"

I'm done with this man. He's not my boss, and I won't sit

around and allow him to push me around. I fold my hands on the desk and lean forward with a wide smile spread across my face.

"I didn't make you look like a fool. You did that all on your own."

"Who do you think you are?" he bellows.

I raise my hand to stop his words. "Part of the team behind Diosa. I was hired for that purpose, not to be your punching bag, sir."

He laughs maniacally. The man is unhinged.

"You're a glorified assistant. Nothing else. You listen to what I say, Raven." He takes two steps toward my desk, and I have to hold my ground and not cower. "It's your first day, and if you're not careful, it'll be your last. Do you really want to have that sort of reputation on you? To be fired from your very first day at work?"

Men like this are exactly why talented people quit the industry. They're not cut out to handle the abuse. I've been through more than most, and I've fought my way through bigger bullies. I won't allow this idiot to ruin anything for me.

Until I know how he's gotten this position and why they keep him, I'll play the game and act remorseful for cutting him down for now.

I plaster on a repentant expression, lowering my head as if I'm ashamed.

"No, of course not. The last thing that I want to do is lose this job. It means a lot to me. Sir, I really am sorry. I didn't mean to upset you. I was just nervous that we'd lose Diosa. I tend to talk a lot when I'm nervous. That's all. I can assure you that it won't happen again."

Lies to appease him for the time being.

Mr. Keller is about to say something else when Charles walks in, eyes narrowed, taking in the current situation. I wonder how much of the conversation he's heard, and I flush at the thought of him hearing me cower to this dickhead.

"Mr. Cavendish," Mr. Keller says nervously. "I . . . didn't see you there."

I swear he is about to bow but then stops himself. Everything about Mr. Keller irritates me, but I smile and pretend nothing is the matter at all.

"Keller," Charles says and nods at him dismissively, turning his attention to me. "Miss Bennett, I'd like to see you in my office. Now."

A sly smile spreads across Keller's face. He's shielded from Charles's view, which is the only reason he's being so brazen.

Coward.

I stand from my desk, straightening the black pencil skirt that molds to my curves, and I don't miss the way that Charles's eyes follow my movement with attention that's a little too familiar to be workplace appropriate.

My cheeks warm, and I thank God he's too focused on my skirt to look at my face.

He clears his throat. "You can follow me."

I don't even spare Keller a parting word or glance as I walk past him. My head is held high, and I work to walk with a confidence I don't currently possess.

Keller has my anger on overload, and Cavendish has my libido skyrocketing with that sexy smolder that's all him.

My mind wars with the two sides of Charles Cavendish. The CEO that's all formalities and professionalism versus the man I met at Silver, whose hands had been all over me.

I dread what's to come. I'd hoped he'd drop our previous encounter and allow us to move on with our lives, but if he wants to see me, someone who's barely a blip on the Cavendish Group radar, it has to be about Silver.

Once in his office, he gestures to the chair in front of his desk. "Please, take a seat."

I sit down, trying hard not to fidget but failing miserably. My hands twist around each other, and my leg bounces.

Instinct would normally have me spouting out words in an

attempt to make this less awkward, but I'm struck mute. No words will come.

This man has the ability to throw me so far off-kilter without saying a word. I'm not sure which way is up at the moment.

"I heard the way Keller spoke to you. Unfortunately, he does have a reputation of being rather demanding with his employees."

"He's an ass." The words come out before I've had a chance to censor them.

He quirks a brow. "An ass? I suppose that's a fair assessment. Although, I don't recommend you tell him that directly."

"I . . . wouldn't. It slipped."

Charles's lip lifts in a grin that sets off his dimples. Heat pools low in my belly, and now I'm really fidgeting.

"He's not bad at his job, but he's not good with people, and he hates it when someone calls him out on it."

"He doesn't seem to like women in general," I say again, without thinking.

"Keller doesn't like anyone who makes him look bad." He shrugs, shifting papers around on his desk. "Personally, I found the whole thing quite amusing."

I have no idea if this is a compliment or not.

"I'm sorry about Mr. Keller, but I saw a hole in the plan, and since there is no account manager—yet—I felt it necessary to intervene before too much time was spent going down the wrong road. Keller isn't my superior, and as far as I've been told, he's not part of the Diosa team. I have a vested interest in this account doing well." The words rush from me, and I'm semi-grateful that they at least seem to make sense.

I gulp, not liking the way he's looking at me. Like he's trying to work out in his head how to gently tell me I need to find another job.

"Did you want to see me to discuss Keller?"

His eyes narrow, and his lips purse together. "No."

"Listen, Raven." He leans forward as though whatever is coming next is sensitive, and he doesn't want anyone else to overhear it.

My back straightens, and I steel myself for what's coming.

"I don't know what your motives were the other night at Silver, but you clearly knew who I was."

My mouth drops open, and the smile is wiped from my face. He can't be serious.

"Are you insinuating that I locked myself in a closet, nearly had a panic attack, and it was all to be alone with you?"

"Sounds right."

"Because I knew you were my new boss?" My teeth grind together.

"I couldn't have summarized it better myself, Rae."

"It's Raven," I snap. "For the record, I didn't know who you were. Some guy named Paxton told me that down the hall were metal doors that were for the VIP restrooms."

His nose scrunches. "What? It was Pax that told you the closet was a toilet?"

"Yes," I say, throwing my hands in the air. "I told you that night."

"I certainly didn't believe you."

"Charles . . ." I look him in the eyes. "May I call you that?"

"I think that would be highly inappropriate, being as everyone else calls me Mr. Cavendish or simply Cavendish."

I wave my hand in the air, rolling my eyes. "I'm pretty sure your hands were on my rear, and your tongue was shoved down my throat. I'll call you Charles." I smile sweetly, watching his features darken in response.

Whether it's due to the reminder of what we did or the way I'm railroading him, I'm uncertain, but I don't care. He has my blood boiling. Accusing me of orchestrating being locked in a damn dark hole to be alone with him . . . it's nuts.

"What is it that you want from me, Miss Bennett?"

My eyes narrow to slits. "Nothing. I want absolutely nothing from you."

He grunts. "Unlikely."

I take a deep breath and lean my elbows on top of his desk. "I earned this job and had it well before Wednesday evening. If I would've known who you were, I wouldn't have gotten within an inch of you."

He smirks as though what I'm saying is laughable. Like he has me all figured out.

Idiot.

"I'm sorry if you feel like I somehow cornered you, but that's not what happened. It was a horrific case of wrong place, wrong time." I take a breath, making sure I have his attention. "I want nothing more from you than to be left alone to do my job. A job that I'll be damn good at."

"Is that all?"

I nod. "When I leave this office, we'll forget Wednesday ever happened. I'll do my job, and you'll do yours. Nobody in this place will know we've ever met. We'll be professional because that's what we are. Professionals."

He considers me for several tense minutes, and I never once break his stare, determined for him to see that I'm serious.

"All right. We're agreed," he says. "I think we better move up finding Keller an assistant and remove you from his temporary help. Let's be honest, if you work for him in any capacity, it's going to end in disaster."

My head bobs in confirmation.

"I actually happen to think that you'll be an asset to this company. Not many people have the balls to speak up and tell a room of executives that their idea lacks foundation."

A genuine smile spreads across my face at the compliment.

"I was just doing my job."

He purses his lip. "No. Actually, you were doing the account manager's job in their absence. That makes you far more valuable to the Diosa team, as it already shows your capability far surpasses what is on your CV."

"Thank you," I say, standing to make my way to the door.

"Going somewhere, Miss Bennett?" His voice is full of humor. "I think we have more to discuss, and I don't recall dismissing you from this meeting."

With my back turned to him, my eyes closed. Being this close to him isn't fun for me. I meant what I said about forgetting Wednesday night, but it's not easy to do. The man has a hold on me that I don't understand.

Yes, he's entirely too handsome for his own good, but it's more than that. His magnetism, arrogant ego . . . *him* . . . all call to me. It'll be a lesson in restraint to keep to my word, but I'm determined to do it.

I open my eyes, turn, and take a seat. "I apologize. I thought we were done."

I have no idea where the conversation is headed. But at least it doesn't sound like I'm going to get fired any time soon.

"You're done with Keller. I need you completely entrenched in Diosa."

"Have you hired the account manager yet?"

He shakes his head. "No. We've yet to find a suitable candidate."

"What about Mr. Keller? He gave me some work to finish up. Am I supposed to tell him I can't?"

"Leave Keller to me. I'll find someone else. There are plenty of eager people out there looking for work. You deserve something a bit more stimulating."

The heat in his eyes is unmistakable, and I can't help the blush that stains my cheeks. He might not have meant that as innuendo, but it certainly sounded like it.

He clears his throat. "Anyway, I will need all the help I can get with this account. We can't mess this up."

"Give me the account. Let me manage it." The words tumble out of my mouth.

"Surely not," he says so nonchalantly that it hurts even worse. "You're not qualified to lead Diosa. This client will open doors for Cavendish that weren't available prior. I can't take chances with previous losses still on the books."

I know he's right, but it still stings.

"You don't have anyone else. At least let me help you with the interview process."

A harsh breath rushes from his chest. "I mean no disrespect, Miss Bennett, but what makes you think you could find someone better than HR?"

"I know Diosa. Qualifications and résumés don't always produce the right fit."

"And you believe you could spot the perfect fit?"

"Yes."

This is the most bizarre situation I've ever been in, and I can admit that I'm in over my head here. But this is my chance to shine. I have to prove that I'm more than somebody's assistant.

"Well?" I prompt, sounding bossy as hell, even though I'm mortified inside.

His head bobs. "I'll give you a chance to lead until we find someone, but if you mess this up even a slight, it's on you."

I don't like his lack of confidence in me, but I can't blame him. He's taking a chance, and we both know it.

"Great. I'll make a preliminary plan ASAP, and if you can get me with HR so I can begin sorting through applicants, that would be helpful."

"I'll have the CVs delivered to your office within the hour. Take the rest of the weekend to work on a solid plan. We'll meet next Monday." He twists his chair, grabbing the phone and raising it to his ear. "Send Keller my way, please."

I grimace. The last thing I want to do is speak to Mr. Keller. Why can't he just call him in? Pushing that down, I internally remind myself that this is all a test. A test I can't fail.

I offer one last smile, stand, and walk toward the door.

"Raven," he calls to my back.

"Yes?" I ask, turning over my shoulder.

"Don't make me regret this."

My lips press together, and I don't say anything as I walk out the door.

The man is insufferable. I can only thank God, or whoever is pulling the strings, that Paxton Ramsey came to my rescue and opened that damn door before things went further. I have no doubt that if we'd had sex in that room, I'd be unemployed right now. Mainly because I wouldn't be able to stomach working with him.

Even though I know it's probably a bad idea, my fingers type frantically, searching through Google to look up Paxton Ramsey. The man really deserves that fruit basket for saving my ass that night.

When I finally find him, I'm speechless. He's an agent who represents many actors and musical talents on both coasts. His company has a satellite office in LA with a small team and is looking to branch into sports.

The men are clearly friends, so why hasn't Charles tapped into his resources?

I fire up another window, type out the e-card and place my order, closing the computer just as a stack of résumés is delivered by one of the HR runners.

Well, this has been an interesting first day.

# chapter ten

Charles

"**S**HE DID *WHAT?*"

The bastard hasn't stopped laughing since he called, right after texting a photo of an obscenely large fruit basket, complete with two sunshine balloons, supposedly sent to him by Raven.

Not for nothing. This whole thing screams Raven. I might barely know her, but the balloons are all her. She's a ray of sunshine—my Rae.

*She isn't your anything.*

"She might be the funniest girl I've ever met," Pax says through his howling laughter. "A damn fruit basket in thanks for saving her from you. How, pray tell, did you manage to leave such a horrible impression on that girl?"

*Bollocks.*

"Tell me again what the card said," I instruct, massaging my right temple with my free hand.

"Mr. Ramsey, it was a pleasure running into you—literally—at Club Silver. I appreciate the tip on the VIP restroom. However, for future reference, not all the metal doors are restrooms, which you learned while saving me from ultimate peril." Pax snorts, bursting into another fit.

"Go on, mate. Get it all out," I say, smacking my lips in annoyance.

Of all the damn people she could've brought into this mess, it had to be Paxton. The one person who will never let this go.

"And for that, I forgive your gaffe," he continues, just barely holding himself together. "Please accept this gift in payment as discussed. You likely saved my job, and for that, I owe you fruit, chocolate, and balloons, at the very least. On another note, while stalking you to send this, I see you are the owner of Factor Talent. I'd love to connect with you at your earliest convenience. Please feel free to call me at . . ."

I jot down the number he recites. I don't recognize it as a Cavendish Group mobile. She's given him her personal number, and now I have it. Not that I'll ever use it.

"Is there not a limit on word count for those damned notes?"

"Of all the things you could be focused on, that's your go-to?" Paxton chuckles. "Please tell me why she's so grateful that I stopped you from fucking her in a closet. This has to be a first."

I huff. "You're a bloody prick, you know that, right?"

"The worst of the bunch. Now talk."

I sigh, knowing I won't get out of spilling all the sordid details. "Turns out Miss Bennett is my new employee."

"Oh, my God," Pax says, losing it again. "This is the greatest thing to ever happen to me."

"Sod off." I scrub at my face. This girl will be the death of me. "Plus, I'm sure the fruit is everything you ever wanted. Now, tell me the rest."

"I'd appreciate it if we could move past the whole closet debacle. Looking forward to speaking with you about how Cavendish Group and Factor Talent could work together in the future. Best, Raven Bennett." He's laughing. Again.

If I could strangle him through the phone, I would. He's getting too much enjoyment out of this.

"Jesus . . . What have I done to deserve this?"

"Too much, I'm afraid. How many months were you on my couch?" He clears his throat. "I've gotta hand it to her. She's the first to recognize a potential partnership that would be advantageous for all of us. You certainly have never brought an opportunity to me."

"I never wanted you to feel obligated to work with Cavendish Group. We're friends."

And that's the truth of it. In this life, I've been used far too many times by people I trusted. They didn't care about my friendship or affection. They wanted me for what I could do for them. Call me jaded, but I have a right to be.

"And that's precisely why we should've teamed up from the beginning. You did with Drew. How am I any different?"

"Drew is a client. What she's proposing would require you to bring your clients to work with us for the Diosa brand."

"Exactly. It's a potential *opportunity* for my clients. One that many would jump at the chance for."

He's right. I'm an arse.

Paxton owns a boutique agency, representing talent across the United States. A partnership with him makes perfect sense, and Raven was the one to move on it.

In a less than appropriate way, but I guess, given the circumstances, she needed to establish a connection with Paxton, and whether she realized it or not, humor is an immediate way to grab his attention. Based on his reaction, he found this beyond hysterical. She's clearly already won him over.

"Don't reach out to her until I say so."

"Why?"

That one word holds so much confusion and something that sounds like annoyance.

"I'm interested to see what she has in mind where Factor Talent is concerned. This would be a huge partnership, and I'd like to be present."

"Don't bullshit me. This has nothing to do with you wanting to be present, dipshit. You can lie to yourself all you want, but don't kid a kidder."

"You're a git," I snap, hating his perceptiveness with the situation.

"That makes two of us," he says. "She seems to have a good head on her shoulders, Charles. Don't run her off."

"I haven't yet, have I?" I bark down the line.

"I'm sure you didn't react well when you saw her in the office."

The bloke knows me far too well. He was there through many of my disappointments in life and the reason I ran to the States to begin with.

"I could've handled it worse."

He snorts. "That's your way of saying you were an asshole."

"I was angry. I assumed she knew who I was from the beginning."

He tsks. "Let me guess, you thought she orchestrated it all. Thought she went into that closet on her own." He laughs. "That was my doing, brother. I told her to go down that hallway. When I saw your text, I realized my error could have put her in the wrong room."

"You took your time," I drawl, recalling that several long minutes went by from when I sent the text to when he opened the door.

Long minutes in the dark with Raven. Her body fit perfectly against mine. The way she melted into me.

Too damn perfectly.

"I figured you weren't hating being locked in a room with a beautiful woman."

He isn't wrong. I would've gladly taken Raven against that door. I'd wanted to do just that the entire night. But something had happened before Paxton interrupted us. She'd already pulled away. Why?

It doesn't matter. She works for me, which means she's off-limits. With everything going on within the company, I need her. Diosa needs her. The past needs to stay in the past.

"Anyway, she's not *Tabitha*. Remember that."

I bristle at the mention of *she who shall not be named*. He knows better than to bring her up, yet he has.

"I'll be happy if I never hear that she-devil's name again."

He sighs heavily. "I know. But you need the reminder. Not all women are out to fuck you."

"She did more than fuck me, mate. She obliterated me."

Tabitha was my Achilles' heel. I was in love, and she took advantage in the biggest way.

"She's an evil bitch, but Raven . . . she's not the same."

That might be true, but it doesn't matter. As long as she does her job and does it well, that's all I care about. It's all I *can* care about.

"And you can tell this from a few minutes in a packed club?"

"It's my job to read people. Raven Bennett is good people, Charles. Be good to her."

"She's my employee," I snap, growing tired at Paxton's need to beat a dead horse.

"Whatever she is, treat her well."

"Go enjoy your fruit, bastard. Don't arrange the meeting. Not until I tell you too."

"Oh, I will."

The line goes dead, and I'm left staring at the photo of Raven's gift.

What the hell possessed her to look up Paxton in the first place? Does she have a thing for him?

Even more reason to ensure I'm in that meeting.

Not because I have an inappropriate attraction to her, but because this partnership is important, and I won't have Paxton putting the moves on her and ruining everything. This is about saving her from him.

*Keep telling yourself that.*

Fuck.

# chapter eleven

Raven

THE LAST FEW DAYS HAVE BEEN A DOWNRIGHT WHIRLWIND.
I know I'm qualified for this position, but I've never worked at a company like this. It feels like I've been thrown into the deep end of a pool without knowing how to swim.

Pandemonium all the time. The new campaign has everyone getting into the office super early and working late. Even now, it's only a quarter to nine in the morning, but I've been here since a little before seven a.m., but others were in even earlier.

Standing from my chair, I stretch my arms up into the air, wringing out my muscles from being slouched in front of my computer for the last two hours.

A yawn escapes my mouth, and I realize just how tired I am.

I need energy, and I need it stat.

Hell, what I need is an IV hooked up to me with a caffeine drip, but seeing as that's not an option, I go for the next best thing and head toward the breakroom on my floor.

People gather around cubicles, chatting about their projects, and I just need a little silence to clear my head. My heels click on the concrete floor as I walk, and when I make it to my destination, I'm happy to see it's empty.

The breakroom is large and modern. White walls with black cabinets and concrete slabs for countertops. Industrial feel, but I like the simplicity of it all after working at the computer all morning.

Large canvases designed with an array of splattered paint adorn the walls.

But that's not the focal point of the room, believe it or not.

Nope, the center of attention is held by a giant state-of-the-art, commercial-grade cappuccino maker that belongs in a restaurant, not in an advertising office.

How I'm ever going to figure this out is beyond me. Where are the directions for this monstrosity?

Letting a curse slip from my mouth, I move until I'm standing directly in front of it, grab a glass mug from where they are sitting beside, and once I'm ready, start to fiddle with the buttons to turn it on.

Nothing happens.

Then I press another one.

And again, nothing.

Why couldn't it just be those little pods in a machine?

I swear I will cry if I can't get a cup of coffee.

My lids feel heavy from staring at a computer, and I need a pick-me-up before Mr. Keller realizes how useless I am right now and shouts it to the world. Even though I'm not under him any longer, he is still checking in on my daily progress. Up in my business every time I make a move.

I press another button.

Praying this is the one.

I'm not even trying to get a fancy fucking drink at this point. Right now, I'd settle for an espresso. Hell, I would eat the beans whole, but I need something.

Finally, the machine comes to life and what I can only describe as the sweet nectar of the gods starts to fill my glass.

The robust smell filters in through my nose, and my blood

pleasure instantly drops with the awareness that I'll be able to function again soon.

Once the machine stops, I lift the mug up to my nose to smell. My eyes flutter closed as a moan escapes my lips.

There is nothing better than coffee in the morning. *I dare anyone to argue with me.*

I'm about to take a sip when I hear a coughing sound.

Or maybe a grumble sounds through the air.

With a jolt, I open my eyes, and when I do, my gaze crashes into Charles watching me from the doorway.

My whole body lurches forward with surprise. Before I know what's happening, I feel the hot liquid splashing over the edge of the mug and pouring onto my white shirt.

Shit.

Shit.

This is hot! Shit.

Charles rushes forward; his steps echo like a freight train, solidifying my mortification.

He's beside me in a second.

Pulling the shirt away from my skin, his hands brush over mine to find purchase on the shirt, too. The expresso is cooling, but it takes me a few seconds to realize I'm okay. I'm not hurt.

As my heartbeat slows down to a normal clip, I hear him speak. "Are you okay?" His voice sounds different, deeper. There's a husky tone that makes me shiver despite the warmth I still can feel from the coffee.

I lift my chin up, and what I'm met with takes my breath away. *Charles watching me.*

No. Watching isn't the right word . . . *transfixed.*

He doesn't blink as our gazes lock, and time seems to stand still. I need to look away, but I just can't break from this man.

Charles Cavendish has his own gravitational pull, and I'm stuck in it.

Seconds pass, and I need to say something, but words feel heavy in my mouth.

He asked me something. *Am I okay?*

Coughing, I give my head a little shake, lifting the haze away.

That's when I look down and see his hand touching mine. Our fingers both grip the material of my damp shirt.

We both drop the cotton at the same time.

He takes a step back. A loud, angry huff escapes his mouth, and the next thing I know, he starts to rummage through the cabinet directly beside him.

The racket he's making could wake the dead, and a part of me dies of embarrassment at the fuss he's making right now.

What the hell is he looking for?

Finally, the sound stops. He lifts up a towel, and I take it in my hand. Our fingers touch, and as they do, his jaw becomes tight. The utter mortification from the way he's reacting to me is unbearable.

*Will the world please swallow me whole?*

"Thank you." Blotting away the coffee, I move toward the other side of the room, needing distance from him.

My heart is hammering way too fast for my liking.

Continuing to clean myself, I notice that he hasn't left the room. "Is there"—I stop my movements and lower my hand—"anything you need?"

He's quiet for a moment. His rigid posture tells me he doesn't like my presence right now.

"No."

"Oh—okay." I blink a few times, confused. "Did you want a coffee?" I mutter.

"No. I don't drink that garbage. I . . . I went to your office to let you know I've pulled together a meeting for the top of the hour. Get yourself together and be there on time."

Before I can say anything in response, he stalks off.

*Who pissed in his cornflakes today?*

Grabbing the half-empty mug off the counter, I take the last gulp.

If I have to sit through a meeting with that grumpy ass bastard, I need all the help I can get.

---

I arrive at the meeting exactly fifteen minutes later with a giant stain on my chest. I tried to cover it with a light scarf I had in my computer bag, but it's still obvious I am a mess.

Sitting at the head of the conference table, the ever-irritable Mr. Cavendish holds court as I try to disappear into my seat.

The way he looked at me before still plays on a loop in my mind.

His warm hands on my shirt. The caring look in his eyes. As much as I try not to think of our connection, it just keeps coming back, day after day.

*You're in a meeting, Raven. Pay attention.*

I need to get a grip. Narrowing my eyes, I try to keep focused.

What are we even talking about?

A fundraiser, maybe?

Oh great, he's discussing raising money for a worthy cause, and I have no idea what he's talking about. This is bad. If he asks me a question, it will be obvious I'm not listening at all.

*Please don't call on me.*

As if he can hear the inner turmoil in my mind, he looks directly at me. His blue eyes are sharp and discerning.

"You can handle that, correct, Raven?"

"Yes, Mr. Cavendish," I answer, having no clue what I'm saying yes to. His jaw tightens at my answer. He knows I have no clue.

"Good. Because this is very important to Cavendish Group. Very important to me."

His tone is sharp, and I know if I screw this up, my future here will be short.

*Is that a bad thing?*

I've only been working here for over a week, and I'm second-guessing if I want to work for this man.

Maybe I can be transferred to a different department. One where I don't have to work for Cavendish directly.

Lost in my thoughts again, I barely notice that the meeting is wrapping up until Charles stands.

Shelby moves quickly and is beside me before I can take a step. She places her hand on my shoulder, telling me with no words to hold back a moment.

Once everyone leaves the room, I turn to face her. "Everything okay?"

"I couldn't help noticing you were spaced out before. Are you okay?" Her eyes dart down to the stain on my chest.

"Yep, just a run-in with an angry coffee machine."

"Okay, good. I was worried about you for a minute. I'd be frazzled, too, if I had to go to a meeting about a gala when it's only my second week." She points to the mess.

"It was not ideal timing, that's for sure."

"Listen, about Charles, I know he's not easy . . ." *That's the understatement of the year.* "But he means well. The money he raises for cancer—"

"That's what we are raising money for?" I ask foolishly as memories of what my father went through seep into my mind.

"Yes, and here at Cavendish, we take philanthropy very seriously. If you need help with making the calls to the vendors for the event, I can help."

*Making calls to vendors. That's what I signed up for.* Good to know.

"I'm sure I'll be okay. I'll be provided with a list and details?"

"Of course. This is important to him. Helping cancer patients get the treatment they deserve—no matter the cost—is central to his need for the business to do well, too."

My chest constricts at her words.

Maybe there *is* more to him than the tough, prickly exterior that he's shown me.

Could there be a heart under that cold, grumpy surface?

━━━━━━━━ ✦✦ ━━━━━━━━

A week later, and it feels like the days have passed in the blink of an eye.

I've been so busy, I have barely had time to see, let alone speak to my friends.

That is until now, and seeing Asher's face across the table makes me realize how much I've missed him.

"This is cool, meeting each other for lunch," Asher says, stuffing a pastrami sandwich into his mouth.

I can't believe I'm starting my third week of working here and this is the first time I've left my desk to eat lunch.

Shelby insisted I take a break after I spent the morning doing research for the Diosa pitch and then leafing through vendors we are using for the cancer fundraiser. There are six months to go until the gala date and a lot of work to do. Once I was done with that, I started looking over résumés and identifying five candidates who could potentially work.

Only *five* out of actual hundreds of résumés.

A lot of talent is sitting on my desk, but none will mesh well with Diosa, based on their former jobs.

"I'm so glad we could get together when Shelby told me to go out for a long lunch. Being Mr. Cavendish's right-hand lady, she leaves little room for argument. I've really grown to like her in the short time I've been with the company."

She's fair and very knowledgeable. She's helping me navigate things while the search is on for my boss, and I've already learned so much more from her than I did with the last part-time marketing job I had during school.

As I eat my lunch, I tell Asher what's happening at the company.

Having a friend to talk to about work stuff makes this journey more exciting.

"Shelby's spending the day scheduling interviews for later this week. Not that anything can happen. Cavendish is leaving for a business trip today, and nothing can be finalized without him."

This means I still have time to nail this presentation and potentially get the job myself.

I might be setting my sights a little high, but you'll always fail if you don't try.

I grin at Asher and then laugh. "I really should be working and not taking a break. I have so much to do."

"Who are you, and what have you done with my best friend?"

I snort. "You know damn well I'm a hard worker."

"You are." He smiles. "I'm proud of you, Raven." He takes another bite and continues to speak around a mouthful. "I don't think I've ever seen you look so smart."

This feels good. Normal. Nothing is weird between us today, and I'm grateful. Asher and I are friends. The best of, and I'm done allowing others to taint that.

"I know, it's fancy, huh? I mean, I'd love to stay in my pajamas all day, but getting dressed up is a close second."

"I must say, I've never seen you wear so much black. Is that a Cavendish requirement?"

"Ha," I say, taking a sip of my water. "After I spilled coffee all over my white shirt last week, yeah . . . black is my go-to choice now. Also, I thought for the first few weeks, I'd tone down my wardrobe. You and I both know that Cavendish isn't ready for my signature look."

He laughs, likely thinking through my assortment of colorful dresses and skirts. I'm not a black and gray kind of girl, and that'll likely help with the Diosa account.

"They're bold and cutting edge. Hopefully, they'll appreciate my knack for color later."

"You really are enjoying it?"

I nod, eyes widening when I realize he isn't caught up on all the events. "Actually, I have a lot to tell you."

"Already? But you've only been there for a few weeks. What could you have possibly gotten into?"

"I kind of got promoted to work on a new account. I'm now the lead analyst for a large new client. I even got a pay raise to go with the role."

His eyes widen, and something very close to envy flits across his face before it disappears.

"My first few days were so boring. I remember just pushing paper around my desk to look busy. How the hell did you manage to get a pay increase already?"

I laugh, remembering what my first few hours were like. "Yeah, I did the paper pushing, too, but there's more." My voice pitches. "They started talking about Summer Smith representing Diosa, and I about lost it."

His hand flies up, signaling for me to stop. "Wait . . . did you just say Diosa? As in Diosa Clothier?"

I nod like a bobblehead. "Yes. It's our new client."

His face sours, and my eyes narrow in response. "What's wrong?"

He folds his hands on top of the table, a typical sign that Asher is trying to control his anger. Why would this make him angry?

"I hadn't heard they'd chosen a marketing team. Bauer was in the running. I was supposed to manage the account."

I swallow hard, feeling bad for gloating. It never crossed my mind that we could be in competition. I should've known since the companies are direct competitors, but this is the first time it's truly settling in.

"I'm sorry, Ash. I didn't realize."

His hand raises again, and he shakes it off. "Not your fault. I guess we need to get used to this. It won't be the first client we battle for."

Something in his voice doesn't sit well with me. Asher is super competitive but never with me. At least he never has been before this discussion.

We sit in silence for several moments, and I hate how thick the tension is. My eyes roam the cafeteria, looking anywhere but at him.

This place reminds me of a cute café. Small, red booths, black-and-white checkered floor. A waitress walking around, taking orders. It feels like I've left the building and am out to lunch. It's a nice touch. It's special. The employees feel valued, like management knows they deserve a break, and the best part is the coffee is delightful since I don't have to make it myself.

"Summer Smith? That's a horrible mix." My head turns to Asher. He doesn't look at me when he says it and continues to shift croutons around his salad bowl.

"Right?" I say a little too excitedly, just trying to get us back to normal. "It's like they didn't do their homework."

"Clearly not. I mean, who doesn't do their homework on their biggest client? It's pretty ridiculous if you ask me. Not like it's hard to do. She's everywhere on social media."

"That's what I said to the executives. I couldn't help myself. I just told them that they did *not* have her demographic right at all. She'd work for one of their lines but not the company as a whole."

"That probably didn't go down well with Cavendish. I hear he's a real asshole."

"Not at all," I snap, earning myself a raised brow. "I mean, he is, but he's also fair."

I try to tell myself I'm not defending Charles as much as I'm defending Cavendish Group. Asher continues to stare at me, so I continue. "I just mean, he isn't horrible. He actually listened to what I had to say and is giving me a chance to pitch my idea."

"What do you mean you're pitching an idea?"

"Until an account manager is hired, I'm helping a lot. He wants me to put together some ideas so we can get started."

"Wait, wait, wait. Are you telling me that Cavendish doesn't have an account manager for Diosa?"

I shrug. "Not yet. Cavendish is overseeing, and I'm the main analyst in the meantime."

"How the hell did Cavendish land that account?" He isn't asking me; he's talking to himself.

A nervous giggle escapes. "Craziest first day story ever."

He grunts. "I'd say. Well, knock it out of the park, Bennett. Show them what you've got."

I release a breath of relief at his encouragement. His earlier attitude is gone, and back is the friend I've grown to love like a brother.

"I shall do my very best. I guess luck is on my side." I think about telling Asher about what happened at Silver, but I change my mind.

I don't want him thinking that I got the promotion simply because I made out with Charles. The whole thing is so against my normal character that I don't want him to know. My little secret that I only plan to share with Lily.

"You really do amaze me, Raven. I told you that you'd climb the ladder quickly, and here you are, already managing to do it." He raises his cup of coffee. "Congratulations on your new job."

I smile, clinking my own mug against his.

"It's nice to have someone to talk to about all this."

"You have Lily, too," he says, taking a sip of coffee.

"Lily wouldn't get it. You've been in my position before."

He grins. "Still am, in a way. So does this mean we're going to make this a weekly date?" he asks.

I cough at the word date, and he narrows his eyes.

*Stop.*

I internally berate myself. We've called outings dates before. Here I am once more, being an idiot.

"You okay?"

"Fine," I say, clearing my throat. "I think that's a good idea. I like this place."

"I'll pay next time. Although seeing as though you've already gotten a raise, perhaps you should pay every time."

"I'm still a mere analyst. You, sir, are the executive. You're still rungs above me."

He grins. "You got promoted on your first day. Just imagine where you're going to be in a year's time."

"It wasn't really a promotion. I'm still an analyst." I roll my eyes.

"Can't you just play along?"

"Fine . . . I'll own the place," I say and give an exaggerated evil laugh, steepling my fingers.

He chuckles. "You know what? I actually wouldn't put that past you. Then lunches will forever be on you."

A group of men, all wearing suits and wheeling suitcases behind them, walk through the door, and my breath catches in my throat.

Charles leads the pack, talking over his shoulders to one of the men I recognize from the meeting. One of the clueless executives.

He commands the room, garnering stares from everyone around us.

It's not just me affected by his mere presence. Go figure.

"What are you looking at?" Asher asks, twisting around to get a look for himself.

"Stop," I whisper-shout. "Don't let him see you staring," I hiss.

Asher turns back to me, eyes wide and a grin smeared across his too-pretty face. "Who exactly am I hiding from?"

I lean across the table. "It's Charles Cavendish."

His brows lift into his hairline. "That's the elusive Cavendish?" He looks over his shoulder, and I slap the table to get his attention.

"Asher," I bite out. "Stop. He'll see us."

He rolls his eyes. "The man's preoccupied, Raven. I can't believe he's so young. Not what I expected."

If that isn't the understatement of the century.

"You and me both," I murmur.

His lip curls. "Do you have a crush on your boss?"

"No." It comes out all wrong, and my cheeks heat. "Of course not. That would be . . ."

"Inappropriate," Asher offers.

"Highly."

My head lifts to find Charles looking in my direction. His face is blank, and I wonder what's going through his head. He holds my gaze for several seconds, causing goose bumps to rise on my arms and my belly to dip.

I hate the reactions he causes. Asher was right. It's inappropriate.

One of the men says something to Charles, and it breaks the connection. I blow out a harsh breath, turning my attention back to Asher, who's staring at me like I have two heads.

"What?"

He shakes his head. "Nothing. Anyway," he says, turning the subject away from Charles. "Tell me about your plans for Diosa. I'm interested in why Summer Smith was so high on their list. Did they even reach out to her?"

I shrug, taking a big bite of my sandwich. "No clue. But it doesn't sound like it," I say between mouthfuls. "I did some research, and apparently, her contract ended with her former partners. Her agent is shopping around. He wants to get another deal on the table for her since she's not going on tour this year."

"Interesting," he says, looking at his phone.

"Do you need to go?" I ask.

His brows are knitted together, and I wonder what he's looking at.

"Not yet. My boss is on a rampage. He must've found out about Diosa."

I press my lips together, not wanting to discuss that any further.

"That was the big deal on the table," he continues. "I'm not due back for another twenty. Tell me, what are you cooking up?"

I have quite a few ideas that I'm putting together, but I'm not ready to share them with anyone.

"I'm still working on it. Very early stages," I say, taking another bite.

The two of us sit for the rest of the lunch break, talking about

Asher's accounts and life in the advertising world. I'm grateful for the reprieve from shifting through résumés.

When we stand to leave, I give him a big hug.

"What is that for?" he asks.

I shrug. "For lunch. It was just what I needed."

He offers me a large smile. "Same."

He pulls me to his side, walking me toward the door.

"You'll always have me, Raven."

That's one thing I know for sure. No matter where life takes us, I'll always have Asher in my life. It's comforting, especially during a period of so much change and uncertainty.

My career is looking up, as long as I can continue to resist whatever strange pull this is between my new boss and me.

# chapter twelve

Charles

MY JAW CLENCHES AS I STALK TO THE LIFT. I TRUDGE ALONG on my path, barely able to control the emotions working their way through my body.

Who the fuck was she eating with?

*Why do I bloody care?*

Is she sleeping with him? Is he her boyfriend?

Fuck.

What do I even know about her? I didn't read through her CV; I just know what Shelby told me. She has her MBA and worked internships and part-time roles in marketing firms to get the experience she has now.

Oh, shit! She could be married, for crying out loud.

Wait, she doesn't wear a ring, so she's not married or engaged.

That doesn't always stop someone, as I bloody well know.

My tongue was in her damn mouth only a few weeks ago. I cannot stop replaying those moments when her lips parted for me.

Yes, she stopped us, but for a brief moment, she didn't . . .

As soon as I reach the lift, I jam the button and wait. My anger is palpable as I ponder if Raven kissed me while attached to someone else.

Wouldn't be the first time I fell into that problem.

The chime of the doors opening pulls me from my thoughts, and I step inside. The door is barely open when I hear a request to hold the elevator. I don't consider who's speaking as I thrust my arm out to stop them from closing.

*Speak of the devil.*

As if conjured by my thoughts, Raven steps into the small space. I move aside, enlarging the distance between us. The farther I am from her, the better right now.

But who am I trying to fool?

There could be an airfield between us, and it wouldn't be enough. I would still find her irresistible. Her intoxicating perfume filters through the air, begging me to approach her, to pull her toward me and inhale. Instead, I fist my hands at my side, willing this ride to be over quickly.

"Are you okay, Mr. Cavendish?"

"Yes," I grit out through clenched teeth.

"Are you sure? You don't look fine."

I inhale, willing myself to calm. "Yes."

"Because if you—"

"Enough!" I snap.

My head turns in her direction, and I see her eyes are wide with shock.

*Fuck.*

"Umm . . . sorry," she squeaks at my outburst. Her chin dips, and she starts to fiddle with the hem of her skirt. Which now draws my attention to how short it is.

Torture.

As we make our ascent to our floor, the air around us grows still, and I'm thankful for her silence, that is until she lifts her head up and looks at me.

"The food in the cafeteria is very good," she says.

"You seemed to be enjoying it." My tone is harsh, and she looks puzzled by my reaction.

Her fingers move again, and this time, her nervous fiddling has her touching her blouse. She doesn't realize it, but the fabric has lifted, and now, a sliver of creamy skin is peeking out, causing my imagination to go into overdrive.

In my mind, I'm hitting the stop button and pushing her up against the wall. She'd moan out my name and the *yes* I desperately want to hear from her again.

I'd capture her lips with mine, suckling on that bottom lip she likes to nibble on in meetings when she's thinking. Raven has no idea what she does to me when I look up and see her pensive.

In my daydream, I'd run my hands down to that tease of a skirt. Feathering my touch under it to feel that exposed skin again. My God, her soft arse was divine.

This time, I wouldn't be forced to stop because of the door. Instead, I'd find her ready for me when I slipped my fingers across her center. The way her body would tremble beneath my touch has me panting for more. Just a taste of her . . .

"Mr. Cavendish." Her soft voice pulls me from my thoughts. "We're here."

With a shake of the head, I follow the direction she is gesturing with her hand and see that the doors are open.

Without acknowledging her at all, I step off and storm toward my office.

I need as much distance as possible.

I'm not even at my desk when my mobile rings with a message. Pulling it from my pocket, I read it.

"Fuuuuuck!"

---

I've been at 5 Herford Street for three days in a row now.

The exclusive club has been my father's watering hole for damn near a decade. He made the conversion from Annabel's, another prominent club, on opening, which secured his feud with Annabel's owner. Yet another betrayal proving my father wouldn't understand the word loyal if it hit him upside the head.

If he's not in his office screaming down the line at someone, he can be found here. The question is, why am *I* here?

I barely take a seat, and a tumbler of The Glenlivet XXV is placed before me. My father's idea of knowing and loving me.

Fuck that shite.

I was summoned to London on short notice, flying out immediately on Monday after lunch. The bastard knows damn well I am in the middle of closing the biggest deal of my career. If the tables were turned, nothing short of murder would pull him away from a client.

Yet when he rings, I'm expected to come running.

I haven't for three years, but something about this request is different. Over the past three years, he hasn't bothered to reach out personally, leaving his assistant to call or send an email. I ignored each and every one.

This time, he rang. Something in his voice was off. He sounded haunted. Hollow.

As the heir to Cavendish Corporation, I've been groomed to take over upon my father's death or retirement since birth, and I can't imagine this meeting is about anything other than plans for the company.

He's likely rewritten his will and made his serpentine bride the new owner.

Good for them. May they both rot in hell.

Three years ago, my future with Cavendish Corporation in the UK came to a crashing halt when my father decided to run a sword through my back.

I hopped on the first flight I could catch and headed to America, taking up residence on Paxton's couch.

Pax and I met at uni and became fast friends. When he heard what had happened, he offered for me to stay with him. He was the one who convinced me to open a satellite branch in New York and stay away from London and my father's betrayal.

Dear old Dad didn't bother to talk me out of it. He even drew up the paperwork, allowing me to operate the New York City branch under a separate part of the Cavendish Corporation. It was no surprise, given the entire reason I fled was his doing.

"Why am I here?" I'm slouched backward in a wing-back chair, trying to give the appearance of nonchalance when I'm quaking inside.

Three years later, I'm still rocked to the core by my father's actions.

He frowns as though my attitude is unexpected and uncalled for.

"It's been three years since you've been home. I thought it high time you visited. And stop slouching. It's unbecoming."

I huff, teeth gritted and bared. "Unbecoming. That's rich from you, Father. You mean to tell me you pulled me away from the biggest project of my career just because it's been too long for you?"

Bullshit. There's more to this meeting, and I intend on getting to the reason sooner rather than later. I've already been in this godforsaken city for too long, the past creeping in around me like shadows in a dark alley.

"Come, son, you can't still harbor that much resentment toward me."

I grind my teeth together, leaning my elbows on the table to get as close to him as I can. "You're wrong, old man. My loathing for you, I'll carry to your grave, mine, and then the beyond as well."

His shoulders deflate, and he sighs heavily, dropping his eyes to the table and shaking his head. "What can I do?"

He picks up his own glass, filled with water.

That is a change.

I haven't been around the man when he wasn't at least two tumblers into his obscenely expensive scotch.

"Nothing," I say through my teeth. "If you wanted to make

amends, you should've done that three years ago. You had plenty to atone for."

He bites the side of his cheek, hazel eyes searching mine, but for what?

"I understand that my relationship caught you off guard."

I laugh maniacally, growing more agitated by the moment. "Glad to see you two have gotten on these past years."

"Charles," he warns, and I throw up a hand.

"Mum just died. How did you think I should behave when her body was barely cold, and you had moved on with that slag?" He flinches, but I keep on going. "I was suffering. And when I needed you. You ran to her. You were *my* family."

"I still am," he says, and I shake my head back and forth vigorously, running a hand roughly through my thick hair.

"Not anymore. Those days are done."

"It's just a woman, Charles."

I bark out a frustrated laugh. "And you think that makes it any better? You have some fucking nerve."

Both of his hands raise. "I am not trying to fight with you, Charles. I've given you your space because I knew I'd gone about it the wrong way. You should've never found out the way you did."

My hand smacks the table with a crack. "I should've never had to find out at all," I yell, earning a reprimand from the bartender that I don't acknowledge. "You should've respected me and respected Mum. Instead, you allowed your dick to get in the way, and our familial relationship is forever in disrepair." I take a breath, trying to rein in my temper. "That's on you and something you'll have to live with. I sleep rather well at night." I cross my arms and sit back again. "In fact, I should probably thank you."

One bushy brow lifts, but he doesn't speak, allowing me to continue.

"You did me a huge favor. Not that it's going to change how I feel about you. For what it's worth, I feel sorry for you, old man."

His eyes close. He looks tired.

"I didn't bring you here for this. It's not that I expected things to go smoothly, but I didn't think you'd still harbor so much anger after three years."

"You don't know me at all, *Father*." I spit the word like a curse. "Now, tell me why I'm here, or I'm leaving."

He takes a deep breath and meets my eyes once more. "I've been working up the nerve to tell you that I'm finally retiring at the end of the year."

I shrug. "Good for you. But why the hell was I brought here so you could tell me you're retiring? A simple email would've sufficed."

"You know why. There are things to arrange. Documents to sign. The company will be yours as it was always planned."

"Don't want it. I have all I need. The paperwork has been signed, making the New York office a separate entity run by me. As far as I'm concerned, London can be given to whatever offspring you may or may not have with her."

He scoffs. "You know damn well there will be no offspring."

"Not my problem. Give it to her for all I fucking care. That's why she married you in the first place."

"Do you think I don't know that?" His voice rises for the first time. "Do you think I haven't regretted my choice from the start?"

"Again, I. Don't. Care. You made your bed. Now sleep in it, old man, and let me get back to my life."

"Your life is here," he barks.

"That hasn't been the case since the day I walked into the office and found you with your pants around your ankles and your dick in that fucking whore." He grimaces, but I charge forward. "America is my home now, and I'm quite happy there." I stand and throw a wad of hundreds onto the table. "Lunch is on me."

He stands on wobbly legs, leaning over the table as though he might be quick enough to grab my arm. I pull back out of reach. "Can we speak again tomorrow?"

I shake my head. "I'm not sticking around. I'm catching the first flight back home." His eyes mist, and I think the bastard might cry right here in the middle of a club for legends. Strong men with backbones of steel. At this moment, he looks broken, and for one quick second, my heart breaks a little more at what we've become. That is until the memories of that day flit to the surface and invade my mind. "You know how I feel. Don't contact me again."

Without another word, I turn on my heels and stalk from the room, feeling a dozen pairs of eyes lasered in my direction. I'm sure it'll be the talk of the club, but I don't give a fuck. He brought this on himself.

He does exactly as he always has. He lets me leave.

Good.

I'm glad to see some things never change.

# chapter thirteen

Raven

Tʜᴇ ᴅᴀʏs ʜᴀᴠᴇ ᴘᴀssᴇᴅ ɪɴ ᴀ ʜᴀᴢᴇ. Mʏ ᴇʏᴇs ᴀʀᴇ ʙʟᴜʀʀʏ ꜰʀᴏᴍ nonstop work and staring at my computer. It's only been a few weeks since I started working on my proposal for Diosa, but it feels like I've been here forever.

I'm exhausted, but I don't regret the amount of work I've put into this project. It's almost time for me to pitch my plan. Charles has been in and out of the office, but Shelby had delivered a message that he'd be returning on Thursday and would like to hear the pitch then.

Having him away has been for the best. I was able to concentrate on my job without distraction and, in turn, have created what I think is a solid campaign strategy. One I continue to tinker with while I wait for his summons.

Rumors have been circulating that he went to London to meet with his father. They say that his father and his wife want to begin traveling the world and that Charles has been asked to take over.

Nobody seems to have the exact story, though.

Some say this is temporary and that his father will be back. Others say Charles will be heading back to London permanently to manage the headquarters, leaving one of the current executives in charge of this branch.

I shudder to think which idiot in a suit will take over.

Clearly, Charles is revered by everyone here in New York, and they're not looking forward to his departure, if there's truth in any of it.

"Good morning, Raven," Shelby calls through the door.

I look up to see she's dressed rather casually compared to her usual dressy look. She's wearing a pair of gray slacks and a scooped-neck white blouse with puffy shoulders. It's the first time she's worn pants in the few weeks I've worked here.

"How was your morning?" she asks, taking a seat across from me.

"Great, thanks. I worked on my pitch the whole time."

Something like relief passes over her features. "Oh, good. I'm taking it you heard the news, and that's why?"

My lips purse, and my stomach flip-flops in response to her words. "News? What news?"

Her smile falters, and she sits back in her chair with a sigh, removing her mobile from her pocket. She goes about searching for something before turning her phone and sliding it toward me. Summer Smith's social media feed is on the screen, and my stomach plummets as I read her announcement.

"We lost another client. Well, not client as she wasn't officially signed, but that no longer matters. She signed with Rothburke Designs."

"What?" I whisper, mostly to myself, in a state of shock. "When?"

"Looks like it happened very recently." Shelby sighs.

Rothburke is another rising company in the world of high fashion. The owner, Sasha Rothburke, is a notorious diva who consistently makes headlines for her less than professional critique of other brands. Most recently, she has made videos discussing the lack of contemporary designs from our client, Diosa. Her spotlight was one of the major factors in Diosa's focus on new digital campaigns.

"This can't be a damn coincidence," she mutters under her breath.

"Were there leaks we were interested in her?"

Shelby shrugs. "Could've been, but these things happen. It's why we need to move quickly on talent."

I slump back into my own chair, feeling sick.

My entire pitch isn't dead, but it's on life support with a massive hole through it. It'll take hours to revise my plan. I should've known better. You always have a plan B and C with pitches of this caliber.

"When is Mr. Cavendish expected to arrive?"

"There is no current word on that. Last I spoke to him, he was en route to the airport," she says, picking at something under her polished pink nail. "He did mention that there were storms in the area, which could delay his flight. He's traveling private, so he will have a longer wait."

Not that I wish storms on anyone flying, but this might work in my favor. The smaller planes won't go out in iffy weather.

I nod, working through a plan. "This is good. I have time to develop another option."

"You sure do," she says, sounding like my very own cheerleader. "Good luck," she says, standing and making her way to the door. "I'll keep you informed on his timing."

"Thanks, Shelby." I don't look up, already beginning my search.

The easiest transition would be a client on Paxton's client list. Someone with a large following but who can grow with Diosa, showcasing the star power of the brand.

I make notes on several ideas, opting to offer a few in my pitch, as I should've done from the beginning. Next, I'll need to tell each of their stories and how it complements Diosa. I need all the hours and minutes to perfect this before Charles arrives, but I know I can do it.

What's the line from that one play? I gotta take my chance? Shot? Something like that.

Hours go by, and I'm still tinkering with the plan. I think it's strong, but I don't like last-minute changes. I'm the type of person who lets things marinate for a day or two, and this current situation isn't allowing for it.

"Knock, knock," Shelby says from the doorway. "I brought you some sustenance from the Thai restaurant around the corner." I perk up at the mention of food. She walks in, carrying a large bag, and I wonder who all she ordered for. "They just delivered it."

My eyes land on the wall clock opposite my desk, and I balk at the time. It's past six. I missed lunch and would've probably worked right past dinner if not for Shelby. My stomach rumbles in protest, and I grimace.

"The cafeteria is closed," she says, making her way toward my desk.

"Oh, my God, you are the best, Shelby," I mumble. "How much do I owe you?"

She waves me off with her free hand. "It's on Cavendish."

I snort in response. "Well, in that case, thank you, Cavendish. But out of curiosity, who all are you feeding?"

She shrugs. "I wasn't sure what you like, so I got a bit of everything." She sets the bag on my desk and makes quick work of setting out the containers.

She ordered all my favorites, not even knowing. Pad Thai, ginger chicken satay, and pad prik have me practically salivating.

Shelby is the coworker and mentor you dream of having in a career. She's given me space to work on my pitch and offered help whenever I've asked for it. I know without a doubt she has my back, and she hardly knows me.

"Any word on his whereabouts?" I ask, trying to help her open containers.

"No, unfortunately. I'm afraid you might be stood up."

I sigh, having feared as much. "I'm sure he's been very busy."

Her head lulls to the side in a *you're probably right* motion.

"I'm not going anywhere until I know for certain he isn't coming."

"I figured as much, which is why I ordered dinner." She places both hands on her hips. "Are you sure you want to hunker down here all by yourself? I'll be leaving for home soon. Everyone else has gone. Building security is downstairs, and they are just a phone call away."

I know she means well, but this is corporate America, and it's still a man's world. She should know that better than anyone, being in the position she is. Tests to measure my capabilities will only continue to come as I fight for my place on the ladder of success.

Rescheduling a planned pitch would be the first major strike against me.

If he told me I had to pitch today, I would. No matter what time it is.

Hell, I'll wait in this damn office until midnight if I have to.

"Yeah, I'm sure. I don't have much of a choice," I say, blowing out a breath. "He begins interviews tomorrow with the potential account managers. I have one last chance to convince him I can do the job."

Her lips form a thin line, and I can practically hear her inner thoughts.

She doesn't think I stand a chance, but she's too polite to say so.

"Well, good night, then," she says, turning toward the door. "If I hear anything, I'll call your office line."

"Thanks, Shelby. And thanks for the food. I really appreciate it."

She offers one last smile and heads out, leaving me in the quiet building alone.

I don't know how long I continued to eat and work, but the sun set long, long ago. Still, there's no word from Charles or Shelby. I've settled in for a long night, determined to sleep here to prove that I'm the best for the job.

On a moan, I swipe at the air, trying to shoo away the fly or whatever other nuisance is swarming around my face. That simple move brings awareness to my stiff joints and neck. One eye flutters open, and I take in my surroundings. My cheek is in a pool of my own drool on top of my desk at Cavendish Group.

*Very sophisticated, Raven*

I shut my one eye that bothered to open, groaning at the knowledge that I'd fallen asleep here. For a moment, I consider just giving in and allowing myself to fall back asleep, but I know it won't happen a second time. I need to get up and attempt to get home and, hopefully, capture a couple of hours of sleep in my own bed.

I stretch my arms over my head, yawning deeply, and yelp at the figure standing next to me.

"Sonofabitch!" I screech, blinking rapidly to adjust to the light. "You scared the hell out of me."

Charles Cavendish stands just to the side of my desk, staring down at me with a smirk.

"Miss Bennett. Care to explain why you're still here at"—he looks at his Rolex, eyebrow rising at what he sees—"two o'clock in the morning?"

The scent of scotch and mint infiltrates my senses, tumbling my stomach into a knot of nerves. Tingles race over my arms and down my spine as I look into the stormy blue eyes of the most handsome man I've ever seen.

For a moment, I wonder if I've dreamed this. Conjured him into my mind, complete with the heated look he's currently singeing me with. If I reach out and pull him to me, would he come willingly? Would he lay me out over this desk and have his way with me like I may have just been dreaming? I want that, even though I know I shouldn't.

"Don't look at me like that, Raven. It won't end well for you, sunshine."

My breath hitches at the way he says my name. His husky voice washes over me like my very own weighted blanket, and I nuzzle into it, feeling the tingles intensify.

*Snap out of the lust haze, woman.*

I internally wage war against my traitorous senses, pissed I'm sitting here making an ass of myself. Shaking my head, I busy my hands, straightening the paperwork spread across my desk. I'm grateful it's only a copy of my proposal and that the real thing isn't currently soaking in my drool.

"I'm sorry. I waited to pitch you on the Diosa plan, and I—"

"Dozed off?" he supplies, and I nod. "Is that the only reason you're here, Raven?"

My eyes narrow on him, and that's when I realize he's half-dressed. His white collared shirt is half-untucked with the first three buttons undone, showing a bit of his muscled chest. The sleeves are rolled up to his elbows, and I swallow as I take him in. He's holding a glass of amber liquid. Likely the bourbon I smelled.

Is he . . . drunk?

"Yes. I waited all day." I stand, grabbing my purse and the final proposal from my bottom drawer, ready to dart from the room to get to air. This man sucks the oxygen from the room, making my breathing labored.

*Pull yourself together, Raven.*

That internal pep talk gets more forceful the longer I stand here idly while I watch him set his drink down.

"I'll see you in the morning," I say over my shoulder, heading toward the door.

But he's quick, grabbing my elbow and stopping me.

He turns me around to face him. Our bodies are so close that our breaths mingle.

Too close.

"Mr. Cavendish?" The name comes out raspy, his proximity doing dangerous things to me.

"Tell me something, Rae," he says, backing me up until my back hits the wall next to the door. "Were you this . . . attentive . . . at all your prior jobs?"

Something about the way he says it throws me off. As though there's hidden meaning in the words. My brain is too foggy at the moment to compute what he's saying but also *not* saying.

"Sir?" I ask dumbly, unable to form a full sentence.

His hand drops from my elbow but lands just at the hem of

my dress, connecting with bare skin. I heat under his touch, and it makes its way up my body to my cheeks.

"Charles," he whispers, and my eyes crook in confusion. "Say my name, Raven." His hand moves, running up my leg and dragging my dress with it.

I suck in a breath, unable to move. To think.

"Ch-Charles."

"That's right, Rae. My *Rae* of fucking sunshine. Say it again. Say my fucking name again."

"Charles."

Before I can say more or move out of his grasp, his lips crash against mine.

I stumble, knees going a bit slack. His free hand grabs my waist, holding me steady as his tongue begs entrance to my mouth.

My lips part willingly, moaning around the notes of oak and mint on his tongue.

A delectable mix of pure masculinity attacks my senses, rendering me completely helpless to stop this.

I'm lost in him, hands grabbing at his crisp, white shirt. Wanting—*needing*—more.

The kiss isn't gentle. It's passionate and raw.

A growl works its way up to his chest, and it only lights the fire more. We're all hands and tongues, and I'm practically crawling up his body.

As quickly as it started, it comes to an abrupt stop.

Charles pulls away, chest heaving. His hands slam against the wall at my head, blocking me in. He stares down at me in a mix of lust, shock, and something darker. Something like anger.

"Did you plan this?" he spits, and my entire body goes rigid.

"W-What?"

"Did. You. Plan. This?" he grits through his teeth, leaning so close, I can hardly breathe.

"No. I . . . I told you I stayed to pitch to you."

He huffs out a humorless laugh. "You stayed the night in the office to pitch to me? Just what were you going to offer up?"

"Yes," I bark, growing more irritated by the second. "What exactly are you accusing me of, *sir*?" I bite.

He straightens, shrugging his shoulder. He grabs his glass and takes a long pull, draining it in one go.

"I guess I know how you managed such impressive endorsements."

I gasp at his insinuation, anger thrumming through every synapse. "Are you accusing me of sleeping my way through my former positions?"

"I didn't *actually* say that."

My hand shoots out, landing against his cheek in a slap that can be heard around the office. His eyes widen, and his hand rises to his cheek.

Inside, I'm quaking, but externally, I stand tall, ready to defend my actions.

He was out of line. Way out of line.

"Let me be perfectly clear, *sir*," I spit. "I earned every single one of those recommendations through hard work and grit. And I won't allow some male chauvinist, arrogant asshole, who's the product of familial nepotism, to belittle my hard work. And if those words are too big for your drunk ass tonight, I'll be happy to say them to you again in the morning."

"But this company is all I have," he says sorrowfully. "I won't let my sunshine take that away, too."

I pull a face, confused by his ramblings.

"What are you talking about?"

He turns on his heel, making his way out of my office. I watch as he staggers down the hall.

He's not just drunk. He's emotionally wasted along with this. What the hell is wrong with him, and who the hell caused this mess?

I consider calling Shelby, but the last thing I want to do is bring her into this mess in the middle of the night. Something is very off with Charles, but I'm not afraid of him or his stupid ideas.

I stop at the vending machine and buy two bottled waters, then head to his office. He's plopped in his chair, nodding off.

"Drink this," I command, twisting the top from the first bottle and setting it in front of him.

He wakes and eyes me warily but does as I instruct, draining the contents. I open the next and slide that one in front of him, and he does the same.

"Do you have any ibuprofen or aspirin? You'll want some for the headache you're sure to have in the morning."

He motions with his head toward his middle drawer. I open it to find a bottle, taking out two and handing them to him. He has a wet bar in his office, so I quickly fill up a tumbler with more water and hand it to him.

"I'm sorry," he mumbles. "I . . . I didn't mean what I said. I don't deserve you. My life needs to stay dark and without a Rae of sunshine."

My eyes narrow on him as he lowers his head to his desk. Within minutes, he's out, as evidenced by the soft snoring.

What the hell happened to him?

I can't very well leave him here alone, so I plop down on the couch on the far wall, setting an alarm early enough to get me out of here before people begin to arrive in the morning.

I won't leave him here drunk and alone. It isn't safe.

He might've been a world-class ass, but I'd never leave someone in this shape. I close my eyes, willing myself to get a few hours of shut-eye on this lumpy couch, but I know it'll never happen.

As soon as my eyes close, I'm assaulted with the memory of earlier. His hands roamed my body. His mouth moved over mine. It was incredible.

It was stupid.

How in the hell do I deal with this?

# chapter fourteen

Charles

HER WARM KISSES ARE MY FIRST THOUGHT AS I COME TO THE next day.

My head is reeling at the memory of being so close to Raven again. The blind need I had for her. The way her body molded to mine. Passion I hadn't felt in years taking over as we kissed.

The way she cared for me afterward.

What the fuck had I been thinking? Raven Bennett is turning out to be my kryptonite.

My employee is off-limits for so many reasons.

I had no business acting the way I did. Drunk or not. The things I said . . .

I'm a prick of epic proportions.

My heart had practically skipped a beat when I'd seen her in the meeting room that first day, quickly chased away by anger and all the questions percolating on why she was there.

The past had snuck up on me like a snake in the grass, shadows from what Tabitha had done falling over the situation and tainting the very air we shared. My first thought was that Raven had infiltrated Cavendish Group to try her hand at pulling me under. Just like Tabitha had.

None of that fucking matters.

Good news is Raven can't break my heart because it was broken years ago.

Funny enough, it wasn't even what Tabitha had done to me that broke me. I could get over that. People move on and deceive you.

No, the one who shattered what remained after Mum's death was my father.

His actions alone.

He was the only family I had left, and that bond should have been stronger.

None of this has to do with Raven at all.

And Raven isn't a snake like that slag of a woman now married to Father. He deserves all the pain she can offer him.

Shelby had hired her, not me, and according to her paperwork, it was long before that night at Silver. I've gone through everything, looking for a reason to terminate her, but I haven't found anything.

All I see is a talented woman who was hired because she'd done a damn good job at her prior internships. Internships that were more impressive than most of the positions the current applicants for the Diosa account manager position held.

Raven showed more potential on her first day than some of the other Cavendish employees have shown after being with the company for years.

The way she'd had the nerve to put up her hand and have her say—despite being in a room full of executives—only impressed me more. If she'd been someone other than the woman from Silver, I'd have promoted her there and then to account manager of Diosa.

She reminds me a lot of myself. Determined. Confident. I like her spunk, and I have a feeling she'll work her way up in the company very quickly without seducing the owner.

This morning, I reviewed her campaign plan, and I have to say, it's incredible. The amount of time and creativity that went into this is something I haven't seen from any of my senior account managers here or abroad. Ever.

Raven Bennett is perfect for the position in more ways than one. And I've screwed it up by not keeping my hands off her. I didn't realize her effect on me until I pressed our bodies together last night. Her hold on my mind has taken over my body, and I don't know what I'll do without her warmth again. She's becoming the only sunshine in my life.

*I'm so fucked.*

When I'm not mired in the London drama, the clients, or what is causing us to lose potential customers, I can't stop thinking about Raven.

She's utterly distracting. My dreams are filled with thoughts of what she must look like naked across my bed. How would it feel like to glide inside her, nothing separating us, just feeling the passion from her body enveloping my rock hard . . .

"Hellooooo. Charlie," Shelby calls, waving her hands in front of my face. "Are you even listening to me?"

I blink several times. I didn't even realize she was standing there, and based on her glare, she is not pleased.

"I'm sorry. What?"

"You can't be serious," she snaps. "You heard none of that?"

"Shelby, I'm exhausted."

"You're still drunk," she barks, crossing her arms over her chest, looking down at me like I'm sure my mother would if she were still alive.

"Please don't start," I beg, rubbing at my throbbing temple. "Yesterday was very much a disaster."

"I don't doubt it was, but you have a damn phone. You should've called."

Her lecture isn't doing anything for my building headache. She stands in the same place for several seconds, glaring down at me and breathing heavily in and out of her nose, until she finally sighs and sits down.

"She sat here all night waiting because you couldn't simply call with an update."

"I didn't know she would do that."

She laughs. A short, derisive laugh that comes out more like a snort than anything else. She whips her dirty blonde hair over her shoulder and stares at me. Her blue eyes are unblinking, and if she were standing, there's no doubt she'd be tapping her foot, waiting for me to speak. I want to tell her to calm down, but I have a feeling that wouldn't go over too well.

"I'm sorry?" It comes out as a question, and Shelby's eyes narrow to slits.

"You aren't sorry. You're hungover and stinking up the place," she barks. "Go home. Shower. Sleep," she says, not leaving room for arguments. "Pull yourself together, and then get your stupid ass back here tomorrow so we can fill these vacancies and keep this company rising to the top."

I've been schooled by my assistant.

"I can't. There's too much to do."

"And you're in the proper shape to actually do it?"

She makes a valid point. Between my headache and wayward thoughts of Raven, I'm damn near useless.

"You're right," I admit, my head lolling back on my shoulders. "I'll head home and come back tomorrow."

She sits back, watching me warily for several tense seconds. "What happened in London, Charles?"

I blow out a harsh breath, groaning in response. This is the last thing I want to get into right now. Shelby has been a godsend to this company and me, but I'm not ready to hear her advice that is overly loud, invasive, and unfortunately, right.

"There are all sorts of rumors circulating. I think it's best if we make a statement before it causes issues."

"What rumors?" I say with a deep sigh.

"That you were called home to take control of the London office."

I nod. No use in denying it. Her eyes widen.

"Seriously? It's all true?"

"It is, but I'm not doing it."

She seems to soften at this. "Well, for what it's worth, I'm relieved. This place wouldn't work without you."

"That doesn't mean that bastard won't press the subject," I say, growing more tired by the minute.

"And that's what had you drunk as a skunk last night and running off one of the best new hires we've had since opening?"

My eyes narrow. "What do you mean, ran her off? Where is she?"

"Not here," she says a little too nonchalantly for my liking.

"She didn't show today? Call?"

"Nope. Haven't been able to get in touch with her."

"Fuck," I growl, banging my fists on the desk.

Shelby jumps in surprise, her hand landing on her heart.

"Jesus, Charles. What on earth was that about?"

I jump to my feet, pacing the floor, running my hand through my hair, searching my mind for answers. I have cocked this up more than I thought possible. Raven's not stupid and is probably making a formal complaint to HR about my actions.

*Not that I don't deserve it.*

I stopped her from leaving, demanded answers, and practically attacked her mouth. Then when that wasn't enough fuckery, I hurled the cruelest accusations right to her beautiful face.

My hand rises to my cheek in memory of her hitting my face.

I earned any visible mark she left behind.

"What the actual fuck did you do?" she says in a voice that promises violence if I say the wrong thing.

"Nothing," I say, waving her off.

"You're going to stand there, hungover, and lie to me? Of all the people in your life, you don't get to push me away." She stands up, leaning over the desk. "You obviously caused Raven to run off."

"You're wrong." The lie comes too easily, but Shelby isn't buying it. Her body language practically screams she's no idiot. "What do you want me to say?" I bark back.

"The truth is always the best place to start."

"Fine! Would you like to hear how I showed up drunk at her desk? What about the part where Raven ran off after I accused her of sticking around the office to seduce me?"

"You have lost your damned mind!" she shouts.

"Shelby, please cease the yelling. My throbbing head is in agony."

"Oh, I'll make it ache far worse, you dumbfuck," she barks.

I prickle at her chastising. Silently praying this stops soon, I continue to rub my temples and whisper, "You do realize I'm your boss, right? You can lose this job right this moment."

Refusing to lower her voice, Shelby continues with the worst bollocking I've had in decades.

"Cut the shit, Charlie. You and I both know you aren't going to fire me, of all people. You caused this mess with Raven, and you need to fix it. Right now."

I close my eyes to stave off the pain caused by our shouting match.

People have started to gather outside my door, signaling we need to quiet down.

"I will handle it," is all I can offer.

"You better because I will walk on you for this. Don't make me keep that promise."

I sigh deeply. "Fine. Now with that sorted, it's time for you to please go back to your desk. If I leave today, you are the only one holding this place together."

I just need her to get out of my office.

Shelby just put a serious damper on my mood, and I cannot handle much more.

It's not her fault by a long shot, but I'm in serious need of meds and sleep. I have a feeling I'll only have time for one of those hangover cures.

She stands and heads to the door. It sounds like she mutters *idiot* under her breath. I wouldn't put it past her.

I watch her barge out, seeing most of the staff on the other side of the door just before she slams it.

I sigh.

The only way I'll get a hold of my life that is spiraling out of control is to start over.

And over begins by getting Raven to come back.

# chapter fifteen

Raven

I'M JUST SITTING AT MY DESK, REORGANIZING THE STACKS OF paper to leaf through the remaining résumés, when Charles walks by my office, stopping in his tracks.

He looks awful.

*Worse than last night.*

"You're here?" he says. I simply nod, feeling far too awkward after last night.

Charles had been a grade A drunk asshole. Not that I'll give him a pass entirely, but something had been horribly wrong with him before he arrived at the office.

Curiosity is getting the better of me to figure out how I can fix this issue. What made someone as cool and collected as Charles Cavendish lose his control?

Trying to tamp down the desire that flows through me when we're in the same room together, I try to answer his question calmly from the safety of my desk.

"I left early this morning to go home to change. Fell asleep. My phone was dead." It's all I offer by way of an explanation. I won't apologize for being late and not calling. It's his fault.

He nods. "I'm glad you got some rest." He stares at me for a few tense moments. "Will you come with me to my office for a few moments?"

My lips purse as I consider my reply. I'm not ready to deal with him, but he is my boss, so what choice do I really have?

*You have the upper hand. He was inappropriate.*

I sigh, knowing it's best to rip off the Band-Aid.

When I exit my office, everyone is staring at me. I wonder what they're all thinking and why they're so interested in Mr. Cavendish and me.

His words come back to haunt me. The insinuation that I didn't earn my raise but took it by opening my legs.

It's like being thrown into an ice-cold pool and held under.

Except it isn't true, and I know it. That's what matters.

"Close the door," he says as I walk in.

I don't say anything. Just sit down. I look up at him, but his eyes avert mine.

Coward.

"You wanted to see me?" I say, getting this dreaded meeting started.

His head lifts. "About last night—"

My hands raise to stop him. As much as I knew this was coming, I am not ready for it. I don't want to discuss it.

"Sir, can we just move forward? I really don't want to discuss it."

He frowns, biting his lower lip as though he's not sure what to say.

"You can call me Charles."

I huff. Of all the things to spit out, that's what he came up with? How about *I'm sorry, Raven?*

Or even *I was completely wrong about you, Raven?*

But as much as I'd like to snap at him, my manners get the better of me. Hopefully, the rest of my face will catch up to my kindness before I shoot him a disdained look.

"Everyone else calls you sir or Mr. Cavendish. I won't take

privileges not owed to my peers." I offer a wobbly smile that doesn't reach my eyes.

He looks at me intently, that deep frown marring his face. "Not everyone else works as close with me as you will."

I have no idea what he means by that, so I just remain quiet.

"I read through your Diosa proposal, and I'm prepared to move forward with you leading the charge as interim account manager until we find someone historically more qualified to fill the position. You'll work closely with me until the account runs smoothly and we can find suitable hires."

"No, thank you, Mr. Cavendish."

His head jerks back, and his eyes widen at what I'd just said. "No?"

"No," I repeat. "Not like this."

This might be the first time ever that I'm willing to walk away from the thing I want most to prove a point, but here we are. I'll take a lot of crap—have in the past—but I won't be called a whore. He might not have actually said the words, but they were insinuated.

He sighs. "Please, Raven, let me—"

"I'm not interested in taking a position because you are atoning for your actions, sir. When I get this account, even if it's just a temporary gig, it will be because I've earned it." I sit back further in the chair, pursing my lips. "Contrary to what you believe, I've earned everything I've ever received. I'm damn good at my job."

My voice holds strong until the last part, when it cracks. I'm exhausted and angry.

"I was wrong, and I'm sorry," he says, leaning forward at his desk. "Your pitch was excellent. The best I've seen. You understand the Diosa brand and potential talent in a way that I don't think anyone else in this office could ever manage. I doubt the applicants I was set to meet today could do it." He takes a deep breath. "Diosa needs you. I . . . need you. On this account," he adds quickly.

I bite my cheek, considering his words. I want to give in and celebrate my winnings, but I won't allow him off the hook that easily.

"I'm not sure I can work with you, Mr. Cavendish. Not after last night."

He nods several times, looking remorseful. "I can't say I blame you, but I need you to know that yesterday was a grave exception. I'll never act like that again. I can assure you of that."

I blink, eyes narrowing in on him. He looks sincere, but still . . . I'm pissed. And rightfully so. He owes me some answers, and right now, I feel justified in demanding them.

"What happened to you yesterday? Why were you so drunk?"

He blows out a harsh breath, head falling back onto his shoulders.

"That's a long story."

I shrug. "I have time, and if you want me on this account, I suggest you start talking." I offer a forced bright smile. "Sir."

He huffs a laugh. "A ray of sunshine even on a cloudy day."

I snort. "Song lyrics are supposed to charm me?"

"It's just the truth. Even angry, you manage to smile."

"It's forced," I say, grinning.

He chuckles, but all humor quickly dissolves as his features darken.

"I was in London, meeting with my father," he begins, and I nod because I'd heard as much. "He's decided to retire at the end of the year and wishes for me to take my place as the head of the company."

I scrunch my nose, eyes roaming over his still posture.

"You don't want it." It isn't a question. I could tell by his body language that it wasn't good news.

"I don't," he admits.

"Why?"

From what I know of Cavendish Corporation, it was always the goal for him to take over one day. It's in the company's manifesto on their website. So why would Charles not want to step into his legacy?

He grunts. "For starters, my father and I don't get along these days."

These days.

As in they did at one time. What could've happened to change that?

I don't get the chance to ask because he continues.

"New York is my home now. I have no intentions of returning to London for any period of time." He folds his hands on the desk in front of him. "Now, let's discuss the new campaign position you will be working on."

"No," I say, and his one eyebrow lifts. "I want to know why you said what you said about me."

His lips purse, and he looks genuinely confused. "About?" he drawls, and I wonder for a moment if maybe he truly doesn't remember that part.

Not that it makes it any less horrific.

"You implied that I've risen in this industry by . . ." My eyes land on the wall of windows behind him as I try to gather courage before I say the next part. Looking back at him, I let a big breath out and quickly utter, "Sleeping my way through the offices."

His eyes widen, his jaw clenches, and then his hands fist together on the table.

"I can assure you, Raven, that had nothing to do with you. In my lousy state of drunkenness, I clearly confused you with someone from my past," he says, rushing on. "Not that it makes my actions any less heinous. But I give you my word. What was said did not and would never pertain to anyone in this office." His head lowers. "I'm bloody embarrassed by my actions."

I snort. "You should be."

His head lifts, and all I see is sadness.

Who made him like this? So jaded and sad.

I nod, wanting to erase that look from his face. Needing to

get on solid ground where he's my boss, one that I respect, and I'm his employee.

"Tell me your thoughts about the Diosa proposal."

One corner of his mouth lifts. "I definitely like where you are going with this plan. We'll need to meet with Paxton and the other agent soon. But I think we're onto something good."

"I didn't say I would take the account manager position."

He huffs. "You're going to pass up the opportunity of a lifetime out of anger?"

My shoulders straighten. "Not anger. Self-preservation. I don't take kindly to being harassed and then given an olive branch by way of a job. That would make your words true, and I refuse."

How did we circle back to this? Oh, I know . . . he's a stubborn ass. I'm meeting him head-on.

"Really?" he grates. "You think I'd give you a job just because we had a row?"

"A row?"

"A quarrel. Fight."

I thought I'd done a good job, but I'll be damned to give in so easily, considering his words and continued assholery.

I grunt. "It was a little more than a *row*. And for the record, I did nothing."

"Well . . . I wouldn't say nothing."

I know what he's referring to, and it has nothing to do with the slap.

"That will never happen again," I say quietly, fearful that the walls have ears and someone will overhear.

"Agreed. Never."

He nods, and then I nod. There's a lot of nodding because what else do you do in a strange situation like the one I'm finding myself in?

"And you agree I *earned* this position, even if it's temporary?"

"I do."

I take several deep breaths, pretending to contemplate my

answer, but the truth is, I was never giving this chance up. I simply needed his reassurance that this wasn't his way of buying my silence for his actions.

"Fine. I'll work with you on this."

He offers me a smile. "We do, however, have one small problem. Well, it's a big problem, really."

My heart is racing, but I'm not sure why. Is he going to say something more about the kiss?

Oh, God, please don't let him bring that up.

"A problem? What's that?"

"Apparently, our biggest competitor, Bauer, is out to sink Diosa. Rumor has it they are looking for a way to steal them. They must know about the clause in the contract. They've already started their campaign for Rothburke, hired Summer Smith out from under us, and they're sinking millions into their plan. The worst part is the men running the advertising company are crooks. They'll be watching our every move, so we need to keep our plans under wraps."

Did he just say Bauer? I knew we were competitors, but not the largest. That means.

Asher.

Oh, no.

The blood drains from my face as wicked thoughts invade my mind, poisoning me.

Just the other day, I'd had lunch with Asher and told him all about Summer. Surely this wasn't because of him? He might be working on climbing that ladder at Bauer, but he's my best friend. He'd never do that to me.

"Are you all right?" Charles asks, face pinched in concern.

"Fine. I'm just hungry and exhausted." Neither is a lie.

"You should go home for the day. Rest. We can start tomorrow."

"No. We're already behind if what you're saying is true. We can do this. We can beat them, but not if we don't get the ball rolling."

He smiles. "Very true. I've started putting some stuff together.

Come around here so I can show me where you saved your mock-ups on the network."

I get up and walk over to his computer. We're so close that I can actually smell him, and the scent immediately takes me back to last night. I try desperately to concentrate on the screen in front of me, but all I can think about is how I felt with his hands moving up my leg.

The way his mouth felt against mine. I gulp and shake my head slightly.

*Concentrate, Raven!*

I reach over to move the mouse at the same time he does, and our hands briefly touch. I jump ever so slightly and notice that he flinches, too.

We are only at the computer for a few minutes as he clicks through several pictures of pieces that Diosa has suggested we use in our ads, but it's enough to set me back on edge.

Can I do this? Can I work this closely with Charles Cavendish?

*You have to. This is your dream job. If you impress him, maybe it can become a real promotion. Not just a temporary fill-in.*

I stand tall, taking a step away from him. "I like them all, but it really depends on who we pick up to wear them."

"I agree. I'll call Paxton and Royal Talent to set up meetings for this week."

"I'll start working on some mood boards for each of those garments. Can you forward them to me?" I ask, rounding the desk and taking a seat across from him once more.

"They'll be sending over the other items for AlteredX and Icon as well," he says, clicking keys on his keyboard. "As soon as they're sent, I'll forward those. You should have the ones we just looked through now."

"When are we conducting the rest of the interviews for the assistant positions?"

He sighs, running a hand back through his thick hair.

"I had them moved to next week. We need to nail the talent first."

I stand, ready to get back to my office and get started.

Charles walks around the desk so he is only inches away from me, leaning back against his desk so we're at eye level.

"You are an incredible asset to this company, Raven. I hope you realize that despite my actions last night, I genuinely mean that. Your passion will be what makes this campaign remarkable."

The word passion lingers in the air, and I swear he's about to lean down and kiss me. A knock on the door has me snapping out of it.

Had I imagined it? Charles is still leaning back against his desk, looking like he hasn't moved.

I shake my head, brush my hands over my skirt, and stand a little taller.

"Thank you for the opportunity, Mr. Cavendish. You won't regret it." Without looking at Charles, I open the door and leave.

The woman on the other side of the door is Shelby, and her eyes widen.

"Oh, you are here today," she says.

"Sorry." I offer a tight-lipped smile.

"Shelby, I'm ready for your meeting," Charles says from behind me, and Shelby glares at him over my shoulder.

"Are you leaving?" she asks.

"Yep," I say and quickly hurry away.

I don't look at Charles at all, and I don't look back to see if Shelby is still glaring at him. I desperately need to get away from this office. From *him*.

It takes a lot to unravel me like that, but the more time I spend alone with Charles, the more I find myself unable to control myself, and that's a huge problem. I got the job, but having feelings for the boss won't help me keep it.

I run to the bathroom and shut myself in one of the stalls. I stand here breathing deeply, in and out, in and out. What would've happened if there hadn't been a knock on the door?

Would he have kissed me again?

Would I have let him?

Did I imagine the whole thing?

*God . . . What is wrong with me?*

He's my boss. I should never have kissed him in the closet that first night. He was a stranger, and that's not who I am. *You didn't know he was your boss.*

This is the last time I think about Charles Cavendish in any way past professionalism. Is he attractive? Yes. Have I worked with plenty of handsome men in the past? Also yes. I can do this. I *will* do this.

I stay in the stall for a full ten minutes, giving myself the pep talk I desperately need, grateful nobody has entered the room to hear my insane rambling. I take a couple of deep breaths and head to the sink, splashing a bit of cold water on my face, feeling better.

*Got to simply keep things professional.*

On my walk back to my office and see that Charles's door is still closed. He seems to keep it shut most of the time, and the blinds are typically down as well, so it's hard to tell what is going on, but as I walk past, I'm almost sure I hear Shelby yell. She does *not* sound happy.

I smirk, wondering how his assistant gets away with speaking to him like that. Most of the men I've worked with in the past had such chips on their shoulders they would never have allowed a subordinate to raise their voice to them.

Charles has had two women chastising him well and good in a mere hour. The door cracks, and a small squeal escapes my lips as I rush down the hallway, not wanting to be caught loitering outside the door.

Hopefully, the rest of the day will not be eventful.

# chapter sixteen

Charles

IT'S BEEN FOUR DAYS SINCE RAVEN TOOK THE DIOSA POSITION, and I've spent the entirety of those days trying to nail down Paxton for a meeting.

The bastard's doing it on purpose, trying to flex his proverbial muscles before agreeing to the meeting.

A meeting he moaned about not having sooner.

We both know he'd rearrange his schedule if any other agency held the Diosa account, but his so-called best mate gets jerked around like a sure thing. Hell, I bet he'd have met anyone else on one of his precious Saturdays to land this campaign for one of his clients.

I asked Raven to meet me in the parking garage on level B so we could walk in together. Paxton chose this God-awful time because he knows I hate meetings before eight o'clock. It's seven, and if not for the espresso, which I normally wouldn't drink, and was crap, I wouldn't be functioning.

I'm an early riser, waking before the sun, which means I hit a wall around eight every morning. It takes a quick workout to get me back in the game.

Today, I needed caffeine.

I'm standing outside my Aston Martin DBS, the one splurge purchase—aside from my penthouse—I've made since arriving in the States, when she strolls up.

"Nice car," she says in such a way that I question what she really thinks. Her face is blank, void of anything resembling awe, and this car is awe-inducing.

"Nice car?" I question, taking her in. "Tell me what you really think of it, Rae."

Her hands land on her hips. "Stop calling me that. Why do you do that?"

My eyes narrow in on her. This really bothers her, but why?

"Rae . . . Raven," I say, motioning toward her. "You know, a shortened version."

Her eyes sharpen. "Well, stop it."

"Has nobody ever called you that before?"

She runs her hands down her thighs, drawing my attention to her body.

She's wearing a black dress that hugs her curves and buttons all the way up the front, paired with a bright pink belt and matching shoes. The pop of color suits her.

"Not for a very long time," she says, pulling my attention back to her face. A flicker of sadness washes over her, and I'm curious who the man was that she allowed to call her Rae. Clearly, it was someone special to her to cause that kind of emotion to show.

"I don't think we're at the nickname level of this working relationship," she says, pulling my attention back to her. She's eyeing me warily.

I shrug, trying to pull off nonchalance. "I think I'll stick with Rae," I say, determined to piss her off, it would seem. "Back to the issue with my car."

She purses her lips and crosses her arms over her ample chest. "It's a nice car."

"But . . ." I press. "I can hear a *but* in there, and I'm very distressed over it."

She laughs. "Men and their cars." She shakes her head. "But nothing, Charles. I like your car."

My chest tightens when she says my name, affecting me in ways it shouldn't. I like the way it sounds coming from her lips. Too much.

"What?" she asks, shifting on her feet.

"Nothing."

"That's not fair." She giggles, sounding nervous. "What are you looking at? Do I have something on my dress? In my hair?"

The smile spreads, and I can't stop it. "I'm only looking at you, Raven. You look lovely."

The words are out before I can stop them. I mean every damn word, but it's not something I should be saying to her.

Her cheeks turn a shade of pink that only highlights her beauty. Her head lowers, and she rocks back and forth on her pink heels.

"You really shouldn't say things like that to me, Mr. Cavendish. We promised we would be professional."

The smile drops from my face, and I clear my throat. "You're right. I was trying to be kind. My apologies."

Her tight-lipped smile is hard to read. In the past few weeks, the bright, bubbly girl I watched at Silver has been reduced to wariness and anger too much, all at my hand.

"Are you ready?" I ask, offering my arm to escort her to Paxton's office.

She nods, walking right past me and completely ignoring my attempt at chivalry.

Probably for the best.

This woman is something else entirely.

We make it up to Paxton's penthouse office on the seventh floor, which overlooks the city. It's ostentatious and entirely Paxton Ramsey's style.

"Mr. Cavendish," Marla, the assistant, croons, leaning over the desk, her large breasts practically spilling from her deep V-neck floral dress.

She's been trying to get into my bed since Paxton hired her, but I'm not interested.

Marla is a ladder climber.

Which is the last thing I'm interested in. She's beautiful and exotic, but sleeping with her would only cause bigger problems for me.

I know her type. Too well.

"Hello, Marla. How have you been?"

She bats her eyelashes, and for a moment, I wonder if she has something in her eye. I chance a glance at Raven and find she might be thinking the same thing, if her tapered eyes and scrunched nose are any indications.

"I've been waiting for your call, honey," she says, just above a whisper.

My hand lands on the back of my neck, the air growing thick with tension. I'm feeling uncomfortable with this conversation being as though Raven is privy to it.

Yet another reason Marla will never receive that call she's waiting for. She's too forward.

Raven clears her throat, pulling Marla's intense stare off me for a moment.

"Oh, I'm sorry," Marla hums. "I didn't see you there."

"Yes, well, it did look like you had something stuck in your eye. Did you get it out, *honey*?"

I stifle a choked laugh behind my fist at Raven's condescending tone that she covers up with the brightest, fakest smile I've seen her wield to date.

"Could you please let Mr. Ramsey know we're here?" Raven continues, dismissing Marla expertly.

She glares in Raven's direction but quickly turns on her heel, stalking toward his office. Within two minutes, his door opens, and Paxton, dressed in his best Armani suit, appears, grinning like a loon.

"It's wonderful to see you," he says, walking straight past me and pulling Raven into a tight hug.

She giggles, patting his back awkwardly. "You, too, Paxton. Thank you for allowing us to meet with you."

He smiles down at her. "It's the least I could do for my fruit-bearing friend."

She offers him a toothy grin. "Glad you liked it."

"Oh, I did. The sunshine balloons were a perfect touch. They reminded me of you immediately."

"Is that so?" she says, and he nods.

"Of course." His hand motions to her. "You're always cheery."

"Dear God," I murmur, rolling my eyes at Paxton's blatant flirting.

They both look at me with varying degrees of interest.

"Glad to see you brought the grump with you," Paxton says, grinning down at Raven.

"I can't seem to shake him."

"Oh, you two are a regular comedy routine. Want me to ring Monty Python to add you to the cast?" I drone. "Can we get on with it, Paxton? I don't have all damn day."

His lips press together as he shoots a look of annoyance at me before ushering us toward his open door. "You used to be fun. Take a seat," he instructs, walking behind his obscenely large mahogany desk in front of a glass wall.

It would be an amazing view if he wasn't on the seventh floor in a city with skyscrapers. His view is another wall of windows, and I can't help but wonder what price he paid to get screwed.

"I looked over your proposal, Raven, and I have to say, you're good. Too good for the likes of him," he jibes at me.

"Thank you," she says, lighting up. Her excitement is palpable as I listen to her jump into a pitch that is anything but scripted.

Her passion is contagious, and her knowledge is impressive. She's a damn force, and I'm spellbound by it.

I'm in a trance, watching her lips move but not hearing a word of it.

"Charles," Paxton says, his voice dripping with amusement.

My head turns as I laser him with a glare.

"What do you think?" he says, crossing his legs and sitting back cockily.

He knows damn well I have no idea what he's talking about, and that annoying grin says he knows why.

"I trust whatever decision Raven makes."

His eyes taper as he considers me. I don't like whatever is going on in that head of his. I can practically hear the accusations, and I tense, waiting for whatever is coming.

"Fine," he says, turning back to Raven. "I'll draw up the contracts for Catelyn and Spencer, but I'd like to throw my hat in the ring for all three accounts."

My eyebrows rise into my hairline. He knows I'm after Jessica Almes since Summer was stolen out from under me.

"News is about to break that I scored the client of a lifetime. The ink is dry, and I now represent Holly Morgan."

My eyes widen, and Raven gasps.

"Holly left World Class?"

Paxton nods, grinning like a Cheshire cat.

Holly Morgan is the equivalent of Summer Smith in the movie business. An actress who will be a great account to work with as she rises through her field.

Holly is known to be classy, beautiful, and perfect for Diosa.

Until today, she was unreachable. World Class wouldn't entertain contracts for her outside of their tight circle. Unless you were in with Richard Cross, owner of World Class Talent, you weren't getting a meeting.

"Paxton, that's incredible," Raven says, sounding shell-shocked. "She's perfect."

"And for my friends," he says, looking back and forth between Raven and me, "she'll be on board."

This is a game changer, and I can tell Raven feels it, too.

"Meet Holly and me at Silver tomorrow night, and we'll close the deal."

"We'll be there," she says without hesitation.

"Great, what else can I help you two with from my balloon-filled office?"

"Nothing at the moment, Pax, but can I use the ladies' room before we head out?" she asks.

"It's the door at the end of the hallway," he says, and I don't miss Raven's raised brow, as if to say, *sure about that,* but she quickly schools her features.

None of us wants to bring up the last encounter we all had at Silver.

When Raven's left the room, Paxton chuckles deeply.

"My friend, you have your hands full with that one."

I purse my lips. Raven has been nothing but professional and brilliant.

"You've got it bad, and you can't fool me."

I scoff. "You're insane. She is my employee. That's all."

He shakes his head. "You're a complete moron, but I'll let you tell yourself these lies." He pulls me into a brotherly hug, patting my back. "Good luck."

I scowl, knowing better than to continue to deny anything to him. He's a dog with a bone, and the last thing I need is Raven walking in on that conversation.

I need her. Cavendish Group needs her.

I won't fuck this up again.

---

"We need to talk."

Trying to clear emails and my head after being at Paxton's office with Raven, I lift my head when a very frazzled Shelby storms into my office. My back goes ramrod straight as I wonder what has her up in arms.

Removing my hands from the keyboard, I give her my full attention.

"Very well." I gesture at her to proceed with whatever news is important enough to interrupt my morning correspondence.

"We lost two accounts." Shelby starts to pace. "Both of the accounts were in the preliminary stages. No contracts signed, but still."

"Breathe, Shelby."

"Breathe? How can you tell me to breathe? Didn't you hear me?"

"I did. But we expected some push back when we started this office and pushed away from the London headquarters."

"How are you not freaking the fuck out?" she scoffs.

"We were bound to lose one or two. Of course, two is not to my liking, but I expected as much. Some clients don't agree with us being in New York. It was a matter of time before they left."

"But that's the thing. It isn't a location issue. Neither client is located in London."

This news has me furrowing my brow. "Explain."

"They both went to Bauer."

Her words have my fist clenching on my desk. "Do we have any of the details?"

"The only thing I have heard is that the campaigns pitched were a bit too similar to my liking."

"And you think this isn't a coincidence?" I ask.

"I don't believe in coincidences."

I nod my head as she continues to pace. "Neither do I."

"Last month, we had a client step away from us and over to them for a 'better option,' and the month before that, they took one of our smaller restaurants." Shelby's footsteps halt, and she stands in front of my desk, arms crossed in front of her chest. "How do you want me to fix this?"

"Number one, you aren't the only person in this office. I'll look into it with some security help. Proceed as if nothing is amiss from your side." Lifting my wrist, I look down at my watch and check the time. So much for spending the rest of the day in the office.

There's always a fire to put out. This loss is barely a spark, but if I'm not careful, it will spread until it becomes an inferno.

"Well, whomever you get, make sure they are doing a deep dive into everyone in this office. I don't trust several people if our campaign was identical to what Bauer produced."

Standing from my desk, I stride over to Shelby and put an arm around her. "You are my fiercest ally, and I know you are upset for all of us. But stressing does no good. Why don't you head home early and take Brad out for dinner. He doesn't need to suffer your cooking every night."

"You asshole. Stop making me laugh. You know I want to stay mad about this."

"I can't let you do that, love. You know I'm the angry one in this relationship."

"No, you are the grumpy asshole who needs to get laid."

"Watch it, Shelby." I give her my stern look. I swear she likes to act like the big sister I never wanted and ended up with when I found her anyway. "I will check in with what I find out on security system options."

Stepping out of my office and down the hall to grab a drink before I make this call, I run smack into someone.

No. Not someone. The only person who keeps invading my mind all hours of the day and doesn't let me get a moment of sleep without her in my dreams.

Her.

Time slows down as Raven wobbles in her black stiletto heels. I see her falling before it happens, and my hands shoot up to bracket around her. Once she's in my arms, I pull her toward me.

Raven feels small in my arms, fragile, and I feel the need to protect her. Keep her safe from all harm. But as I inhale the soft fragrance of lilacs, I know I can't do this.

*You need to let her go. You cannot be enough for her.*

With a cough, I steady her body, then drop my arms and step away.

"Thank you, I—" she says, but I cut her off.

"If you can't walk in women's shoes, Miss Bennett, maybe you should try something different. We don't have that strict of a dress code. Maybe trainers would be best from now on."

Based on the appalled look on her face, she opens her mouth to argue. I don't wait to hear what else Raven has to say, as it won't help this feeling I have when I'm such an arsehole to her.

I'm already gone.

Thirty minutes later, I'm pulling up to the nondescript building in the meatpacking district. Parking my car, I look back at the navigation.

There is no way this is the place. This hole in the wall needs security; it's not a security center.

But Drew Lawson told me this guy was the best. Called him a world-renowned hacker who runs his own security business. Comes from a well-known family that is legit in real estate.

I must get to the bottom of who is trading in Cavendish Group secrets. Cameras, computer spying, the whole works are needed in my offices, and I can't have anyone finding out.

I have no choice but to take Drew at his word. Hopefully this bloke is as good as he's supposed to be. We don't have time to spare losing clients, especially now with London becoming an issue.

Stepping out of the car, I look for the address, but I don't see it. I do see a door, though. I'm not even a few steps away when the door opens.

Fascinating.

"You can come in." A voice says from fuck knows where. The brick? There must be a built-in camera and intercom somewhere I can't see.

I step inside the door and am transported into what I can only describe as a high-tech lair that would make a Bond villain jealous. I walk farther inside, and as I do, I see a man who looks to be my age sitting in front of a full wall of monitors.

"You must be Charles Cavendish," he says as he swivels his chair to face me. "I'm Jaxson Price."

# chapter seventeen

Raven

"Y OU DID WHAT?" MY MOTHER CHOKES AROUND THE SIP OF margarita she had just taken.

We're in the middle of discussing my day, and somehow, we got around to the part about how I went to a meeting with Paxton. Then the topic turned to how I went about securing said meeting, leaving out the whole Silver ordeal. Obviously.

"I sent him a fruit basket and asked for a meeting," I repeated with a one-shoulder shrug.

"A fruit basket?" my mother asks, looking at me as though I've lost my mind.

I offer a toothy grin. "He's mentioned before that he's partial to fruit."

"You've spoken to him before?"

Teresa Bennett doesn't miss a damn thing. Ever.

Lily chuckles, piecing together when I would've learned that news. We share a look, and I hope she can see that is *not* something I want to be brought up around my mother.

Mom and I have always been very close. We tell each other nearly everything. But I don't want her to know about my lapse in judgment at Silver. It's so unlike me, and I know it would taint her views of me working with Charles.

For reasons I don't even want to dissect, I don't want her thinking poorly of him. I'm an adult and capable of making my own decisions. As is he. But my mom's old school when it comes to romance, and I know she'd find my actions in the club to be very scandalous.

"It all worked out," I say, bypassing her question. "I landed some huge wins for the company."

Thankfully, she doesn't call me on it.

I continue to work through the details of the meeting, filling them in on every last piece, except for who we were bringing on as the talent.

They both begged, but I remained silent. I explained what we were up against without calling out Bauer and that I was under strict secrecy. When they heard the penalty would be losing my job, if not worse, they both said they understood.

I could tell they were disappointed. I am, too. I'm so excited about Holly Morgan potentially working on this campaign, but it's not something I can share, especially before the ink's dry.

"My baby girl, moving up in the world." Mom smiles brightly, motherly pride beaming from her. I return the smile.

Lily engages my mom in a conversation about her area of town, and I zone out.

Thoughts of Charles are invading my peace and setting me on edge. The man has taken up too much of my energy this past week, but I can't say I hate it.

He's an enigma, carrying around secrets that I'm desperate to uncover.

I swipe my tongue across the rim of my glass, gathering the salt on my tongue before tipping back the lime margarita, eager to think about anything other than Charles.

It's our weekly taco Tuesday, complete with a pitcher of regular and peach margaritas. We've been doing this for the past few years, and I refuse to stop the tradition now due to my job, even if I had to cancel the last few weeks.

"Tell me about your boss," Mom says, and I take another sip, sighing around the strong bite of lime.

"What's there to say?"

Lily snorts. "A lot," she says under her breath, and I fix her with a look of warning.

Her eyes half-roll, but she doesn't say anymore. But my mom hears everything, and she didn't miss Lily's remark.

"Spill," she demands, and I wince.

"I've only seen him once, but he's not easily forgotten," Lily says with a giggle, leading me to believe Lily is already feeling very good from the margaritas. "He's one of the most handsome men I've ever seen."

My mom looks at me with a raised brow. "He's attractive?"

*That's an understatement*, I think to myself.

"I guess. If you like grumpy ass British men," I say, hoping that'll be the end of the conversation.

"British grump, eh?" Her teasing tone tells me she sees right through my false indifference.

"Ya, today the asshole told me if I can't walk in adult shoes, I need to wear 'trainers.' Ugh. So embarrassing."

Mom laughs because she knows me too well. And based on the way she's staring at me with that knowing look, I can tell that I'm going to get the third degree once Lily is gone.

*Great.*

Lily left shortly after eleven, taking an Uber across town. Mom stuck around, which wasn't unusual on a Tuesday.

Since Dad died, sleepovers have been a normal thing for us.

We were lying on my bed, watching an old episode of *Frasier*, when Mom decided to catch me off guard.

"You gonna tell me about this crush you have on your boss?"

I roll over to face her. "I don't have a crush on him. Why would you say that?"

She smacks her lips, searching my face. "I know my daughter, and I know that starstruck look you get in your eyes. It happens every time Henry Cavill comes on the TV."

I roll my eyes. "You are ridiculous. Charles and I work closely together. I respect him and how hard he works."

"And . . ." she drawls.

"*And* he's doing great things for Cavendish Group here in the United States. And I can't help but admire his tenacity."

She snorts. "Tenacity? Goodness, me, bringing out the five-dollar words. That's more than a crush."

I grab the pillow from behind my head and whack her with it. She squeals, grabbing her own pillow. Sometimes we act like children, but it's just how we are.

It wasn't always like this. We had a typical mother-daughter relationship throughout school. One day, I loved her, and the next, I hated her.

She was always the strict one. When she said no, I always went to Dad, and he'd give in, earning himself a scowl and the cold shoulder for a couple of hours.

Their fights never lasted long. They were the true definition of love, and it broke my mom's heart when dad died.

It broke mine, too. We were a solid unit, and the world only made sense with us all together.

We both fall back onto the bed, laughing at our shenanigans. My mom grabs my hand and squeezes, and I know the moment is about to get heavy. That's her telltale sign that a serious conversation is about to begin.

"Promise me you're not falling for your boss."

I look at her. *Really* look at her, wondering why this bothers her so much.

"Would it be so bad if I were?"

She presses her lips into a straight line but doesn't say anything.

"I'm not, but I'm just curious why you're so bothered by the idea."

She blows out a harsh breath. "From all that you've said, it sounds like heartbreak waiting to happen, baby girl. He's the heir to the entire Cavendish Corporation, and the headquarters are in London. His home."

I don't say anything, but I give her a look that says *and so.*

"What happens to you if he goes back there? Would you go to London?"

I bark out a strangled laugh. "Mom, I told you nothing is going on between us. It's ridiculous to even consider what I would do in a situation that will never happen." I take a breath and offer a small smile. "But you know I'd never leave you."

She would never admit it, but I know, deep down, that's what really scares her. The thought of being alone is my mom's biggest fear.

"Not that it matters. You and I both know wherever I go, you go. It's not the first time you've packed up and followed me," I say, offering a bigger smile, but she doesn't return it.

"I'm worried about you. This is your dream job. In your dream city. You worked so hard to get here, and I know how easily a man like Charles Cavendish could creep under your skin." She said his name as though it were a disease. "I don't want you to give everything up for a man because nothing lasts forever, love. You've got to take care of yourself first."

"Mom," I say, looking at her long and hard. "What's really going on?"

Her bottom lip trembles, and a tear drips from the corner of her eye.

"You know I loved your father more than anything, baby girl, and I will never regret the sacrifices I made to be with him, but I gave up *everything* the moment he smiled at me. I'd do it all over again, but life is short, and we're not guaranteed our happily ever after."

Tears stream down her cheeks now, and I reach out, swiping

them away. She hiccups a sob, and I pull her head into my chest, holding her while she cries.

I doubt tequila has played a part in her current state, but I also know she's never really grieved the way she needed to.

After several seconds of allowing her to have her moment, she lifts her head, rubbing at her eyes. "When your dad d-died, I didn't even know who I was anymore. All the dreams I had before meeting him were no longer an option for me, and I felt lost."

My father did become my mom's identity. His friends were hers. Where he went, she went. Looking back, I can see now how unhealthy that was. My mom didn't have her own life, so when Dad died, she lost everything.

"I don't want you to ever feel the way I do. Like a piece of you is missing. I want you to love, baby girl, don't get me wrong. I do. But I am *petrified* of your heart breaking like mine was..That's my issue, not yours. So don't listen to me. I'm a cynical old bat."

I laugh. "You're hardly old, Mom. You can relax. I'm going to be fine. I'm not falling for Charles. I'm following my dreams."

She sighs. "Guard your heart. That's the best piece of advice I can give you."

I squeeze her hand. "I will. I promise."

"You're all I have left of him," she says. "Not only do you have his eyes, but you share his name." She closes her eyes. "Ray would be so proud of you."

I can't help my own tears from falling. My dad was the only person who ever called me Rae. They chose my name because my dad said he always wanted me to have a piece of him. It's an honor I've carried my entire life. One I cherish above all.

"I love you, Mom."

"Me, too, baby girl. Me, too."

# chapter eighteen

Raven

Tacos last night might not have been the best idea after all.

Okay, it wasn't the tacos. The margaritas may be at fault.

My head has been aching all morning long. My fault for chugging that last margarita, hoping to avoid any additional conversations surrounding Charles.

Luckily for me, mom didn't bring up the topic again, instead choosing to discuss how Lily finally opened up to my mom about her feelings for Asher before she had left for the night.

Poor girl didn't realize the can of worms she was opening. I'm not sure what it is about Asher that sets my mom on edge, but it's clear she doesn't exactly care for my best friend. Which is very peculiar and so unlike her.

She likes everyone.

Now, I'm back at my desk earlier than I need to be, staring at the résumé of my one o'clock interview. This candidate seems like a perfect fit for Icon.

She has a firm handle on advertising and marketing, but more importantly, she spent almost a decade modeling. I think she will get along well with Catelyn Davies, a former Victoria's Secret model looking for her next big role with Diosa. At least, that's my hope.

It's imperative I have the right team in place. In my absence, this person will run the show, reporting directly to me. If they mess up, I've messed up.

I like to pretend I'm more confident than I really am, but the truth is I'm petrified of losing the account. I want to prove to Charles that he hired the right person, despite my lack of experience. Thankfully, he'll be joining me in these interviews. In a sense, he'll have to share the blame with me if we choose incorrectly.

That fact does the trick in easing my worry.

I head toward his office, hoping to review some last-minute questions for Rochelle, the interviewee, but his door's closed.

Turning to head back to my office, I hear the door creak open and turn to watch a smartly dressed man with a horrific comb-over exiting. I catch a glimpse of Charles through the door, and he looks angry.

And, if I'm not mistaken, I swear I heard Charles yell, "Idiot," before opening the door. Shelby's just getting back to her desk, and I shuffle my feet toward her, trying to get out of the older man's way.

Charles catches my eye, and I quickly look anywhere but at him.

"Who's that man?" I ask Shelby, and her eyes darken.

"I don't know, but it's not good. There was a lot of yelling, mostly Charlie." I raise a brow at her. "I'm sure we'll find out soon," she says as Charles stalks toward us.

I can feel my heart pounding in my chest. What's going on that has him so irate? This isn't good going into a round of interviews. Very important interviews for a very important client.

"One of the new analysts canceled," he grits through his teeth. "It appears she accepted a job at Bauer."

I swallow a lump in my throat.

"I've moved the other interviews up and added a couple more to the mix. Meet me in my office in ten."

He doesn't wait for a reply, spinning on his toes and stalking toward his office, slamming the door behind him.

Shelby whistles. "Good luck with that, Raven."

I spend the entire ten minutes preparing to deal with a broody Charles. Things with Bauer seem to be getting worse. First Summer, now potential employees. Maybe this is part of the corporate game, but it feels personal.

I knock on Charles's door right on time, not wanting to send him over the edge by being late.

"Come in," he barks, and for a moment, I consider faking ill and going home for the rest of the day.

From this side of the door, he sounded more grizzly than man. I pop open the door, peering my head around the corner.

"Are you ready for this?"

He pulls a face that tells me the answer is no.

"I have better things to be doing."

This stops me up short. He was the one who insisted he be a part of the interview process. Not me.

"I *can* handle it if you would rather sit this one out," I offer, hoping he'll take the bait and I'll be spared his ire.

No such luck.

"No," he snaps, typing something on his keyboard, striking at the keys a little rougher than necessary. "This account is too important. I have to ensure we have the right people for Diosa."

My jaw sets at his condescending words. Like I can't handle the interviews and choosing the best candidates myself.

*What an ass.*

I want to lash out, but I know it's no use arguing with him right now. He's got to be stressed.

"We'd better get going. Our first interviewee is probably waiting for us in the conference room."

"Yes, security brought him up from the lobby, and he's waiting in there." He stands without saying another word and shoots right past me.

"Well, all right then," I say, following him like a puppy dog.

"Who's up first?" he asks over his shoulder.

"Reagan Miller, sir."

He bobs his head. "Right, my choice."

I have to stop myself from rolling my eyes at his words.

When we enter the room, an attractive man sits across the table.

Reagan Miller has to be at least six feet, three if not four inches, with blond hair and blue eyes. Tall and lean, and did I mention *very* attractive?

"Reagan Miller? I ask, completely ignoring Charles as he shoulders past me to the head of the table.

"Yes, ma'am. That's me."

I nod my head, extending my hand. "Thank you so much for coming today." Charles turns, eyeing Reagan and then me suspiciously, and I wonder what the hell's gotten into him.

Finally, he extends his hand, shaking Reagan's. "Yes, thank you for meeting with us. We're conducting several interviews, so, if you please, I'd like to quickly refresh myself with your CV."

"Absolutely," Reagan says. "If I can answer any questions about my qualifications while you browse, please hit me with them."

Charles looks over the paper with a raised brow, and I slap his thigh under the table to wipe that look off his face. It's light enough to get his attention but not alert Reagan.

He looks at me out of the corner of his eyes, but when I don't say anything, he flips through Mr. Miller's résumé.

"How about you tell us a little bit about yourself." I start the conversation feeling wholly uncomfortable.

"I had a short stint playing as a quarterback in the NFL," he tells me. "But an injury to my back cut that short."

"I'm sorry," I offer, and Reagan smiles.

"It's all good. I went back to school. Graduated from Stanford with my MBA."

"That's . . . impressive." I can't keep the awe from my voice.

Reagan Miller is good-looking, talented, and smart. He's a catch, and even I can clearly see that.

"Thank you." His husky voice is low and sexy, and I giggle.

Like a damn schoolgirl with a crush. Reagan grins, and my cheeks warm. Charles clears his throat, shooting me a quick scowl.

"You have no experience." It isn't a question. Charles is being rude.

"Actually, I've been working as a medical sales rep for the past five years. It's there on my résumé."

I bite my bottom lip to stop myself from laughing. Reagan isn't allowing Charles to bully him around, and it's very amusing.

"How were you able to work and get your MBA?" Charles asks, sounding like a mega jerk.

"I already had my bachelor's degree from UCLA, and that's all that was needed for the medical job. The hours are flexible, and I was able to juggle both school and work." He leans over, pointing at his résumé. "As you can see, I was President's Club the past three years while maintaining a 3.7 GPA."

"You do realize that the position you applied for is a marketing analyst. You would be taking a deduction in pay. Why would you want that?"

"Yes, sir, I realize that. I'm looking to get out of the med device business. It's cutthroat and demanding."

"And you think this job isn't going to be just as cutthroat and demanding?"

I kick Charles in the shin. His head turns to me, and he glares.

I don't know why he's being so combative. This was his choice. He's the one who squeezed Reagan in for an interview.

"No, sir. Not at all. I know it's a tough gig. I've always been interested in advertising sales, and Cavendish's reputation is growing. I want to be a part of it. I think it would offer a unique experience with huge growth opportunities within the company."

"Very well stated," I offer, hoping to make Reagan feel a little more comfortable.

"And if I can be frank with you, money isn't really an issue, as I invested wisely with the NFL salary given the two years I played. I'm willing to take a pay cut to get the experience in an industry I'm passionate about."

"I love to hear that," I say, ignoring the scowl on Charles's face.

Charles grunts. "All right. Let's start the questions."

I look at him in confusion, and the next thing I know, he's full throttle into an interview method we already discussed would not be the right way for these types of discussions.

Steam is practically coming out of my ears. I'm so angry.

The way he's acting is absolutely ludicrous, yet Reagan handles him like a superstar, answering every question he's asked like a pro. My anger quickly melts away as I sit back with a smirk, enjoying the way Reagan is soaring and Charles is getting pricklier.

We both shake Reagan's hand when the interview is over, and I escort him to the lobby.

"Thank you for coming today, Reagan. It was very nice meeting you."

"I'm not getting the job, am I?"

I blink, not having a clue how to answer that. "Mr. Cavendish and I have many applicants, but we'll be in touch soon."

He nods, offering a tight-lipped smile. "I really want this job, Miss Bennett. I hope you can convince him to take a chance on me."

I offer him a smile. "We'll be in touch."

He walks out, and I can't help but think that he could really be an asset to Cavendish. Except I think Reagan and I both know that Charles had something against him from the moment he saw him.

"Charles, what the hell was that?" I ask, barging into his office without so much as a knock on the door.

His brow rises. "Pardon me?"

"Why were you trying to antagonize him? If you were trying to be an asshole, you succeeded."

His head jerks back. "I did no such thing."

"Don't act like you weren't being entirely rude back there. And why? He was your choice. You're the one who arranged for that interview."

"He's horrible for the position. Every woman in this company would be too busy gawking and flirting to do their job. You included."

"What?" I shriek. "Have you lost your mind? What is wrong with you?"

Me? Flirting? Okay. Maybe I was a little. But that's beside the point.

I take a deep breath. "I wasn't flirting, Mr. Cavendish. I was excited by the experiences he brings. Imagine him working on the AlteredX line. A former NFL player would be amazing."

He groans, running two hands down his face. "I'm sorry, but I don't agree. I think we need to move him out of the running."

"You're making things very hard. You and I need to fill these positions, and that man nailed that interview. So whatever shit you have going on, pull yourself together and be professional."

I spin around and tear the door open, preparing to storm out.

"Shut the door now, Raven." His voice is low and threatening.

I look over my shoulder to see him stand from behind his desk and stalk toward me.

I turn, placing my back against the door, but it's no use. He stomps right up to me so our breaths mingle, placing both hands on either side of my head.

"Do you think I wasn't being professional?"

"Not a bit," I say softly. "You were being a dick."

His eyes widen, and one side of his lips raise. "A dick?"

"Yes. A big, huge dick."

"Raven, you have no idea how big of a *dick* I can be."

That one word is full of so much innuendo I'm not sure what to do. He lowers himself so our lips are a mere inch apart. If I moved even slightly, our mouths would touch.

My belly flips, and tingles caress my skin.

I want his mouth on mine again. The one that fills my dreams at night.

I need it.

Recognizing I absolutely am in charge of this moment, my hands lift to his chest, and I softly push him back, making enough room for me to escape without incident.

"Please excuse me, Mr. Cavendish. I need some fresh air."

He moves back even farther.

"By all means. Run away, Rae. Again."

I don't even bother to scold him. I run because that's the best thing I can do for us.

# chapter nineteen

Raven

Tonight is all about securing Holly Morgan and making sure Paxton has this contract signed, sealed, and delivered.

Since it's Pax, we are at Club Silver with a VIP experience that is another level entirely.

Behind the closed white satin curtains hiding us away from other patrons, we are seated on white couches with cloud-like cushions. Knowing how packed the club is, this amount of privacy is very welcome.

Bottle service offers only top shelf, and whatever your heart desires is on tap. After taco night, I'm keeping it simple and playing safe with Tito's and soda.

I'm speechless at the level of attentiveness our hostess provides, although there's no doubt it has everything to do with our host, Paxton.

She eyes him like a snack she intends to devour later, and I don't doubt he's prepared to allow it.

Every time she moves past us, I don't miss how he eyes her long, tanned legs. She wears a black leather miniskirt that just covers her assets and a white halter top with the name 'Brittney' across the chest in glitzy silver lettering. Can't blame the lady for playing Paxton's game when he slipped her a hundred-dollar cash tip.

Holly Morgan and Charles sit on the couch next to me, their heads lowered together as they talk about God knows what. Her head falls back, and she laughs at something he's said. Her dainty hand lands on his thigh, a little too familiar for my liking.

What is he doing?

Securing the deal by flirting?

How the hell will that not end in disaster?

"Don't worry about that," Paxon says, scooting closer to me. "It's not worth getting a wrinkle between your eyes."

"I don't want him to mess this up because he's improper."

"Improper?" Paxton says with a grin.

I nod briskly. He sits back, putting one arm above my shoulder on the couch, leaning in closer like he's about to impart classified information and doesn't want anyone else to hear.

"That man is the epitome of professional."

I flash him an *are you serious?* expression.

He chuckles. "If you're thinking about what happened between you two, don't. Your situation is entirely unique. A case of not knowing who each other was." He takes a long pull from his bottle of Stella. "If he would've known that you'd been hired at Cavendish, he never would've touched you."

I bristle, and I'm not even sure why. He hasn't said anything insulting.

"Calm down, killer. I'm not saying he wouldn't want to. He just wouldn't cross that line. The New York branch of Cavendish Corporation means everything to him."

"Why?" I ask, curious as to why New York trumps London.

London is his home. It's where his family is.

"That's not my story to tell, and frankly, if you two are going to be working together, it's probably best you don't ask."

"Why?"

"Is that your favorite word? You don't get overtime bonuses for asking more questions, Raven."

I bite my bottom lip, trying to stop the smile from spreading. "No, I'm curious, and curiosity doesn't require long-winded questions."

He smirks. "Curiosity kills."

I roll my eyes. "Whatever. Just answer the question."

"Do you think you two could actually carry on a relationship of any sort while working together? He's the boss."

He makes a very valid point. One I've thought about myself.

"We're not going to have any sort of relationship. But I would like to understand him and his motives a little more."

"Take my advice, keep yourself at a distance. For both your sakes."

I chew on my cheek, wanting to ask *why* yet again, but refrain. Paxton has been nothing but kind since I first met him, and if he's warning me off his friend, I have to believe he has both our best interests at heart.

Besides, it was never a question.

We kissed.

We touched.

We moved on.

"And I really don't have to worry about that?" I ask, nodding my head toward Holly and Charles. "I ask purely for the sake of Diosa."

"No. I'll let you in on a little secret. Holly Morgan is married."

My brows knit together. "And . . .That doesn't bother everyone."

"Her husband owns a bank. An entire bank. Cavendish, for all his wins, can't outdo 'owns a bank.'"

"Got it."

I relax a little, knowing that Charles can put out all the charm in the world, and it won't do any good.

Not that I care. I don't. This is work.

It's strictly about Diosa.

*Keep telling yourself that, Raven.*

"You should talk to her. She'll appreciate your viewpoint on the campaign. If anything, I think you'll be the one to seal the deal with her, and not for any reason other than your passion. She'll see it, and I know it'll excite her. It's contagious."

I smile widely at the huge compliment.

"I wonder what they're talking about," I say, watching as Charles's eyes lift to the ceiling in what appears to be thought.

"Holly had a list of questions for him. She's very excited about working with Diosa, but she won't sign on the dotted line unless she feels she can do the brand justice and the brand can, in turn, benefit her brand. Money isn't everything for Holly. Images are important. Representation is important. And the values of the company are most important of all."

I nod. "I can't wait to talk to her. I have a lot of ideas, and I think she'll be very happy with the direction I'd like to go."

"I saw your initial mock-ups, and I have to say, I'm impressed. What did you do before working at Cavendish?"

"I finished up my MBA and did an internship with Saks Fifth Avenue. I also worked part time in the Bloomingdales corporate office. After that stint, I helped with a couple of the boutique brands that Macy's has picked up recently."

He whistles. "How did you land those?"

"I was at the top of my class, and we had to do pitch wars. Mine came out on top."

"Very impressive, Miss Bennett."

My eyebrow rises. "Now I'm Miss Bennett?" I chuckle. "So formal."

"When entertaining clients, I need to be semi-professional."

I snicker. "Good luck with that." I stand, smoothing down my skirt.

"Where are you off to?"

Smirking, I lean in. "I'm going to give another go with the VIP,

157

VIP, super-secret restrooms." I look around, playing at mysterious. "But nobody can know."

He laughs. "I should wish you good luck. Keep clear of the metal door."

I press my lips together. "No worries about that. It was a once-in-a-lifetime mistake."

"Sure was," he says, and something in his gaze tells me he doesn't believe that for a second.

I shake my head, making my way from the private room.

The club is packed, like the Wednesday night we first met. The bass is thumping, and bodies are pressed together on the dance floor. The air is thick with perspiration, perfume, and pheromones.

I'm headed toward the secret hallway when I spot a familiar face standing with a group of men at a tall table. Asher has his head bent in, talking with a man with facial hair trimmed neatly.

Three other men are huddled around, watching Ash and the beard with interest. They're all dressed in their suits from the day, likely having come here straight from work.

Asher has been working late hours, according to a text he sent the other day. Ever since Summer Smith took the contract, they've been in full swing, shooting commercials and arranging interviews with popular publications.

He didn't share much about the campaigns, but it's probably for the better.

I don't want to inadvertently steal his ideas because it's easy to do. It happened many times during pitch wars when friends who'd been study partners had pitched to each other.

It was inevitable that something was going to end up in another pitch. It wasn't even done maliciously.

I wonder whether I should interrupt what looks to be an intense conversation and decide against it.

I miss my friend, but it appears we're both here with colleagues, and if I'm really being honest, a part of me doesn't want him to find out about Holly Morgan.

Not that I believe he leaked the information about Summer, but because, like the incidents with pitch wars, the same thing could happen. It could be a slip of the tongue that he mentions to someone else within the office, which leads to Bauer coming after yet another collaboration.

I remember Charles having mentioned that the men behind Bauer were shady, and I know it's best to keep my head down and pretend I didn't see Asher.

It makes me sad, but I'm an adult working in a competitive field, and whether I like it or not, he works for the competition, making us on opposite sides of the line.

Just as I reach the back hallway and the first door that actually is a bathroom, another hand reaches for the handle at the same time. Jumping, I step back and look up to see Charles.

"What in the world are you doing here? Go away. I need to use the restroom."

"Not happening Raven." He looks at me all serious while I stand gaping at him.

"Are you off your rocker?" I chide.

"No, I need to be the first to go in. You know, to make sure the lock works." His words register, and I can't help but bark out a laugh.

"How is it you can be such a dickhead and then the next minute so funny?"

"Talent. Now get in here."

He pulls me into the small restroom before I have time to protest. He's so close in this small space, but I don't want to move away from him at all. That pull is back between us, and it's all-consuming.

Hands around my waist, he leans down. "We agreed nothing could happen at the office. We never said anything about away from work." His words tickle my ear.

Why does everything he says drip with hunger and make me thirsty for him?

"Well, Mr. Cavendish, if you want to break the rules, you should kiss me now."

He leans back and looks into my eyes. I don't know what he sees, but his hands cup my face. The warmth of his palms feels so wonderful I want to keep his hands on me all the time.

"Sitting next to you tonight, I had to let you know that you truly are my Rae of sunshine," he whispers and places the sweetest kiss on my forehead.

Then, as suddenly as he stepped into the room, he's gone, and I'm left reeling from a moment I have no ability to unravel.

# chapter twenty

Raven

WHY IS TODAY THE LONGEST DAY EVER?
It's only noon. I'm never going to make it.

Seated in the office café, I'm eating my turkey sandwich and thinking about last night. My thoughts continue to yo-yo between work and Charles. Both have me smiling like a gleeful idiot.

So many amazing things happened last night.

For work, I finally got to talk to Holly, and she's incredible. It's always a risk you run with talent, but it seems we hit the lotto with Holly. She had some incredible ideas to piggyback off what I shared with her, but I was admittedly distracted the whole time.

After the sweet feel of his lips on my forehead, the tension in the VIP room was excessive. The little things that happened had me keyed up for hours afterward. His hand brushed against mine and burned me to my bones. Like a moth to a flame, I'm begging for the heat again.

Something that most would think so innocent felt so intimate. My core clenched, and my body ached for more. So. Much. More.

Goose bumps spread over my arms, and my stomach dips. My thighs clench together, and my eyes dart around, hoping that nobody can tell what I'm currently feeling.

White-hot need.

*Focus on anything else.*

I get out my phone and send Asher a message, needing to distract myself from thoughts of Charles Cavendish. It has the intended effect. A douse of cold, killing my libido.

Thank God.

**Me: You busy later? Let's do dinner. I don't feel like cooking.**

The truth is, I'm desperate to find out what's going on over at Bauer.

They've pulled some really interesting moves recently. Maybe Ash will open up, and I can figure out if he really did take my information about Summer and use it against me.

Plus, recon for Cavendish seems like a job that needs to be done, and I'm the perfect person to do it.

Not that I'll share what I learn with Charles. I'd never do anything to jeopardize my friendship with Ash, but it would give me some insight into what they have cooking—if anything—where Diosa is concerned.

Surely his boss, and the other people working there, could easily have found out that Summer was on the market. It didn't necessarily mean that Asher told them.

I don't want to come right out and ask him if he's involved in taking her away from us, just in case I'm wrong.

I really hope I am because it would kill me if he betrayed me for a job. Not that it matters whether I straight up ask or not. I'll know when talking to him face-to-face.

I've known Asher for a very long time, and there is no way that he'd be able to hide anything of this magnitude from me. I'd know straight away if he was.

**Asher: Obviously. I have two hot dates. I'm hoping both come back to my pad.**

**Me: Playboy idiot . . .**

My hand hovers over my phone, trying to decipher if he's

messing with me or if he really has two girls lined up for the night. It wouldn't be the first time Asher engaged in such behavior.

**Asher: Okay, fine . . . I don't have anything going.**

**Me: Why do you mess with me like that?**

**Asher: Maybe I want you green with jealousy.**

**Me: It would depend. Are they blonde or brunette?**

**Me: Better yet if you tell me they're both redheads. I have a serious girl crush on that girl from Jurassic World.**

**Asher: You're killing me, Raven . . .**

**Me: So . . . dinner?**

**Asher: Did you get another promotion? Is that why you're asking me out?**

I chuckle.

**Me: When did I say that I would pay? Lily is busy. I already checked.**

**Asher: Lily is busy? So I'm just your second choice, then. Is that how it goes?**

**Me: Pretty much. And I really don't want to sit alone. So is that a yes?**

**Asher: . . .**

**Me: I see you typing, but I don't see a yes . . .**

**Asher: Obviously, it's a yes. You know I hate cooking.**

**Asher: But mainly I miss you. Dinner it is.**

I laugh. Asher always makes me laugh. There had been a time when I wished I could look at Asher differently. If he could be tamed, he'd be the perfect guy. But alas, he's like a brother, and I'll never see him as anything but.

**Me: Miss you, too, buddy!**

**Asher: So 7pm? Let's do pizza.**

**Me: PIZZA! Don't you want to do something a bit more sophisticated?**

**Asher: Not really. Do you?**

**Me: No. I love pizza. Okay, see you at 7. I better go. Work, work, work.**

**Asher: Later, babe . . .**

I roll my eyes because Asher can't shut off his flirting. It's in-grained in him. I'm immune.

I switch off my phone and slide it back into my bag. A night with Asher is just what the doctor ordered. The two of us almost always drink a little too much and laugh a little too loudly, and it always ends up being a fun night out.

I wish I could open up to Asher about the night at Silver and who Charles really is. I wonder what he'd say. Would he be enter-tained by my crazy news? Or would he flip out and prove my mom and Lily right?

I don't want to find out. Ever.

I look up and see Charles walking through with some of the executives. Those earlier sensations wash over me, and I squeeze my legs together once more.

Our eyes meet, and he grins, causing a riot of feelings. A blush creeps up my body, and I smile, lowering my eyes to my plate. The last person who needs to see the lust I'm wearing like a second skin is my boss and his cronies.

Thinking about Charles is a constant struggle between profes-sionalism and the thought of wanting to rip off his clothes. I need to get a grip on myself, but being this close to him isn't making it easy. I've reverted to a teenage girl with raging hormones, and it's embarrassing as all hell. Even if I'm the only one who realizes the effect he has on me.

Maybe I need to rip off the Band-Aid and jump back into dat-ing. If I could find a diversion with another guy, it could help me get back on track.

Focusing my attention on someone else can't be a bad idea.

Asher has tons of hot friends. None of them interest me, but maybe I haven't given them a chance.

Yes, I need a distraction from this weird mess I've found my-self in. Anything to push Charles out of my head.

Lost in my thoughts, I actually jump when my phone rings. It's a number I don't recognize, and I almost ignore it, assuming it's another annoying telemarketing call, but at the last second, I cave.

"Hello, this is Raven," I say, waiting for the person on the other line to speak.

"Raven, it's Charles."

His husky voice washes over me, and I almost groan, but I stuff it down.

Way down.

I look toward where I'd just seen him moments ago, but of course, he's no longer there. Had I manifested this damn call?

*This is nuts.*

"Raven?"

"I'm here, but how did you get this number?" The question comes out a little snappy, and I instantly regret it. How is it my fault I'm unable to control my reaction to him?

"It's in your new hire paperwork."

My hand smacks against my forehead. "Oh, right," I say, feeling stupid. "What can I do for you?"

"I need you to work late tonight. Holly's on board, but she has some scheduling conflicts. We need to get her photo shoots arranged ASAP."

"Tonight?"

*Dear God, this is not what I need.*

Distance after those feelings last night. A new distraction . . . that's what was on the menu. Not time spent alone in a dark office with a man I'm struggling to keep my hands off.

"Yes. Tonight," he drawls as if I'm slow and he's annoyed by it. "We'll need to work until we have it all ironed out. Late nights are part of the job," he says, sounding like a complete ass.

His attitude does the trick, and my lust is overturned with annoyance at his less than cheery disposition. I can get whiplash from the directions this man takes. It might be part of the job, but can't a girl get a simple please?

"Why do you have to be so damn grumpy? I need to cancel

the dinner plans I had for the evening, but I'll be here for as long as needed."

He's quiet for a moment, and I wonder what he's doing on the other end.

"Fine. I'd like you to work this afternoon on contacting all the publications we'll want to feature Diosa and Holly in. Book those shoots for any time within the next forty-five days. Interview questions can be sent over immediately. If we can do the shoots here and send them the proofs, even better."

"On it," I say, jotting as much of this down as I remember.

That will easily keep me busy the rest of the day.

"Come to my office straight after you finish that, and we can get started. For the rest of the week, I'd like you to work on interviews and getting the other two accounts and talent set up with different publications. This is most important."

"Will do."

"I'm sorry to interrupt your plans, but this is important."

He doesn't sound like he's sorry at all. What about the part where he interrupted my lunch? Do I get an apology for that?

"Raven, did you hear me?"

"Yes, and no worries. This account comes first, sir." I say 'sir' a bit surlier than necessary, and I don't doubt he heard it, based on the way he clears his throat.

"Good. Thank you, Raven."

I put the phone down and stare at it for several minutes. I got my thank you, although he practically snarled it.

Charles is making it very clear that he's my boss, and if nothing else, he's treating me like everyone else in the office.

Ugh. In the office. God, I hope he doesn't play this Jekyll and Hyde routine every time we go somewhere.

I sigh as I realize I need to cancel on poor Asher after I practically begged him to come out with me.

This is important for my job. I have to make a good impression.

The only way I'm ever going to succeed is if I work hard. He'll understand.

But spending my evening with Charles . . . stuck in his office with nobody else around . . . no thank you.

I gulp and quickly change my stream of thought.

I won't think like that again.

It's not healthy.

It's not right.

Yet it's all I'll think about for the next several hours.

Fuck my luck.

I get to work sending Asher a message to inform him about the change of plans.

Asher is naturally upset but assures me he'll be badgering me tomorrow for another dinner date.

I finish up my lunch, throwing it into the trash and making my way back to my office. My phone beeps, and I look down to see one last text from Ash.

**Asher: I'm proud of you, Raven. You're kicking ass at Cavendish.**

I know in that instant that he definitely wasn't involved in the Summer debacle.

Not Asher.

He wants me to win just as much as he wants to win. He's my cheerleader and confidant, and it's one thing I don't have to worry about ever losing. We're in things together.

The evening rolls around quickly, and I nervously make my way to Charles's office. I glance around and see that only two people remain. One is packing up, and the other is Shelby, who'll undoubtedly leave within the hour.

"Hey, Raven. Getting ready for a long night with the boss man?"

I lean over her desk and whisper, "What kind of mood is he in?"

She smirks. "Lucky for you, he's in an exceptionally chipper mood this afternoon."

My one eyebrow lifts. "Dare I ask why?"

She shrugs. "No clue. But thank God for small miracles."

Thank God is right. If I had to endure his grumpiness for any amount of time tonight, I might go off the deep end. His moods give me whiplash, and I'm bound to snap one of these days.

"I'm going in. Have a good night."

"You, too," she says, raising her brows.

I knock and wait until he calls out for me to come in.

"How did the afternoon go? Did you get things sorted with the pubs?" He assaults me with questions before I can even make it fully into the room.

So, this is how it's going to go?

Twenty questions, interrogating me on the job I did, because heaven forbid that the man relinquishes a modicum of control. As if I can't do the job to his expectations.

I plaster on the largest smile I can muster and jump into the details, hoping it shuts him up.

"I did. Holly is booked with *People*, *Elle*, *Cosmo*, and *Women's Health*."

I focused all my energy on getting all four booked out within the next two months, getting ahead on the job he asked me to make my project for the whole week. He might not be used to people getting shit done, but I'm not those people. I'm a go-getter, and I'm damn good.

"Spencer and Catelyn will team up for a double feature in *People* and *Cosmo*. I've reached out to a few additional publications, and I'm just waiting on their response. I'll look for some smaller magazines, including online publications, to focus on AlteredX and Icon as well."

He nods, not looking up from his computer. "Good. Send me a list of all pubs you've reached out to."

My lips slam together, and my teeth grind at his less than

impressed response. Now he needs a spreadsheet of who I've contacted? "I didn't realize I was going to be micromanaged."

He looks up at me, brow furrowed. "I'm not micromanaging, Miss Bennett. I'm asking so I can send Sergio an update. I told him I'd keep him in the loop."

Shit. I didn't mean to say that out loud.

My cheeks warm, and I fidget in my seat, wanting to crawl under the desk. I tamper down the embarrassment and dive right into work, hoping the tension dissipates soon.

"What is it you'd like to work on now?"

His jaw ticks, but he eventually looks away from me, eyes back on his computer screen. "I think it's best if we nail down the ad locations and get some copywriters on board to have the scripts done by this time next week. Holly needs to shoot the commercial before the eighth of May."

I pull out my phone and check the calendar. Forty-five days as of tomorrow to have this all ironed out and the first commercial shot.

That's pushing it. Really pushing it. But I won't say that to Charles.

"When will she be available for more shoots? I'm assuming we'll roll out a new commercial every ninety days?"

"That sounds about right. She said she could be ready in August."

"Hmm," I murmur, thinking things through. "We need a location that can provide four wardrobe changes and be spliced to create multiple ads. To be on the safe side."

"Very well. Any ideas?" he asks, eyes remaining fixed on his computer.

"I have everything I've mocked up on this flash drive if you want to see it," I say, waving the drive in the air.

He finally looks up and reaches out for the drive.

"Let's take a look," he says, motioning for me to move my chair around to sit by him.

My anger prickles.

He hasn't even seen what I've done, and he's already acting like it won't be good enough. I'm two seconds away from steam rolling from my ears, and if he bothered to look at me, he'd see how far he's pushing me. But he doesn't. He's back to looking at his damn computer, acting like I'm not here.

He plugs the flash drive in and opens up the file. I wait as he watches the presentation, sorting through the mood boards and locale photos I've arranged in various folders on the drive. I'd put together a slideshow for three separate shooting locations and the aesthetics I felt would work best. The sound of him clicking through it makes me anxious. Finally, he gets to the last slide and stops it.

When he looks up at me, he grins. My heart thumps in my chest.

That grin.

His mouth.

Snap out of it. He's an ass.

"You've worked hard on this."

*Obviously, asshat.* "Very hard, sir." The words come out happy, even though I'm spitting nails internally.

"Sir?" He lifts a brow. "I think you can call me Charles after hours, Raven."

Now it's Charles? This irritable man is driving me mad. I don't know which side of him I'm going to get from minute to minute.

A smirk spreads across his face as a myriad of emotions pass through me. I have no doubt he can see them all.

That smirk.

It undoes me.

Drives me crazy.

"This looks like something my other account reps would've spent months on. Not a few weeks. I'm impressed, Raven. This is truly amazing."

Damn straight. Now will you have some faith in me?

I don't say it out loud, but I should. I need to stand up for myself.

"It still needs a bit of tidying up, though," I say instead. "I didn't get a chance, but I have written down a few ideas on how we can tweak it."

He nods. "Which location would be your top choice?"

I'm struck speechless by this question. He went from acting like I was incompetent to asking for my opinion in the span of minutes.

I flush under the weight of his stare.

Getting to dream up something this big was massive, but actually having a say when so many variables are at play is something else entirely.

Despite the enigma across from me, I'm in heaven even having this conversation.

I take my notepad and move my chair next to him.

"I'd love to shoot AlteredX in Italy." I flip to a certain slide and start pointing out why. "The beautiful backdrops and the ocean make me want to go exploring. We can have a group of yoga students behind Holly on the beach." I shrug. "With that backdrop, I could be convinced to throw on yoga pants and join. Plus, yoga is most popular in Italy. It suits."

He steeples his fingers, resting his chin on top. "Do you think we could sneak in shots for Diosa and Icon as well?"

I nod my head vigorously. "Of course. Italy gives us so many options."

We spend the next hour reviewing my notes and making changes on the computer. Charles comes alive when it comes to organizing and planning. He rolls up his sleeves and jumps right in, which is completely opposite to the CEOs I've worked with in the past.

Those men and women were happy to sit back and simply oversee. They worked on landing accounts and rubbing elbows. They never got into the nitty-gritty unless it was to bitch about this or moan about that.

Watching him work and seeing his passion for this makes me like him even more.

Not good.

"Here," he says, standing. "Let's trade seats. It will make it easier."

I rise, brushing against him as I move past to take his vacant seat. Those pesky tingles rush through me at the brief touch, and I turn my head so he doesn't see the blush creeping up my neck.

I focus on the job, organizing and adding to the various files as Charles calls out ideas. We work in harmony, and the hours fly by.

His leg brushes against mine, and a shiver races along my spine, but I ignore it, continuing my work. Being professional. Proving that I'm the right person to lead this account.

I have to.

At eight thirty, Charles orders pizza, and I don't say no when he opens a bottle of wine. I'm not sure this is proper office behavior, but I won't look too much into it. He is the owner of the company, and if he's okay with wine, who am I to turn it away?

For my own sanity, I tell myself this is the least I'm owed for working this late.

Not that I need to worry. Despite this rather intimate setting, we only speak about work matters. We never once veer into personal territory, which I know is for the best.

"I think we've got this pretty nailed down," I say around a bite of cheese pizza.

He grins. "You've got a little something there," he says, pointing at my mouth.

My tongue swipes out, wiping away the sauce from the corner of my mouth. I grab a napkin and dab at my lips to ensure no more sauce remains.

"I think so, too," he says. "Once we have our team in place, we'll be set."

"About that . . ." I wasn't going to broach the subject, but I really think Reagan deserves a second thought.

His résumé is impressive, and he handled Charles well. He'd be perfect, and I'm not willing to let this drop and lose out on him.

"I really wish you'd reconsider Reagan. We need him."

Charles purses his lips, leaning back into his chair. "Give me three good reasons."

I blow out a harsh breath, annoyed that I have to sell him on something that should be a no-brainer.

"I looked up his net worth. He didn't need his MBA, and he doesn't need this job. He wants it, which means he'll work hard."

Charles grunts. "And?" he drawls.

"He's well-spoken, good at sales, well-dressed . . . should I go on?"

I'm determined, and it's coming through in my tone. For a moment, he's not the owner of the company. He's a coworker who's being an idiot, and only God knows why. My elbows are on the desk, and I'm leaning over, probably looking like I'm about to strangle him.

Charles's eyes darken. "I have a feeling you're going to, whether I want to hear it or not."

I don't even flinch as I continue. "He held his own against you, even when you put him through the gauntlet. He can handle talent and run a tight ship."

"Anything else?"

I shrug. "He's smart, Charles. He'll do well on the Icon team. I think Spencer will love working with him."

Charles takes a few deep breaths, seeming to consider what I've laid out in front of him. Eventually, he nods. "Fine. Hire him."

I squeal, covering my mouth with my fist, trying to rein in my excitement at getting my way. "This is so exciting. You won't regret it."

"I already do," he says, grabbing another slice of pizza. "But we need these spots filled. As much as I hate to admit it, out of all the candidates we've met so far, he's been the best, and I agree, he'll run a tight ship."

"He's certainly my type." My hand flies to my mouth. "I'm sorry, that's not what I meant. I was trying to say he's the type. *The* type," I repeat to emphasize where I went wrong.

Charles grins. "Do your cheeks always turn that lovely shade of red?" On cue, my cheeks heat even more.

"They do not," I say, trying at denial. Grabbing the glass of wine, I take a large sip.

"They do, and they are currently." He takes a deep breath. "Will there be a problem with you working closely with Reagan?"

I choke on the wine, spluttering into my napkin and looking like a complete fool, I'm sure.

"What? No. You know I'll keep it strictly professional."

His one eyebrow lifts in an *are you sure about that* expression, and my eyes blink several times. He sets down his pizza and leans over the table.

"I must admit I'm growing tired of that word."

"What word?" I practically whisper.

"Professional." He nearly growls the word.

"Oh?"

It's the only word I can squeak out. I'm thrown off balance, watching his eyes burn with something very close to lust—but that can't be right. I'm imagining it because I want it to be.

Stop.

"Extremely tired of it," he drawls, his eyes never wavering from mine.

I shrink under the intensity of that stare and only slightly relax when his eyes drop to my lips. I instinctively run my tongue over the bottom, and his eyes darken to molten pits.

Shit. What am I doing?

We might be working well together, but there's no doubt that there's a pull to him. Something I'm fighting hard against. It's been like this since Silver, and I'm finding it very hard to avoid.

I turn to face the computer and try to veer the conversation back to the plan.

"I think we're almost done," I say awkwardly.

"I think you're right." He sighs. "Thank you for staying late with me, Raven. I know it's a last-minute ask."

Awkward doesn't come close to describing this moment. The air is thick with tension, and I want to run from the room. Save myself from doing or saying something monumentally stupid.

"Raven," he presses when I don't say anything.

"I don't mind," I offer lamely. "This job means a lot to me. This account means a lot."

Charles touches my arm, and I turn to face him. "That's good to hear. Because this job means everything to me, and not many people seem to get that."

His hand lingers on me, heating my insides to inferno levels. Our eyes meet, and we search each other's faces. I'm not sure what he's hoping to find, but at this moment, I want to give in to this fierce attraction.

To kiss him.

To feel his hands roam over my body.

I want him to finish what he started in that closet at Silver.

I won't be saying no even though I should.

His eyes lower to my lips again, and I instinctively lean in.

He doesn't hesitate.

# chapter twenty-one

Charles

**M**Y MOUTH CRASHES AGAINST RAVEN'S, HER LIPS PARTING TO allow me access. Our tongues collide, and a moan rushes up her throat.

The need to rouse a symphony of those noises from her is intrinsic.

Nothing soft or tentative about this feeling. The coil broke, and we're giving in to the temptation we've both been avoiding.

Our kisses turn hungrier, my arms wrapping around her waist, pulling her onto my lap. My cock, straining against my trousers, begs to be set loose.

My hands drop and then move to the hem of her dress, dragging it up until it's bunched around her hips. My fingers coast gently along the edge of her delicate knickers, moving until they're at her heated center. Her breath hitches at the contact, and I know she wants more. Below the lacy material, I can feel the moisture, and it causes my cock to jerk. I don't remember ever being this rock hard.

So long. So very long since I've wanted a woman like this. I need more.

Pushing the fabric aside, I run one long finger up her center, drawing a breathless sigh from her, breaking our kiss. Raven's arms rest on my shoulders, and she leans back with her eyes closed.

She is the picture of every one of my dreams.

Except now she's real. Raven is here, wet and ready just for me.

I want this.

She wants this.

I'm not fighting it anymore.

As I lean in to kiss her, I push one finger into her pussy, and she whimpers in response.

"Am I hurting you?" I whisper, and her head shakes.

"Words, Rae."

"No. Please," she begs, and I stop with the inquisition, pumping my finger inside her.

When she's adjusted to easily fit one finger, I add another, and she makes little noises that almost undo me. Her walls tighten around my fingers, and I'm dying for it to be my cock inside her.

Raven is into this just as much as I am. It's evident in every moan and cry of pleasure. I'm ready to say to hell with the consequences and take her on my desk.

Why shouldn't we do this? We're adults.

*She's your employee.*

My mind wanders to a time three years ago when another woman, who I thought loved me, proved she was only after my money and resources.

Moans.

Cries of pleasure.

Tabitha laid out on a desk with a man who wasn't me between her legs.

That reminder ruins everything. An effective dose of cool water drenching my libido.

I can't put an end to this fast enough.

"Fuck," I say and pull back, leaving a fraction of space between us. "We can't."

Raven's eyes are wide, and I quickly turn away, not wanting

to see the look of confusion that will surely bleed into hurt at any moment.

"W-What's wrong? Are you okay?"

"I'm fine. We just have to stop."

"I thought . . . I thought you wanted to—"

"I don't want you." I regret the words as soon as I say them. They're a lie.

I wanted it with every fiber of my being.

But I can't say those words as they will only cause more confusion to her head and my heart.

Too harshly, I state, "This was a mistake, Raven. I'm the owner of this company."

She glares at me with a fire in her eyes I've never seen. "How many times do I have to tell you I didn't know that when you had me against the door at Silver," she snaps.

"That might be true. But you know now," I bite out. "We need to be better. I don't know what you were thinking."

"Me?" she cries, eyes widening. "Excuse me. You seem to forget that you're the one who always backs me into this position," she snaps.

Her typically sunny disposition is gone.

Embarrassment, hurt, and anger rise to the surface.

I deserve her ire.

"You know what? It doesn't matter. You're right. We shouldn't have done this." She blows out a harsh breath. "Again."

"Raven. I—"

"Don't," she bites out. "I don't want to hear any of your fucking excuses."

This conversation is difficult with her still on top of me. My hands itch to reach out and touch her.

Fucking hell.

"No excuses. I acted improperly, and for that, I'm sorry."

She seems to realize she's still on my lap and springs up like I caught fire and she's trying to escape the flames.

"You did, but at least you had the strength to end it just in time," she says, eyes lowering to the floor. "Glad you were able to do what's best for us both."

The need to say something to wipe the look of mortification from her beautiful face is intense. This wasn't one-sided. I wanted her just as badly.

"I'm truly sorry," I say, trying to meet her gaze.

Her head shakes, and her lips tremble.

"Nope. I don't want even more apologies. Let's move on and forget all about this slip in sanity."

"Raven," I say, shaking my head. "Don't. I didn't mean . . ."

I can't finish the sentence. I'm not setting out to embarrass her more than she already is. I'm not a complete knob.

She takes a deep breath and closes her eyes, appearing to rein in her emotions. When they open, I see resolve, and it breaks me a little.

"Charles, can we do this?"

I pull my bottom lip into my mouth, trying to determine what she means. When she doesn't elaborate, I ask, "Do what?"

"I happen to like it here, and I really don't want to jeopardize my job. You're my boss. Is working this closely going to be awkward?"

My chest tightens as the sadness laced around her words seeps into my soul. I realize how much pain I've caused her. How much of an arse I've been.

"I know you do," I say. "We can do this. We won't be provoked again."

I'm sorry about the kiss. Sorry about the way I made her moan at my touch. Sorry about every stolen kiss, every moment touching her beautiful skin.

*Bloody liar.*

"Let's call it a night. We've covered a lot today." I sigh, standing from the chair.

She nods. "I think that's for the best."

She keeps herself busy by rounding up her stuff while I remove her flash drive from my computer.

"I'll work on the finishing touches and get with the creative team to finalize the scripts to send to Holly, Spencer, and Catelyn early next week," she says. Her tone is back to professional, and I loathe it.

It might be what's best, but it doesn't change the fact that I don't want things to be this formal with Raven. I want her to feel comfortable around me. To act herself.

*Too late for that, prick.*

"We'll need to get their approval quickly so we can book travel," I say, going along with her choice of topic.

"Agree. I'll make sure the documents ask for approval within forty-eight hours. Holly will have to be okay with that since it's her schedule forcing us to move quickly."

Her take-charge attitude at the moment is beyond attractive. Instead of running out of here like a blubbering mess, she's pushed down the awkwardness and has managed to act like a true professional.

*Despite your actions.*

I groan, and she eyes me warily, thankfully not voicing her thoughts.

"Thank you, Raven. I think we have a solid plan. I'm almost certain all three of them will give their approval."

"Me, too," she says, moving toward the door.

The shift from making out in my office to discussing Diosa is jarring, but she handles it like a pro.

Good.

Hopefully, we'll be able to move past this.

"Good night, then," she says, glancing my way one more time.

"Good night, Raven."

I watch as she slips out the door, leaving me alone in the quiet office to replay what had occurred here earlier.

Pouring myself a tumbler of whiskey, I throw it back, the liquid burning all the way down. I quickly pour another, hoping to chase away these errant thoughts.

I have to forget about the way she feels.

The way her body molds to mine perfectly.

The taste of cinnamon on her breath.

Trying to forget about Raven Bennett isn't going to be difficult. It's going to be impossible.

*I'm a selfish motherfucker.*

I throw the tumbler across the room, and it bursts into a thousand tiny pieces against the wall.

My mind is jumbled with ideas and questions about why I can't have her. Why it would be a horrible idea to throw my cares to the wind and take her like I want to.

Then I remember the look on her face when I pulled away.

The hurt.

The shame.

I might be a bastard, but I won't ever be the cause for that look on Raven's face again.

I'll stay away because it's what's best for her.

It's what's best for the company I've worked so hard to build and the people it supports.

The people who count on me in the office and at the cancer center.

I must do the best for all of them.

# chapter twenty-two

Raven

I'M SO ANGRY WITH MYSELF THAT I COULD SCREAM. I KNEW TO be careful around Charles, but I'd let my guard down yet again.

The moment I get home, I slam back three shots of tequila, needing to feel anything but the overwhelming shame.

I try to call Lily, but she's not answering.

I dial Asher next, but he's also ignoring my calls.

*He's pulled away, too.*

Turning on the TV, I attempt to watch an episode of *Friends*, but I can't concentrate. My mind whirls with everything from memories of how his fingers felt inside me to the look on his face when he ended it.

Anger had pulsed from him.

As though I'd somehow been fully responsible for *his* actions.

He was the one who gave in.

It was his mouth that crashed against mine.

His hands slid up my thighs.

His fingers damn near pushed me over the edge.

I switch off the television, throwing the remote onto a chair across from me before pouring two more shots and slamming them back.

The prior shots are already affecting me. My head is starting to swim, and my toes tingle. A sure sign that I'm one shot away from total insobriety.

Good. I need the escape from my own mind.

How dare he pin everything on me?

He may not have said the exact words, but his expression—his body language—practically screamed it.

He looked at me as though I had orchestrated the kiss, which seemed to be his MO. I might've leaned in, but I didn't force him to make the next move.

If he's truly blaming me for his lack of control, that's bullshit.

Before I can think better of it, I dial my mom's number.

"Raven?" My mom's voice is thick with sleep, and I immediately burst into tears.

Regret pulling me down.

*Good grief.*

I did *not* need those last two shots.

I'm so emotional, and even with my mom cooing soothing words into the phone, I can't stop the torrent of tears flowing down my face.

"What's wrong, baby girl?" she asks, and I cringe.

What did I think would happen when I called her after midnight, crying like a lunatic?

"Is this about your boss?"

I want to crawl into a hole as soon as she asks. How is she so perceptive?

Sure, she knew I was working late tonight with him, but why did her mind immediately go to Charles?

I don't bother denying it. It would be pointless anyway.

"I messed up, Mom."

"What happened?" There's no judgment in her voice, only concern. She's always been my rock. The person I know would never turn their back on me, no matter the mistakes I make. The very last person I ever wanted to disappoint.

I burst out crying again before I even have a chance to say anything.

"Raven. Talk to me. What's wrong?" she presses.

"We kissed. I . . . let things get carried away."

The memory of what we did crashes against me, and I nearly buckle over. I feel sick to my stomach.

"Take a deep breath and tell me everything," she says, sounding alert for the first time since I called.

"I-I can't. I don't w-want you to know," I say through hiccups.

She sighs. "There isn't a thing in the world you could tell me that would make me think less of you, Raven Marie. I love you unconditionally."

Those words break the last of my resolve.

*Unconditionally.*

I tell her absolutely everything, and it only makes me feel worse.

The shame is intense, and now that my mom knows the whole truth, guilt wracks me, despite her words of assurance.

"Why didn't you tell me about this before?"

She's hurt. I can hear it in her voice. I've never kept secrets from her. Not since my dad died.

I sigh. "How many daughters talk so openly about these things with their moms?"

"I'm not interested in what other people do, Raven. You know I'd never judge you. You're an adult. You've always been open with me."

"I know," I cry. "I guess I was just . . . ashamed," I admit. "You warned me not to go there, and I didn't listen."

And therein lies my biggest regret. I'd been warned, and for the first time in a very long time, I didn't listen to her.

"It sounds like it was unavoidable. The universe was throwing you together from the beginning."

"Mom, please don't start," I beg.

She's always been very spiritual. She believes some people are placed in our paths for a reason. The last thing I want to hear is that the universe wanted something to happen between Charles and me. We're not destined like she and my dad were. We're simply a momentary lapse. A mistake that should've been avoided because I'm smarter than this.

"He's my boss."

"And you had no idea who he was that first night. We can't help who we fall for."

It's something I've told myself numerous times. That way, the situation doesn't feel so taboo. But I didn't fall in love. I fell into a lust trap. Something a stronger woman could've easily walked away from.

"I didn't ask for this."

"Exactly," she says.

"I don't have feelings for him. It was a one—okay, two—time thing."

I'm on a roll, stamping down my hurt and forging a will of steel.

"You don't?" My mom cuts in, confusing me.

"Don't what?"

"Have feelings for Charles?"

She doesn't sound convinced. If anything, her voice has a hint of challenge, and I don't like it.

"Of course not," I bite out, tone full of indignation. "It's lust, pure and simple. He's charming, gorgeous, and a smooth talker with that stupid British accent of his. Probably has a string of girls he beds, here and across the pond. I practically threw myself at his feet, begging to be one of the numbers."

That thought is a serious blow to my ego. I'm not that girl. I don't do random hookups with men I have no shot at a future with.

What was I thinking?

"You know me, Mom. That's not the sort of thing I would allow. It is so out of character."

"Mm-hmm," she says, not saying a word more, so I continue.

"A simple fling is supposed to remain just a one-time thing.

After the night at Silver, I never should've seen him again. This is New York City, not some small town."

"True," she offers.

"It's not every day that your fling turns out to be your boss."

"Excellent point, Raven. I'm glad you're coming to terms with the fact that fate made this happen."

I completely ignore her. That's one thing we'll never agree on. Fate had nothing to do with this.

"I told him not to kiss me again."

At least, I think I did. It was strongly alluded to, at the very least.

"And he didn't listen?" Her tone turns lethal. You don't mess with her baby and get away with it. "You don't want a guy like that. If he does this often, he's not for you. No matter how good-looking or charismatic he is."

"Right," I say.

"You want someone who will treat you like the prize you are."

"Absolutely," I say, sounding like a cheerleader getting pumped up by her captain before a game. "You're right. I definitely deserve better than that. And I'm glad I've put a stop to it."

"I suppose it's going to be awkward for a while, but there's nothing much you can do about that. Eventually, everything will go back to normal, and you'll forget this whole sordid thing happened."

Unless it doesn't.

What if Charles ends up being like all the other stuffy executives who mess with their employees and run them out of the office when they're done with them?

"What if he makes my life miserable?" I voice my concern, and a tear leaks from the corner of my eye.

"Do you really believe he'll do that? Is he truly that bad?" Her voice is soft.

I consider the question, thinking back on all the moments with him. Charles doesn't seem like the type. He gave me a chance even after realizing I was the woman from Silver. He listened to my ideas and got on board. He's always been fair. His company means everything to him, and I believe I've proven my worth.

"No, I don't." I don't even have to think any more about it. "He's not a bad guy at all, Mom. I'm just . . . angry with myself."

"You two messed up. That's all. People make mistakes all the time. And he probably feels as awful about it."

I'm sure she's right. After the anger abated, his eyes shone with remorse. I'm sure he wishes as much as I do that he never did what he did.

With time, we'll get back on equal footing and do our jobs.

"Thanks, Mom. I'm sorry I called you so late."

"I'm glad you called." She sighs heavily. "Have I ever told you how I met your dad?"

I think back through all the stories over the years and realize I have no idea exactly how they met.

"No. You haven't, actually."

"I ran into him at the local pool. We hung out all day and hit it off immediately. I knew within an hour that I wanted to know him better, but I was in a relationship." She huffs a laugh. "The next day, I went back to the pool, hoping to see him, and was shocked to find my boyfriend there with him."

"What? How is that possible?" I sit back on the couch, kicking up my feet and getting comfortable to hear this story.

"Your dad was childhood best friends with Curt, my boyfriend at the time. They'd lived next to each other until your grandparents had sold their house and moved across town. Your dad went to another school, but he remained friends with his old neighbors. Curt was supposed to be at the pool that first day, but he got sunburned, and his mom made him sit the day out. If that hadn't happened, your father and I might never have had that day to build a bond."

"I've never heard that story," I say, smiling at the thought of my dad macking on his friend's girl. Clearly, he didn't realize it at the time because that wasn't Dad. He was loyal to the end.

"It was a sore spot for your dad. I broke up with Curt the next week and started dating your father. It ruined their friendship, which he never quite got over."

"Did you regret causing that rift?"

I grimace as soon as the words come out. They sounded harsh, even though they weren't meant to be.

"I did, but your father tried hard not to let me. We were meant to be together, no matter who was hurt in the process. We had a love that couldn't be stopped, Raven."

"What does this have to do with me?" I ask, wondering how we went from discussing my slipup to hearing the story about her and Dad.

"I'm just saying, don't close yourself off to happiness."

My mouth drops open.

"Are you suggesting I should pursue Charles?"

She warned me away from him, but this story and her words have me second-guessing what I'm hearing.

Maybe it's the tequila fog.

Maybe it's wishful thinking.

Either way, I'm thoroughly confused.

"No, baby girl, I'm not suggesting anything. I'm simply saying what's meant to be will be. You can't stop fate. You might as well not fret about things you can't change or avoid."

"I don't like that saying."

"Tough, buttercup. It's all true." She laughs. "Either you two will learn to keep your distance and everything will be fine, or it won't."

"None of this is reassuring, Mom," I groan, pulling a pillow over my head.

"Who knows, Raven. You could even find that you aren't supposed to stay away from each other. Maybe this *is* fate drawing you together."

My thoughts are already too cluttered with warring emotions. I don't even want to begin to consider that.

"Unlikely." It's all I say, hoping to drop the conversation. "Thanks for listening to me. I better get to bed."

"Get some rest. Call me tomorrow."

"Love you, Mom."

"You, too," she says before the line goes quiet.

I slink my way to my bed, not bothering to get undressed. My body is heavy, my head swimming.

Despite my state of drunkenness, sleep doesn't come easily.

Between the alcohol and thoughts of Charles, my mind refuses to shut off.

If only I didn't care about this job. I'd call off and avoid him altogether.

There's too much to do, and I've never been one to run away from my problems.

I'm not about to start now.

# chapter twenty-three

Raven

NOT EVEN COFFEE COULD RECTIFY MY ZOMBIE PERSONALITY the next day. Walking slowly into my office, bags under my eyes, thoroughly disheveled, I am literally a *Walking Dead* cast member.

Nightmares about hooking up with your boss in the office will do that to a person.

I pulled myself together in fifteen minutes, having to run out the door to catch the subway, but didn't make it on time.

There was a moment when I thought I might scream out loud for everyone to hear. The anger and frustration mounting on my shoulders weighed me down, threatening to spill over.

I had to wait for the next ride and barely made that because I'd been too distracted. If I were a smart girl, I would've called it a day and crawled back into bed.

My white blouse is wrinkled, and my navy blue skirt is a tad shorter than I'd typically wear to work. I'd been half-asleep when I'd pulled it from the closet, so I'll spend the entire day pulling it down, self-conscious and full of self-loathing.

Somehow, I manage to tamp down the emotions and pull myself together.

Not wanting to be seen, I slink into my office and shut the door, throwing myself into my work. It motivated me to get here, and it will get me through the day. I work for over an hour before the events from the night before creep in.

No matter how hard I try, I can't shake my mom's words about fate and the story about her and my father's meeting. I'd never put too much stock into things of that nature, but I couldn't negate the fact that everything that had occurred with Charles and me had seemed too implausible to be anything less than fate.

Not that I believe Charles and I are meant to be. We're not. We can't be.

If anything, we're star-crossed lovers, destined to die a slow and painful death.

*Drama queen.*

I have to admit, though, how we keep being pulled together is strange. Neither of us seems to be able to stop. It feels as though some unseen force is pulling the strings and thrusting us together.

Then pulling us apart.

Are we just avoiding the inevitable?

Maybe we should let things happen and deal with the fallout.

Allow ourselves to taste a slice of the forbidden fruit before the snake comes along to fuck shit up.

I blow out a breath, willing myself to concentrate on my work. There's a lot to do and little time to do it.

I'm sending the creative team an email asking to meet this afternoon. I'll need every hour I can squeeze to formulate ideas ahead of time. As good as our marketing team is, I'm better. I understand this account more than any of them.

We're on a time crunch, and I need all hands on deck.

Otherwise, I'd do the heavy lifting all on my own. I'm determined to nail this, and I'd be lying if I didn't admit I'm a bit of a control freak.

Thankfully, the creative team had been given a heads-up by Charles and was more than ready for my email. They'd agreed to a three o'clock meeting, right before the end of the day, which gives me plenty of time.

My phone pings, pulling me away from my computer.

**Asher: Lunch?**

I want to see him, but there's no way I can fit lunch in today. If I'm lucky, I'll have a couple of minutes to hit the vending machine for a less than fulfilling snack.

**Me: Can't, sorry. I have a tight deadline chasing me.**

**Asher: Sounds scary. I can't wait to hear all about it.**

I'd love to be able to talk shop with someone who gets what I'm doing, but Asher isn't the right person. Whether I like it or not, he's competition. Until this campaign is over, I'm keeping my ideas and whining to myself.

**Asher: Dinner?**

**Me: I'll probably be working late. Can I text you later?**

I won't. I know that the last thing I'll be up for tonight is dinner out and having to balance time with my friend and dodging his probing questions about my work.

**Asher: Sure. I'll be free.**

**Asher: Listen . . . I need to talk to you about Summer. I messed up.**

Dread fills me because, without a doubt, I know what he's going to admit.

He was the one who leaked the Summer info to Bauer.

Bile coats my throat, and my stomach plummets to my feet.

**Me: Are you fucking kidding me, Ash?**

**Asher: I'm sorry. It wasn't intentional. I've been sick over it.**

**Me: And you decide to tell me via text????**

**Asher: You guessed. I wanted to tell you in person.**

Fucking typical of Asher to chicken out and drop news like that via text.

It's his MO.

Every time he sleeps with a girl and doesn't want round two, he ends it with a text.

It's his way of dealing with it without actually feeling the fallout. He's a coward. It's one thing for him to pull that shit with hookups, but I'm supposed to be his best friend.

**Me: Fuck this shit.**

I put my phone on silent and stuff it into my purse.

What the fuck was he thinking? How could he? And to allow that to happen via text?

I trusted him, and he betrayed me.

I feel sick to my stomach because no matter what Asher's involvement in this was, I'm the one who shared the information with him. This is just as much my fault.

I pull out my AirPods, needing to drown out my own thoughts. The last thing I need over the next few hours is distractions. Asher hurt me, but he didn't ruin this account. We can still nail it. Make it better.

I have to concentrate. Soothing music spurs my creativity. I think best when one of my favorite singers croons in my ears.

I press play and get back to work, losing myself in the music for the next few hours and pushing thoughts of Asher and his betrayal to the back of my mind.

---

The meeting with the creative team went better than I expected.

Apparently, my attention to detail and extreme OCD made their jobs easier.

*Big surprise.*

They asked for four days to complete everything, which would put us ahead of the original timeline.

Charles had told them that this account took priority, so they had their entire team—ten people—working solely on this campaign.

I'm relieved. Exhausted and ready for bed, but relieved nonetheless.

Despite the shit show of a day it's been, this one thing went well, and I'm going to hold on to that.

I hit the trusty vending machine on the way back, grabbing a bag of Fritos and a Diet Coke, ready to get back to my office and dive into securing publications for Icon and AlteredX. It's four o'clock, and the office is already thinning out for the evening.

I settle at my desk when there's a knock on my door.

My shoulders stiffen, nervous that it's Charles on the other side. I've avoided him all day, which is likely due to his own attempts to dodge me.

Good. It's for the best.

"Come in," I call out.

"I need help," Shelby yells from the other side, and my brows knit together.

I head to the door and open it to find her standing there with the largest bouquet I've ever seen.

"Who pissed you off?" she asks, pushing past me and walking into the office to set the obscene floral arrangement on my desk.

"Is there a card?"

She blushes, giving away the fact she likely read it.

"Sorry," she says, grimacing. A firm confirmation that she did, in fact, read it. "I couldn't help it."

I smirk, plucking the card up and reading it.

*I'm sorry. Can we start over?*

There isn't a signature, but I know immediately who sent them. My stomach plummets, thinking about what a mess he would've put us in had he signed it.

What the hell was he thinking?

Shelby looks at me expectantly, waiting to hear who sent them.

"My friend, Asher." I shrug. "We had a bit of a falling out, and he said some things he shouldn't have."

I lie because I have to, but I feel bad instantly.

Shelby has been good to me, and here I am, blatantly lying to her face.

I despise keeping secrets and hate lying even more, but it can't be helped.

This is one thing I'm not sharing with anyone.

"Well . . . looks like he has a massive thing for you," she says, and my head snaps to her.

"What do you mean?"

She looks at me like I'm dense.

"Nobody buys an arrangement that size unless they're in love."

I pale at her words because this is anything but love. This is an act of buying my silence.

No. Love is definitely not a factor here. Guilt is more likely.

It's also a ploy to ensure I'm not going anywhere because he knows he needs me.

Well, to hell with that.

I don't want anything from him.

"Oh, boy, looks like the flowers aren't cutting it. That guy must've really screwed up."

I smash my lips together, knowing that isn't the case.

"It was both of us," I say, not wanting to tell one more lie.

This part, without mentioning who it is, I can share.

"We kissed when we shouldn't have, and it ruined everything," I explain.

She purses her lips, searching my face. Her eyes narrow in on me, and sweat builds at my temples. Does she know? Could she suspect? I'm about to say something when she shrugs and continues.

"Sounds like he has good intentions. Why are you still angry?"

I blow out a breath. "It was the wrong place to send me flowers. I don't want to mix work and my personal life. He knows that and should've considered how embarrassed I'd be when receiving this." I motion toward the offending flowers.

She chuckles. "If you don't want them, I can put them in the foyer."

"No." The word snaps from my lips without a thought.

Shelby's eyebrows shoot to her hairline, but a slow, knowing smile creeps across her face.

"So, maybe the guy does have a chance after all?" She smirks, and I wince.

"I'm . . . conflicted."

Her head bobs, and a slow smile plays upon her much too curious face. "Mmmm-hmmmm. Navigating feelings is a real pain, huh?"

Giving them up to the foyer would be for the best. It would send Charles a strong message, too. But the truth is, I don't want to part with them. It's ridiculous, considering the reason they were sent to begin with, but I want them.

*So dumb, Raven.*

"Let me think about it," I say, and she smiles.

I don't ask why she's smiling because it's obvious. She knows those flowers will be sitting right here on this desk tomorrow morning. Am I that easy to read?

"I'm headed out. It's girls' night, and I asked to leave early," she says, making her way to the door.

"Fun. I'm jealous. I'll be here. Working." I shift the flowers to the other side of the desk, giving me a clearer view of the door.

"Again? You have my sympathy." She rocks back on her heels, clearly ready to get out of here.

"See you later, Shelby."

I wave a hand, looking back down at the paper sitting in front of me, determined to get my work done and get out of here before nine tonight. I'm hungry and tired, but due to my distractions this morning, I'm behind.

I sit at my desk for well over an hour, trying to work, but my gaze keeps landing on the flowers. They're gorgeous. Easily the prettiest I've ever been given.

Hydrangeas have always been my favorite.

My mom used to have several bushes at our old house, and I always loved them. Hers were a brilliant shade of blue, but these green and white blossoms, intermixed with pink roses, make for an elegant combination. Sophisticated. Just like the sender.

My mind drifts to Charles, and I wonder if he chose this exact bouquet or if the florist did. I hate that it bothers me to think he left it in someone else's hands.

Why do I care?

I shouldn't.

But I do, and it pisses me off. *He* pisses me off.

The mind games aren't fair. He could've simply said the words or done as I suggested last night and moved forward. Act like it never happened.

He didn't have to send me these flowers and toy with my head even more.

I'm out of my seat and headed in his direction before I can think better of it. I'm coming unhinged, and I blame him.

No matter how many times I tell myself I can move forward and work alongside him, it's not true. He's under my skin, and I can't think of anything else.

I'm so screwed.

# chapter twenty-four

Charles

R AVEN IS MY POISON AND ANTIDOTE ALL IN ONE.
I can't get her out of my mind.

I know better. I've learned from experience. But I can't stop the flood of feelings that invade me when she's near. I'm unraveling, and it's entirely the five-foot-four-ish blonde ray of bloody sunshine's fault.

I've never had such a visceral reaction to a woman. Why the fuck is this happening now? This isn't like me.

I have rules.

Reasons to keep women at a distance.

My work is my life, and I've been more than fine with that these past three years.

Having been let down by people before, I made a promise to myself that I would never let it happen again. You can't be hurt if you keep people at a distance.

*A very far distance.*

Allowing people in has never been comfortable for me. I don't like to get too close to anyone. After losing my mother and experiencing the excruciating pain that came with her loss, It was easy to be a loner. I don't care to ever endure that level of pain again.

When I find myself getting in deep, I always pull away.

I'd started that process the day I'd proposed to Tabitha and realized what I'd done.

Add to that, I didn't love her.

It was a relationship of convenience, and I'd allowed her to strong-arm me into taking it to the next step as a power play. Nothing else. Love would never have been a factor. It would've been like every other prearranged marriage throughout time, made solely to solidify two strong family lines carrying on.

A step I never wanted. Especially with her.

Only I'd been made the fool. There was no merging of two great families. She was an accomplished liar, attempting to climb the ladder of high society. A broke socialite, trying to hide the fact that her daddy's cash was well and truly gone.

Raven is different. She's been the one to pull away until last night. She didn't seek me out at Silver and lock herself in a bloody cloakroom to seduce me.

A series of chance encounters brought us to this moment.

If I were a religious man, I'd think God put her in my path.

Rubbish.

Nobody put Raven Bennett in my path. It's utter bullshit and a coincidence.

Raven has repeatedly warned me off and asked me to forget our mistakes. But that's the problem. They don't feel like they're mistakes with her. Stopping last night was difficult. It went against my very being.

My body literally ached for her hours later. I couldn't sleep.

I have already had a taste of what she feels like against me, and I want more.

The very idea of never having her mouth on mine again drives me completely insane.

My reasons for stopping were for the best. She *is* right. I'm her boss, and we need to keep things professional for the sake of Diosa and the future of the New York office.

Everything rides on the success of this branch. I refuse to go back to London with my tail tucked between my legs.

I have the means to begin my own company, but it would take years to build up the reputation that my father and I have worked for decades to build at Cavendish Corporation.

Diosa is the key to securing my future here, and I need Raven to help solidify that future.

Her ideas are what will keep the account for us because I know others are poaching. Diosa signed a contract, but their attorneys made sure to add a clause that it was all pending approval of the campaign.

Things have been done so ass-backward with this account. Typically, the pitch would've been made and the campaign finalized before the contracts were signed, but the launch of their new products changed their timetable and forced them to find their marketing team, and for us to have to scramble.

Raven practically ran from my office last night, and I'm petrified. What if she quits and leaves us with no project for the Diosa team? She's here today, but that doesn't mean she hasn't already started looking elsewhere.

I need to make amends, and I do it the way all men do when they've messed up well and good.

I send her flowers.

Searching through the website, I find exactly what I'm looking for. The largest bouquet of hydrangeas and pale pink roses.

I fill out everything, leaving the card short and simple.

***I'm sorry. Can we start over?***

No signature. I don't need anyone in the office to know who sent them. Only Raven.

They'll be delivered after lunch today, and hopefully, she'll know I didn't mean to make things uncomfortable. She'll see that I'm not a bad guy. That I want her to stay.

At least I hope so.

My door flies open, catching me off guard.

A livid Raven storms in, shutting the door a little harder than necessary.

"What the hell is wrong with you, Mister? What were you thinking?" she practically screeches.

I'm not sure what she's talking about, and she must realize it because her eyes narrow.

"Ugh. Why do you think I'd storm in here? The insanely large floral arrangement you sent me a clue?"

My head tilts to the side, wondering why flowers would cause this reaction. It's completely opposite of what I was aiming for.

"Are they ugly? They didn't look ugly on the website. Why don't you like them?"

"My God, you are obtuse. It's not the actual flowers, Charles. You sent them to the office where everyone can see them. It's completely humiliating."

Every time she says my name, another piece of my resolve snaps. It does things to me I don't even understand.

A lazy smile spreads across my face. "Getting flowers is humiliating?"

"When they're from you," she snaps. "What if someone found out? What would they say?"

I scoff. "I don't give a damn what anyone says. I owe you an apology. It's nobody's bloody business."

Her arms cross over her chest, and my eyes roam over her.

I grin, standing from behind my desk and walking toward her.

For every step forward I take, she takes a step back.

"I didn't sign my name to the card. Nobody will know they're from me," I insist.

"That's not the point, Charles. We said we'd forget about it. This isn't forgetting." She sounds tired, and I hope my actions aren't the cause.

*Of course they are, dickhead.*

"Did you get any sleep last night?"

Her eyes close. "It's completely obvious I didn't sleep. Why are you asking questions you know the answer to?"

"I didn't either," I admit, and her eyes crack open.

"You didn't?" she says, peering up at me with wide cornflower eyes.

I shake my head back and forth slowly, taking the last couple of steps until we're almost chest to chest.

"You haunted me all night."

She swallows, eyes hooding. "Charles." My name slips from her lips on a moan, and something in me snaps.

Fuck it then.

I pull her against me. "Tell me you want this, Raven."

"You can't keep doing this yo-yo game with me. I . . . We . . ."

I take a step back, and she grabs the collar of my shirt, pulling me forward once more. "I know we shouldn't, but I don't want to stop this. Let's start over again."

Before either of us can change our minds, my hands grip her thighs as I lift her. She squeals, but I silence her by crashing my lips to hers.

She doesn't resist, meeting me halfway and wrapping her legs around my waist while I carry her backward toward my desk.

The office is empty. Everyone left within the last hour.

There's nobody to stop this. Nobody to interrupt.

I sit her on the desk, pressing my mouth to her throat. "Tell me you want this as much as I do, love."

Her breathing is heavy, and her pulse races under my lips.

"I do. I need you. If you stop this time, I'll combust."

"This time I'm not pulling back."

I hope the fallout isn't earth-shattering because I'm too far gone for Raven. I can't stop this collision course we are on.

I kiss a line down her neck and across her collarbone.

"Lift your arms," I command, and she does.

I drag the white shirt over her head, discarding it somewhere behind me. Stepping back, I take her in. Perfect pale skin and ample breasts covered by a lacy white bra. My hands make quick work of removing that, too, as I continue my trail of kisses until I'm at the swell of her breast.

I pull a nipple into my mouth, my tongue alternating between flicks and sucks. She moans, which drives me on. Her ankles lock behind my back, pulling me into her. My cock strains against my trousers in reaction to being this close to her.

My arm circles her waist, holding her in place while my free hand massages her other breast. I grind my full length against her center, and she cries out.

"Please, don't stop this time," she begs.

"No way in hell."

My lips crash against hers again, and I sweep my tongue over hers, relishing the taste of mint on her breath. She moans when my hand runs up her thigh, trailing over her panties.

Her hands land on my chest, pushing me away, and for a moment, my heart stops. But it quickly restarts when she lifts her hips to pull her skirt and knickers down her legs, discarding them over my shoulder, where her shirt lies on my floor.

I take her in, completely bared to me.

She's more than I could've dreamed up. She's everything.

"Raven, I—" I shake my head at a loss for words as she sits up, wrapping her arms around my neck.

"If you say a word to stop this, so help me, Charles . . ."

A growl tears through me, need steamrolling me into feeling things I never have felt before. Possessive. I want to own Raven. If only for tonight.

"No. I'm not stopping this," I say, running my tongue over my bottom lip as I take her in. "Tonight. Right now. You're mine."

I take a step forward, brushing my lips against hers.

"I've got a bad feeling about this," she whispers.

"Very bad," I agree. "Horrible idea, but I don't fucking care. Do you?"

Please say no.

I might die if she ends things now. But I won't move forward without her consent.

"Take off your clothes."

She only has to tell me once. Within seconds, my trousers, briefs, and shirt have been discarded, and I stand naked before her.

Her eyes widen, and her teeth rake in her bottom lip.

My mouth claims hers again, and she pushes her breasts into me. My muscles tighten under her palms as she strokes my chest. My heart pounds as she wraps her fingers around my cock with one hand and palms my balls with the other.

"Bloody hell, Raven." I groan against her lips. "That feels—"

Her hand moves up and down my shaft, and I'm not sure how long I can allow her to do it.

I sweep papers off my desk, leaning her back and putting both palms on either side of Raven's head.

"You're so beautiful, Rae," I say, smiling down at her before I lean in for another kiss. Her hands skim over my chest and run up to my shoulders. I shift, moving between her legs, and line my cock up with her center.

I look into her eyes. "Last chance, sunshine."

She shakes her head. "Do. Not. Stop."

I push myself in, stopping when I'm halfway to allow her walls to adapt to my size.

"Please," she begs, and I push in, my dick slamming as far as possible. A moan of pleasure escapes her, and I take that as permission to move.

I rock in and out, loving the way her body forms to my cock, squeezing every time I pull out.

"Fuck," I say, building in pace. Her mewls push me on.

I'm so immersed in Raven that I forget about where we are.

Everyone might have left, but this building is open twenty-four seven. Anyone could walk in on us.

I couldn't care less at this moment, and that should terrify me. Not once have I mixed work and pleasure. My company means too much to fuck it up with meaningless sex. Everything with Raven is different, and that's the scariest bit of all.

Raven's fingernails dig into my back, bringing my mind back to the here and now. All thoughts of this being a bad idea disappear as I relish the sting from her nails. I pump into her harder, drawing more exquisite noises from her kiss-swollen lips.

Her legs squeeze my hips tighter, and I know her orgasm is building.

"Kiss me," she says, pulling me down to her. I grab her hands, pinning them above her head as I lean down, swiping my tongue across her bottom lip.

"Charles."

My name on her lips makes me want to give her anything and everything she asks for.

I kiss her passionately for several moments, slowing my thrusts in the process.

"More," she says, voice heavy with need.

She writhes beneath me, back arching off the table as I pull all the way out and slam back into her. I begin a punishing pace as I work to push her toward the edge.

My body tightens, my own release building as I drive into her.

She cries out, but I don't stop.

I'll take every moan of ecstasy. Every single ounce of pleasure I can muster.

Her pussy tightens around me, and I know she's falling over the ledge. I'm close behind.

One thrust.

Two.

Total bliss.

I spill into her, collapsing on top of her.

We lie here quietly for several minutes, breathing heavily and lost in our thoughts.

My body is wrung completely. I'm thoroughly spent.

Being with Raven was more than I hoped for.

*You didn't use a condom.*

My stomach plummets with that realization.

*Arse.* I'm a *complete and total arse.*

I sit up quickly, and Raven comes with me. "Charles?"

The fear in her voice has my nerves settling minutely.

"We didn't . . . use protection."

She lets out a harsh breath, looking relieved when I'm anything but.

"I'm clean. Haven't been with anyone in two years."

I nod. "Me, too." Her one eyebrow lifts in a teasing manner. "Well . . . in regard to the clean part."

She winces, and I know she probably doesn't want to think of me with other women. Knowing she's been celibate for two years makes me happier than it should.

"What about birth control? I'm so sorry, I didn't think about . . ."

"We're okay. I have an IUD."

I breathe for the first time in minutes, relieved that at least she's responsible.

"Forgive me. Your health should be my first concern."

She smiles the best smile. "Forgiven."

I pick up her skirt and shirt from the floor, handing them to her before I work to locate my discarded clothing.

We're silent the entire time we're getting dressed.

My mind is mush from what was quite possibly the best fuck of my life. Memories from moments before swirl through my head.

Raven's legs wrapped around my waist.

Her tight pussy clenched around my cock.

The sounds she made while I was fucking her.

Sublime.

"A-Are we all right?" she stammers, drawing my attention back to her.

She's worrying her bottom lip, and I have an intense urge to hold her and release any concern she feels.

"We're more than all right, love." I pull her into me. "We're exceptional."

She studies my face. "You don't regret what we did?"

I should. I *really* should.

I grin. "Do you?"

She shakes her head. "No."

I place a kiss on her forehead, breathing her in as I do.

"Neither do I."

She sighs. "Okay."

It's all she says.

No questions about what's next or what we are. No declarations of feelings or demands for the future.

One last kiss and a smile before she makes her way to the door.

"I'll see you tomorrow."

I'm gobsmacked.

Raven might very well be the perfect woman.

"I'll see you tomorrow," I say, rubbing my chin and trying to smother a grin.

She offers me one more brilliant smile before waving and making her exit.

This woman is definitely going to own me if I'm not careful.

# chapter twenty-five

Raven

I'M A MESS.

I thought giving in to temptation and finishing what we started would cure the insane need I have for Charles, but all it's done is create a bigger monster.

Now I'm left wondering what's next and trying to put labels on something that can't be named.

Nothing has changed.

He's still my boss, and I'm still his employee.

I'm not normally one for a fling, and I know this will never be more. I'm not stupid enough to think it will be, but I can't get him out of my head.

*You're an idiot, Raven.*

I'm sitting at my desk, looking through the mock-ups marketing sent, and I can't focus. I should be excited to work at my dream job and run a campaign that, months ago, I could've only imagined overseeing.

All my mind can conjure is images of Charles between my thighs, pushing into me.

The sounds of our bodies merging.

The sensation of his breath on my neck.

That deep, sensual voice echoing across the room as he came undone.

I can't escape it.

I never want to.

The horrible reality—I want to experience it again.

Knowing full well that's impossible, I want a label.

I can't have Charles *and* Cavendish Group.

It won't work.

Some people can block out what others think of them, but that's not me. It would be devastating if my colleagues thought I only got this promotion by sleeping with the boss.

It's not true. But since when does the truth matter in this world?

Wouldn't I think that, too, if it were someone else in this position?

I work too damn hard to be accused of something so heinous. Charles's power or position doesn't interest me. It's the man.

The whole grumpy-ass package.

I wonder if I got him away from the office, he would loosen up a fraction. He's damn good at his job and seems to have a good sense of humor. A caring nature exists below that gruff exterior; I can see peeks at times.

I come out of my daydream with a screech and jump when my phone rings.

I see it's Asher and contemplate between sending him straight to voicemail or screaming down the line at him. He's the last person I want to talk to, but I can't ignore him forever. We have history, and despite my anger, deep down, I know it was an accident.

Hazards of working for competitors.

I answer.

"Asher," I say, with as little affection as I can muster.

I might be speaking to him, but I'm not about to forgive him immediately.

"Raven. Hi," he says, sounding awkward for what might be the first time ever. "You've been impossible to track down."

"That happens when your best friend stabs you in the back."

He sighs. "You know that's not what happened. I'd never—at least not intentionally."

"I know, but it's going to take me a bit to come to terms with that."

"I understand." He's quiet for a moment, and I'm about to ask if there's anything else when he finally speaks again. "What are you up to today? Could we grab lunch? Talk?"

My petty side screams to say no, but the other half—the loyal to a fault part—of me says we need to hash things out. I've never been one capable of holding grudges, even when it's more than justified.

"Sure. I could do that."

I hear his harsh breath, a sure sign he's relieved. "Thank you."

"I was going to make it an earlier lunch today. I have a lot of work to do."

"That works for me. I'll meet you in the cafeteria at eleven?"

"Perfect. I'll see you then."

I end the call without saying goodbye. Looking at the clock, I have two hours before I meet Asher, so I will myself to banish thoughts of Charles and concentrate on the materials in front of me. We're on a deadline, and I won't mess this up.

---

The marketing materials the creative team sent were amazing.

The first draft was beyond expectation. They got our vision immediately and ran with it. I had a few minor tweaks, but it took me less than an hour to list them in an email and get them sent back.

Shanda, the head of the team, said that the changes should be done by the afternoon for final approval.

I think Holly, Catelyn, and Spencer will love the vibes we've created for the first four campaigns. Fun, flirty, sensual, and sophisticated. All words that come to mind when you think of all three Diosa lines.

This afternoon, Reagan will come in to fill out his new hire paperwork and get set up in his cubicle. I have two more second interviews for the AlteredX assistant and my personal assistant after Reagan arrives.

By my calculations, we'll have our team in place, new hire work done, and I can hold my first team meeting. I'm very excited to see it all coming together. Feels almost too good to be true.

I swing by to see Shelby before heading down to the cafeteria to meet Asher. Charles's door is shut, and my eyes remain fixed on it for too long.

"Everything okay?" Shelby calls from her perch.

I pull my eyes away from the door to answer. "Yes. I just came to let you know I'm heading to lunch. I'll be back by the time Reagan and my interviews arrive."

"Perfect," she says, looking down at her screen. "Charlie won't be able to make it today. He had a last-minute meeting added to his calendar that he can't miss."

"Oh, okay," I say, dread seeping in.

Is he already avoiding me?

"You'll do fine," she says, misreading my emotions. "You might very well appreciate him not being there. You can choose the people you want without dealing with his grumpy moods." She cups her mouth with her hands. "He's got one hell of a temper today."

My eyebrows tip in. "Really? Any idea why?"

Now I'm really freaking out. Is what we did finally setting in? Does he regret it now?

She shakes her head. "No clue, but I have a feeling it has something to do with the meeting that was added to his calendar." She leans over conspiratorially, lowering her voice. "Something is going on with his father."

My eyebrows lift into my hairline this time. That I did *not* expect.

"Is everything okay?"

She shrugs. "Haven't the slightest idea. But I did a little

research." Her cheeks turn beet red when she realizes her words make her sound nosy as hell. A trait I'm beginning to believe is just Shelby's way.

"The man he's meeting with is Mr. Cavendish's attorney. The senior Cavendish," she emphasizes. "From London."

When I don't say anything to that, she continues. "The same man who showed up out of nowhere last week." She puckers her lips. "Something is definitely going on across the pond."

Interesting. I know he's gone to London, and it's no secret that he's the heir to the entire corporation.

"Do you think he'll be taking over sooner rather than later?"

She makes a motion with her head that wobbles between shaking and nodding. "I don't know, but this office will miss him if he leaves. I can't think of one of the current executives that could do this job the way he has."

My nose scrunches. "Not one of them is fit to run this company," I say before I can think better of it.

She giggles. "Don't say that too loud. These walls have ears."

I grimace, thinking about what these walls have heard over the past twenty-four hours.

"I better get going. I'm meeting a friend for lunch, and I'm gonna be late."

"Enjoy a long lunch, Raven. You have to take care of yourself, and you've been working too many hours. You need a break. I don't want to see you back here before twelve thirty."

"Yes, Shelby, I'll leave on an extended lunch, even though I will feel guilty the whole time." Rolling my eyes, I rush down to the cafeteria, finding Asher waiting for me.

"Raven," he says, jumping up from his seat.

We do this awkward dance. To hug or not to hug. Eventually, Asher makes a move and pulls me into a tight embrace.

"I've missed you," he says, lingering a little longer than necessary, and I swear to God, he breathed me in.

This is the longest we've ever gone without talking to each

other when we're angry, and I can tell he's very bothered. He's been with me through so much, and I can't help but admit that this divide between us has been excruciating for the whole day it's been a thing. I'd like to get things back to normal with my friend, even if it means forgiving him probably quicker than I should.

He's a good guy, and there is no way he would purposely betray my trust.

We take a seat, and he slides my sandwich over.

"You know me so well," I say, looking down at the turkey pocket wrap, complete with Fritos and a Diet Coke.

"Well, your palate hasn't changed since you were eighteen. Easy to get it right."

I snicker. "That is true." I take a sip of the cold cola. "Tell me what you've been up to," I say, trying to keep the conversation about him.

"You know. The same old, same old. Work, sleep, repeat."

"I saw you at Silver the other night."

His eyes widen. "You saw me, and you didn't say hello?" His face falls, and I can tell he's hurt.

Shit.

Why do I open my mouth?

"I was there for a work event, and it looked like you were in pretty deep conversation with some suits. I didn't want to interrupt."

His mouth forms an O, and he nods. "Yes, I was there with some colleagues. We were discussing a new account that's keeping all of us very busy." He takes a deep breath. "But you know I'll always make time for you, Raven. Always."

"I know, Ash."

"Please forgive me." The words rush from him in one breath. "My boss was talking about approaching Summer again, and it slipped out. All I said was she already took a gig, and we shouldn't waste our time." He smashes his lips together, shaking his head back and forth. "As soon as it came out of my mouth, I felt sick to my stomach."

He's telling the truth. I know without a single doubt. He looks crestfallen, and I'm internally smacking myself for avoiding him as long as I did.

"We're fine, Ash. I can see it was an honest mistake. One that I could've easily made myself. We're good," I press, hoping he knows I mean it.

He cracks a small smile, looking a tad bit relieved.

"For the record, the collaboration with Summer has turned into a bit of a nightmare. She's a fucking diva."

I suck in the side of my cheeks, biting down so I don't say anything.

"Cavendish Group dodged a bullet with that one," he murmurs, and I can't help but internally do a victory dance.

We're on such a short timeframe that the last thing I need is the divas. Holly doesn't seem like that at all.

"I'm sorry to hear that. I've got to say, I'm relieved not to have to deal with her."

"I can assure you, you should be relieved. Hopefully, you guys got someone better." He takes a drink of his iced tea. "To be honest, I wouldn't even be surprised if she breaks her contract with Bauer." He grimaces. "Please don't repeat that. I could get in so much trouble."

Both of my hands rise. "I won't say a word."

"So . . . we really are . . . okay?" he asks, looking uncertain.

I smile. "Yes. We're really good, Ash."

He takes a huge breath. "Good, because we have some planning to do."

I lift a brow. "Planning?"

"You do realize that Lily's birthday is coming up, right?"

I gasp. "Oh, crap. I completely forgot." My palm slaps against my forehead. "I haven't talked to her in days. I'm the worst friend."

I lay my head on top of my hands. Asher leans over, patting the back of my head.

"This is why you have me. To remind you of the stuff that you forget while trying to navigate corporate America."

I chuckle. "Thank God for you, then."

"Thank God, indeed." He grins at me.

I laugh, my head falling back on my shoulders. It feels good to be back to normal with Asher. It's been too long. Even before our fallout, I've practically tiptoed my way around him since my mom and Lily planted false ideas in my mind about his feelings for me.

It was unfair because I should've known better. I should've just talked to him.

When my eyes lift, they land on a figure over Asher's shoulder. My heart stops for a moment before galloping.

"What's wrong?" Asher asks.

I gulp. Charles is walking in the doors. And he isn't alone. On his arm is an impeccably dressed woman with long, blonde hair and scarlet-red lips.

"It's . . . well . . . it's my boss."

"Oh, shit. You're allowed to be here, right?"

"Yeah, it's my break."

He sits back. "Hopefully, he won't see you."

Asher seems completely oblivious to my inner turmoil.

"Nope. He saw me. He's coming this way."

I want to slink into my seat and disappear. I haven't seen him since yesterday, and based on his current company, I'd rather not.

Charles approaches, wearing a dark navy suit, similar to Asher's, but on him, it looks tailor-made. Why does he always have to look so perfect?

"Raven," he says, never once looking at Asher. "Aren't you supposed to be in an interview?"

"Hello, Mr. Cavendish. Nice to see you," I say, keeping the bite out of my voice and things ever so professional. I can tell it annoys him. "My interviews are later. It's still my lunch break. I'm here with my friend, Asher Anderson," I say, motioning toward Asher and forcing Charles to acknowledge his presence.

He nods at Asher as if sizing him up before the showdown in the ring. It's ridiculous.

"Nice to meet you, Mr. Cavendish. Raven has told me so much about you."

I kick Asher under the table, and he grunts.

Charles looks my way with a raised eyebrow. "Is that so?"

"I've told him about the company and how much I enjoy my job."

*Please go away. Please go away.*

Things couldn't get any more awkward if I stood on the table and stripped down to my panties. The tension is high, and I'm not even sure why.

Because of what we did? Or is it about the woman he's with, or maybe Asher?

Either way, I want this unease to end.

"Glad to hear you're enjoying the *company*," Charles practically purrs, and my face heats at his hidden innuendo. "This is Angela," Charles says, as if he suddenly remembers the woman next to him. "She's an advisor to my father in London. She came to see the New York office."

Interesting. His father's attorney and now an advisor is here, too? What is going on?

"Hi, Angela, lovely to meet you. This is Asher," I say and smile affectionately at Asher as I do.

Something that sounds almost like a growl escapes Charles's throat, and all eyes turn to him. He coughs, and Angela claps a hand on his back.

"Are you okay, Charles?"

I hate that she calls him by his first name. So familiar.

"Fine," he chokes out. "We better leave you to it. Have a great day," he says and walks off, never officially acknowledging Ash.

I watch as he finds a table not too far from us. Not close enough to hear us talk, but definitely close enough to watch us.

"That is my boss. The CEO of the company."

"I gathered as much." Asher chuckles. "He's . . . intense."

"He's something all right," I mutter under my breath.

He shrugs, glancing toward Charles. "He's known to be rather private."

"Yeah, you won't find anything about him on the internet."

"You stalked him online?" Asher's mouth forms a straight, thin line.

"No. Well . . . yes. When I was interviewing for the company. I tried to find out all I could about him."

He bobs his head. "Makes sense. He's acting a bit strange," Asher notes, looking over that way again.

I turn my head slightly and see that Charles is watching us. I turned back to Asher with wide eyes.

"Yeah. He's weird. So full of himself. Anyway, let's eat our food."

"Good idea. I'm running out of time," Asher says.

We spend the rest of our lunch eating, laughing, and being far too friendly with one another.

At one point, I look up from my food and find Charles standing in the archway leading into the cafeteria, staring daggers at the back of Asher's head. His pinched features are set in a fierce scowl. The blonde from earlier is gone. My back straightens, and my shoulders roll.

What the hell is wrong with him?

I recall what Shelby had said. How he has a meeting with his father's attorney.

It's not until later, but maybe he's just angry about having to have his whole day rearranged?

Either way, his current glare is pointed directly at me, and I am doing everything I can not to shrink under the weight of it. I've done nothing.

Well . . . aside from that whole sleeping with the boss thing.

*Oops.*

He flips around and heads back in the other direction, leaving a chill in the air in his absence.

"Something wrong?" Asher asks, looking over his shoulder.

"Everything's fine," I say, plastering on a fake smile. "I was trying to think about what we could do last minute for Lily."

"She likes that mom-and-pop restaurant in Little Italy."

I grin. "You just named most of the Italian restaurants there. Which one?"

"Oh, hell. I don't remember. I'll look on my computer when I get back, but I can make reservations for the three of us." I nod, and he continues. "Let's go on her birthday. Six work?"

"I'll make it work." I sigh, thinking about all the work I still have to do. "What are we getting her this year?"

It's been a thing between the three of us for years. One wacky gift and one super sentimental. I'm typically the one who works on the wacky gift, while Asher is the sentimental one.

"I found this really pretty bracelet and necklace set through Tiffany's. I think she'll like it."

I bob my head. "Perfect."

"And, of course, we should set up a massage and facial at that spa you two love."

"Yes. That we have to do!" I say excitedly. "Why don't you let me book that, though, since I'll go with her."

He smiles widely. "My girls need pampering."

"That we do, sir. That we do."

He steeples his fingers. "Now for the wacky gift, what do you think?" he asks. "Edible undies? Purple bunny vibrator?"

I smack my lips together. "Why does your mind always go there? It's a wacky gift, not a dirty gift." I knock on his head twice with my knuckles. "Hello, Asher. Is anything up there but dirty thoughts?"

He chuckles. "No."

It's all he says, and I can't help but laugh.

I check the time. "Oh, shoot. I've really got to get going now. I have a full day of work this afternoon."

"Oh, yeah? Anything fun?"

I hesitate for a moment, questioning whether I should say anything. This is how the last fiasco happened.

"Never mind," Asher says, lowering his head. "I get it."

"I'm not going to say much other than I'm trying to hire some additional staff. I trust you, Ash, but I just think for my career, I can't keep blabbing. Someone may get the wrong idea about both of us. I don't want that for you."

"Good point."

I stand, pulling him into a hug. "I probably won't see you before Lily's birthday, so keep in touch."

He squeezes me a little harder, placing a kiss on my temple. "I'm glad to have you back," he says into my hair, and I sigh, feeling the same.

I missed him.

"Me, too."

"Can I take you to dinner ? Just you and me. To make things up to you?"

I bite my bottom lip. "I'm not sure, Ash. Things are crazy right now."

His face falls, and I hate it. We have hardly seen each other since I took this job, and I'm not okay with that.

"Let me check my schedule and get back to you."

"Don't work too hard, babe."

Stepping back out of his grip, I grin up at him. "You know I can't promise that."

After a light punch to his shoulder, I head back to my desk, ready to get this day over with and get home.

After seeing the way Charles stared at me, I am not in a hurry to see him.

Which makes me sad.

Ugh. Sleeping with my boss was such a mistake.

# chapter twenty-six

Raven

MY INTERVIEWS ARE COMPLETE, AND BOTH PRISCILLA AND Carmen have been officially offered positions.

Reagan is with Human Resources, working on his paperwork now, and I have a meeting set for the team in two weeks so they can go through training first.

It's been a productive day, and I'm feeling good when my desk phone rings.

"Cavendish Group. This is Raven speaking."

"Raven, it's Shelby," she says.

"Hey, Shelby. What's up?"

"Mr. Cavendish would like to see you in his office. Immediately."

And just like that, my good mood evaporates.

I'd avoided him and thoughts of us the whole second part of the day, but this was inevitable. I can't hide forever, and I don't want to.

I've never been the type of girl who's okay with a one-night stand. I made an exception for him, but it didn't feel right.

This may not be able to go anywhere, but I sure as hell am not gonna run away from my actions.

I square my shoulders, straighten my bright pink dress and yellow belt, and head to get this over with.

*It will only be as awkward as you make it, Raven.*

I give myself mini pep talks the whole way there, but it's no use. My hands shake at my sides, and my mouth is dry.

I take a deep breath just outside his door before knocking briskly. He calls out for me to come in.

He doesn't even look up when I enter, typing away on his computer.

"Shut the door and take a seat, Raven." His harsh tone causes my back to go ramrod straight.

This is how it's going to be? *Good to know.* "Why do you want me to close the door?"

I don't do as he's asked.

Instead, I cross my arms over my chest in defiance and glare at him. When he finally realizes I haven't moved from just inside the door, he looks up, brows knitted together.

"Because I want to talk to you alone. I'm your boss. That's a normal occurrence."

My shoulders roll back, and my cheeks heat. "Yes, I know you're my boss. That part has already been clearly established."

"Shut the damn door, Raven." Now his voice sounds tired, and I wonder if this has something to do with the advisor he was with.

I shut the door but don't move to take a seat.

"So, did you have a nice lunch?" he asks, but something in his tone doesn't sit right with me.

My eyes narrow. "Yes, I did. Thank you."

"I could see that," he says sarcastically.

"Then why did you ask, *sir*?"

He huffs. "It's rather forward of you, bringing a man who works for the competitor who has stolen things directly from us into *my* cafeteria. Are you feeding him information?"

My head whips up in response, wondering what's gotten into him.

"You're kidding, right? You looked into him."

"You failed to mention that your boyfriend works for Bauer."

"Asher is my friend. Has been for a long time. Who he works for isn't a factor in that."

"He doesn't seem to be on the same page with you on the status of your *relationship*. He wants more."

My hands land on my hips. "Then he's in for a rude awakening then."

He shrugs. "Poor sod. You should really have that discussion with him soon."

"With all due respect, *sir*, what I do in my personal life is none of your business."

He smirks, but doesn't look up at me.

What the heck could possibly be so important that he can't put it aside for a few minutes to have this fight like an adult?

"Going to sit?" he practically purrs, and I want to slap him.

I narrow my eyes, confused by the shift in his mood.

"I'm perfectly fine right here. What did you need, Mr. Cavendish? Surely, you didn't bring me in here to discuss my lunch."

He tries and fails at smothering a smile, folding his hands on top of his desk. He leans forward.

"It's Mr. Cavendish today, is it?"

"Well, I don't know, sir," I say with a little too much sass. "I haven't seen you since yesterday, outside of that moment in the cafeteria when you seemed to glare holes into my head." I huff. "So, yes. I feel like *Mr. Cavendish* is appropriate for the situation."

He sighs. "I'm sorry, Raven. Please take a seat."

I do as he suggests, not because he asks, but because my legs are getting tired of standing on these horrific stilettos.

"You wanted something?" I drawl, putting the ball in his corner and needing to fill the silence.

"About lunch," he starts, and I cut him off.

"Yeah, about that . . ."

He shakes his head. "I'm sorry if I acted like an arse, but I was caught off guard seeing you with . . . *him*."

He's jealous. It's the only explanation for this behavior, then and now.

Oh, what an interesting turn of events.

"You are an ass. Asher is my friend."

"I don't like him."

"I don't give a damn. He's been a part of my life since I was eighteen and has been there through my darkest times. He's not going anywhere."

His jaw clenches, and his hands ball into fists on his desk, but eventually, his features slacken, showing he's capable of being an adult.

"I apologize."

"I accept your apology. But for the record, jealousy isn't masculine."

He barks a laugh. "Noted."

"Is that all you brought me in for?" I say irritably.

"I've booked a short trip to Italy with Holly to scout out locations."

My head jerks back. "Holly?"

I'm not sure what I was expecting. It's not like I'm miffed about him going somewhere with another girl, especially Holly, but I'm the account manager. Why am I not going?

He nods. "We don't have time for both of us to go, and I need you here, Raven."

I know he's right. As much as I'd love to be whisked off to Italy, this isn't a fairy tale. It's our job.

"If you could send me a list of the landmarks and places you'd like to see in the ads, I'll grab the shots. Photographs of the real area are not something that we find on Google. We need the true angles of exactly how we'll want the photos done. I think having Holly in the mock shots will really help the team nail this when it's time to actually shoot."

"You're bringing a photographer with you?"

"I'm more than capable of handling a camera, love. I do own an advertising agency."

His words may be condescending, but his tone isn't.

And love?

Dear God, I could get used to him calling me that.

"You can work a camera? Interesting."

"I can work a great many things," he says, smirking, but I don't so much as smile back.

This easy flirting with him is all well and good, but I still feel rocky, not knowing where we are. I refuse to ask him to define this new normal between us, but it doesn't stop me from wondering.

His smile drops as he realizes I'm not taking the bait.

"Listen, Raven, about—"

"Oh, God. Please don't." I groan, throwing my head into my hands and not loving how this conversation is starting.

As much as I wanted this to happen, now that it's here, I'd do just about anything to avoid it.

"Let me finish," he says, and I slump forward in my chair. "I don't regret a thing. A part of me feels like it was always destined to happen."

My breath hitches as I remember my mom's words.

Fate.

"Anyway, I don't do relationships, and there's a very good reason for it. The relationships I carry on are short-term, and the women always know going into it."

My stomach sinks to my feet. Nothing is worse than getting the *I don't do relationships* talk after sex.

"I recognize I didn't offer you the same courtesy in explaining how I work, and for that, I apologize. Especially given the fact that we work together."

My eyes shut tightly as I battle to fight off the deep embarrassment seeping in. If he notices, he doesn't show it, moving forward with his talk.

"I don't want things to be rocky between us."

Obviously. Hasn't that been the issue all along? We hook up. Things are strained here at work?

"What you're saying is this won't happen again, and we'll move on and forget it. Do I have that right?" I ask evenly and without any inflection.

I don't want him to think I'm angry because I figured it was a one-time thing.

"That's not what I'm saying," he says with a sigh. "I don't know what I want, Raven."

He brushes his hands back through his hair. "I'd be a liar if I said things didn't feel different with you."

I scoff. "You don't need to feed me lines for my sake, Mr. Cavendish. I'm perfectly capable of handling the truth."

His lips purse. "I'm not giving you lines. I wouldn't say something that I don't mean. I'm not promising you a happily ever after. I really wouldn't mind stopping the one-time-only rule for a bit with you."

My heart skips a beat, and warmth spreads up my legs.

"We need to separate work from whatever this is between us," he says, and I nod, unable to form words without squeaking. "Say something," he commands.

I take a deep breath. "What happened here in the *office*, it can't happen again," I whisper, not wanting his nosy—albeit amazing assistant—to overhear.

"Agree."

"We don't put any labels on this," I say.

"Yes. No labels." He offers me a small smile. "We take things slow, and if they progress, they progress."

"If they don't, we act like adults, and we go on to knock the Diosa account out of the park," I continue.

"Precisely," he says.

I quickly change the subject, not wanting to have this conversation here in the office anymore.

"When do you leave for Italy?"

"As soon as I can arrange my flight. But I'll be leaving soon. A one-week whirlwind in the three cities you provided as the best locations to showcase the athletic wear and the designer look at the same time. You are brilliant, do you know that?"

He looks at me with such sincerity. It's difficult to see myself that way sometimes. To know someone who wants to kiss me also thinks I'm intelligent has my heart swelling. Quietly I say, "I appreciate your words."

"Of course. I mean it. Shelby will send over the full itinerary based on your locations, so you'll know how to reach me if you need to."

"Thank you, Mr. Cavendish."

He pulls his top lip into his mouth, trying to hold off a laugh.

"Behind closed doors, I'd prefer you call me Charles."

"Not Charlie," I ask, grinning.

"I bloody hate that name. Shelby knows it. It's her power play, and I need her on my team, so I allow it."

"Charles, it is." I smile, standing to head back to my office to check on Reagan.

He stands and walks around the desk, walking with me toward the door.

My hands are on the doorknob when his arm darts out, catching my free hand, turning me around, and tugging me into his firm chest. I yelp at the move, and he smothers the noise with his mouth.

The kiss is short, being as though we're in the office and Shelby is just behind the door.

"I'm sorry," he says, leaning his forehead against mine. "I know we said we wouldn't do this in the office, but I couldn't help it."

I place a chaste kiss against his lips and step out of his grasp.

"I'll allow it this once. Have a safe trip, Charles."

I'm floating on a cloud the entire walk back to my office. I don't know what's going to happen in the long run, but I'm relieved to know it wasn't a one-time thing. No matter what happens between Charles and me, I have a feeling I'll be okay with simply having had any amount of time with him.

# chapter twenty-seven

Raven

"YOU LOOK BEAUTIFUL, RAVEN."

I stare at Asher standing at my door. He's wearing a dark gray suit with a blue tie, and his hair is slicked back instead of the unruly, just-got-out-of-bed look I'm accustomed to with him.

"Uh . . . thank you," I say, questioning whether I'm underdressed.

After spending too much time in the office and giving one final kiss to Charles before he got ready for his flight in the morning, I texted Asher, and let him know I could meet him after all.

Then I threw on a yellow shift dress with a red belt and nude heels. I thought I'd be overdressed for a night out with Asher. Boy, was I completely wrong

"Why are you staring like that?" he asks, smirking.

I motion to his body. "Because you're in a suit. It's Thursday, Ash. Where the hell are you taking me?"

"You're dressed perfectly. Stop freaking," he drawls. "You'll easily turn all the heads in the place."

I purse my lips. "Flattery will work with me." He smirks but doesn't say anything, so I continue. "Since when do you wear a suit when going to dinner with me?"

"Since I fucked up and need to redeem myself."

"Damn straight. Take me to a Michelin star restaurant or lose me forever."

He laughs, "You're a nut, but you *will* be getting fine dining tonight."

"That sounds spectacular." My eyes scan his suit once more. "It's only fair that you should get to experience luxury, too, Ash. You look like a Bond, and a Bond boy only gets the best."

"Bond? I like it," he says, and we both chuckle.

When we arrive at the restaurant, I gasp. This is no pizza joint, not that I thought he'd wear a suit to grab a pizza. But this is one of the fanciest restaurants in Midtown. I know he feels bad for what happened, but this is too much.

I turn to face him before we get out of the car.

"La Grenouille? Are you serious?"

He shrugs. "I know you've always wanted to come here."

He's right. It's been on my bucket list for a long time. Not that there aren't better French restaurants in the area, but the ambiance is what calls to me. Rather than the trendy, uber-modern restaurants the rich and famous typically choose in this part of the city, I prefer the old-world style.

"Asher, you didn't have to take me here. This is so expensive."

His chin drops to his chest. "No. I did. I feel awful for what happened. I know a fancy restaurant won't take that away, but I feel like you deserve to go somewhere nice and on Bauer's dime while we're at it."

I snort. "Bauer, eh?"

He shrugs. "I'm wining and dining with a potential client."

"Well, I don't agree with that. Isn't that kind of like stealing?"

"No, I'm serious. After what we did to steal a client, we kind of deserve it."

"I'm not going to win this argument, but if that's the case, what are we waiting for?"

He squeezes my hand as he helps me out of the back of the town car we rode here in.

It's nice to have my best friend back.

"Asher," I say, looking around in awe. "This is amazing."

And I'm not lying. The restaurant is absolutely beautiful.

My eyes don't know where to look. The gilded restaurant with pink walls and flowers that rival any I've ever seen is something out of a fairy tale. The photos online don't do it justice.

We make our way to our table, and I look at Asher. A laugh bursts from my lips.

"What's so funny?" he asks.

"This. I mean, it's a far cry from our usual restaurant."

"Hey, don't talk badly about Pizza Sam," Asher says.

Pizza Sam is a place we frequent for its incredible pizza as well as for its location in Queens.

"I would never talk badly about Pizza Sam. It's only the best pizza place in the world. That's right—the world!" I say, and we both chuckle. "But seriously, this is nice. Very nice."

Asher orders us a bottle of wine, and when the server comes back and pours us each a glass, we toast to a good friendship.

We spend the evening dining on world-class food and the finest wine I've had in a long time. No expense is spared, and I wonder what Asher's expense limit is. I don't ask, even though I'm dying to know, because I don't want to discuss work.

I know that the owner of Bauer is from a family legacy in the oil industry. Money isn't an object for them. It never has been.

Not that it's any different for Charles. He might not be an oil tycoon's grandson, but he isn't hurting for money. His father has been uber-successful in the United Kingdom. Then again, I know little about Charles's family. For all I know, he's a billionaire, too.

Charles.

My mind strays from the gorgeous surroundings and back to Charles.

I wonder if he's all packed for Italy.

I never had time to look at his itinerary. I was too busy closing out the week and preparing for tonight with Ash.

I grab my phone to pull it up quickly and flush when I see I have a text message from Charles.

**Charles: I hope you're relaxing.**

**Me: I'm out to dinner with a friend.**

**Charles: You'll have to tell me all about it later. Have fun.**

**Me: Thanks for the text.**

**Charles: I found myself thinking of you.**

"What has you smiling like a loon?" Asher asks.

My head snaps up to him. I stuff my phone back into my bag.

"Sorry about that. It was . . . my mom. She's being her typical self." I lie because I'm not ready to share Charles with anyone. Especially Asher. "She says hello."

He smiles.

"I'm not sure your mom likes me."

I frown, hating that he picked up on my mom's skepticism surrounding him.

"What makes you say that?"

"I don't know," he says. "It's just that she always looks at me like she doesn't trust me."

"She does not."

Another lie, but one to avoid hurting his feelings.

"She's just an overly curious woman. I'm sure you're misreading it."

"Let's hope," he says. "But in the end, as long as you trust me, that's all that matters."

I know he's referring to Summer, and as angry as I was, I said I was over it, and I am.

"I do."

Asher smiles, but it drops quickly, and he suddenly looks nervous.

"What's going on?" I ask.

I have a feeling he's going to bring up the whole situation, which I really don't want to talk about anymore. But he doesn't.

Instead, he clears his throat and looks down at his plate. He can't look me in the eye.

"The thing is, Raven . . . uh . . . I know we're friends. We've been friends for a very long time. And right now, it might not be great timing, considering we just had a fight, but there's something I need to tell you."

No. No. No.

My mom and Lily's warnings ring loud and clear, and my stomach sours. I know without a doubt he's going to tell me he likes me.

I feel panic rising inside me. Everyone was right. My mother was so sure, and I thought she was nuts, yet looking at him now, I know she wasn't.

"Let's enjoy the night and talk about whatever's on your mind after? Can we do that?"

He takes a deep breath, nodding. "That's probably best."

I exhale, closing my eyes while he's distracted. That was close, and I can't have that talk with him. Not now. I need to think through how I'll let him down easily. I need Asher in my life, and this could be the very thing that severs our friendship for good.

It makes me feel sick to my stomach.

I take my sweet time eating and even order dessert, determined to drag this night out and avoid that conversation for as long as possible.

Fully stuffed and a glass of wine on the wrong side of sober, we make our way toward the waiting taxi.

The entire ride home is strained. I watch Asher from the corner of my eye, and I catch him staring at me every time. His hand lands on my knee, and I tense.

It's not like it's the first time he's touched my knee, but now that I think he actually has feelings for me, it feels . . . wrong.

I don't remove it, and when the taxi pulls up to my apartment, I realize that was a mistake.

It's only when I step outside into the shock of cool air that I realize I'm thoroughly drunk. I grab his arm to stabilize myself, and Asher stares down at me in a way that suggests he's misreading my proximity to him.

I flush, a mix of the wine and weather combining, and Asher's eyes darken.

"Raven," he says way too huskily.

Before I can take a step back, he leans in to kiss me. My hand claps across my mouth, effectively halting his advance.

"I'm going to be sick," I say, turning around and running toward my door.

I'm not. It's all an act to get out of this horrible situation. All that innocent flirting has put me in this spot. It's always been our way, but now that potentially real feelings are involved on his end, it has to stop. I'm sending mixed signals, and it's not fair.

I have nobody to blame but myself.

I drank too much and, in turn, sent the wrong signals.

"Raven," he calls to my back. "Can I help?"

I turn around slowly. "I just need to be alone. I don't want you to see me get sick."

He smiles down at me. "Please text me in the morning."

"I will," I promise, opening the door to step in. "I had a good night. Thank you."

"You're welcome."

He leans in and places a chaste kiss on my head. Like he typically does.

Then he's gone, and I truly feel sick.

Inside the comfort of my home, I flop onto the bed and cry.

What have I done?

I grab my phone and call the one person I can tell about this.

"Mom . . . I messed up, again," I start.

"What's wrong, baby girl? Are you okay? Is it work?"

"Yes. No. Oh . . . it's everything."

She sighs. "Start at the beginning."

For the next thirty minutes, I bare my soul to my mom, not leaving out one detail.

There is silence on the other end of the phone, and for the first time ever, I can't bring myself to care what she thinks. I didn't do this on purpose.

"What a mess," she finally says. "I really hoped I was wrong about Asher."

"Me, too," I cry. "I don't like him like that. This is going to ruin everything, and I just got him back."

I burst into tears.

I'm making a mess out of everything these days.

"I should've told him how I feel, but I couldn't break his heart."

"You should have. Asher is your best friend. I don't always think he's a good guy, Raven, but if you are set on making amends, I will support you. He'll eventually come to terms with it."

"You think?"

"Eventually."

That's Mom. She never overpromises or tells you what you want to hear. She's straightforward and blunt at times.

"I should be so lucky that a guy like Asher likes me," I say, sniffling.

"We can't help falling for the people we do, Raven. You can't regret not feeling the same way that he does. In time, he'll find who he's meant to be with."

"I know you're right, but it doesn't stop it from hurting all the same."

"That's a sign that you care. You're a good friend, baby girl. He'll realize that one day."

Hopefully, this doesn't ruin our friendship in the meantime.

Right before I fall asleep, I realize Asher left me alone, knowing I was drunk and thinking I was going to be sick. The man I want to end up with would've played the knight in shining armor and refused to leave me for fear I'd drown in my own ick.

And this is why I'll likely end up single with ten cats.

It's too late to call Asher tonight, but I have to make plans to meet up with him before dinner with Lily to clear things up.

It'll definitely have to be done face-to-face. This means we're in for a very uncomfortable interaction. I try to put it out of my mind and fall asleep, but it's no use. Sleep doesn't come.

# chapter twenty-eight

Raven

NINE O'CLOCK IN THE MORNING IS TOO EARLY TO DEAL WITH Asher.

Thursday night with him has me wanting to avoid him as much as possible.

When I get to the office, I settle myself in front of the computer and start working. An hour into the workday, everything is derailed by one simple message from Asher.

**Asher: I had such a great time with you.**

**Asher: I hope you're feeling better. xxx**

God, I really fucked things up. I don't see him that way, and I know I never will. Now, I've not only led him on, but poor Lily, who is clearly in love with him, is bound to find out. And right around her birthday week to boot.

**Me: Great night. Feeling better.**

**Me: Let's meet soon.**

**Me: I have some things I need to talk to you about.**

**Me: Got to get back to work, but maybe tonight?**

I don't put any x's at the end of my message, and I hope that he can tell by my tone that I'm not trying to flirt with him. My head is throbbing, and it's going to be hard to concentrate. As I attach my phone to the charger, it starts ringing with Charles's name on the screen.

"Hey, aren't you supposed to be on a plane, or is it one of those fancy kinds you can make a call from?"

"Supposed to be is the operative phrase. I need you to get yourself to the hangar address I just texted you. You are coming to Italy with me."

"Wait. What? What do you mean I need to get to the hangar? I thought you had this all under control?"

"Had. I *had* it under control until Holly arrived and puked all over me."

"What?" I hold back a laugh, but barely. He sounds so mad, yet the idea of him covered in goo is too good not to laugh.

"Hardy har. Laugh it up. Holly has a sickness bug or food poisoning. Pax is getting her picked up and checked out. But we already have the plane and hotels booked at the three locations. Now, are you meeting me at the hangar, or do I need to ring Shelby for a free trip to Italy?"

"All right. All right. I'll get to the airport, but I need to go home and pack."

"There are shops in Italy. Just get here. We don't have all day to hold the plane."

Forty minutes later, I pull myself out of the taxi with my computer bag and now-overstuffed purse after raiding the market across the street from the office. I'm not traveling anywhere without a toothbrush and my preferred toothpaste.

And deodorant.

"About bloody time." Charles gives me one of his smirks, letting me know he's teasing.

"I'm only brilliant with marketing plans. Last-minute travel has never been my go-to. You are lucky I have a current passport and carry it with me."

Bending down, he gives me a soft kiss on the cheek. "I shouldn't say it, but I'm very glad Holly got poorly. Now I have you all to myself in Italy."

"Hey, we're supposed to be working. We have a lot to accomplish in a week. Milan, Venice, and Rome are all going to take time to navigate to and around."

"Knowing Shelby, she has that all worked out to within a five-minute window. But the nights are for relaxing," he almost coos to me as we board the plane. "Now, how do you feel about the mile-high club?"

"I don't fly well. I'm sleeping on the plane, and you shouldn't even think of touching me. It may be the second time someone retches on you in one day."

"Fine. I'd rather not change clothes again, thank you very much. I have some calls to make and work to do on another client opportunity. You rest, and we'll be there before you know it."

# chapter twenty-nine

Charles

W E ARRIVE IN MILAN AND HEAD STRAIGHT FOR THE HOTEL. Once settled in my room, I allow my lips to part into a smile.

As always, Shelby did an amazing job in picking out the hotel.

The location is sublime. It's right off the piazza, facing Il Duomo. It will be perfect for what we have in mind for the shoot.

Milan is the focal point of the Diosa luxury segment. Lake Como and Rome for the athletic line and Venice for Icon's consumers.

Raven's insight is refreshing. She created a sharp look to tie the three brands together, yet each still has a distinct feel.

Pride swells inside me at the hard work she's done, pride and another feeling I don't want.

A feeling that I no longer thought I was capable of.

I care about her. And not as her boss.

How is it possible that in such a short time, she has made me want to break all my rules? This slip of a woman jump-started my heart.

*Stop.*

*There will be none of that.*

No way in hell will I be made a fool of again.

Not after the last time. *Not after Tabitha.*

I'm still living with the mess that tramp made.

Even now, I'm picking up the pieces of the shit storm she's created in London. No. I can't allow myself to let Raven in.

*Too fucking late.*

Despite my attempt to distance myself emotionally from her, to keep my walls up, I still wonder what she's doing.

*I ache to see her.* To bask in her *light.*

Things are darker when she's not around. I head to the door when I hear a light knock. Opening it, my breath catches in my lungs. She's magnificent.

"Rae." That's all I can muster. Her beauty has left me speechless.

She smiles, a soft one that is almost shy, before looking down. "Thank you for the clothes. How did you know my size?"

"I have my ways."

"British and a spy . . ."

"Don't even go there," I laugh out, well aware she's about to make a Bond joke. "Let's just go to dinner." Raven rolls her eyes, and I smile.

Taking her hand, we travel down the lift to the main lobby and out into the piazza. "Up for a short stroll?"

"Sure. What did you have in mind?"

"I know of a divine restaurant. I think you will love it."

"Lead the way," she says, and together, hand in hand, we make the short walk to Ristorante Savini.

Raven's footsteps stop, and I look over at her to see her shake her head. "Charles, I am not dressed for this place. It's way too fancy." She touches the floral cotton dress I purchased for her.

"There's no dress code. And if there were, you'd still be fine."

She nibbles her bottom lip, and when she does, the desire I'm barely able to tamp down whenever I'm in her presence is back.

"Rae, you have no idea what you do to me, do you? Let's go eat so we can get on with other things."

"What kind of other things, Mr. Cavendish? I thought the evenings were for rest and relaxation," she coos playfully.

"Oh, they are. All in due time, sunshine."

As we sip our wine after our extravagantly delicious meal, I can't help but want to know more about this alluring woman across from me.

"Why Columbia for your MBA?" I ask, and the change of topic has her eyes going wide, but she's quick to recover.

"You mean besides the 96 percent graduation rate and a 94 percent placement rate? Well, it came down to location. I always wanted to live in New York, and I knew my mom loved it there." Her gaze meets mine. "My mom moved to New York to be with me," she clarifies.

"You are close with your mum?"

She nods. "Yeah, we've been each other's rock the last five years." She worries her lip as a somber look washes over her features.

"Is this because of your dad's passing? You've spoken of it before." For all the time I've known her, worked closely with her, she's barely spoken of him, let alone her family. "When did he . . ." my words trail off, my own emotions of losing my mum making my throat feel dry.

"Seems like yesterday"—she inhales— "but in reality, it was a long time ago. He got sick my freshman year of college."

"You can talk to me."

"I know. It's hard, though, no matter how much time has passed."

Leaning forward, I place my elbows on the table. As painful as it is for her to tell this story and for me to hear it, I want to know everything about her. Everything that has made her the woman she is today.

"My freshman year wasn't how I expected it to go. Dad was tired all the time, but we thought nothing of it. Then he complained of pain, reoccurring pain in his back. Nothing made it better. Then the weight loss started. That's when we got scared. Once the jaundice showed up . . ." Her hand lifts and wipes away a stray tear that has trailed down her cheek. "By then . . . well, by then we were too late. The doctors diagnosed him with pancreatic cancer."

Fresh tears well in her eyes. I reach my hand out to take hers. I need to feel her.

Comfort her.

Comfort myself, too.

She doesn't know what the account of her father's illness is doing to me right now. The feelings that are rising to the surface as she speaks.

There's a connection between us.

Raven knows what it means to lose a parent. She knows the loss that drives me. The loss that eats at my soul.

"I'm so sorry."

"Thank you. It was devastating to see it all happen so quickly. Trying to go to school. Trying to take care of Dad as he started palliative care. Then taking care of Mom when he went to hospice. She couldn't do everything for him, and that seemed to bother her the most. They were special, my mom and dad. Always two peas in a pod. Her heart shattered when he passed. I'm glad I got to see them in love, though. Even at the end. That was a precious treat."

I almost can't breathe as I grasp Raven's hand tighter.

When the feel of her hand isn't enough, I pull her chair just a little closer. I need to feel her warmth. In the middle of all that loss, she found something a 'precious treat.'

She's astonishing.

My free arm reaches out, and my finger swipes away at the tear running down her cheek. Our gazes lock, and a silent moment passes between us.

"What about you, Charles?" she breaks the silence. "What's the real story with you and your dad?"

"Ha. That bastard." A hollow and bitter laugh escapes my mouth.

"Please talk to me."

"It wasn't always strained, the relationship between my father and I," I tell her.

"You had a happier childhood, too?"

"It wasn't atrocious. I think Father worked too much, and that put a strain on Mum." I try to pull back my hand from hers, but she's not having it. Instead, she looks me in the eye and then curls her fingers around mine tighter. "But that's another story. I don't want to talk about *him*."

"Tell me about your mother, then. After they divorced, what does she do now?"

"There was no divorce. Like your father, she also passed away."

# chapter thirty

Raven

STUNNED SILENCE AT HIS WORDS.

I didn't know she passed away . . . wait, *did I?*

No.

I would have understood him better if I had, and now, like a missing piece of the puzzle being found, I feel like I can finally understand Charles better.

This affinity we have for each other goes deeper than just chemistry. Deeper than lust. Deeper than attraction.

Somehow, it makes sense, though.

"If you don't mind me asking, how did she pass?"

"Cancer. Not pancreatic. She had breast cancer. Went undiagnosed for entirely too long. By the time she was in with the doctors, a treatment plan was no longer an option."

"Charles—" I say, but he shakes his head. The look he gives me is full of sorrow, but also, it's a silent request not to take pity on him. Not to feel sorry, which I understand. "I'm so sorry you have had to endure this kind of loss."

"Thanks. When I came to New York and got settled in, I promised myself I would do something good with the company profits. Hence the fundraiser. It will be at my family home in the Hamptons."

"Hamptons, huh?" I say, trying to focus on a line of conversation to help ease the somber mood that has settled in the air. "I didn't know it was there."

Charles lifts an eyebrow. "Were you distracted, Miss Bennett?"

"Maybe a little."

"Why ever would you be distracted in one of my meetings?" He gives me a wicked look. The moment for sharing has passed, and now the usual heat I feel when Charles is around is back with a vengeance. "I want to kiss you right now."

"What's the problem with that, Mr. Cavendish?" I draw out, my voice low and seductive.

"Oh, Miss Bennett, if I start . . . I'm not stopping."

Pulling my gaze from Charles, I find our waiter and raise my hand to motion him over. "Can we please have the check?" I ask when he's close enough to hear.

"Good choice." Charles smirks.

*God, that smirk.*

But it's the laugh that follows that does me in. After opening up about our shared loss, for him . . . it means everything.

"You don't laugh like that in the office. Why not? I feel I could make it my ringtone. Actually, it'd be perfect, too, if you'd speak as my ringtone," I chide playfully.

"Is that how it is Raven? You only like me for my accent?"

"There are a few other reasons I enjoy your company."

His pupils dilate. "Should we go back to the hotel and quantify those reasons?"

"Quantify. For science. Sounds like a plan. Let's go." I stand and immediately, I'm pulled into his arms.

Tipping my chin up, I look at him. His gaze sparkles with mischief. A look of lust, longing, and want. But I also see something else, something I didn't see two hours ago.

*Understanding.*

He knows my heart now, and I know his.

The question is, what will we do with that knowledge?

# chapter thirty-one

Charles

Back in the hotel, I don't bother with pleasantries. Instead, I whisk Raven straight to my room.

No words are spoken as I open the door, pull her into the suite, and lead her through the master bedroom to the bed.

"This is forward, sir." Her arse hits the mattress.

"I think we're well past formalities, love. Unless, of course, you insist I woo you first."

She giggles, and it is possibly one of the sweetest sounds I've ever heard.

I'm happy when she's happy.

It's a feeling I haven't felt in a long time.

I like it.

"I want to do this right," I admit to her. We are both sitting on the bed, fully clothed, holding hands, fingers entwined.

"Nope. This works," she says.

I lean in and kiss her, pulling her closer to me. She feels good in my arms.

"Rae. You are so beautiful." I reach over to unbutton her shirt. "But you'd look even lovelier without this on."

She chuckles. "Why do you insist on always calling me Rae?"

"Why do you insist on asking me that every time?" I retort.

She gets quiet for a moment, and I tip her chin up with my finger. "What's wrong?"

"Nothing. It's just . . . only my dad has ever called me that."

The pitch of her voice sears my soul.

We're kindred spirits.

Both feeling too much.

Joy.

Sadness.

Anger.

Does my calling her *Rae* make her angry? "Now I understand. Would you prefer I not call you that?" I hope not because I'm quite partial to the nickname.

"Would you actually listen?"

I squeeze her hand in mine. "Of course, I would. Had I known before, I would've stopped."

That makes her shake her head. "No. I don't want you to. I like that *you* call me Rae."

"Good. Because I don't want to stop."

"Why?"

"Because you are my Rae." I shrug. As if she should understand what I mean. She furrows her brow, clearly confused. Separating our hands, I cup her cheek. "Because, dear Rae, you are my *ray* of sunshine."

Abruptly, she stands, and I'm at a loss for why, until she pulls the dress over her head. Her knickers and bra are next, leaving her completely bare in front of me.

"No distractions?" she purrs.

I'm immobilized, staring at every square inch of her.

"None," I promise, swallowing. I lay her back, marveling at how beautiful she looks spread out on my bed, but the look of hunger I see in her eyes has me jumping to action.

My clothes are discarded, and I hover over her, wanting to take my time with her.

"Please," she begs, and I waste no time lining my cock up with her core.

In one abrupt move, I push into her. A groan escapes.

Gazes locked, I give her a second to adjust, and once she exhales a small breath, I then slide in the rest of the way.

Her muscles clamp around me.

She's so tight.

So wet.

Too perfect.

I push in at a steady pace, and she meets my thrusts every time. We're creating a symphony with our bodies.

"Raven," I groan, thrusting harder. Deeper.

Her fingers dig into my arms, and it only undoes me. I'm a possessed man, slamming my cock so deep inside her, I don't know where I end and she begins.

I slam into her without mercy, and she continues to beg for more. I know it won't be long.

A primal moan escapes her lips as she tips over the edge.

Something like a growl bursts through my chest as she contracts around me. Thrusting a few more times, I pour into her, coming harder than I ever have before.

Afterward, we lie side by side, and I turn to face her.

She smiles up at me and yawns. "Sleep. We have all the time in the world."

---

Days have passed, and things are now different between Raven and I. We have unlocked something precious, but we aren't naming it. Aren't calling it out. Not standing on ceremony, needing to claim a relationship status.

A hollow feeling weighs in my gut.

*Wasn't that what you wanted?*

Yes. That's what I wanted. To not put labels on things.

*But clear definitions can be nice.*

Despite that need for labels niggling through my mind, I try to keep focused on work.

We have accomplished a lot.

We went up to Lake Como and captured pictures on a boat while cruising around. The sportswear images ended up perfect.

Then we traveled through the ancient streets of Venice, finding lots of shops with colorful windows. The perfect backdrop to promote the ICON line.

We've become inseparable and insatiable.

To the point I don't want to see the trip end.

Now in Rome and done with the Diosa shoot, I had hoped that we could spend a bit of time sightseeing together, enjoying the city, but unfortunately, my father's legal team has rang. I have to head to London. Raven will return to New York alone.

I don't like the idea of separating from her. I feel lost knowing that tomorrow we'll no longer be together.

A heavy feeling weighs on my chest.

When Raven is around, she's the light.

As if summoned by my thoughts, I hear a knock on my door. I know it's her. Opening the door, I pull her inside and then shut the door behind her.

Still in the foyer, I don't even say hello; instead, I kiss her soft lips.

"Charles," she breathes in between licks and nips.

"Yes, Rae?"

"You don't want dinner?" She pulls her mouth from mine, and I groan at the loss.

"Not tonight. I've got room service on the way later. I want you all to myself one last time."

"Last . . ."

"Well, for a night or two at most."

"Oh, yeah. Of course. You need time alone when you get back to the city. I get that."

I place a finger on her lips, stopping her rush of words. "Rae. It's not that, love. I have to go to London in the morning. It just makes more sense to send you home."

"Oh. Oh. Okay." She nods. "You don't want me with you in London," she whispers, and the tone of her voice feels like a knife in my chest.

Cupping her cheeks in my hands, I smile down at her. "I want you in London with me. I'd love to show you around my hometown. But we have work to do to finish this campaign. I need you back in New York, but tonight, I need you here. With me. I need to fuck you."

"Okay."

Slowly, I back away and move us toward the bedroom suite. I stand her next to the footboard of the massive mahogany frame.

"Turn around. Let me help with this zipper."

She gasps as my warm fingers touch her skin, then I remove her dress, slowly.

I work the thin material off her body until she's left in just her knickers and lace corset.

*She's a goddess.*

Sliding the lace off her, I lean in to where I know she's desperate for me, and swipe my tongue against her skin. "You taste intoxicating. I cannot get enough of you."

"Charles." My name on her lips sets me ablaze.

I need her.

Her intelligence. Strength. Humor.

I need each piece of her. I tell her that with my ministrations. Making her squirm and push until I break her control. Raven falls apart as she comes on my mouth with unbridled restraint.

Once she comes down from her high, she unties her corset and gets on the bed. Without any more delay, I remove my clothes, move onto the bed, and cover her with my body.

Raven reaches up and touches my cheek. The caress breaks

down any of the last barriers I may have had left. A feeling I've never felt weaves its way through me.

What is this?

*I won't say it.*

I will not say those words out loud.

It's too soon. It's not right.

But God, it feels so right when I slide into her warmth.

Complete.

We are fated.

I was meant to be in that cloakroom.

# chapter thirty-two

Raven

MY FINGERS HIT THE KEYBOARD AS I SET ABOUT OPENING MY morning emails.

Things will be busy today with Charles stopping in London on his way back from Italy, so I need to get to work.

With a quick glance, I see I have over a hundred emails waiting for my response. My head shakes, and then I look at my half-empty mug of coffee. I'm going to need a refill pretty soon if I'm going to read through all of these.

I'm about to take the last few sips when I hear a commotion coming from the elevator. A few seconds later, Keller places a gorgeous bouquet on my desk. The look on his face as he places it down can only be described as murderous.

"I'm not your assistant," he hisses.

Reaching for the flowers, I pull out the card.

The card simply reads: *I missed you, but I will see you soon.*

Now I'm even more confused . . .

Who will see me soon?

I was supposed to see Asher, but he wouldn't send me this, would he?

I hear the sound of a cough, and I see that Keller's brows pinch together as he studies me.

"Who are they from?" he asks, his voice tight.

"No clue." I shrug.

"You must have a clue?" he presses. I shake my head. I'm about to say something when I hear people talking.

Keller huffs and storms off, and I'm confused by why, but then, as if the waters part, I see Charles and I know longer care about what crawled up Keller's ass.

My breath catches at the sight of Charles walking down the hall. His gray suit hugs him just right, and my mouth waters.

I stand and head to intercept him before he walks into his office. When I'm standing right beside him, I lean in and whisper, "What are you doing here? You're supposed to be in London."

"Change of plans. We have work we need to do."

I lick my bottom lip, having a hard time focusing on his words, as my eyes trail down his torso, raking him in.

"That was fast," I say, lamely.

"I can be when I choose to be."

There's so much innuendo in those words that I'm having a hard time not blushing.

He looks ever so briefly at the flowers and then at me.

I'm fighting the urge to run to him and pull him in to my arms. This thing between us is turning into an inferno, and I don't want to put it out.

I need more time with him.

He shrugs, tipping his chin up. "Nice flowers. Was there a signature?" He smirks and walks off, leaving me wanting.

Was there a signature?

I pick up the note and reread it.

*I missed you, but I will see you soon.*

No signature.

He'd told me he wouldn't sign his name so people in the office wouldn't know the last set of flowers were from him.

That smirk . . . Oh, my God. Every time he has that heated look. *It's too much.*

The flowers are *not* from Asher. They're from Charles. *I missed you.*

He missed me, and that does crazy things to me. My stomach tingles, and my whole body feels light.

I don't know what to do. Or how to respond. For a while, I just sit here, staring at the pink roses, smelling their sweetness.

I missed him, too, and it's killing me that I can't go to him and show him just how much.

I sigh, moving the flowers to the corner of my desk, and head toward Charles's office. We might not be able to have a proper reunion, but I want him to know the gesture is appreciated and that I feel the same way.

I know we said we wouldn't mess around at the office, but a kiss won't hurt. Right?

It's lunchtime, and Shelby is surely away from her desk.

It's now or never.

Charles's door is open when I arrive, and I walk right in, closing the door behind me, beckoning for him to come to me.

He grins, standing from his desk and making his way toward me.

"What's this about?"

I grab his collar and pull him into me, pressing my lips against his. When my tongue pushes past his lips, tangling with his, a groan makes its way up his throat.

We're tangled in each other for several minutes before he breaks the kiss, placing his mouth on my neck and running his lips up the curve of my neck to the shell of my ear.

"Raven, you are delicious," Charles murmurs. "I want you. Now," he growls.

I chuckle, pushing him back lightly.

"I only wanted to thank you."

He pulls back, smiling down at me. "That was some kiss, love," he croons.

He's smiling so wide, and part of me wants to throw caution to the wind and beg him to have his way with me right here.

"I love them, but you should probably stop doing that."

"No."

"No?" I say, repeating his words.

"I'm not going to stop. I like sending you flowers."

I smile. "Hydrangeas are my favorite, but the pink roses are a very close second."

"So bigger is better?" he teases.

"It has nothing to do with the size of the arrangement. Hydrangeas remind me of home. Where I lived with my parents before Dad died."

Charles doesn't say anything for a while. He just stands there, watching me.

"Will you tell me more about him?"

I breathe a sigh of relief. "One day soon, I'll tell you all about him. But right now, I'll keep up the mystery."

"I'd like to know all your secrets."

"I bet you would. What about you, mister? Do you have skeletons in your closet?"

"That is definitely a conversation for another time." He sighs. "Can we pretend it's just us? Maybe have a go again on my desk?"

I grin. "No chance. We've been in here alone for too long as it is. This office has ears, according to Shelby."

His eyes widen. "This I must hear."

I might be messing around with Charles, but I'm not about to narc on Shelby. She's been too good to me, and she seems to be good for him, too. Cavendish Group needs her.

"That's all she said. Not sure what she meant by that." I look into his blue eyes and say the first thing that comes to me. "I missed you, too."

He smiles. "I believe a proper hello is in order, Rae."

"I thought that's what just happened." I motion back and forth between us, and he grins.

"I have more in mind, love. More like Italy. Things that can't happen here."

I blink, thinking about all the things he could be talking about, and heat crawls up my neck.

"Have dinner with me tonight?" he says, and the reply is almost immediate.

"I'm hungry." I shrug as though it's no big thing. "I could eat."

He smirks. "I'm paying."

"Of course, you're paying. You asked first. That's how the rule works." I wink to show I'm only teasing.

I don't need him to pay. It's not about that.

"Will we be leaving straight from here?" I ask, quickly looking down to survey what I chose to wear today.

"If that's all right?"

"Fine by me. I'll head back to my office and finish up my stuff." I turn to open the door, and he pulls me in for a searing kiss.

"I'll swing by your office around five."

"Perfect."

---

The rest of the day flies by, and before long, Charles and I are seated at a table in an exclusive club for the New York elite.

I've heard of Zero Bond and always wondered what it would be like, and now I'm here. With Charles. It's surreal.

I take a sip of my cosmopolitan, recognizing that the top shelf really does make a difference.

"The high resolution prints of the Italy photographs came in. The backdrops turned out stunning. I'm in awe of your skills."

He smirks. "My skills are quite legendary. I aim to satisfy, love."

"*Love,* is it?" a voice full of sugar and venom says.

I don't miss how Charles stiffens, face darkening to something sinister.

My head pops up to see a beautiful woman dressed to the nines in a red Gucci dress from this season. It's ostentatious and obscenely expensive.

Who is she? And why is she looking at Charles like she is very well-acquainted with every piece of him?

I already hate her.

# chapter thirty-three

Charles

"Tabitha," I whisper, not wanting to summon the demon if this is some twisted nightmare.

"Charles," she coos. "Imagine running into you here. I had no idea this was your locale of choice these days."

Bloody cow. She knows damn well where I frequent, and it's no coincidence that she's here.

"Tabitha, you and I both know that is utter bullshit. You're a bloody stalker."

She throws her head back and laughs like a maniacal villain. "You're always so dramatic, darling."

She speaks loud enough that everyone in the vicinity has turned to stare.

"Tabitha, keep your voice down." I turn to Raven. "Do you mind if I talk to Tabitha alone?"

"Of course not," she says, but her narrowed gaze and stiff posture tell me she'll have many questions when we're alone.

I want to strangle the bitch. It's not enough that she played me for an utter fool, but she has to continue to cause problems.

Tabitha walks out the front door, allowing it to slam in my face.

I've never so much as raised a hand to a woman, and I'm not about to start now, but Tabitha Murphy could tempt God.

"I see you've downgraded. What a joke you've turned into," Tabitha hisses.

I look at her and wonder, not for the first time, what on earth I had seen in her.

Her tits are practically falling out of her plunging neckline, and every single thing about her screams fake.

She'd been arm candy, something I hate to admit. There is simply no point denying that I'd slept with her because of it and stuck around because she was a convenience.

"I didn't. Not even close," I grit through my teeth. "And before you say anything more, I want you to hear me out. You need to leave this city and never return."

She throws her head back and cackles. "Oh, Charles. You are a delight. I forgot how funny you were."

"I'm not playing around, Tabitha. You're not welcome here."

"In New York City?" She motions around. "You're nobody here, Charles. You don't make the rules."

"I can make your life miserable, and you bloody well know it."

"Why don't you save us both the time and stop thinking you have any power over me. I moved up in the world while you slunk away to the ghetto to mend your broken heart."

I take a threatening step forward, and she shrinks under the weight of my glare.

"Go the fuck home," I growl.

She pouts her lips. "Why? So you can go on screwing the help?"

"Excuse me? Just how the fuck do you know anything about her?"

"You are a man, Charles. You're predictable. I expect you to do the same all over again. You work too much to find someone out of the office. You never did know how to have fun."

"Guess what, Tabitha. Not everyone is a cunt like you. Things are different with Raven. She hasn't gotten to where she is by spreading her legs for every dick with a wallet."

"Why you—" She leaps forward, and I catch her by the arms, holding her in place.

"Watch it, *Tabby*. Put those claws of yours away," I spit the name with hatred.

"Are you saying she's your fucking girlfriend?"

She jerks her hands out of my grasp and straightens her dress. And then like the unstable person she is, she suddenly turns her face into a demure look as she says, "I can't believe you, of all people, are breaking company rules. Kissing your employees . . . tsk, tsk."

"I kissed you in the office, Tabitha. And in case you forgot, you were *my* assistant, and I was your fiancé."

Completely ignoring me, she picks at her fingers and continues her chattering. "I feel like someone should know about what is going on."

"Who are you going to tell? I think you're forgetting New York is my company."

"I'm going to tell anyone that cares to listen. You might not be affected, but she will. The tabloids will love this news. Especially considering how private you've been since arriving in the states."

"You won't."

"Won't I? And why not? Do you have a better offer for me?"

"Because I'll ruin you. I'll drag you through court for decades."

"Do your worst." She gives me a coy smile.

"I will ruin you. Stuart will love to help me take you down."

Her eyes widen at the mention of my father's attorney.

"You've been speaking to Stuart, have you? Well, two can play this game, Charles. I wanted to reconcile, and you just want a war? Fine. I'll give you one."

"You don't have a chance."

She doesn't say another word, slamming her shoulder into mine as she passes, heading back into Zero Bond.

I stand in the warm June air, wondering how I'm going to explain Tabitha to Raven.

What a fucking mess.

The walk back to the table is tense as I try to decide what I'm willing to share with Raven.

That week in Italy meant something to me. We aren't defining things, but I really do like her. I want to protect her. Enough to want to shield her from Tabitha's wrath. Enough to want to see where this thing goes.

"Are you all right?" she asks, appearing concerned.

There's no anger present on her delicate features, and it's such a contrast to the girls I dated earlier in life.

My ray of sunshine, even after a less-than-friendly run-in with a crazy cow.

"Fine, love. Did you decide what you'd like to eat?"

She gnashes her lips together but doesn't press, looking back at the menu with furrowed brows.

"Everything looks delicious."

"Then everything you shall have." I smile, but she doesn't return it.

She sets down her menu and looks directly into my eyes, momentarily paralyzing me.

"You know I don't need you to do elaborate things for me, right? That's not why I'm here with you."

My lip twitches. "I know, and that's likely why *I'm* here with *you*." I sigh, grabbing her hands across the small table. "I've told you I haven't done relationships. That includes taking women to dinner or buying them flowers. I haven't done those things for anyone in a very long time."

"Why me?" she asks, her voice small and full of doubt. As if the very idea of me being here with her was some cosmic joke, and she was about to learn of it.

"I'm not certain. I just know you're a bright light in a rather gloomy room."

"There you go with the poetry."

I smirk. "It's the God's honest truth. I adore spending time with you."

She smiles. "Me, too."

By some act of God, Raven doesn't ask about Tabitha, and I'm more than happy to avoid it.

"Will you tell me about your family?" I ask, recognizing the double standard.

She doesn't seem to care, though, and that warms my heart even further.

Her face lights up as she tells me all about her mother. It's easy to see they're very close.

I listen with rapt attention, soaking up her positivity and general goodness.

She's so different from Tabitha. Different from anyone I've ever met. She's an old soul trapped in a twentysomething body.

"I should have asked this so many times before, but how old are you, Raven?"

"Twenty-six. I'll be twenty-seven in September."

"Twenty-six feels like a lifetime ago for me. Today, at thirty-three, I feel like you have your shit together more than I do."

She has her own place, a well-paying job, and is comfortable in her skin.

I have the money, the place, and the prestige, but I don't always like who I see in the mirror.

A man who runs when times get tough.

A man who consistently runs away from any sort of affection.

*Not a man at all.*

A boy, crying internally for the life he was robbed of by the people he loved most.

I'm not good enough for the treasure sitting across from me.

# chapter thirty-four

Raven

"I'M SO EXCITED FOR ALL OF YOU TO FINALLY BE MEETING," I say, looking out at our Diosa team. "Reagan, can you stand and tell everyone a little bit about yourself and what your position here will entail?"

Reagan stands, smiling at the two women who aren't hiding how they ogle him. "I'm Reagan Miller, former NFL linebacker. I'm married to a beautiful and successful woman. We have two children; Addy is three, and Carl is two."

I can practically taste the unshed tears of my two newest team members as they learn that Reagan is, in fact, married. And to a model, no less.

"I'll be assisting Raven in managing the AlteredX account. I feel my years in athletics will help with the athletic brand."

He takes a seat. "Thanks, Raegan. Pricilla, you're up."

The dark-haired, five-feet-two-inch beauty stands, offering a small wave to the room. "I'm Pricilla, and I'm happily single with zero children. I went to school at NYU and can't wait to travel the world one day," she says, looking at something in the distance with a dreamy look on her face.

I turn to find that Charles has graced us with his presence, thus the cause of the dreamy look. Late, but at least he's here.

"I'm assisting with the Icon line. I'm a fashionista with over one million Instagram and TikTok followers, so I have a lot to bring to the team."

She plops herself down in her chair, and I motion for Carmen to take her turn.

"Hey. I'm Carmen, and I'll be assisting Raven with the Diosa luxury brand. I'm a former Victoria's Secret model and *Playboy* centerfold." She winks at Reagan, and I internally groan.

I'm sure HR is going to have a field day with this if Reagan says anything.

I make a note in my notepad to speak with the girls individually and to loop in HR on the rules of the office, specifically pertaining to sexual harassment and relationships with colleagues.

I am such a hypocrite.

Walking around the room, I pass out the folders with the pictures that Charles took in Italy and the mock-up for copy and placement.

"Look this over with a fine-tooth comb. You're each responsible for your own brand, but I'd appreciate you looking at them all. In the event of an emergency, you'll need to be ready to jump in on any campaign for any of the Diosa lines."

They all murmur their understanding while flipping through.

"I'll need any changes or suggestions by two o'clock on Friday. Any questions?"

All three of them have their eyes on the mock-ups, eagerly browsing through already. The various expressions of awe and excitement give me relief. These three are perfect for this job, and I can't wait to see what they bring to the table.

"Okay, if nobody has any questions, you're free to head back to your workstations."

They all pile out, and my eyes scan the room for Charles, but he's gone.

I wonder why he didn't offer any words of welcome. I've thought about Charles all day. I miss him. Not that I could've said that with a room full of people.

I can't stop thinking about being in his arms again, and it's a serious workplace hazard.

With just half an hour to go until the end of the day, I decide to send him an email and take a chance.

*Dear Mr. Cavendish,*
*I have a few things that I need to discuss with you regarding the Diosa project. I'm working on the next phase and could use your eye. Are you free this afternoon to discuss this?*
*Raven.*

The reply is immediate.

*Hello Raven,*
*Yes, this afternoon suits me. I'm working late tonight, so come in whenever you are free.*
*Sincerely,*
*Mr. Cavendish*

I smirk, knowing it probably pained him to write that signature. I'm giddy at being able to spend some time alone with him. We'll be at the office, so we can't do anything, per my own rules, but at least we can talk and simply be in each other's presence.

I wait until every person has left the building. Then I make my way over to Charles's office.

"Mr. Cavendish, sir. I'm here for our meeting," I say, grinning.

He laughs. "Come in, shut the door, and lock it."

I do as instructed, and two hands grab me by the waist and spin me around. We're chest to chest.

"What is this really about?" he asks.

"What do you mean?" I say innocently, batting my eyelashes.

"Well, you waited until everyone had left the building . . ."

"They have?" I say, feigning ignorance. "Wow, it's later than I thought. I hope you don't mind me taking up your time?"

"You're playing games, Miss Bennett." He grins down at me. "I approve."

I lean up on my toes and place a kiss on his mouth. He immediately pulls me tightly against his chest and kisses me with fervor. I feel his impressive length harden, and my core clenches with need, but I force myself to pull away from him.

"No more of that," I whisper. "We're at the office." I bite my bottom lip.

"You are such a tease," he quips, moving a piece of hair behind my ear.

I laugh. "And you're not?"

"I'm a lot of things, love. But a tease?" He scoffs. "I think not."

"Then what would you call yourself, Mr. Cavendish?"

His lips purse, and his eyes narrow in on me. "First of all, I thought we established that behind closed doors, I'm Charles."

He runs his hand through my hair, and I lean into his touch.

"Hmm," I say dreamily. "Charles." His name rolls off my tongue, and his eyes darken. "What else?"

"Aside from that?" He jabs his tongue into his cheek. "A desperate man."

"Desperate," I faux gasp. "Surely, you're not desperate for a woman."

"Yes. I am," he says in the most serious tone I've heard in a while. "The truth is that I've never met anyone I've connected with on more than a sexual level. You're the only woman who has ever challenged me. That makes me desperate for you."

"That sounds horrible." I place my hand on his cheek.

He frowns. "I'd like to know where you stand on all of this. You do not seem as distressed as I am."

My teeth grip my bottom lip as I squint one eye in concentration. "Our current location makes it difficult for sure."

"That was your rule," he growls.

I tip my head to the side, eyes roaming his body with hunger. "I might just give in."

"Is that right?" His eyes brighten. "What do I need to do, love? Tell me, and it's yours."

I can feel my heart rate increase. "Hmm. Let me think about that," I tease.

Charles smiles and I walk to his side of the desk, motioning for him to join me. When he's seated, I sit on his lap and look at him.

"Raven," he warns. "I'll respect your wishes, but if you continue to toy with me, I can't be held responsible if I snap."

"A little snapping never hurt anyone."

I throw my arms around his neck, crashing my lips to his. I moan at the feel of his tongue against mine. His hand caresses my breasts through my blouse, and I'm aching for more. He never pushes things further, respecting my decision.

I'm not sure whether to scream or beg, but I'm about to do both.

He pulls away just for a moment. "I know what you want, but not here, love."

I groan, knowing I've taken this game further than I should've. We're in the office, and I haven't changed my mind about messing around here where anyone could catch us. It's just that I lose my mind when he's this close.

"You're right. We can't, but it's not that I don't want to."

His head falls back on his shoulders as he blows out a harsh breath. "But it's the office, and we should keep this private."

"I'm sorry. I shouldn't have—"

He waves off my next words. "Please don't apologize. I was in it with you."

"I wish we didn't have to hide this."

"Me, too," he says.

"I don't want people in the office to think I got this job because of it."

"I understand. And I agree with you."

My mind drifts to unpleasant possibilities, and as much as I don't want to darken the mood, I think it's past time we discuss what happens if things go south.

"Charles, if things don't work out, we need to agree to end it on mutual terms. We both need to promise we won't let it affect our work relationship."

"Of course, but that is not something I want to think about now," he says and grins at me. "Just let me kiss you."

"We said not in the office."

"How about not in the office after today?"

"Only if you promise to take me to my favorite place for something sweet. You know I can't resist a good snack."

"Anything you want, love. But you're my favorite dessert."

He dives back in and kisses me gently, alternating between sucking on and nipping my bottom lip. I'm so keyed up I can hardly stand it. I rub against his leg, chasing an orgasm that's just out of reach.

His hand moves below my shirt, pulling down my bra and kneading my breasts. He pinches a nipple between his fingers. I cry out, and he smothers it with a kiss.

I continue to ride his leg unabashedly as his hands move over me, causing a riot of sensation.

"Will you come for me, Raven?" he says, lifting my shirt and taking one nipple into his mouth.

My head falls back on a moan as my orgasm builds.

I'm rocking against him so hard that it's only a matter of time before I shatter, coming all over his expensive pants.

In one motion, he lifts me into his arms and places me on the edge of his desk, lifting my skirt and pulling my panties down my legs. His hand lands at my center and rubs feverishly before he inserts one and then two fingers. I fall back onto my elbows, watching as his fingers pump in and out, pulling my orgasm closer.

One pump.

Two pumps.

I fall apart.

"Charles," I whimper, continuing to rock back and forth, riding out my pleasure against his hand.

He pulls me flush against him, and I practically sag into his arms.

I'm sated and thoroughly exhausted.

"That was . . ."

"A new experience," he says.

I look up into his eyes. "Yes."

Embarrassment should set in at any moment. I rode his leg right here in his office like a horny teenager.

But embarrassment never comes.

Because Charles makes me feel safe.

# chapter thirty-five

Raven

"HAPPY BIRTHDAY, DEAR LILY. HAPPY BIRTHDAY TO YOU."
We bellow the birthday song at the top of our lungs,
drawing every other person in the place into our shenanigans.

After we finished dinner at the restaurant in Little Italy, we
headed back toward our neck of the woods to a karaoke bar around
the corner from Lily's place. We've spent the past hour singing all
of Lily's favorites, and I'm exhausted.

"Thanks, guys. I'm so glad you two are celebrating with me."

Lily's about one drink away from sloshed. Before too long, we'll
need to take her home and tuck her into bed.

"We have presents," I say, setting the misshaped gift onto the
table.

Asher follows suit, placing his much smaller and beautifully
wrapped gift next to it.

"One wacky gift." I grin, handing her the larger of the two
packages.

She narrows her eyes suspiciously at the item.

"Is that a Nerf gun? Please tell me we're about to bust out a
game of Nerf wars right here," she says, hiccupping.

"That will lead to arrests, and we're all adults now, remember?" I whine.

"Yeah, no guns." Asher chuckles.

She unwraps the gift I chose, a dirty word coloring book complete with a set of colored pencils. The snort laugh that rips through her chest is hysterical. It's a sound I didn't think possible for Lily's petite frame. Guess I picked correctly on the gift or she's just super drunk.

"Oh, boy. Someone needs to go home," I utter.

"Not before she opens the sentimental gift." Asher pushes the small white box with a giant pink and white polka dot bow on the top.

She unwraps it quickly and gasps at the Tiffany pendant. An item that we've both eyed for months.

Of course Ash remembered.

I shoot him an impressed head bob.

"It's gorgeous."

"And so are you," he says, turning his megawatt smile on my friend.

He doesn't even realize she's googly eyes over him as he jumps up from the table.

"I need to piss."

My nose scrunches. "Men," I mutter, and Lily giggles.

"Where have you been?" Lily whines. "Since you got that job, I hardly see you."

I grimace because she's right. I've been slacking at keeping in touch. My mind has been so preoccupied.

I glance around to ensure Asher isn't loitering.

"I'm kind of seeing someone," I whisper.

"You're what?" she bellows, and I clap my hand to her mouth.

"Shh. I don't want anyone but you to know."

Her eyebrow rises, and I remove my hand.

"Why not? That's exciting."

"It's . . . complicated." I blow out a breath.

Her eyes narrow, and her head tilts to the side. "Oh, no. Raven . . . tell me you didn't hook up with the hot stranger turned boss."

I bare my teeth in an *oops,* expression.

"Gah! You totally did. Tell me all about it."

"I will, but not here. I haven't told Asher about him yet, and I don't want him to find out tonight."

She bites her cheek. "Why?"

I don't want to lie to Lily, but this is her birthday. I'm not about to ruin it by admitting that I was wrong, and Asher does, in fact, have feelings for me.

"Work stuff. I'll tell you about it next Taco Tuesday."

She bobs her head, grimacing. "I need to go home. My head hurts."

"You're leaving?" Asher asks, walking up behind us.

"Birthday girl is out," I explain. "Can you make sure she gets home? I have an early day tomorrow."

"Sure." He shrugs.

I grab my purse and stand to leave, eager to escape before anything can get weird. Asher's hand darts out, grabbing my arm.

I freeze, sending a prayer up to heaven that he doesn't go where I'm afraid he's going.

"Can we talk? Like tomorrow night, maybe?"

This needs to happen sooner rather than later. It can't be avoided.

I take a deep breath. "Yeah. We can plan on it for now."

Tomorrow night, I'll have to break my best friend's heart.

Shit.

---

The next morning, I'm entrenched with phone calls and meetings with our client about how the launch project is going. I barely remember to come up for air at noon and head to the break room for some much-needed caffeine. I successfully pour myself a coffee without spilling it and turn around to see Charles in the doorway.

"Look at you mastering client relations and coffee pouring. Too bad the latter is not available for an increase in salary, Ms. Bennett."

"You know, it's weird. For such a picky-ass Brit, you are funny at times."

"Picky? Well, I have been called worse."

"What's your day been like? Mine has been too busy, and I'm ready for a bottle of wine at home tonight."

Ducking out the door to make sure no one is listening, he leans closer and whispers, "Any chance you would want company with that wine?"

"Are you saying you want to come over, Mr. Cavendish? Is there a project you would like to work on?"

"Very much so. I think there are sheets and sheets of data analytics to pore over, don't you?"

"Data. Hmmm. Not the D-word I was thinking of . . ." I trail off as I look at the lust building in his blue eyes. "I'll text you my home address and see you tonight. Around say eight?"

"Abso-fucking-lutely," he says with a wink as he turns and walks away.

A wink.

God help me. I'm going to lose my heart over a wink.

Ten minutes to eight and I can't stop fussing. I keep looking in the mirror to make sure I look okay, and I spend an unnecessary amount of time cleaning the apartment. Anything to keep me preoccupied while this nervous energy practically chokes me.

"Hello, love," Charles says when I open the door. He leans in and kisses me, handing me a big bunch of white hydrangeas.

"Oh, you are very good at this whole buttering me up thing," I say and go to put the flowers in a vase.

"You look beautiful," he says, smiling down at me before his eyes wander around the room. "Nice place."

"Thank you. It's small, but I really like it."

"You've done a lot with the space. You're bloody brilliant with décor."

I blush under his compliment. "It's home." I shrug. "Want the ten-second tour?"

"Please."

I take him around, showing him each space, and telling him about all the updates I've requested from management. It takes minutes, and I have no doubt that his place is something else entirely, but you'd never know it. His eyes are wide and his smile genuine as he takes in every space.

"And that's it. I'm assuming you live in some fancy townhouse," I say as we settle down on the sofa together in the living room.

He laughs. "What makes you say that?"

"Oh, you know, you're only the CEO of a huge advertising and marketing firm. I mean, no big deal."

"I have a nice flat. But it's not huge." He shrugs one shoulder. "Maybe I'll invite you over someday," he teases.

"Maybe I'll decide to feed you tonight."

He laughs, throwing his head back. "I see how things are. Tit for tat."

I make my way toward the kitchen. "Would you like some wine?"

"Please," he calls back.

I quickly pour two glasses of Pinot Noir and head back to the loveseat, plopping down next to Charles.

"Exactly," I say, taking a sip of wine. "This is nice, Charles."

"What?" he asks, pulling me into his side.

"This. Us," I explain. "It feels so normal."

He's very quiet, and for a moment, I wonder if I'm coming across as too pushy. We said slow, and he's made it perfectly clear he's not a dater.

"It's just that we've experienced possibly the weirdest start to a relationship ever, and this bit of normality is actually quite welcome."

"Quite," he agrees. "We have done things rather backwards, haven't we?"

I laugh. "Epic understatement."

"I have a question."

"Bloody hell. Why do I get the feeling I'm about to be interrogated?"

I chuckle. "Nothing like that. It's just that I'm curious. Have you done something like this before?"

"Like what?" he asks, brows furrowed.

"Sorry. I'm talking about that first night. When you kissed me in the closet?"

His lips form a straight line, and for a moment, I think he's going to refuse to reply. "Are you sure you want me to answer that?"

"I'm just curious."

"Would you believe me if I told you it was my first time?"

I tap my chin, faking contemplation.

"I wouldn't believe you. Not a chance."

He chews on his cheek. "I've done a lot of things in my life. Some I'm proud of and some I'm not. Since I've chosen in the past not to get involved long-term with women, things like that tend to occur more. It's safer."

"Safer?"

I'm treading into unsafe territory. The further we go down this hole, the more jealous I'm beginning to feel. It's an odd sensation. One I have to admit I don't particularly like. The truth is, I don't want to think about him with anyone else.

"Those women were looking for a good time. They weren't looking for Prince Charming."

I nod, getting what he's saying but mostly keeping myself busy so I don't combust.

"With you, it somehow felt . . . different. I feel almost like it was serendipitous."

I smile despite the pit in my stomach. He's managed to remove the jealousy by making me feel special. "I feel like that, too."

"Tell me about the last relationship you had," he presses, turning the subject away from himself . . . again.

It occurs to me that this is how it always goes. A little bit about Charles and a lot about me. I want to push back, but I'm afraid to ruin the night. It's not often we have uninterrupted alone time, and the last thing I want to do is push him.

"I've been single for a while." It's all I offer.

"Why?"

"I was concentrating on finishing my degree. I didn't have time to date."

"You haven't dated at all in the past year?"

"I mean, I went on a few dates, but nothing serious. The last serious guy I dated was during undergrad. Sophomore year. We were together for almost two years."

"Two years? What happened?"

"He moved to a different state. Different college. We tried to keep it going, but it all just fizzled out after a few months. I don't think either of us minded. It was one of those relationships that had died long before it officially ended."

He grunts as if he knows all about that.

"Neither of us knew how to end it. His moving just gave us an excuse. How about you?"

But Charles is saved by the bell.

The doorbell.

It rings, and we both jump in surprise.

"Expecting someone?" he asks.

"No."

This is strange. I never get random visitors, and of all nights, it has to be tonight.

I peek through the hole to find Asher on the other side. The very last person who I had expected. He's holding a bottle of wine in one hand and the biggest smile I'd ever seen as I swing the door open.

"Asher? What are you doing here?"

"I thought . . . you said," he stutters over his words. "We agreed to talk tonight. Remember?"

"Oh, shit! I completely forgot. Please forgive me. I'm the absolute worst. Can we talk tomorrow instead?"

"Sorry, did I interrupt something?" he asks. He looks me up and down. "You look nice. Going somewhere?"

"Uh . . ." I murmur again. I have no idea what to do, so I just stand there, looking like an idiot.

Asher peers in and sees Charles sitting in the living room with a glass of wine. I'm suddenly very aware of the scene in front of me. Even the lights have been dimmed.

"What's going on?"

"I'm sorry, Ash. I forgot and invited Charles over for dinner."

"Your boss?" His tone is sharp.

"Yes." I shut the door, stepping out into the hallway with Asher.

"Why can't I come in?" he asks, narrowing his eyes. "Am I interrupting more than a work dinner?"

"No. I just . . . shit," I say, opening the door back up and swinging my hand forward to motion Asher in.

"Asher, this is Charles. Charles, this is my best friend, Asher. Wait . . . you already met in the cafeteria. Never mind, I forgot," I say, completely flustered.

Asher looks at me. "Is something going on between you two?"

His question hits like a dagger to the heart, catching me off guard and throwing me backward. This is not how I wanted things to play out with Asher.

I'm not even sure how to answer that. We'd decided to keep things on the down low, and with Charles sitting right here, I'm not sure I can be honest.

"Uh, well . . . It's just . . ." I trail off.

Asher raises his eyebrows at me. "It's just what, Raven?"

"Don't keep the man in suspense, love," Charles says, making his way toward us.

I grimace at the look in Asher's eyes.

"What about the date we went on?"

Asher sounds hurt, and it's breaking my heart.

"What date?" Charles asks, pulling me into his side.

"It wasn't a date," I say to Charles and turn to Asher. "It wasn't a date."

When I repeat the words, Asher looks like I've struck him.

"You've got to be kidding me," he snaps.

"Asher, I'm sorry. I wanted to tell you."

"That's why you agreed to meet up? You wanted to explain to me that you're seeing your boss? Fuck, Raven. Fuck!" he yells, raising the bottle of wine to his forehead. "I can't believe you."

"Ash, please. You're my best friend. I—"

"You're sleeping with your boss," he bites. "Who are you even?"

Charles takes a threatening step forward, and my hand flies out, hitting his chest to halt his progression.

"I don't bloody care who you are. You won't speak to Raven like that. Not while I'm here."

"And who the fuck do you think you are?" Asher says through his teeth.

Charles takes a deep breath. "Listen, mate, go home. When you've calmed down, you two can have this conversation peacefully."

"Don't fucking order me around, *mate,*" Asher barks, moving closer to Charles.

Charles is at least two inches taller than Asher, but Ash isn't letting that stop him. He stands in defiance, looking up at him. "You'll just fuck her and then fuck her over, and I'll be left to pick up the pieces."

"You don't know anything about me. I'd never hurt her."

"Oh, yeah? I know what you guys are like. You think you're all big shots with your fancy job and your big paychecks. You think you can have any woman you want. You think the whole world needs to bow down for you."

"Asher. Please," I beg.

"Raven wants you to leave. Best be on your way," Charles says calmly.

"Why should I leave? Why don't *you* leave?" He turns to me, looking half-crazed. "Raven, tell him. Tell *him* to leave."

I look at Asher and sigh. "Just leave, Ash."

The look of despair on Asher's face right before he turns to walk away will haunt me for a long time.

# chapter thirty-six

Raven

"CARE TO EXPLAIN WHAT THAT WAS ABOUT, LOVE?"

My lip quivers, and I lose the battle, falling apart. Charles's eyes widen as his arms dart out to pull me against his solid chest, cocooning me in his warmth while a torrent of tears cascade down my cheeks.

"Shh. It will be all right, Rae," he coos into the top of my head.

Charles directs us toward the couch, placing me down and taking the seat next to me, keeping me tucked into his side while I work to get my crying hiccups under control.

After several minutes, I'm finally together enough that the tears have slowed to a trickle, but my heart hurts.

The look on Asher's face.

His defeated posture as he walked away.

I broke him.

I broke us.

"Would you like to talk about it?" Charles says, and I take a deep breath, blowing it out with a whoosh.

"Not really, but I suppose I owe you some answers."

He doesn't say anything, and I know I have to give him something.

I scoot out of his embrace, turning my body to look at him. I'm sure my face is puffy and red, but he doesn't seem to notice. His eyes are kind as they stare into mine.

"Asher and I met freshman year in the dorms. We became fast friends," I start, trying to determine how much I want to tell Charles.

I'm not trying to hide anything, but Ash and I have a long history. I didn't want tonight to be spent like this.

"We've been inseparable since."

"Did you have a relationship at one point?"

I shake my head. "Never. It was *never* like that with us."

Charles's eyes narrow.

"It truly wasn't . . . until recently."

His posture stiffens, and my hand darts out to land on his chest. "Nothing has happened between us, and it wouldn't as far as I'm concerned. I don't have feelings for him like that. He's like my brother. Our other best friend, Lily, is in love with him. Has been for a long time."

"Why do I get the feeling that his affections for you are entirely different?"

"My mom and Lily have been saying for some time that they thought Asher's feelings had shifted. I've been avoiding it because the thought of that nearly destroyed me. It would ruin everything."

"It appears it's too late for that. The man looked utterly gutted."

I wince, closing my eyes. "I know."

I sigh. "The last thing I want to do is upset you more, but I must ask, what date was he referring to?"

My stomach drops. This is the one thing I did not want Charles to find out. I messed up when I told Asher about the account. It's my fault we lost Summer. But I can't lie to him. I need to own up to it.

"It wasn't a date. Something recently happened, and he took me to dinner as an apology."

"What happened?"

I chew my bottom lip, looking down at my lap. "I told him about the Diosa account and how we were bringing Summer on board."

His back straightens, and his eyes harden into slits. I rush on with my explanation.

"We've always talked about everything. I didn't think about the ramifications."

"He works for Bauer," he practically growls, and I slink backward in response to his anger.

He has every right to be mad. This is enough to get me fired, and I wouldn't blame him if he did. I signed confidentiality paperwork, and I broke it.

"He told his upper management." It's not a question. Charles is speaking out loud, putting all the pieces together.

"Yes."

His eyes close, and his jaw ticks.

"I don't think I need to tell you how bad this is, Raven."

I nod, gulping.

"I take full responsibility for losing Summer."

"Why didn't you tell me immediately? Were you trying to lose the account for us?"

My head jerks back, his tone and words together catching me so off guard. I expected him to be angry, but this is something much worse. He actually thinks I'd purposely sabotage Cavendish?

"You can't be serious, Charles. I'd never."

He jumps up from the couch, pacing the room.

"I don't know what to think. Here I am, opening up to you, going off to Italy for the project, getting closer, and you've been having clandestine meetings with the competition. Giving confidential information away to your arsehole of a mate."

"Clandestine meetings?" I say, standing up and crossing my arms over my chest. "Are you serious? He's my best friend. Someone I've met up with regularly for far longer than I've worked for you." I spit the words, growing more angry by the second.

How dare he accuse me of such a thing? I've worked my ass off for this account, and he actually thinks I would do that to hand it over to the competition? Fuck that.

Charles's hand sweeps back through his hair, pulling at the roots. He looks more frustrated than angry at the moment.

"Charles," I say, taking a step toward him, and he takes a step away from me.

That hurts.

I slump back down onto the couch, curling my legs underneath me. "If you think that lowly of me, just leave."

Charles stops his pacing, turning to look at me. "What do you expect from me? I've told you that this company is my life, and what you did could've directly impacted us. If we lost Diosa, it would set us back years. Do you understand that?"

"Of course, I do," I snap. "Why do you think I worked so damn hard to find a replacement? I take ownership of my part in losing Summer, but if you haven't noticed, we're better for it."

He scoffs. "You don't know that. Summer could've made the whole campaign take off."

"And Holly won't? She's just as big as Summer and without the damn diva status."

Some of the fight appears to bleed out of Charles.

"We shouldn't have had to scramble to get talent. We had Summer, and now Bauer does."

"You're right, and that's on me, but don't stand here accusing me of trying to sink Cavendish. I've worked too damn hard on this account for you to spew that bullshit."

His hands run down his face. "You're right. You have."

I let out the breath I was holding, not saying a word and allowing him to work out his thoughts.

"I believe that you didn't intend to tell Asher, but you do see how your relationship with him poses a real concern for me?"

I nod. "It won't happen again. Ever," I promise.

He grunts, and my desire to argue with him rises again. I

understand his anger, but the way he reacted was more than I would've expected after what we've shared so far.

He takes a seat next to me on a harrumph, and I turn toward him.

"You hurt me, Charles. The fact you truly believed I was capable of sabotaging this account cuts deep."

His eyes bore into mine for several tense seconds as he sucks on his teeth, seeming to think on my words.

"I have trust issues," he finally offers, turning his head from me.

My eyes narrow in on the side of his head as I wait for him to elaborate.

"People I cared for hurt me deeply. They trampled over my trust and threw our relationship to the wolves without a second thought during one of the most difficult times of my life."

"Do you want to tell me about it?" I ask hesitantly.

"Not tonight, if that's all right with you."

I purse my lips but nod.

"I'm sorry, Raven. The man showing up caught me off guard, and then your admission to the Summer fiasco brought back hurt that I've worked years to stuff down."

"I'm sorry, too," I offer, placing my hand on his leg. "For all of it."

He offers me a small smile. "I want to try to enjoy this stolen moment with you. Is there still a chance for that?"

A grin spreads over my face. "I'd like that."

He pulls me against his chest, placing a kiss on top of my head.

"Don't hurt me, Raven."

His voice is small and vulnerable, and it catches me off guard. Who hurt him, and what exactly did they do?

"Not if I can help it."

Pulling away, I lean up to press my lips to his.

I spend the rest of the night in his arms, allowing him to chase away the hurt and sadness. Thoughts of Asher are momentarily gone.

If only it could always be like this.

My body wrapped around Charles as he shows me just how much he cares.

It's sublime.

It's everything I need.

# chapter thirty-seven

Charles

"Hello."

I can't help but grin at the sound of her voice. Even on the phone, she sounds like my own personal brand of sin.

"Raven, it's Charles. I need you to assist me with another account today."

"Absolutely," she says brightly. "What do you need me to do?"

"I'll text you the address."

"Oh . . . we're going to the office?"

I smile, hearing the confusion in her voice. Without seeing her, I know her dark blonde eyebrows are furrowed, and she's biting her cheek.

"I'm already on my way. I'll arrange for a car service to pick you up in fifteen minutes."

"Okay, sure. Is everything okay?"

"Everything is perfect," I say. "See you soon."

I disconnect the call and get to work setting things up. We aren't meeting with a client today. I'll actually be the car service picking her up.

The date Friday night turned into a nightmare, with her love-sick best friend spoiling the night. I won't allow anything to ruin this opportunity we have together.

After the chaos, I'm determined to make it up to her. I had every right to be upset about her slip to Asher on the Diosa account, but I understand how easily it could happen. She wasn't intentionally trying to sink the campaign.

I constantly have to remind myself that she isn't Tabitha.

I spent the rest of that evening focused on her pleasure. Anything to wash away what could have turned into a completely shitty evening. I wanted to erase *him* from her memory, at least temporarily.

It was plain to see how much she cared for Asher, and if I'm honest, I loathe it.

I arrive forty minutes later at her door.

Her eyes narrow. "I thought there was a driver and we were going to see a client."

I smirk. "I *am* the client."

Raven laughs. "Oh, yeah? And how may I be of assistance?" she says as she walks toward me.

"You can enjoy an afternoon date with me. To make up for Friday night."

Her lips purse. "That wasn't your fault. You don't have anything to make up for."

"I do. My reaction was out of line. Besides, we were interrupted. I won't let that happen today, love."

We hop into my Aston Martin and drove down to the Jersey Shore. There's an arcade that Paxton always talks about as though he's a kid frequenting it, and I want to see how Raven acts when I present her with such a date.

In true Raven fashion, her eyes light up, and she squeals in happiness.

At that moment, it occurs to me that I've never met a woman like her. So spontaneous. Ready to take on anything with a smile.

If I had ever suggested such an outing to Tabitha or any of the women I'd bedded through the years, this never would've happened. They would've refused. Arcades and fun were beneath them.

Fancy dinners, galas, and anything that would raise their status were acceptable.

This?

Never.

Raven and I have been playing games for hours, and I've never had so much fun.

I've never been a fun person. Never.

Life is easy with Raven, and she makes me want to have fun.

She goes with the flow and makes any day better just by simply being there.

I've never felt this free, and it has everything to do with her.

"I cannot believe how exhausting it is to play games like that. I don't remember being so tired when I was a kid." I stretch my arms over my head, relishing the pull of my muscles.

"Yeah, but that's because you moved your entire body while playing the games. You know you don't actually need to swerve when you're turning? You just have to press the controller. That's all," she says, smiling wide.

"Ah, you're taking the piss now. But you'll see . . . there's a method to my madness. At least, I'd like to think there is."

She stares at me for several long seconds, and I wonder what's going through her mind.

"You're cute," she says, reaching over to push a strand of hair that has fallen over my eyes.

"Why do you say that?"

"You just are."

"You didn't think I would be the type of guy who would sit for hours playing games with you?"

She shakes her head. "Truthfully? No, I didn't."

"And? Are you glad that I am that man?"

She beams. "So very glad. You're sort of the whole package, you know."

"Only sort of?" I tease. "You wound me, love."

She chuckles. "For now. I mean, I'm only getting to know you. But so far, you're in the clear running to be the whole package."

I smile. "I'd like to get to know you even better, and I have an idea."

It's percolating as I stand here, and I'm trying to work out all the details in my head. She looks at me with an expression that says, *get on with it.*

"The presentation will be done by Thursday. There's nothing more we can do. It'll be in the hands of your assistants to line up everything. You can approve their work from anywhere."

"So . . . what do you have in mind?" Her eyes shine with curiosity and excitement.

"How about you come with me to the Hamptons? We can spend the day relaxing."

"The Hamptons? Seriously?"

I might be losing my mind. I've never taken a woman to my family home here in the States. Only Tabitha, and that had been a nightmare.

The poor staff had been ordered around and snapped at, even when they'd completed their tasks satisfactorily because nothing was ever good enough for the mardy cow.

"We'll have the place to ourselves; the family won't be around. We can talk about the plans for the Gala. And trust me . . . it's the best place to relax after finishing a big project like the Diosa campaign. Think cocktails. Think swimming pool."

"Think sex?" she suggests.

I laugh. "It appears you've got the gist of it. So, are you tempted?"

"Tempted? Nah. I'm provoked into making all the work disappear so I can have this time with you."

I grin. A weekend away with my girl in the Hamptons is just what the doctor ordered.

Besides, it will only further prove that Raven is different and worth going all-in with.

# chapter thirty-eight

Raven

I'VE RECEIVED ABOUT TWENTY MESSAGES FROM ASHER SINCE that night. I know I was an asshole for what I did to him, and I'm not sure how to make it right. Losing him would feel like losing a limb.

He's part of me, and I have to make this up to him.

I'm back at the office, working furiously to finish the presentation. We'll give it to them tomorrow, and I've never been so nervous. It's damn good, but with the tight timeline, we can't afford any major rewrites or creative differences.

Holly didn't seem like a diva, but if she pulls anything crazy, I might lose my mind. We've worked so hard on this, and I'll be devastated if any of them truly hate it.

More than impressing the talent associated with the project, we have to nail this with Sergio Di Rosa. The legend himself will be present, and that adds a whole layer of fear.

Charles calls me into the office, and when I arrive, he's pacing up and down the small space. He looks frantic.

"Charles. Stop pacing. What's going on?" I ask.

He holds up his hands in despair. "I just heard from Paxton.

He says Bauer has stepped up their game. They found out about Holly. Everything about her," he stresses.

"What do you mean?"

"Well, apparently, Summer is very unhappy with them. The agent had to beg her to finish her contract, but she's threatening to pull out. They approached Holly, and they knew about her scheduling conflict and were more than willing to pay her double what Diosa is and meet all her scheduling needs."

"No," I gasp. "How?"

He shakes his head. "I have no bloody idea. Apparently, according to Paxton, their presentation was incredible."

"But he's your friend. How could he?"

"It's business, love. It's half the reason I didn't approach him to work together before. When talent is involved, things can get messy. He's their agent, not their boss."

"What now? Is the Diosa campaign screwed?"

"Holly and Paxton canceled the meeting for tomorrow. She's supposedly poorly," Charles seethes, and my stomach falls.

I feel ill.

I can't believe this. I honestly thought we had this in the bag.

"I don't know what to say. I'm speechless."

"Me, too." He looks at me as though he's got something to say but quickly looks away.

"What is it?" I ask, stepping forward.

He rocks back on his heels. "You didn't share anything else about the Diosa campaign with Asher . . . right?"

I can tell he's struggling to ask the question, but it doesn't matter. It's clear the thought entered his mind, and that only makes my chest ache as anger and anxiety flare.

"You're serious? We talked about this, Charles. You know everything."

His hands fly up. "I know. I just . . . had to be sure. You must understand my predicament, considering."

"Considering what?" I snap. "That one time I mentioned in

a conversation with my best friend that I was excited because we might land a superstar? It's a far damn cry from handing over my pitch."

He sighs, jaw ticking. "I know. I am sorry I asked. I simply needed to hear from you that it wasn't the case. Please understand—"

"When did they reschedule to?"

I cut him off, trying to avoid a bigger fight. He has reason to ask, and as much as I want to lash out at him, I can't. I put the doubt there in the first place.

His head shakes as though he's trying to clear his mind. "When did they reschedule to?"

"The meeting," I snap a little too harshly.

"Monday, nine o'clock." He runs his hands back through his hair, pulling at the roots. A move I've seen him do far too often lately.

"We should probably postpone going to the Hamptons," I say, lowering my voice and looking toward my feet.

"The presentation is ready. We're going," he says firmly. "But we should probably limit it to one night."

Relief swims through me. He still wants to go with me. Despite everything, we're going to have some alone time.

"That makes sense," I say, stuffing as much happiness into my voice as possible, considering we'd just been arguing. "Get back late on Saturday and have an entire day to rest before the pitch."

"You still want to go?" he asks, and it's filled with hope.

I nod. "Of course, I do."

He smiles, but it doesn't reach his eyes. The events surrounding Diosa are surely weighing heavily on him.

"What did Sergio say about the change?" I ask.

"He was concerned. Wanted to know that we could get Holly on board." He sighs. "Sergio saw the mock-ups, and he's obsessed with the campaign we've created around Holly at this point. If we have to change talent, it will be a hard sell for him."

"I don't understand how this happened."

"Someone in this office is feeding Bauer information. It's the only way," he grits through his teeth.

"It's not me, Charles. I swear it."

He grabs my hand. "I know you don't think it's you, Raven. I'm willing to gamble it all that this has nothing to do with you."

I squeeze his hands. "How do we figure out who it is? Can we do that?"

"I'll have the security team comb through incoming and out-going emails. That will be the best way to snuff them out."

"Do you have someone?"

He bobs his head. "I'll make the call to get the data. Price Security has been looking into a few things, but it's time to dig through and see what they've found." He steps toward me, keeping a few inches between us. "I know our pitch is good. You've worked so hard. I'm sorry this is happening to you, as well."

"This isn't your fault, Charles. We'll figure it out. There is no way Bauer can beat us. I'm sure of it. Holly will change her mind after seeing what we have for her. It's going to be fine." I take a deep breath. "I will spend every waking moment making sure it's per-fect. You have my word."

I'm not entirely sure how much I believe my words, but I want Charles to know that it's at least possible to bring Holly around. Even if we can't, we'll find another talent.

Charles smiles. "You're brilliant at this job, you know that, right?"

"Now, that is something that I like to hear. Praise from the boss man himself." I grin up at him, just barely refraining from press-ing my lips to his. "But you can thank me after we win the talent," I say with confidence.

"And how, pray tell, would you like me to thank you?" he asks, voice lowered, eyes wide and two dimples popping.

I step onto my toes and let him pull me into his arms, even

though we're in his office. With everything going on, I need his touch as much as I hope he needs mine.

"Well, I'm sure you can use your imagination for that. But I can give you a little glimpse for now . . ."

"Here? Isn't that against your rules?" he teases.

I reach up and pull his face closer to mine. We'd promised each other that we wouldn't do anything at work anymore, but it's hard to resist the odd kiss every now and again.

"To hell with the rules."

I smile as he leans in and deepens the kiss.

"Charlie Edmond Cavendish," a woman squeals from the doorway.

We turn around in a panic at the sound of the voice, and I quickly break away from Charles as I see Shelby standing there, watching us in what I hope is mock horror.

"Shelby, I . . . "

"Got caught kissing the boss?" She smirks.

"It's not what it looks like," I say, panicking.

"It's my fault," Charles lies, trying to cover for me, but it's pointless.

Cat's out of the bag, and the nosiest person in the office bore witness.

"Shelby, I'd appreciate your silence on the matter," Charles says. "Raven and I have just started seeing each other, and I promised we wouldn't let it affect work. We agreed to keep things away from the company, and we really should not have kissed in the office. I'm so sorry that you had to walk in on that."

"Don't worry about me, sir. Raven is very good at what she does. As long as that doesn't change, I don't see the harm in it."

I sag in relief, not finding a stitch of insincerity in her words.

"Although I must say, it did catch me off guard. You two have played the role of professional rather well."

Charles smirks. "It's been bloody difficult, if I'm being honest."

She smiles at Charles. "Well, I'm just happy to see you smile, Charlie. It's been . . . well, I'm not sure I've ever seen it."

"You lie," he drawls. "I'm delightful."

"A ray of sunshine, sir."

He shakes his head. "No. That's her," he says, looking at me.

It's such a tender smile. One that melts my heart and sends butterflies flying in my belly.

When he looks at me like that, there's not a doubt in my mind that I'm falling for him.

Hard.

"I'll let you two get back to work," she says, her voice dripping with mirth.

"We are. We will . . . work, that is," I stutter.

"Of course, you are, my dear."

She winks, walking from the room and leaving me to wonder how long it will take for the office to know our secret.

# chapter thirty-nine

Raven

"AH, SO THIS IS HOW THE OTHER HALF LIVES?"

My eyes are wide as we pass mansion after mansion. These places aren't even the permanent residences of their owners. It's the kind of wealth I can't wrap my head around.

"Pretentious and entirely too much flexing? Yes . . . this is how that half lives."

I snort, looking over at Charles, who doesn't bother turning his head to peer at the massive estates. Why would he? He lives in one.

"I think I could get used to it." I shrug my shoulders.

We drive in silence for another couple of minutes as I take in the opulence surrounding me. I'm lost in thoughts about the times Charles spent here. Who did he bring? What did they do?

Ugh. Don't go there.

"This is it," he says as we pull up to quite possibly the biggest house I've ever seen.

He clicks a button, and the gates open to allow us access to a sprawling three-story mansion with that old-world feel I adore.

The grounds are meticulously manicured, and a large fountain sits in the middle of the circular drive. As I step from the car,

I can hear the waves crashing somewhere in the distance, and I ache to explore.

"We're going to stay in the guesthouse. I find it to be cozier."

Something in his voice gives me pause. Like maybe this place doesn't hold the best memories for him. Which makes me question why we're here.

I don't have time to ask as he begins to spout off details.

"There are two residences on the property, which is a little over four acres. There are two pools and a tennis court."

"Wow." It's all I can manage as I spin in circles. "It's incredible, Charles. When was this built?"

"The 1900s. But you'll find that the inside of both places has been recently updated."

"I . . . don't have words. I'm speechless."

He huffs a laugh. "I've spent many a summer here. Some of my fondest memories are from times spent on these grounds."

Okay, so maybe I was wrong, and he does like this place.

"Lifestyles of the rich and famous, huh?"

He chuckles. "Not quite. But it is a lovely place."

"It's so weird for me to think that this is normal for you. You really do have a different life from what I'm used to. Yet you're surprisingly normal for someone used to all this."

He pulls a face. "Normal? I don't want to be normal."

"Normal doesn't mean boring, Charles," I explain. "Now, come on, let's go to one of the pools you've told me all about."

"Now? You don't want a tour of the grounds? The houses?"

"I believe you promised me some extra fun. Not that I wouldn't be dumbstruck by all there is to see around here, but I just want to spend time with you. Alone."

His eyes widen, and a smirk breaks across his face.

"You always surprise me, Raven." He shakes his head, his hands lifting to his mouth, blocking the dimples I love to see. "Come on. Let's get you in your swimming costume."

"Well . . . don't get too excited. I do plan to scope out the house while changing." I grin, and he mimics the expression.

When he unlocks the door and sweeps out his hand for me to enter, I run into the house like a child who has just discovered a candy store. I can hear Charles laughing at me as I run from room to room, checking it out. I've never seen a place like this in my life. I feel like I've just stepped into the middle of a movie scene.

The foyer is wide open, with a circular staircase leading to a landing on the second floor. A large ornate table sits in the center with the largest floral arrangement I've ever seen, and I wonder who keeps up the place while they aren't here.

The floors are white marble, and I have to slow my pace so I don't wipe out. The place is floor-to-ceiling white. The only touch of color comes from the décor. It's stunning.

"Is this for real?" I ask when I make my way to the back of the house.

It's nothing but window after window, giving an incredible view of the back.

Tall trees surround the entire backyard, blocking us from the view of the neighbors. The property is large enough that it's likely unnecessary, but it's nice to know we're hidden from the world and can do as we please.

I don't even bother to go into a room to cover myself as I strip down and put my bikini on. He laughs the whole time.

Charles stands in front of me with a big towel, wrapping it around me.

"Your towel, my lady."

I almost die.

It's like one of those big, white hotel towels, and it's wrapped around me twice. It's luxurious in a way I'm not used to.

A girl could definitely get used to this, though.

Charles is in his red swim trunks, and my mouth dries at how spectacular he looks in them. His chiseled chest is on full display, and my eyes trail down and over his six-pack abs, right down to the V that dips beneath his shorts.

Too damn hot for his own good.

Together, we walk over to a pool that is quite possibly the fanciest pool I have ever seen in my life. It seems to go on forever as it weaves around rocks that form tunnels that lead to a grotto.

He jumps in, pulling me with him.

"Charles," I scream, right before I'm submerged.

When I surface, I see that we've splashed water everywhere, and even the towels are soaked. He's laughing, but I'm not.

"How are we supposed to dry off?"

"It's sunny, love. I'll get you another towel while you sunbathe."

"That works," I say, nodding my head in approval.

"You're very easy to please." He grins, which appears to be a staple on his handsome face today.

It looks good on him. The tense posture and rigid features that he wears around the office are gone. He looks younger, lighter.

"This is pure luxury. A girl could get used to this lifestyle." I swim up toward him.

His eyes darken, and his lips form a thin line.

"What's wrong?"

He shakes his head. "Nothing. I'm going to grab a drink. Would you like something?"

"Please," I say, watching as he walks off.

I think back over my words, wondering what I could've said or done to make him react that way. I'd simply complimented the place.

Then again, the lifestyle is probably the exact reason he doesn't date. Plenty of women wouldn't see Charles for the catch that he is, beyond the money.

He's back quickly, handing me a drink. The hardened look is absent, and I thank God for that. The last thing I want is for this short trip to be ruined.

"A glass of champagne, mixed with pool water, for the lovely lady."

I take a sip. "Ah, how did you know? My favorite drink of all time."

He smirks. "It's Prosecco, sans the water."

"My hero."

The rest of the day is magic. We spend it poolside, eating the most incredible food made by a private chef.

Charles had made a call to have Andre available to feed us. He stops by every now and again with platters, more champagne, and anything else our hearts' desire. Then he made himself scarce again. It's hard not to get swept away by the extravagance of the place.

We're lounging by the pool, and my eyes blink open when I feel someone hovering above me.

Charles grins down at me. "You look ravishing."

I rise up on my elbows. "That so?"

He nods. "I'm starving."

"You just ate," I tease, shielding my eyes from the sun.

"Yes, but I want you, Raven."

Liquid fire heats low in my gut, and I'm suddenly hungry, too. Hungry for him.

He lowers onto his knees, scooting my body to the end of the chair so my legs dangle over. As he pulls down my bikini bottoms, my core coils with an intense need, and I'm aching for what's to come.

He doesn't make me wait.

His mouth descends on my center, lapping, sucking, nipping.

My back lifts off the chair with a moan, and I fear Juan will hear. I tense, and Charles must sense it.

"Nobody's going to hear you, love. Let go."

He moves back to my center, adding his fingers to the mix. He inserts one, pumping in and out of me as I buck against his hand, all the while continuing his pattern.

Lap.

Suck.

Nip.

Oh, God!

He inserts a second finger, and my pussy clenches around both.

"Charles," I cry out, and his fingers work harder. Faster.

I'm coming apart, and it's the greatest form of ecstasy. No drug could ever compare to the things Charles does to my body.

He continues to lap at me as I grind against him, riding out the orgasm.

I'm limp against the chair, riding the high.

"Your turn," I say, rolling to the side.

He shakes his head. "Not now. Rest. There's plenty of time."

At some point, I doze off, relaxed and happy.

---

The sun is still high in the sky while the two of us are lying on the sun loungers with big, floppy hats and drinks at the ready.

Another platter of food is delivered poolside. I'm not sure I can eat another thing until I see the decadent desserts.

"So how often have you brought other girls here?" I ask while biting into a chocolate-covered strawberry.

The words are out before I can take them back. The truth is, I don't want to know. It's the last thing I want to think about. He's quiet, and I think he might dodge the question, but he doesn't.

He turns to face me. "This is the third time."

"Oh?" I say, sounding disappointed.

*What did you expect?*

For him to say that he'd never brought a girl to the Hamptons before?

I guess I should be grateful for the honesty.

"And how was it?"

Why on earth I think that's a good question to ask is beyond me. I'm clearly a glutton for punishment or really trying to push his boundaries.

"Terrible," he admits. "Not like this at all."

"You mean they didn't run and dive-bomb into the pool?" I tease, needing to ease the tension I've caused.

He laughs. "They certainly didn't. They were more interested in making sure they got the perfect tan or putting together the perfect cocktail. Or taking endless photos to put on their social media accounts and brag to the world." He sighs. "Don't get me wrong, I understand that this is quite the place. But it's more than that."

"What do you mean?" I ask tentatively, feeling like he's finally going to open up.

"They were most interested in telling other people about how splendid their life is rather than spending time with me." He shakes his head. "I don't know."

He felt used for his money.

"I'm sorry, Charles. It sounds like you've dated some real divas."

He grunts. "I've dated a lot of fake girls in the past."

"You don't think I'm fake?" I ask.

"Raven," he grates. "I think you are the furthest thing from fake. My mother would've loved you. You're the sort of girl I would be proud to show off to the world."

For a moment, I'm speechless. His praise means everything to me. The fact he found me worthy to meet his mother made my chest ache. She clearly meant so much to him, and I can feel his pain at her loss.

"That's quite the compliment, Charles."

His head turns to me, his eyes boring into mine. "I mean it. Wholeheartedly."

I take a deep breath, looking at my surroundings.

"I get it now."

"Get what?" he asks, sounding confused.

"Why you don't date. Why you have strict rules surrounding sex." I sigh. "You've had horrible taste in women in the past."

He burst into laughter, pulling my chair closer to his and grabbing my hand.

"You are very right, love. I had terrible taste."

I smile. "You're amazing, Charles, and it has nothing to do with this place. You're talented and passionate. You give people a chance to prove their worth. You don't care about bloodlines and prestigious schooling. You allow people to shine when other CEOs wouldn't. You let *me* shine."

My cheeks heat, having voiced such a private thought.

"You shine all on your own, Raven."

I inhale, taking in the fresh air and basking under the warm sun. "I'm having the best time with you, Charles. Thank you for bringing me here."

"I've never enjoyed this place more. Truly. Thank you, Raven."

I turn away and put my glasses back on, enjoying the rays on my face. Charles places his hand on my belly, and the two of us just lie here in comfortable silence.

I'm lost in thoughts of how perfect this day has been. Not just the luxury of the place but the company. I've never had this much fun with a person.

I got to see a side of Charles Cavendish I don't think many get to bear witness to. He's charming, funny, and a lot of fun. He let loose, and it was wonderful to see.

"Raven?" Charles says, pulling me out of my internal musings.

"Hmm," I murmur, completely content.

"I think I'm falling for you."

I sit up, dislodging his hand from my stomach.

"What?" The word comes out husky.

He swings his legs over the edge of the chair to face me. "I'm falling for you, Raven Bennett. Against all my rules, you've broken down the walls I thought were fortified."

He places his hands on my cheeks, staring into my eyes. Blue on blue.

Hope and anticipation.

Lust.

Longing.

Love?

"I believe you could be the woman who brings me to my knees. I could love you one day, Raven. Hopelessly."

My heart races, and my stomach skydives into my core, leaving me nearly panting. I can't believe he's saying these words to me.

It all happened so quickly, and the odds have been stacked against us.

I feel like we've gone from zero to a hundred in just a few weeks, but it doesn't matter. I feel the same.

Say something.

I will my mouth to move—for any words to come out—but I'm too scared to speak. Too scared to learn that this is a dream. One I'll come crashing out of, destined to hit rock bottom and die from a broken heart.

Just like Mom warned.

I want to take things slow. As wonderful as it is with him, we still have a lot of obstacles to maneuver. He's my boss, and I'm very aware that being with him could impact my career. It could create problems for the whole of Cavendish.

Getting swept up in the moment would be so easy. So . . . foolish.

I don't want to say anything and ruin the moment, so I say the first thing that comes to mind.

"Thank you."

So many emotions cross over Charles's face, finally hardening into stone. His eyes darken like they do when I know he's angry.

He clearly hoped that I would say more, and at this moment, I wish I had.

"I think I'll go change," he says, his voice flat and emotionless.

Without another word, he leaves me sitting by the pool, the setting sun my only company.

# chapter forty

## Charles

W HO THE FUCK SAYS THAT?
*Thank you.*

Those words gnaw away at me, reminding me of another time right here in this very fucking place when I was crushed.

This house was my mother's sanctuary. My father thought staying here would be beneficial to her while she was undergoing treatment at Sloan Kettering for her first bout of breast cancer. She couldn't travel back and forth from the United Kingdom because she was too weak.

She loved the ocean, and my father thought the sea would help cure her.

He was desperate.

We all were.

We tried to make memories that would last a lifetime, knowing we didn't have much time with her.

The last time I was here was right after she died. I told Tabitha I needed to get away.

I wanted to be somewhere I could feel close to my mum.

Tabitha and I were already engaged, and I'd been considering breaking it off. Right before my mum died, she begged me to find love. To be happy like she was with my father.

I'd promised, and I'd planned to truly give things a shot with Tabitha. We'd been happy enough. I enjoyed her company, and she enjoyed mine. Surely, we could fall in love if I allowed myself to be open to it.

And I was.

I needed her to pull me out of the darkness that descended when my mum died. My father was too far gone himself. Tabitha was my person, and I was going to lean on her strength to get through.

When we pulled up, a dozen cars were waiting in the driveway. Tabitha had organized a party, of all things. It wasn't to keep my mind off everything. It was to entertain herself while I grieved alone in another wing of the house.

She'd left me to my own darkness while she partied with New York socialites, cementing her status in the States.

She didn't give a shit about me.

She wanted everything I had. Most importantly, my last name.

Something she'd never have after that week.

It had taken every ounce of courage I had to open up and give my heart to Raven, and she'd stomped all over it.

*Thank you.*

Those words had my teeth grinding and my hands balling into fists.

Did she not feel the way I did? Could I really have been such a prat to believe she could care for me as much as I did her?

Well, I was going to bloody well force her to admit she felt the same. I'm done running from my feelings.

I stalk toward the front of the massive house, searching for Raven, when I hear her small voice.

She sounds sad. Broken.

"Asher, please answer." Her voice shakes, and I remain hidden behind a wall, eavesdropping like a damn tosser.

"Please let me explain," she continues, crying down the line, and my shoulders stiffen at the emotion in her voice. "I love you."

*I love you.*

Words I wished to hear from her lips that went unsaid.

*Thank you.*

My jaw ticks, and I have to prevent myself from falling into a fit of rage.

She told that fucking arsehole she loves him, but she couldn't even tell me she cared for me. Was I blind to believe she was different? Could she have pulled one over on me so thoroughly?

Rage consumes me, threatening to pull me into a darkness I haven't experienced in a long time.

Because I haven't given a fuck about anything since the last time I felt like this.

I allow the anger to flow through me for a few more seconds before I decide to confront Raven.

Stepping out from behind the wall, I walk toward Raven, whose back is turned to me.

"Everything all right?"

Her eyes are wide and filled with unshed tears.

She's fucking crying over him?

I steel my resolve, seeing things for what they are.

She's no better than Tabitha.

She played me for a fool, and I allowed it.

No more. This ends now.

# chapter forty-one

Raven

COME ON, ASHER. PICK UP. PICK UP.
I've been trying to get in touch with Asher since everything went to hell with Charles. I realized that by saying nothing, I was ruining everything.

Both men deserve better from me, and I'm determined to make amends.

I have to.

It's eating away at me.

Asher deserves to know the truth. That he'll only ever be my best friend, and I can only hope that'll be enough for him one day.

Charles needs to know I feel the same way.

More even.

I'm not just falling. I'm *in love* with him.

Spending the day away from the office and just enjoying each other has solidified it. I've never been in love, but the way my chest feels tight and my belly tingles in anticipation every time he's near tell me this is something real. Something I'd be an idiot to ignore.

But it's not just that.

It's the way I feel in the quiet moments with him. Like I don't have to fill the silence. I can relax and bask in the comfort he provides. It's the way I want to make him happy. To make him smile.

I want to give Charles Cavendish all of me. Whatever will ensure that lighthearted man never leaves. The one I got to experience the day at the arcade and here at this house that holds so many memories for him.

I likely ruined things with him, but I can fix it. I have to.

Asher will tell me how to fix this. He's always been my voice of reason, and once he gets over his hurt, he'll be there for me through this, too.

I need him to know how I feel about Charles. He needs to know that this isn't just a passing thing.

I love Charles.

If Charles will hear me out and forgive me for holding back, I have every intention of holding on to him. I don't want a fling. I want forever.

Not now, but someday.

Asher is not picking up.

"Everything all right?" Charles asks, walking into the room, voice full of steel.

I whip around to find his hands are in his pockets, and his face is void of emotion.

Shit.

This is not good.

"I'm fine. I just can't get ahold of Asher. He's not answering any of my calls."

"I didn't realize you were still at odds."

I sigh. "We are. I know you saw a bad side to him, but he's not like that at all. It's my fault anyway."

"How so?" His biting tone causes me to wince, but I forge on, hoping to turn things around.

He takes a seat on a chair facing me.

I shift on my feet uncomfortably, looking down at Charles, who still has a blank face. "I might've led him on unintentionally."

Charles's eyes narrow imperceptibly, but I don't miss it.

"You led him on. How?"

"He was making his feelings more noticeable. I ignored it. Instead of coming clean and telling him there was no chance, I stayed quiet."

Charles's shoulders stiffen, and I wonder what he's thinking. Is he misunderstanding my silence from earlier?

How could he not?

"Charles. About earlier," I say, but he shakes his head.

"Not now, Raven."

"When? I can't go on feeling like this. It's horrible."

He huffs a humorless laugh, and I tense.

"I think we both know this was never going to work, Raven."

My heart stops.

My body sags.

I feel like I'm going to be sick.

"Getting to know you was fun, but it wasn't meant to last. I don't do relationships." He glances around the room, and his eyes manage to darken more.

What is he remembering that has those shadows clouding his handsome face?

"This place reminded me of that." He shrugs. "The sex was great."

I stare at him. Did he really just say that to me?

"Seriously?" I snap. "That's all you have to say to me?" My voice pitches, and Charles doesn't even flinch.

"Oh, come now, Raven. Surely you'd say the same. Italy. The office. Here. It was just really good sex. Now you can leave."

"Charles, you don't understand. I—"

"Don't," he snarls. "Don't you dare try to backpedal."

Knowing Charles, even after a short time, I'm aware that anything I say at this point would come across as forced. He wouldn't believe me, and it would only make things worse.

I've well and truly messed up, but I don't care.

I have to say the words.

"I've fallen in love with you." I say the words, but it's too late, and I know it.

He bares his teeth as the anger pours from him.

"I. Said. Don't," he grits.

Dread pools, and I'm petrified we can't come back from this.

After all the nuggets of information he's given me about his past and the hurt he's felt by those he's loved, I fear I've added my name to that list.

Something I will regret for the rest of my life if that's the case.

"Your bags are packed, and a car is waiting for you out front."

My mouth falls open. He's kicking me out?

"You are not just sending me packing. We are going to talk through this. Charles, I—"

"I don't want to hear anything more you have to say, Raven. Please leave."

"No. You said if something happened between us, we would handle this as adults. This is as immature as it comes. You will not do this to me."

"I won't do this to you? Isn't that just rich? I won't kick out the woman who lied to my face repeatedly?"

My hands rest on my hips. "When did I ever lie to you, Charles?" I challenge.

"When haven't you? From the first moment at Silver, you were next to Asher. But somehow the man working for Bauer didn't recognize me?"

"No, I told you I didn't know."

"Bullshit Raven. Everything has been a lie. And I fucking fell for it."

"Italy was not a lie."

He inclines his head. "Oh, and Holly just magically got poorly before we were supposed to go for her shoot. Did you and Asher work that up? Get her to play that card?"

"I didn't even know I was going to go. You called *me*,

remember? I didn't have clothes. My God, why won't you listen to reason? You said you wouldn't do this. *You* are the liar. A liar and a goddamn coward."

"I'm not the one who said *thank you* to the man you just fucked but called your boyfriend and said *I love you!*"

"That's not what . . ."

His jaw is locked. "I said no more," he grits out.

"I'm not going until you say this isn't going to affect work. You promised."

"I promised you nothing. Now get out."

"Charl—"

"Leave!" he bellows, and I swear the house shakes on its foundation from the force of his rage.

Rage he's directed at me.

Tears spill down my cheeks, and I choke back a sob.

Charles's shoulders rise and fall, showcasing the strength of his anger. It's not abating.

I've hurt him. He might mask it under a layer of rage, but that's pure pain radiating from him. And I caused it.

I have so much to say, but it won't do any good tonight.

I won't provoke more betrayal from him. He doesn't deserve it.

Without a word, I move toward the front door and find my bag sitting there. My heart is in my throat, and my knees wobble. I'm two seconds away from breaking, but I don't want it to be here.

I rush from the house, the tears turning into a river of grief as I throw myself into the car and watch the house and Charles slip out of view.

My heart is left in Charles's hands.

# chapter forty-two

Raven

IT'S BEEN A WEEK SINCE I LEFT CHARLES IN THE HAMPTONS. Luckily, the meeting was pushed back because I don't know if I would've been up for seeing him so shortly after what happened.

I've not seen nor heard from him. Shelby told me he's been working remotely, and I wonder if he stayed in the Hamptons.

I've worked tirelessly to keep my mind preoccupied, but it's no use. I can't stop thinking about the look on his face. The one I caused.

A part of me had believed that if I just gave him some time, he'd come around. But an entire week has gone by, and my heart still hurts, knowing that things are well and truly done.

There's a knock on my office door, and I call out for whomever it is to enter.

My heart jolts when Charles walks in.

He's still wearing that hard expression. His eyes are cold and emotionless. I gulp, not sure what to say or do.

He shuts the door behind him, not making any move toward my desk.

"You're back." My voice is small and unsure, but he doesn't react.

"I got back today," he explains. "I came to work out the details of this situation."

My eyes narrow as I try to work out what he means.

"I promised that when things ended, we'd be professional and find a way to move past it." He puts his hands in his pockets. "I intend to keep that promise."

"You do?"

He nods. "You're important to the Diosa account, and Cavendish isn't prepared to let you go on account of my momentary lapse of judgment."

My head jerks back with the force of a slap to the face.

"You're an asshole," I choke out.

His eyes narrow. "What exactly did I do, Miss Bennett?" His voice is low and threatening.

"This isn't the place to discuss this," I snap. "People will hear us."

"This is the only place we'll be discussing this. I'll say whatever I wish whenever I wish. Hell, I'm allowed to scream at you if I so please. They won't have any idea what's actually being said behind that door."

"Shelby will." My voice pitches.

He scoffs. "Shelby will be paid handsomely to remain quiet about this affair."

My body goes cold.

Affair.

Something quick and quiet. Something taboo and dirty.

I'm really going to be sick.

"You're a pig," I screech. "Demeaning what we shared is low."

"I demeaned this?" He barks a humorless laugh. "You're bloody crazy."

I jump up from my chair, leaning across my desk. Anger rises with something darker, sure to send me over the edge.

"Have you ever actually looked at yourself in the mirror?

Because I'm starting to think that you have no idea what a prime idiot you really are."

"*I'm* the idiot?"

I step around my desk, stalking toward him. We're toe to toe.

"Yes," I spit. "You're a grumpy, arrogant asshole."

"Funny. You said the complete opposite last week. So which is it, Raven?"

I glare at him for several seconds, and without thinking, I slap him across the face.

I almost laugh at his shocked expression. That's before his face reddens in anger and his fists ball at his sides.

"Did that make you feel better?" he growls.

"Yes. It felt really damn good," I say, sounding small and unsure.

"Whatever was between us is over," he says through gritted teeth.

"Agreed. You'll never touch me again."

He stares at me for several tense seconds before turning around and storming out, leaving me to stare after him.

I take a deep breath and calmly sit down, get out my file, and attempt to do my work. I'm not going to make a scene. I'm not going to cry.

It's pointless to think this as the tears start to run down my face in a waterfall of grief.

What have I done?

I can't be here. Can't be this close to him.

I might not have said the words, but how the hell did it turn into this?

His anger.

The resentment.

Where did it all come from?

There's a knock on my office door, and my heart skips a beat, hoping Charles has come to his senses.

"Come in," I say, my voice wobbling.

The beautiful woman from Zero Bond walks in, and I quickly wipe away my tears.

"C-Can I help you?"

She saunters in, looking like a cat stalking its prey. She's wearing a beige Chanel suit, looking sophisticated and gorgeous.

"Do you know who I am?" she purrs.

I shake my head, which elicits a Cheshire cat grin.

"Charlie is so secretive. I shouldn't be surprised." She takes a look at the flowers he sent last week. They're on the verge of hitting the trash can for several reasons.

"Are those from Charles?"

"Yes," I say, and wonder who she is and why she's here.

She narrows her eyes. "Hmm. Not surprised. I've received the same flowers from him on multiple occasions."

"The same?"

I'm so confused and devastated that I wonder if I'm even awake. This entire encounter is incredibly bizarre.

"The very same." She takes several steps closer, picking at her red-painted nails. "I feel it is my duty to tell you what went on between Charlie and me."

"What do you mean? What went on?"

I feel nauseous, sensing that something earth-shattering is about to be imparted. Not that it matters. We're over. My stomach literally lurches. "What do you mean?" I force myself to ask again.

"I mean he was my fiancé."

My world tilts, and I have just enough time to grab my trash can before the contents of my stomach spill out.

"And I came to get him back, so it's time for you to leave."

# chapter forty-three

Charles

THE SOUND OF FOOTSTEPS HAS ME LIFTING MY GAZE TOWARD the entrance to my office. "What are you doing here, Tabitha?"

She takes a seat across from me, making a show of crossing her legs.

"I came to talk," she coos. "Thought it was long past due."

"Get the fuck out."

I don't bother looking up at the bitch. My skin crawls with her proximity alone. After the fight I had with Raven, I'm a coiled wire, ready to snap. If she doesn't heed my warning and leave, she'll feel my full wrath.

She tsks. "Is that any way to speak to your *mother*?"

"You're not my anything," I grit through my teeth. "You might be fucking my father—"

"Wrong. I'm married to your father." She twirls a piece of her hair, and an evil grin spreads across her face.

My eyes narrow in on her, full of fire and warning, but she doesn't so much as flinch. That sick smile, plastered all over her fake face. She's nothing more than a plastic shell of the woman I once tried to love.

"What are you up to?"

She shrugs. "I was in the area and wanted to say hello. I miss you, Charlie."

I growl. "Don't call me that."

She whimpers, pursing her botched lips. "You used to love it."

"Never."

She takes a deep breath, blowing it out loudly while picking at her fingers. "I met your pretty plaything again. What's her name? Robin?"

My stomach sours at the thought of this vile woman being anywhere near Raven.

"I find it interesting that you failed to tell her about us. About all the times we fucked." She giggles. "Sorry to be crude."

"She's not my anything. You managed to spoil that."

"Me?" Her hands raised to her heart like she was offended.

"Your lies. Your manipulations. The way you ruin everything you touch." I take a heaving breath, trying to rein in my temper. "You made me distrust every woman who dares to get close to me. You've ruined me."

When Raven hadn't returned my sentiments, the poison seeped in, surrounding me with memories of Tabitha and how she'd only been interested in my wealth.

"Oh, come on. Don't act like I didn't do you a favor. The best thing I did was saddle up with Daddy Warbucks."

"You're vile."

"Think what you'd like, but I do care for him."

"You don't care about anyone but yourself."

"So hostile. Did you really love me that much?" She blushes. "I'm flattered."

I laugh sardonically. "It has nothing to do with you. For all I care, you could've bloody well shacked up with the pope. It was my father who destroyed me."

"Yes, that did break him, too. I must say, you men are quite the tender hearts. I wasn't prepared for that."

"Get the fuck out of my office!" I yell, and she has the common sense to jump.

"Calm down, Charles. I only came to warn you that your father is ill."

My breath hitches.

"You came all the way here to tell me that? Like I care."

Tabitha would never take time from her busy life to drop in and warn me that my father's ill. It's just another one of her sick games. She hasn't been able to pit us against each other in some time, so I have no doubt she's been concocting something.

"It's his heart." She says it like it's not really a big deal. As though she were really just in the area and thought she'd drop a bomb on me and watch it explode.

I won't give her the satisfaction.

"You bitch," I seethe.

"Sir, is everything okay?" Shelby asks, rushing into the office, eyes wide.

When she gets a look at Tabitha, her eyes narrow to slits.

"You," she grinds through her teeth. "I didn't realize we were entertaining Satan today, sir."

I snort, and Tabitha's eyes cut to Shelby. If looks could kill, Shelby would be on death's door.

"Everything is fine. She was just leaving."

Shelby nods. "There's a call for you on line two, sir."

I nod, picking up the phone but never moving my eyes from the snake in front of me.

"Cavendish."

The voice on the other line speaks, but I hardly hear a word. Instead, I'm watching, and I don't miss the small smirk.

She's pure evil.

Her warning wasn't a lie for once, and I'd wasted my time fighting with her.

Fuck.

I don't know how to feel. I'm running, but my legs feel like lead. For as angry as I am, and for all the resentment I've harbored, those words felt like someone stabbed me in the heart with a dull blade.

*Your father's had a heart attack.*

*It doesn't look good.*

My father's attorney told me my father was ill, but I sent him away.

Stuart told me that Tabitha was gunning for more inheritance, blackmailing my father with something that had him considering lifting the prenup.

I'll strangle her.

I booked the first flight I could manage, but it left me with little time to make it to the airport. They've already called last call over the speaker, but I'm not giving up.

Not until that door is slammed in my face.

My feet pound against the floor, and my arms pump as I weave in and out of people in my way.

I don't offer apologies, and I don't look back. My mind is set on my father.

If he dies, our unfinished business will haunt me.

I have too many questions. Too many things I want to say.

He can't die. Not before I can tell him that I forgive him.

That it was never about her, but the sting of my father choosing her over me when I needed him most.

Thankfully, I make it just as the attendant is closing the door. She lets me in, seating me in my first-class chair.

"Can I get you anything, sir?"

"Double scotch on the rocks, please."

I need something that reminds me of him.

A memory to hold.

I check my phone once before we take off, and I find that I have no calls and no texts.

What was I expecting?

The things I'd said to Raven are unforgivable.

She can't understand the trust issues I have due to my past.

It wasn't fair because I know she's nothing like Tabitha.

At some point along the way, I've fallen for her. I don't know when or how, but I did.

It's been a whirlwind, and for someone who doesn't believe in love at first sight, I'm starting to think that's exactly what I experienced the moment my eyes found Raven across the room at Silver.

But I ruined that with my toxic words.

I tarnished everything we could've had by allowing Tabitha's venom to flow through me. To make a home in my veins and turn me cold and incapable of love.

No. Not incapable.

Raven proved that wrong.

Because I do love her. It took me losing her to realize it.

Laying my head back on the seat, I prepare for the flight, my stomach twisting in knots, knowing the mess I'm about to walk into and the devastation I left behind.

# chapter forty-four

Raven

"To hell with boys," Lily says, raising a glass of bourbon on the rocks.

We skipped right over our typical drinks, going straight to the strong stuff.

I know it's not what I need. It'll only dull the pain for a while.

It hurts.

I understand my mom's anguish a little bit more. Although mine is only a fraction of what she experienced.

I filled Lily in on all the events, not sparing a single detail, and she listened.

"What was the bitch's name?" she growls.

I shrug my shoulders. "She said her name is Tabitha."

Lily pulls my computer toward her and starts typing away. Within five minutes, her eyes look up and meet mine.

"Is this her?"

She turns the computer around, showing me a picture.

I nod.

"This is bad," she says. "There's a whole lot more to the story."

My eyes narrow. "Tell me."

"Are you sure?"

"Positive."

She clicks keys, eyes scanning the screen.

"According to a few London tabloids, her name is Tabitha Murphy. She's a London socialite whose father squandered every last penny they had."

My eyebrows rise.

"So she's a money-grubbing whore?"

"And then some." She cackles. "She was smart and got a full-ride scholarship to Cambridge. Used that circuit to rise up in the ranks, attaching herself to wealthy businessmen and aristocracy."

"Wow. How in the hell did she end up with Charles?"

"Hard to tell. Her list of suitors is long, but none lasted more than a few months."

"They likely caught on to her gold-digging ways," I say, and Lily grunts in agreement.

"The worst part," she says, taking a breath. "Not long after the engagement between her and Charles ended, she married Charles Cavendish."

My head jolts back. "They got married?"

Bile rises in my throat, and I think I'm going to vomit right here.

She shakes her head slowly back and forth. "*No.*" She stresses the word, and my nose scrunches in confusion. "She married his father."

My mouth drops open.

Everything that Charles said about his rules and staying away from relationships filters through my mind, making complete sense.

She did a number on him.

"His father?"

"Yeah. Pretty low, right? The woman's a snake."

My head shakes back and forth. "She's worse."

Lily nods. "Raven, I'm going to level with you. I think he probably has many demons brought on by her. A lot of self-doubts. When he bared his soul to you, and you didn't re-ciprocate, all that came crashing around him." She sighs. "I'm not saying the way he acted was right, but this makes it a little clearer."

I hurt him.

Made him feel like he didn't matter to me while basking in the material glamour surrounding me.

Just like she did.

"I need to make things right."

There's a knock on my door, and Lily stands to open it.

Asher enters, walking right to me and pulling me into his chest.

It's the first I've seen him since our fallout, and it breaks me further. Tears roll down my face, my heart breaking and mend-ing at the same time. I'd missed Asher so damn much, and his coming here despite all that means the world to me.

"Are you okay?"

"No," I whimper. "Not at all."

He hugs me tight, cooing words of encouragement in my ear. When I'm finally calm, he pulls back.

"What did he do?"

The anger pouring off him is intense, and although it's mis-placed, my chest swells with love for him.

"Nothing. He did nothing," I cry. "It was me. I ruin every-thing," I admit. "I'm so sorry, Ash. I didn't mean—"

He hugs me tighter. "Don't. It's okay."

"It's not," I cry. "I hurt you."

He sighs, placing a kiss on top of my head. "We can't help who we love."

Sadness.

It radiates from him, and I wonder if there will ever be a day when we can return to how we were. I stay wrapped in his arms, crying tears of grief, terrified that things will never be the same between us, but mostly, crying for the loss of a love I don't think I'll ever experience again.

Because feelings that deep don't happen twice in a lifetime.

It might've been a whirlwind romance one step short of instalove, but it was our story. Charles and I were meant to fall for each other. I know that without a shred of doubt.

"Are we okay?" I whisper into Asher's shoulder.

"We will be." He kisses me on top of my head again. "I promise."

I hold on to that, allowing him to hug me while I cry until there are no more tears to spill.

Hours later, they're both still with me. We've ordered pizza and switched to water from the alcohol.

"I need to tell you something," Asher says, and my back straightens at his tone. "It's the last thing I want to be telling you, considering this," he says, motioning to me, "but you have to know."

"Tell me," I whisper.

He takes a deep breath. "Bauer got ahold of your presentation, and they've already pitched it to Holly . . . and Diosa."

I gasp. "When?"

"It just happened."

My head swims, and I feel the world spin around me.

"You have time, Raven. Come up with something better. Something fresh," Lily says, taking up the role of cheerleader.

"She's right," Asher chimes in. "Bauer can only capture clients with shady practices. You can do it, and I'll help."

I offer him a small smile, hardly able to conjure one.

Not only were Charles and I destined to meet, but I must've been destined to lose this account as well. The fates have turned their back on me, cursing me to a life of misery, so it would seem.

"Whatever is going through that head of yours, stop," Asher commands. "You don't give up on us, Raven Bennett. You fight."

"He's right. You're strong, and we promise to help," Lily offers.

A genuine smile spreads across my face because while everything else around me falls apart, I'm still blessed to have these two at my side. Ready to fight with me.

Asher offered to take on his own company to help.

The odds might be stacked against me, but they're right. Raven Bennett isn't a quitter. I'll fight to win back Diosa and save it for Cavendish.

I'll do it for myself.

I'll do it for Charles.

"Let's do it."

# chapter forty-five

Charles

"**Y**OU'VE GOT TO BE KIDDING ME."

My hands slam down on the desk as Dr. Amberly checks my father's vitals.

"Not at all. He's quite fine. A bad case of indigestion." He packs up his stethoscope. "He'll live to see another day."

"Why did Stuart think you were dying?"

My father sighs. "Tabitha. You know how she worries."

I scoff. "She's not worried, you idiot. She's plotting."

He shrugs. "Wouldn't be the first time, now would it?"

"She was at my office when I got the call," I bellow. "She did this."

"You're probably right." He sighs, sounding exhausted.

Something is very wrong here. What are the chances I got called home for a false alarm while she was sitting in my office?

I don't like it.

"Where are you going?" my father calls out to my retreating back.

"To find her and figure out what her angle is."

"Charles, please stay," my father begs. "I have things I want to discuss with you."

On the flight here, I'd prayed. Actually prayed that he'd be all right so we could have this conversation. Now I have the chance.

I take a seat across from him, slinking back into the chair. Bone weary.

"Go ahead and speak," I command.

"I never told you about how I met your mother," he starts, and my teeth grind together. "She was my assistant."

I narrow my eyes, and he keeps talking.

"She was the only person in the office who would challenge me. When I was wrong, she told me so. I liked that." His eyes get a far-off look. "She was everything to me, and when she died, I died, too."

I remember those first days. It was painful to watch. My father was broken. He laid over her body in the casket and wept. If we allowed him, he would've crawled right in with her and allowed them to throw the dirt over them both.

"I'm not trying to make excuses, but I want you to know that Tabitha preyed on me when I was at my lowest. It wouldn't have mattered who it was. I would've clung to them. I was lonely and broken."

"I know, Father. I've come to terms with that."

I had. It wasn't easy, but the truth was, I never cared about her enough to allow it to eat away at me. She'd done enough damage, tearing my father away from me. I wouldn't allow it a moment longer.

"I hate her," he grits through his teeth.

That stops me up short.

"I wish more than anything I could remove her from my life permanently, but she's a leech."

I huff out a breath. "I'm sorry. That's not what I want for you. It never was."

"It's what I deserve. What I did—" He chokes down a sob. "I'll never forgive myself. Now it's too late."

My head shakes. "It's never too late. We can start again. I can help you leave her."

327

"She'd find a way to torment us still. There's no escaping the devil, son."

His words ring true. Even after these years I've been away, she's still got her talons in me. Showing up at Zero Bond, attaching herself to my father. Leech is a good word for the bitch.

"Between you, me, and Stuart, we can make her pay, Father. All you have to do is say the words."

"Help me." His plead washes over me, and determination replaces all the anger and hurt I've harbored.

We may be far from fixed, but I have faith that we'll find our way back for the first time in a long time.

I'll help him get rid of her once and for all.

"Have Stuart draw up the paperwork and hire a company to pack her things. We'll have her out of here in no time."

He smiles.

"Thank you, son."

I nod. "I'm going back to uncover whatever damage she's done in New York."

She'd talked to Raven. She said she had. What the hell could she possibly have said?

"What's wrong, Charles?" my father asks, and I turn back to him.

"I met someone. Someone . . . I care very much for," I admit.

A smile spreads across his face. "That's wonderful, son. I'm thrilled to meet her."

I shake my head. "I allowed my past to ruin things. We're done, and I fear that Tabitha might have put the final nail in the coffin. I'm just not sure how."

His eyes cloud over, hate for Tabitha evident across his entire face.

"Whatever she's done, we'll make her pay," he promises, and I nod. "Don't allow love to slip through your fingers, Charles. It only comes around once, and whoever this girl is, I can tell she's the one."

I purse my lips, unwilling to think about that right now.

I've caused so much hurt. I've allowed Tabitha to destroy my one shot at happiness without doing a thing. It was the memory of her betrayals that seeped into me and poisoned my thoughts toward Raven.

Sorry isn't enough. It won't fix things between Raven and me because I'm not fixed. Before I can offer her anything, I need to work on myself. I need to understand that not everyone is after my money.

Raven never was.

I have to be open to being loved.

Raven loved me.

"I'm going to make Tabitha pay," I promise before I stalk from the room, ready to take on pure evil.

# chapter forty-six

Raven

CHARLES WALKS INTO THE OFFICE AND STRAIGHT INTO A BOARD meeting with the directors, likely hearing for the first time that we lost Diosa.

I groan, having missed out on my opportunity to tell him I had nothing to do with it. I'm desperate to find out what is happening in that room and can barely concentrate on the rest of my work.

People keep asking me why the board is meeting, and I can't answer them. It isn't public knowledge that the Diosa account is on the rocks. People don't know the pitch was compromised—stolen by Bauer. I know that I'm coming across like an idiot, being as though I work directly with Charles, but I don't want to say too much until I figure out what is happening.

I still can't believe it. How did the opposition get our presentation? I couldn't even blame Asher because he had never even seen it. There is no way he could've gotten ahold of the file.

I can't figure it out. But somehow, somewhere, it's been leaked. And because I'm the one who created most of it, I feel responsible.

The board is going to hold me accountable.

I might lose my job.

I've already lost so much.

Charles and now Cavendish.

An hour later, Shelby calls my desk phone.

"The eagle has landed. The eagle has landed."

"What?" I ask, thoroughly confused.

"The board has adjourned, and Charlie is back at his desk."

Now's my chance to pounce. I have to ensure him that I have no idea how Bauer got the file.

"Thanks, Shelby."

I rush from my office, practically running down the hall to Charles's office.

"I didn't do it," I say, storming into Charles's office.

He's been gone for two days, and it looks like he went to war in that time.

"What?" Charles asks.

"I didn't leak the information to Bauer. I'd never do that."

"How do I know you're telling the truth?"

I take a step forward. "If that's what you really think of me, you don't know me at all because I would never do that to you, Charles. I wouldn't do it to this company either. I just want you to know that. And . . ."

But I don't get a chance to finish. Charles holds up his hand to stop me.

"God, I know you didn't do it, Raven. I would never think that. But I must be honest with you—the board of directors thinks it is your fault. They've somehow figured out a connection between you and Asher. They think Bauer placed you here as a mole."

"That's the most ridiculous thing I've ever heard," I snap.

"For what it's worth, I told them it wasn't you. But they're skeptical. The email sent to Bauer was traced back to your computer."

"That's impossible because I didn't send it."

"We checked your computer. It definitely came from the company computer."

"But it wasn't me, Charles. I swear."

"I know. You don't have to prove anything to me. But this

doesn't make you look good. Who would do something like this to us?"

I think for a moment, trying to make a list of suspects, but nobody stands out. Shelby would never, and nobody else has access to my office.

"Charles, what about cameras?"

"What do you mean?"

"Are there surveillance cameras here? Is there any way we can find out who got onto my computer?"

I watch his facial expressions change from confusion to elation.

"Fuck. Brilliant. I forgot about the cameras." He grabs my hand. "Come on, let's go see the security team. They can show us."

We run down to the security room to find a slovenly man sitting behind a computer, munching on Doritos.

"Ryan," Charles calls out.

The man levitates off his seat, chips flying everywhere, but it doesn't stop Charles.

"I'm glad you're here. Tell me, are there cameras in all the rooms?"

Ryan grunts, shoving his chips aside and sucking off the cheese from his fingers.

My stomach sours at the sight.

He obviously doesn't get many visitors. When he's done cleaning his fingers, he nods. "Yeah. Jax had me put cameras everywhere but your office. What area are you interested in?"

"Good. Good. Would we able to look through the ones pointing at Raven's desk?"

"Who's Raven?" the man barks.

"This is Raven." He motions to me. "She sits on the main floor. She's basically facing my office."

"Raven," he says, tipping his chin up as though he's the coolest guy here.

Who the hell is this man?

"Uh . . . yeah. Sure. Which day would you like to look through? And what time?"

Charles rattles off a day and time frame, and Ryan gets to work.

"Okay, should I just fast forward, and you can tell me when you want me to stop?"

"Yes, that's perfect," I say, wanting him to get on with it.

I'm dying of suspense.

"Take a seat and get comfy. It might be a while."

It takes about thirty minutes to finally see something that makes us both scream, "Stop!"

Ryan pauses and then rewinds the tape for us. We all sit in silence as we watch the scene unfold in front of us.

And there it is, as clear as day.

Tabitha Murphy.

She came to my office and purposely upset me, hoping I'd leave. It gave her the perfect opportunity to break into my computer and forward the files.

We watch as she sits in my chair for several minutes, messing with my computer before closing it and chuckling to herself.

"Who is that?" Ryan asks.

"Someone trying to sabotage me," Charles says through his teeth.

The anger permeates the room, settling over all of us.

Even Ryan drops his too-cool-for-school attitude and sits up straight.

"Isn't that your ex-fiancée?" Ryan asks.

"The very one."

"Wow, someone sure is bitter."

I huff. That's the understatement of the year. She's evil incarnate, and she used me in her attempts to take him down.

I'm about to turn away and stop watching when another person appears in the footage. My eyes narrow as I try to see who it is.

When the man turns his face, my mouth drops open.

It's Keller.

The rat bastard.

He's the one feeding inside information to our competitors. The mole trying to take us down from the inside. He and Tabitha have been working together this whole time.

"Fuck," Charles grunts. "Ryan, can you make me a copy of that?"

"Certainly, sir, I'll do that right away."

Ryan seems very pleased that he has done something good for the company. He makes a copy and hands it to Charles, and the two of us make our way back upstairs. I feel relief wash over me.

"So, what are you going to do?" I ask.

"I'm going to speak to the board of directors right now. I need to call the police."

I nod. "Good. Take them down. Once and for all."

"Good idea."

"Any word from Paxton? Did he know about this?"

He blows out a tired breath. "He claims that Holly went behind his back and organized the whole thing with Diosa, alongside Bauer."

"I'm having a hard time grasping the level of betrayal. Holly seemed so nice."

He huffs. "This is business, love. Nice doesn't factor in."

Love.

I know I shouldn't get my hopes up about him using that term of endearment, but I can't help it. It felt so natural. So . . . normal.

But now isn't the time to speak to him about our fallout. Right now, we need to try to win back Diosa.

Going to his office, I close the door and call Asher, who is clearly in a huge panic after our last conversation.

"Raven. What's going on? Is Charles going to out me to Bauer? I'm going to lose my job, aren't I?"

"I'm sorry you got mixed up in all of this. I'm not sure if your name will get brought up, but Charles has assured me he'll do his best to keep your name out of it."

He sighs. "I'm not sure I want to work there anymore. Not when this is how they operate."

"Maybe Charles can hire you here. I'll speak to him about it."

He grunts. "You think after our start that would be a good idea?"

I take a second to think this through, but I know the answer.

Charles isn't the type to mix business with personal issues. If Asher is good at the job, Charles would hear him out.

"I think he would."

"We'll cross that bridge when we get there," Asher says.

I spent the next half-hour telling him about how I met Charles and how Tabitha used our relationship to gain access to my computer.

"Wow. That's . . . insane."

"It really is. She's a nightmare."

The line is quiet for several seconds.

"Do you love him?" Asher asks.

Without hesitation, I answer, "I do."

"Then I'm happy for you, Raven. I really am."

"Thank you, Ash. I hope you'll find someone who makes you feel this way someday."

"I'm sure I will."

"There's always Lily," I say, grimacing when I realize I've said that.

I promised myself I wouldn't interfere in their love lives, but here I am, butting in.

"Who knows?" he says, catching me off guard. "How's the presentation going?" he asks, changing the subject.

"It's coming. Diosa agreed to give us the final meeting before they decide to break their contract with us."

"What did Sergio think about everything?"

"We didn't tell him, anything about what happened. Figured it would only sound like a lame attempt on our part to soil his relationship with Bauer. If we win this, we want it to be a clean fight on our end."

"It was only ever a clean fight on your end, but I respect that. Cavendish is the better company, hands down."

"Can we chat soon?" I say, needing to get busy.

"For sure. Raven, it's good to have you back," he says.

"It's the best," I agree. "Pizza soon?"

"Always pizza."

I place the phone down and smile. It feels so good to be on speaking terms again with Asher, although I feel terrible that his job is on the line. And all because of some jealous girl who will never be happy, no matter what, or who, she has.

I stay in the office until Charles comes back forty minutes later.

"I hope you don't mind that I stayed here. I just didn't feel like going back to my desk."

"It's fine."

When he doesn't say anything else, I continue. "I wanted to find out what's happening before going out there. I can't even imagine the sort of rumors flying around about me."

"Your name is cleared, and the police are involved." He sounds exhausted. "They are both facing some serious jail time."

"Good."

"The board has been turned back to your side. They apologize for thinking otherwise. I showed them the tape, and they agreed it's out of our control."

"That's a relief," I say, laying my head back on the chair.

"Anyway, afterward, I called Bauer. That's why I took so long. I wanted to make it clear that they'd be brought up in the police report."

"How'd that go?"

He grunts. "The man is a bloody prat. I hope their shady business dealings come to light, and he suffers for it. I don't mind competition, but not like that."

"Do you think Asher will lose his job because of his connection to me?"

"He will."

My head lowers. "I thought so."

"Raven, we need to discuss Diosa," he says. "The board is not happy. We can't lose this account."

"I've been working on a new pitch. It's been all hands on deck, and we're ready to present. I called Sergio personally, and he's agreed to give us the last pitch."

His eyebrows shoot up to his hairline. "You've been busy."

"I wouldn't let us lose this account, Charles."

He nods. "Will Holly be there?"

I shake my head. "She couldn't be reached."

He heads for the door without another word.

"Where are you going?"

"I'm going to have a talk with my mate, Paxton."

*Good luck, Pax.*

# chapter forty-seven

Charles

"**P**AXTON!" I SHOUT, RIGHT OUTSIDE HIS OFFICE.

Marla stands from her desk, looking scared.

"Mr. Cavendish, he's in a meeting. Can I help you with something?"

This might be the first time the silly bitch doesn't use her flirtatious tone with me.

"His client went behind my back and brokered a contract with my competition. I want answers, and I want them now."

She shrinks back, picking up the phone and dialing someone. Likely the police, given my abrasive attitude.

"Mr. Ramsey, Mr. Cavendish is here to see you. It seems very important. He's rather pissed."

"Oh, darling, I'm more than pissed. I'm bloody raging."

"He's bloody raging, sir." She turns red. "Oh. All right. Okay. Sure."

"Can you wait for thirty minutes?" she asks.

"No. I will not wait for thirty minutes. You tell him to drop what he's doing, or he'll lose his best mate."

She presses the phone to her ears. "Sir, he won't be delayed. He's threatening you." She takes one look at me and purses her lips. "He said to come in. But don't start throwing punches, or I'll call security."

"I'll do my best," I say.

The truth is that I don't want to lose my cool. Paxton has been a brilliant friend to me, and I'd hate to lose that.

This is the exact reason I didn't approach him about his clients sooner. These sorts of things never end well for friends, and here we are. I'm yelling in his office.

"What's happening, brother?" the tosser asks.

"You allowed Holly to make a deal with Bauer and take Diosa with her? How could you do that, mate? I thought you were a man with integrity."

"What are you talking about? Holly hasn't signed with Bauer for anything. She hasn't even met with them. At least not that I know."

"Then she did it behind your back. It's been confirmed by Sergio De Rosa himself that Bauer pitched to them—with a stolen plan, no less—with her attached."

"No fucking way. That can't be. Holly would've had to come to me for contract negotiations."

I scoff. "Holly is obviously making deals without you."

He sighs. "Look, man, I'm sorry."

The more I speak to Paxton, the more it becomes clear that he had no idea what Holly was up to.

"She stole my client for her own means. She never would've landed the Diosa ad if not for me," I snarl.

"That is very true. I'll get to the bottom of it, and if this checks out, I'll drop her. Without a second thought."

"You'd drop your biggest client?"

He places a hand on my shoulder. "Talented people come around every day. New stars rise with the moon. You're my brother, and I don't work with people who fuck with my family."

I've never wanted to hug another man more than I want to at this moment. In a few simple sentences, Paxton has restored my faith in humanity. He's proven I'm not a complete idiot when judging someone's character.

"Thank you, Pax. That means the world to me."

"Make no mention of it," he says, taking a seat and kicking his feet up on the desk. "Out of curiosity, how did you find out?"

"Asher Anderson, Raven's best friend. He works for Bauer, and he gave her the heads-up."

He nods. "But you said they stole the pitch. How?"

I laugh darkly, and one eyebrow on Paxton's face rises.

"Tabitha broke into Raven's office with help from one of my employees and emailed it to Bauer."

He whistles. "That bitch. Please tell me she's behind bars."

"Soon. Very soon, I hope."

"What can I do to help?"

"Do you have any backup talent to replace Holly?"

He grins. "I've got talent for days, brother."

# chapter forty-eight

Raven

THE MOMENT OF TRUTH IS UPON US.

Diosa is here and ready to hear the pitch. We've got one chance to nail this and convince Sergio to stay with Cavendish.

Summer Stine and her agent are running a few minutes behind. Apparently, that is nothing in the entertainment industry, but it is still rude to me.

Paxton had come through big time.

After Summer broke her deal with Bauer, her agent dropped her, and Paxton was right there in the wings, waiting to snatch her up. He convinced her to give Cavendish another go, and she agreed.

I'm nervous about her since Asher mentioned she was quite the diva, but when are superstars not? At her level, we'd be hard-pressed to find someone better.

I can handle her.

When she arrives, she practically glides into the room.

Summer Stine looks different in person. I searched through thousands of Instagram photos to ensure that she could do the new campaign justice, and I have to say, she's even better in person.

She has a natural beauty that goes underrated these days.

She'll be perfect.

She extends her hand to me. "I'm Summer. You must be Raven. It's a pleasure to meet you." Her smile is wide and seems sincere.

I'm starting to wonder why Asher thought she was a diva. She certainly doesn't act like one.

"The pleasure is all mine."

I make the introductions and then get everyone seated to hear the pitch.

I move through the slides that boast mood boards and set photos for each brand. I tell the story of how each model with be the face of their particular brand, but it will be an interwoven story. It'll show how all three lines, Diosa, Icon, and AlteredX, are brands for all women.

Every person in the room remains quiet through the thirty-minute pitch, and not a single question is asked. I'm growing nervous because, typically, there'd be a semblance of interaction. The silence is unnerving.

Do they hate it?

I finish by outlining the time schedule for all three campaigns. It's a year-long contract, and each campaign would require the talent to fly out to various locations for photo shoots for the ads as well as for publications.

"Does anyone have any questions?"

My voice wavers slightly, my nerves getting the better of me.

We worked so hard to pull this together, but we didn't have enough time. We don't have on-scene photos like before. Instead, we used stock images.

"I have to say," Summer speaks, "I'm impressed."

My head turns to her.

"I heard about what happened to your last pitch, and I must admit, I didn't believe you could pull together something as incredible as the last in such a short time." She smiles, looking toward Sergio. "I was wrong. What do you think?"

"I must agree. This is very creative. Unique." He bobs his head. "I love it."

Air rushes from my chest as my eyes meet Charles's. He's smiling, and I can't help but return it.

"I'm in if Sergio is."

"Give me a day to check with my attorneys, but I agree, Cavendish is the right fit."

"Thank you."

They all stand to leave. Sergio is escorted out by Charles, but Summer makes her way to me.

"You have a very bright future ahead of you. I think I need to follow your career." She smirks. "I can't wait to see if Pax has more campaigns from Cavendish."

"That's very kind of you, Ms. Stine."

"Please"—she waves me off—"call me Summer. I hope we can have a great working relationship," she says. "I broke off my contract with Bauer because they didn't appreciate my input. They wanted more makeup. I wanted less. They thought I needed to lose a few pounds. I thought I was fine the way I was."

"What? That's sick," I say. "No wonder you quit. That's ridiculous."

"Especially these days." She sighs. "It's no matter. I just spoke to an attorney, and I plan to sue Bauer."

"Good for you."

She smiles. "I'll be in touch."

When the office is quiet, I sit in the dark, basking in the glow of potential success.

We might not have officially won them back, but it sounds promising. We've done all we can do, and now we wait for word from Sergio.

Everything is on the up and up, except nothing feels right.

As much as I want to celebrate, I can't.

Charles and I are still at odds, and it's killing me.

"Raven," he calls from the door.

I look up, and my breath hitches at the sight. He looks worn but no less handsome. He's my dream in reality. The one thing I'll never be okay with losing.

He takes a seat next to me.

"Charles, I—"

"Please," he says, "let me go first."

I nod.

"I'm sorry about the Hamptons and what happened afterward. You did nothing wrong, Raven. It was my past sneaking up on me."

"I know," I say, and his eyes narrow.

"You do?"

"I did some digging and learned all about the time you spent with Tabitha. I know that she married your father."

He blows out a breath. "Yeah, that was very difficult. But not in the way you think."

"Tell me."

"I never loved Tabitha. It was a relationship of convenience. One that kept going because I cared so little for her. I did whatever I wanted. There was no reason to break things off because we were hardly together."

"You had to have loved her at some point. You asked her to marry you."

"I didn't. Marriage isn't always about love, Raven. Sometimes, it's a simple business transaction. Families marry their children off to other important families as power plays."

"She was the daughter of farmers."

Not that I don't think farmers make a good living but compared to Cavendish? It seems unlikely.

"Her father owned half of London's untouched land. The amount of pull he had was vital to the growth of Cavendish."

"You would've married her just for that?"

He shrugs. "Like I said, love wasn't a factor."

"That seems cold."

"I didn't use to think so, but since I've met you, I realize what a long, horrible life it would've been." Standing up with a sigh, he says, "You don't have to say anything, Raven. You don't have to feel the way I do. But I want you to know that I'm not falling. I've completely fallen in love with you."

My breath hitches, and my heart pitter-patters in my chest.

"From the moment I saw you across the room in Silver, you've been all I think about. My world is dull without you, and I can't go back to that. I won't."

"Charles—"

"Not yet," he says, shaking his head. "Let me finish."

I close my mouth, biting my lip to contain myself. I don't want to let him tell me what to do, but I am desperate for his words.

"I don't need you to tell me you feel the same way. I don't need you to promise me a future. All I need is your reassurance that we'll see where this goes. That you'll give me a chance to prove that I'm not the arsehole who spouted those horrible things to you. I will make it up to you, Rae."

I don't allow him to say another word. I can't.

My heart is pounding, and my legs are shaking with the need to be in his arms.

I launch myself at him, slamming my mouth against his.

We're tangled together in Cavendish Group, and I couldn't care less.

If we're going to do this, it isn't going to be a secret. I lost him once, which taught me that I don't care what people think. I'm amazing at what I do, and if I have to prove that through hard work, so be it.

It's been my way all along anyway.

I pull back. "I love you, Charles. It was never a question."

"I love you, Raven Bennett."

We fall against each other, losing ourselves in this dark office. Our tongues tangle together, and our hands roam, but we don't take it any further. It's not about sex. It's about finally being on the same page. Finally knowing that this is real.

We're meant to be.

It was fate bringing us together all along.

# epilogue

Raven

FIVE MONTHS HAVE PASSED SINCE THAT AWFUL NIGHT IN THE Hamptons.

The day that Charles admitted his feelings, and I was a coward.

We put the past behind us and vowed to grow together.

To love fiercely.

I'm driving with Asher to the Hampton house. Charles had to go there a day early to meet with the caterers, so we're meeting him there.

Asher and Charles spoke soon after the whole incident with Bauer. They get along really well now.

I'd even say they've grown to be decent friends.

Asher lost his job, as expected, and came to work with us at Cavendish.

Suprinsigly, everyone has been very supportive about Charles and I.

I guess it's hard to be angry with me when everyone was still reeling over everything else that happened. Plus, with Keller gone, I took over his vacant role in the compnay.

Let's just say the entire company really hated that guy and I'm a welcome replacement.

Asher's been an amazing addition to the team. The Diosa campaign was a success and they have signed on for even more work.

"I feel so posh," Asher says as we make our way up the drive to the house.

Asher gasps as we round the corner, and the house is in view.

"I told you so," I say.

"Wow, I know, but it's even bigger than I thought it would be."

"Oh, trust me, you're going to feel a whole lot more posh when you see what's waiting for you. The place is crazy. I can't wait for you to see the pool and all the work we have done for the Gala decorations."

I'm talking a mile a minute, so excited to be coming back here. It's time to start new memories to erase the last few.

"This is the Hamptons. Lily would love it here."

Lily couldn't make it because of some work wedding she had to attend. Asher and I were bummed but understood. She has to play nice.

"When was the last time you were here?"

"Not since everything went downhill. I'm ready to move forward. Now that Tabitha and Keller have been found guilty of fraud, I'm ready to do something good. The trial took too much out of all of us. With them in prison for their crimes, tonight's charity auction needs to be a success."

"It will be successful and we'll have a blast. Based on the size of this place, you and Charles won't even know I'm here and vice versa . . . thank God."

I laugh. "Why do you say that?"

"I don't need to be subjected to your extracurriculars."

I slap his chest. "You're just jealous that you won't be enjoying extracurriculars this weekend."

He smirks. "Fair point."

"I'll just hang with Summer the whole time while you two get up to your fuckery," Asher says.

I chuckle, not bothering to deny it.

Summer is working on a couple of campaigns with us, Diosa being the largest. They officially signed Cavendish Group. It's been a very beneficial relationship for us all. Paxton doesn't hate the arrangement either. His commission is bonkers from Summer, let alone the other clients we have scheduled for marketing campaigns.

I smile up at the big house. It's so good to be back at the place where Charles had first told me he was falling for me. If only I hadn't ruined it by not saying it back. But it's okay. Everything worked out in the end. There are a lot of cars around, and I look at Asher.

"Wow. This is going to be amazing for funding." I state.

"Everything looks really nice, Raven. You and Shelby do a great job at party planning. That should come in handy in the future."

"What do you mean? The charity event is only once a year, and it rotates locations. We won't have another thing to celebrate in this grand of style for a while."

"Yea, umm—right."

"What are you hiding, mister?" I ask as we get out of the car and head to the front doors.

"Nothing, nothing." Putting his hands up in the air, Asher continues, "I swear I don't know anything."

"You are the worst liar, *ever*. You're lucky we're both dressed up. You look too good in a tux for me to hurt you, and I like these heels too much."

"You'd probably fall and break an ankle. Then Charles would really kill me tonight."

"You are being secretive, and I don't like it."

We make our way outside, and there, in front of the large pool where Charles and I made love one day so long ago, is a group of people all waiting for us with champagne glasses in their hands.

I see Charles in the front, smiling at me.

"What's going on? I thought we'd be showcasing the silent auction items by now?" I ask, smiling so wide my face feels like it might break.

"Looks like there's been a change of plans, Raven." With a wink, Asher steps off to the side.

Charles walks up to me and gets down on one knee.

"Raven Bennett, you've made me the happiest man in the world. I love absolutely everything about you. From your sunny disposition to your mad marketing skills, you are the woman I was born to love."

Then he takes out a small box and opens it to reveal a shining oval-shaped diamond ring.

"Raven, will you marry me? Make me the happiest man alive?"

Overwhelmed with what is happening, I collapse onto the ground in front of him. I can't seem to find my words, which didn't work out for me last time. I take a deep breath, look into his aqua eyes, and smile.

"You shook my foundation from the first moment I met you. In the dark, you are my light. I've never met anyone quite like you. You're a rare find, Mr. Cavendish."

"Mr. Cavendish?" he says, smirking.

"Charles," I coo. "I love you with every piece of me, and I wouldn't be happy living a life without you."

"What's your answer?" Ash calls out, and everyone laughs.

"I think I'm rambling now," I say, and Charles smiles. I place my hand out and reply, "Yes. Very much yes!"

Everyone applauds as Charles puts the ring on my finger and leans in to kiss me. We stand up, and it's only then that I see who's here. My mother and Lily are among the throngs of people.

"Mom!" I run forward and hug her.

"Hi, my girl. Congratulations."

"What are you doing here?"

"Charles invited me. And I got to spend the day alone with him, visiting, as he set this surprise up for you. The more time we spend together, the more I know he's the perfect man for you. I'm so happy for you, baby girl. You look so beautiful and happy." She leans in and places a kiss on my cheek. "I think you found your Ray."

I burst into tears, hugging my mother so very tight. The mention of my father and her love for him sends my emotions through the roof. I've always wished for a love like theirs, and I've found it.

"We're all here for the week," Lily says, coming up behind me.

"The week? That's the best news ever," I say as I step back from Mom and wipe away the tears.

Charles walks up to me, and I wrap my arms around him.

"Thank you. For all of this," I say.

He grins and takes my hand. "Now, there are two other people I want you to meet," he says. He walks me over to a man who looks exactly like an older version of Charles, and I know instantly it's his father. All the way from London.

Charles has been helping his father with his divorce proceedings. It's been a long road, but he looks good.

"Gwen, Dad, I want you to meet Raven. Raven, this is my dad and his wonderful girlfriend."

"It's such a pleasure to meet you. I've heard so much about you, Mr. Cavendish."

"All good things, I hope?" he asks. "Please, call me Charlie."

"Only good things. How is France? Are you enjoying your travels now that you're feeling better?"

Charlie retired at the end of the year, placing a trusted executive as acting CEO for the London branch until my Charles figures out how he wants to proceed moving forward.

For now, he's promoted Shelby to the UK office.

The divorce from Tabitha went through uncontested, mostly due to her criminal charges, which in turn activated parts of the prenup agreement.

Charlie is now able to live his life again without the stress that woman caused to the whole family. He always wanted to travel, and Italy was his first stop, on a suggestion from Charles. That's where he met Gwen.

"France is delightful. But it's always good to be here, especially when celebrations are to be had."

"We're so glad you could make it. Enjoy," I say, leaning in to kiss Charles's cheek. "I'm going to check in with Ash."

He nods.

On my walk to find him, I see Shelby standing by the auction tables and wave to her. Shelby smiles a deep genuine smile and I'm so happy despite her work schedule abroad she was able to still come to the event that she helped plan.

Turning in the opposite direction, I see that Lily and Asher are in the corner laughing about something, sipping on champagne.

Asher has been dating Lily for the past four months, and I have a funny feeling that after seeing the engagement, they might follow our lead soon.

I might've thought it fast at one time, but love has no timeline.

It's strange to think about how much has changed in six months.

I leave them be, wanting to give them some alone time.

Charles comes up behind me.

"Is everyone really staying for an entire week with us?" I ask.

Charles smiles. "They are. Is that okay?"

"Sure, I mean . . . we have our own wing. It's not like they can hear us, right?"

"Raven," he growls into my ear. "Are you worried about being deprived of sex?"

"I mean . . . obviously. We can't be here in this house celebrating our engagement and not be together-together. It wouldn't be fair."

He smirks. "I'm sure we can find somewhere to sneak off to. A cloakroom, perhaps?"

I smack his chest, grinning like a loon.

"Wouldn't that be something," I say, reminiscing about that first night.

"I can't believe you're going to be my wife," he says.

I look at my ring. "I'm so happy you will be my husband. Does this mean I finally get to move in with you?" I ask. The two of us have been talking about it for the past month, but we haven't yet come to any decision.

"I have a team back in New York, packing up your flat as we speak."

"What? You're serious?"

"I won't sleep another night without you by my side, Raven."

"You and your poetry."

"Only for you."

I sigh, melting into the man I'll get to call my husband. If you would've told me this is where we'd be one day, I might've called you nuts.

Fate has a way of working miracles, and Charles is mine.

From this day forward, I'm going to prove to him that he's more than what he earns. He's a man who loves fiercely and deserves that love in return.

Today.

Tomorrow.

Always.

# acknowledgments

I want to thank my entire family. I love you all so much.

Eric, Blake, and Lexi you are my heart.

Thank you to the amazing professionals that helped with Provoke:

Melissa Saneholtz

Suzi Vanderham

Jenny Sims

Jaime Ryter

Champagne Formats

Hang Le

Mo Sytsma

Jill Glass

Kelly Allenby

Thank you to Shane East, Vanessa Edwin, Kim Gilmour and Lyric for bringing Provoke to life on audio.

Thank you to my fabulous agent Kimberly Whalen.

Thank you to my AMAZING ARC TEAM! You guys rock!

Thank you to my beta/test team.

Mia: Thank you for always fixing my blurb.

Parker: Thanks for always being my sound board.

Leigh: Thank you for listening to me bitch.

Vanessa: Thank you for being the best.

I want to thank ALL my friends for putting up with me while I wrote this book. Thank you!

To the ladies in the Ava Harrison Support Group, I couldn't have done this without your support!

Please consider joining my Facebook reader group Ava Harrison Support Group

Thank you to all the Booktokers, bookstagramers, and

bloggers who helped spread the word. Thanks for your excitement and love of books!

Last but certainly not least. . .

Thank you to the readers!

Thank you so much for taking this journey with me.